continued . . .

"A fun read . . . The pace moves right along, running poor Simon a little ragged in the process, but providing plenty of action. If you liked *Dead to Me*, it's a safe bet you'll like this one even more." —Jim C. Hines, author of *Red Hood's Revenge*

"A fun, interesting, and witty read. It is something a little different, with a male protagonist, tongue-in-cheek attitude, and interesting mystery."　　　　　—*Urban Fantasy Land*

"It has a little bit of everything for the paranormal junkie . . . unique from a lot of the urban fantasy genre. This is a fantastic series."　　　　　—*Bitten by Books* (5 tombstones)

"Nice touches . . . There is a lot to like here."　　　　—*VOYA*

"Clever, well-paced, and attention-grabbing."
—*Errant Dreams*

DEAD TO ME

"Simon Canderous is a reformed thief and a psychometrist. By turns despondent over his luck with the ladies (not always living) and his struggle with the hierarchy of his mysterious department (not always truthful), Simon's life veers from crisis to crisis. Following Simon's adventures is like being the pinball in an especially antic game, but it's well worth the wear and tear."
—Charlaine Harris, #1 *New York Times* bestselling author of
Dead in the Family

"Part *Ghostbusters*, part *Men in Black*, Strout's debut is both dark and funny, with quirky characters, an eminently likable protagonist, and the comfortable, familiar voice of a close friend. His mix of (mostly) secret bureaucratic bickering and offbeat action shows New York like we've never seen it before. Make room on the shelf, 'cause you're going to want to keep this one!"
—Rachel Vincent, *New York Times* bestselling author of *Alpha*

Ace Books by Anton Strout

DEAD TO ME
DEADER STILL
DEAD MATTER
DEAD WATERS

DEAD WATERS

Anton Strout

ACE BOOKS, NEW YORK

THE BERKLEY PUBLISHING GROUP
Published by the Penguin Group
Penguin Group (USA) Inc.
375 Hudson Street, New York, New York 10014, USA

Penguin Group (Canada), 90 Eglinton Avenue East, Suite 700, Toronto, Ontario M4P 2Y3, Canada
(a division of Pearson Penguin Canada Inc.)
Penguin Books Ltd., 80 Strand, London WC2R 0RL, England
Penguin Group Ireland, 25 St. Stephen's Green, Dublin 2, Ireland (a division of Penguin Books Ltd.)
Penguin Group (Australia), 250 Camberwell Road, Camberwell, Victoria 3124, Australia
(a division of Pearson Australia Group Pty. Ltd.)
Penguin Books India Pvt. Ltd., 11 Community Centre, Panchsheel Park, New Delhi—110 017, India
Penguin Group (NZ), 67 Apollo Drive, Rosedale, North Shore 0632, New Zealand
(a division of Pearson New Zealand Ltd.)
Penguin Books (South Africa) (Pty.) Ltd., 24 Sturdee Avenue, Rosebank, Johannesburg 2196,
South Africa

Penguin Books Ltd., Registered Offices: 80 Strand, London WC2R 0RL, England

This is a work of fiction. Names, characters, places, and incidents either are the product of the author's imagination or are used fictitiously, and any resemblance to actual persons, living or dead, business establishments, events, or locales is entirely coincidental. The publisher does not have any control over and does not assume any responsibility for author or third-party websites or their content.

DEAD WATERS

An Ace Book / published by arrangement with the author

PRINTING HISTORY
Ace mass-market edition / March 2011

Copyright © 2011 by Anton Strout.
Cover art by Don Sipley.
Cover design by Annette Fiore DeFex.
Interior text design by Laura K. Corless.

ISBN: 978-0-441-02011-9

ACE
Ace Books are published by The Berkley Publishing Group,
a division of Penguin Group (USA) Inc.,
375 Hudson Street, New York, New York 10014.
ACE and the "A" design are trademarks of Penguin Group (USA) Inc.

PRINTED IN THE UNITED STATES OF AMERICA

10 9 8 7 6 5 4 3 2 1

*For my grandparents
Ray & Edna Van Valkenburg,
who have supported me all along*

ACKNOWLEDGMENTS

Welcome to book four in the Simon Canderous series, dear readers. Thanks for dropping by once again. Glad you made it through the zombie-filled streets.

It takes a village to bring a book to fruition . . . a haunted, creepy, fog-filled village. It's time to thank some of those villagers personally for ushering *Dead Waters* into existence, including: everyone at Penguin Group, most notably the creepy crawlies who inhabit paperback sales; my editor, Jessica Wade, beater-upper of bad writing whenever it rears its ugly head in my manuscript; production editor Michelle Kasper and copy editor Valle Hansen; Annette Fiore DeFex, Judith Murello, and Don Sipley, for an action-packed jacket, complete with gargoyle and Simon's trusty retractable bat; Erica Colon and her crack team of ad/promo people; Jodi Rosoff and my publicist, Rosanne Romanello, who parade me out from time to time to interact with the public; my agent, Kristine Dahl, and Laura Neely, at ICM, who keep track of the kind of details that make my head all 'splodey; the Dorks of the Round Table—authors Jeanine Cummins and Carolyn Turgeon; the League of Reluctant Adults, for continued support and stocking of the bar; glamazon Lisa Trevethan, for her eye in all things beta; Jennifer Snyder, webmistress of UndeadApproved.com, the unofficial fan site that knows more about me than me; my family; and last but certainly not least, my wife, Orly, who puts up with long hours of me ignoring her while I bring these books to you. She has the patience of a saint and my undying love. Now, let's see what shenanigans the gang down at the Department of Extraordinary Affairs is up to this time, shall we?

You consider me the young apprentice . . .

—The Police

It is imperative that all departments register the next of kin for any and all incoming apprenti and interns, as well as make sure they have signed their insurance waivers.

—Memo to the general field force of the Department of Extraordinary Affairs

1

I wanted to be home. I wanted to be in my nice comfy bed in my nice swank SoHo apartment with my beautiful girlfriend, Jane, at my side, not dressed up in my three-quarter-length leather coat, sporting my trusty Indiana Jones–style satchel. I certainly didn't want to be using the retractable metal bat hanging from my belt as we answered a late-night haunting emergency in an antiques store at the Gibson-Case Center on Columbus Circle. Sadly, it was a rare day when I got what I really wanted.

The motif of the store was that of an old-world warehouse, maybe New York dock houses circa 1900. The interior was massive, blocked off here and there with partial walls that broke the space up into a cluttered maze of furniture.

Jane let out a quiet whistle. "I feel like I stepped out of time," she said.

I nodded in agreement. "It looks like the gathered treasure hoard of a secret Time Police."

She looked back over her shoulder at me, continuing off into the darker depths of the store. Her long blond hair was still half-crazed looking from the warm September winds that had whipped at it along Central Park West. "Is that an actual division of the Department of Extraordinary Affairs?"

I grinned. "I love that in our line of work, that *is* a serious question, but no," I said. "I think maybe I caught it from an episode of *Doctor Who*." I had hoped for a little laughter out of her, but all I could get was a weak smile. "You know, nothing good comes from skulking through a closed-up shop in the middle of the night," I whispered. "Especially if it's a favor to someone."

"Especially if that someone is undead," she said. "Still, it could be worse."

I stopped skulking along for a minute and looked at her in the low, dull red cast down from distant EXIT lights. "How? How could it be worse?"

"Technically we're not on the clock with the Department of Extraordinary Affairs tonight, right? So, as you said—this is a *favor*. Doesn't count as work, so . . ."

I smiled, despite the creepiness of our surroundings. "No paperwork," I said. "I won't have to spend half my night documenting this. Score one for us."

Jane nodded, clapping, but I grabbed at her hands, stopping her. The sound echoed out in the silent stillness of the store for a moment before dying completely.

"Sorry," she whispered.

I looked around the store. "Antiques," I said, cringing a little. "Why did it have to be antiques?"

Jane squeezed my hand. "You going to be okay?"

I nodded. "I understand your concern, hon, but I'll be fine."

Jane didn't look convinced. "It's just that . . . I know how your psychometry gets. I don't want it triggering while we're taking care of whatever is haunting this place."

"I know," I said, putting my nerves aside. "I'm like a kid in a candy store, except that kid would be less likely to go hypoglycemic." New and simple objects could trigger my psychometry, but every damned thing in here had so much history bound to it. If I used my power to read the past on any of this collection of goods, its richness would drain my blood sugar in no time.

"I can catch you if you pass out," Jane said with a smile.

Despite my trepidation in the still spookiness of the store, her words calmed me. I let go of her hands, pulled out a pair of gloves that helped dampen my powers, and slipped them on before starting off through the maze once again. "Although," I said, looking at some of the pieces, "I'm not sure I *want* to control my powers. The quality of this stuff really speaks to the ex-thief in me. It makes me want to—what's the word?—re-thief."

"Focus, hon," Jane said. She reached inside my knee-length leather coat and pulled back the left flap of it, revealing the holster at my side. She pulled out the foot-long metal cylinder and handed it to me. "Here, this should help."

The weight of my retractable bat felt good in my hand. I clicked the safety off it by hitting Jane's initials on its keypad—*JCF* for Jane Clayton-Forrester—and it sprung to its full lethal length. There was power in holding it.

We continued creeping along as quietly as we could. The navigation was hard going but it became easier to see as a faint glow rose beyond a long bank of armoires up ahead. Jane stopped in her tracks as she rounded the corner, using one of her hands to steady herself against the closet. "Whoa," she said, her eyes widening.

I hurried ahead through a clutch of tables to join her and looked for myself. The store opened up into an empty circle in the middle of the cavernous space with an old-fashioned barber's chair at the center of it. The black leather of its seat had intricate waves of color, the type of flame details you usually saw on a hot rod, not a chair. That wasn't what had Jane's attention or mine now. Floating unsupported at least fifteen feet above it was a swirling mass of intricately arranged lamps. The bulk of the structure was made up mostly of Tiffany-style lamps of every shape and size, their bulbs burning softly.

"Take notes," I whispered. "For instance . . . lamps should *not* float in the air like that."

"Ya think?" Jane asked. "No offense, but I think that floating lamps fall more into my job expertise in Greater and Lesser Arcana Division."

"Maybe," I said, "but Aidan Christos called me in for this favor, so I'm gonna handle them."

I told myself I was being chivalrous, not sexist, but truth was I couldn't live with myself if I put Jane in harm's way. Sometimes it was a good thing to pull what little sway my seniority in the Department gave me over her.

The semisolid form of a girl in her early twenties, roughly my age, faded into the chair at the center of the circle. Her long black hair was shagged out in a hipster mess and Jackie O sunglasses covered half of her face. She wore an ink-stained wifebeater that left her collarbones exposed, giving her an Iggy Pop look of emaciation. Her arms were covered in tattoos and one of her legs was irreverently slung over the left arm of the chair. Low-cut hip-hugger jeans and heavy black biker boots completed her look. Not bad-looking for a hipster ghost. She didn't move from the chair but cocked her head back and forth from side to side like some strange and curious bird.

"Jeremy?" she said, craning her neck forward. "Is that you, Jer?"

The floating mishmash of lamps overhead hitched in their circular pattern, several of them rattling against one another like glass teeth clacking together. A few colored panes of Tiffany glass came free and rained down onto the shop's floor.

I collapsed my bat down and slipped it back into its holster at my side. It didn't really feel like the right approach for dealing with a transparent biker chick. Instead, I advanced into the open circle and approached the chair.

At the sound of my footsteps, the woman tensed and stood up. She peered through her sunglasses in my direction as I approached. "Jeremy?" she asked once again. "I've missed you." She gave a warm smile and the circle of lamps overhead rose to a steady glow and sped up in their swirling circular pattern.

I had no clue who this Jeremy was, but I did what kept me alive most days—I winged it.

"Yep, it's me," I said, not sure if I should be trying to disguise my voice or not. "Good old Jeremy."

The woman cocked her head to the other side. "Where have you been, Jeremy? You sound so . . . different." She took a few shambling steps toward me.

I circled around behind the chair, putting it between the two of us. Sure, she could probably walk right through it if she wanted, but it felt safer to me anyway. Her spirit slid itself into the barber's chair, her hands clutching the arms of it possessively.

"Sorry," I said. "I'm getting over a cold. I've missed you, too." I needed more information if I was going to fulfill Aidan's request and rid the shop of its unwanted ghost. I stripped off one of my gloves and pressed my hand against the cool leather back of the chair. I pushed my psychometry into it, feeling the power roll down my arm until I felt it snap in connection with the chair itself, and then my mind's eye pressed into the history of the chair, feeling for significant moments in it. As the past snapped into full-color resolution, a piece of the woman's story unfolded to me.

The barber chair sat in the middle of a dimly lit tattoo shop after hours. A pixie-cut blonde with a lot of curves and barely enough clothes to cover them was leaning over a ratty-looking dark-haired hipster boy I assumed was Jeremy. She crawled up onto his lap, straddling him before kissing his neck. There was really nothing left to do but sit back and enjoy my psychometric equivalent of Skinemax.

Just as it was getting good, the shop door flew open. The blonde sat up, startled, nearly falling out of the chair as she pushed herself up off of Jeremy.

Before she could get off of him completely, the tattooed woman stormed across the shop and grabbed fistfuls of Pixie Cut's short blond hair before slamming her to the floor.

"Bitch," she hissed, and turned back to Jeremy. "Not in my store and *definitely* not with her."

Jeremy pushed himself back into the chair like he was trying to escape through it. My powers meant that I felt her deep love and, much worse, her deeper pain at his betrayal. The tattooist pounded rageful fists against him over and over. Jeremy took it, too stunned to move, until the tattooist went for a shot at the family jewels, shaking him out of his dazed stupor. He pushed her away, standing up. "Get the hell off me, Cassie."

The violence in his voice stopped the tattooist in her tracks. The anger melted away from her face. Jeremy didn't care, pushing past her and moving to help the blonde up off the floor.

"You're going to help *her*?" Cassie shouted. This set off a new fire in her eyes and she leaned over the barber chair, snatching up one of the tattoo guns. She stepped on the foot pedal and fired up the needle on its piston. She engaged the pedal's lock with a flick of the toe of her boot, and then turned and lunged at Jeremy.

Pixie Cut screamed. Jeremy spun, barely having time to put his hands up to guard his face from the blow. The shriek of the machine sounded like a jigsaw revving as the needle darted in and out at lightning speed. The woman was out to maim.

Thankfully, the cord of the tattooing device was shorter than the distance to her boyfriend, and it pulled free from the wall. The rhythm of the machine slowed, but not before the woman landed a solid hit against Jeremy's arm, drawing blood as well as a jagged black line of ink. Jeremy grabbed crazed Cassie's arms and forced them down to her sides. She struggled, but her histrionics were draining her, leaving her powerless.

Jeremy stared at her in disbelief, and only after she had stopped struggling completely did he let go of her. He backed away slowly, the blonde rushing to his side and throwing her arms protectively around him.

The tattooist stood there in shock. Her pain in the moment was a thick swirl of mad emotions coursing through me. Tears flowed hot down her face . . . There was a mania in her head that made it hard to keep myself separate from her jumble of irrational thoughts. Her fingers ached from clutching the powerless tattoo gun. She looked down at it, and then dove for the outlet where the cord had pulled from the wall. It roared to life and she stared down at the pulsating needle, before raising it to her face. Whatever she was going to do next, I couldn't watch. I pulled my mind's eye back to the present.

The ghost woman—Cassie—was still sitting right in front of me in her tattooing chair, her head craned up to look at me. Her face was still half-hidden by the sunglasses. I could guess why.

"What did you *do* to yourself?" I asked. I couldn't help it.

The tattooist gave me a wide, grim smile. "I couldn't bear to see him with another woman," she said, "so I didn't want to see him at all. But you're not him. You're not Jeremy."

Residual sensations of her anger and jealousy forced themselves on me, the tattooist's raw emotions overpowering my own. The return of a person's psychometric emotional state was such an unfamiliar and unbidden force, so violating, that I staggered, grabbing for the barber's chair.

"Look out!" Jane shouted. The floating structure overhead shifted and faltered. It continued to whirl around, but with the woman's growing agitation, it jerked unsteadily in its course above us. Standing under it didn't strike me as the smartest idea right now, either, and I backed away from the chair as bits of glass started falling from the unstable array of floating lamps above.

The woman cocked her head off in the direction Jane had spoken from. "Is she here, too?" the woman said, the rising anger in her voice cutting into my ears like glass. "Your little blond friend?"

Although Jane wasn't Pixie Cut, and I wasn't Jeremy, it really didn't matter. All that mattered was that crazy Cassie had switched her focus to my girlfriend.

"Jane!" I shouted over the falling debris from the structure above. "Run!"

Jane stepped out from behind the armoire that hid her, moving for the aisle, but her footfalls echoed out as she did so. The tattooed woman flicked her wrist and several floor lamps tore themselves free of the structure and flew through the air toward Jane. Two of them smashed into armoires near her, but one found its mark and tangled itself between Jane's legs, sending her tumbling.

"Crap!" I yelled. I didn't wait to see where Jane landed. I was already running off in her direction, seeking cover as I went.

Lamps of every size flew past me as I ran. The dull *thump* against my leather jacket from two smaller ones pushed me forward, but I kept running and dove for the safety of a large chest of drawers. Jane's looked out from beneath one of the nearby beds. When I hit the floor, there was a crunch of broken glass under my coat, and I rolled toward Jane as she pulled me under the bed.

"You okay?" I asked her.

"Oh, you know," she said, with a nervous smile. "Just busy cowering."

"Mind if I join you in a quick cower?"

Jane laughed, letting out some of her nerves. "Be my guest."

I took a moment to catch my breath, and then rolled onto my stomach, putting my back against the bottom of the sturdy old bed frame. "We stay here too long, I think we're going to die."

I pressed up on the bed, driving the headboard down into the ground and lifting the feet of it.

"I hate antiques," Jane said, grunting as she joined me in pushing up the bed. "So damned heavy."

"But sturdy," I reminded her, hoisting the bed into a protective wall position with one last burst of survival adrenaline. "Good for cover. Good for living." I quickly told Jane everything about the lovers' triangle I had witnessed in my vision.

"Maybe the haunting is totemistic," Jane offered when I was done.

I looked over at her, the word barely registering in my mind.

Jane shrugged. "I've been reading up on totems in Arcana," she said. "Objects embedded with ritualistic properties. Think about it. You got your reading off the energy imbued in that chair, hon. Her pain is wrapped up in that. What if the chair is the object holding her here?"

It made sense, and I could have kissed her for suggesting it. Destroy the chair, release the spirit. I felt around my inside coat pocket, searching for something but coming up empty-handed.

"Damn," I said. "No good. Most of my tricks are in my regular work coat."

I looked down at the bag Jane wore strapped over one of her shoulders. "Please tell me you have more than makeup in there?"

Jane nodded. "I still have some bits of my D.E.A. welcome kit in my purse," she said. She pulled out three self-unraveling Mummy Fingers bandages, six rune stones, and a stoppered vial, the same kind Connor used all the time to coerce spirits into submission.

"Perfect," I said, pointing to the vial. "Run for the chair. Coat the damned thing with it."

"And what are you going to do?"

"I'm going to do what I do best," I said, "and see how much damage I can take."

Jane gave me an unsure smile. "Is this something they teach you in Distractions 101?"

"Just make sure you get to the chair," I said.

Jane nodded, wrapped her arms around my neck, and kissed me. While it was much appreciated, I felt a weird surge of rage and realized that the tattooist's anger and jealousy were still in control of me, running strong in my head, to the point where Jane's kiss almost tasted like the betrayal Cassie had caught Jeremy in. I eased Jane back away from me, trying not to push.

Jane didn't seem to notice, gave me a thumbs-up, and ran off along the outside edge of the room.

I pulled out my retractable bat before running back toward the outer edge of the circle where all the action was taking place. As I went, I made as much noise as I could, slamming my bat into anything and everything. It hurt my soul to bash away at antiques like this, but let's face it— the room was already half-destroyed from Cassie's lamp carnage.

The tattooist followed the sound of my progress with her ear cocked, sending more and more lampish destruction my way.

"Go ahead," I said, stopping at a spot on the edge of the circle opposite the chair. I readied my bat. "Let it all out. I can take it."

"Oh, can you?" she said, raising her arms up. The woman's body was shaking now, her chest rising and falling like she had just run a marathon. Her hair rose up in snake-like waves all around her, floating in the air like she was underwater. The tattooist unleashed her full fury at me. Stained glass panels and bulbs shattered all around me. Like mighty Casey at the bat, I swung to deflect each and every item the woman launched at me, but my arms were already tiring.

Across the room, I still didn't see Jane, but what I did

see was a set of drawers moving out toward the old barber's chair. The hint of a blond ponytail stuck up behind the unit and the sound of my bat crashing away masked its movement. When the drawer was in place, Jane popped up, unstoppered the vial, and coated the chair.

"Step away," I called out to Jane and ran for the chair. The tattooist followed the sound of me scrabbling across the broken glass and sent her assault after me, which was what I wanted. As I slipped behind the chair, one of the Tiffany floor lamps headed straight for me and I brought my bat down hard on its still-glowing light. It smashed apart, the red-hot filament falling into the chair, which in turn ignited the liquid. The chair went up like a dried-out Christmas tree mid-February.

"No!" the tattooist screamed out, all of her focus turning from me back to the chair. She ran to the already burning mess and threw herself into it, the flames rising up all around her, not even affecting her ghostly form.

A wave of heat washed over me, forcing me to back away. The tattooist raised her arms, crying out as her chair went up in flames. Her cries echoed out, and then faded as her spirit did the same. The second she vanished, the sound of wrenching metal came from above and the entire floating structure came crashing down on top of me, the room going dark except for several small fires that broke out from the fall. There wasn't time to move or dive for cover and I was driven to the ground, the thunder of it all deafening me.

As I lay pinned on the floor, the store's sprinkler system kicked and I welcomed the coolness. It was actually refreshing as I spent the next few minutes watching the room descend back into darkness and figuring out how to untangle myself from the treacherous twists of metal and shards of glass. When I finally was able to stand, the pile of broken lamps was waist deep.

Jane groaned nearby.

"You okay?" I called out.

"My hair is full of broken glass," Jane said somewhere off to my left, "but other than that, yeah. I feel like fiber-glass insulation." The sounds of her freeing herself filled the room with a metallic clatter and more crunching of broken glass.

As my eyes adjusted to the dark, I took in all the carnage around me while I tried to calm my racing heart, but then I realized I wasn't calming. Part of me was still full of the tattooist's anger and jealousy. It wouldn't shake off, clouding my mind instead.

Jane knocked on something wooden, hollow, but I was too caught up in trying to recover myself that I didn't bother to look over at her. I assumed she was still behind the dresser that she had snuck out behind before everything fell on us.

"Not only is it sturdy for defense against Tiffany lamps," she said, "but it would look lovely in your bedroom, just underneath the windows along the left side. Don't you think?"

I fought to clear my head, focusing on the antiques all around the room to bring me back to reality. The damage around us was incalculable. I tried coming up with a number in my head to price it all, but I couldn't even begin.

"Simon . . . ?"

Jane's uncertain tone brought me out of my thoughts. I turned toward where she stood, still behind the low set of dark wooden drawers. Now that I had a moment to look them over, they were lovely with slim, tapered legs and a sleek, mid–Century Modern look to them.

"What?" I asked, perhaps too sharp, but I couldn't help it with the distraction of Cassie's raw anger and emotions upon me still.

Jane's brow wrinkled at my tone. She hesitated before speaking, and when it came out, her voice was small. "I just thought this might be nice in your place," she said. "You know, for me. To hold my stuff, rather than just that drawer you gave me in your dresser."

"We'll see," I said, distracted. The image of the woman taking the tattoo gun to her own eyes danced across my mind and I shivered.

Jane gave a fake pout. "*That* sounded less than enthusiastic."

I sighed. "You'll have to forgive me," I said, testiness thick in my voice. "I just watched a love-crazed woman gouge her own eyes out over a guy, so picking out furniture seems a little trivial to me right now." Snapping at Jane was oh, so easy right now given all Cassie's feelings of betrayal, vengeance, and jealousy flooding through me. Why couldn't I shake it off? "We'll discuss it later. Let's just try to get out of here without severing a major artery. Step carefully."

By the time we picked our way out of the debris, we were soaked through from the sprinkler system. As we approached the front door of the store, my phone vibrated. I checked the text message. DEA NOW PLS. SPCL ASGNMNT U & CONNOR. AQ.

"We have to go," I said. "Downtown to the Lovecraft Café and the Department of Extraordinary Affairs."

"Not back to bed?" Jane asked, looking even unhappier than she had a minute ago. "We're not even on tonight. What's wrong? Please tell me it's not another zombie infestation."

I pulled up the gate and held it for her. Jane's face was a grim mask as she ducked under it. "Possibly," I said. "I have to go in, anyway. A call came in, requesting Connor and me specifically."

My stomach sank. Given the tattooist's emotions still coursing through me, I was glad for the text, secretly hoping it *was* about a new zombie outbreak that needed dealing with. At least then I could get out some aggression with my retractable bat.

2

We stepped out of the antiques warehouse and back into what looked like an empty shopping mall. The space was cavernous and modern, and rose up several levels above us. Off in the distance floor-to-ceiling windows showed the traffic going around Columbus Circle.

"Very disorienting," I said. "Coming out of that old antiques shop that feels like it's down on the docks and back into the modernity of the Gibson-Case Center." Cassie's emotions faded as I took in sights other than the mess we had left behind in there.

"Surreal," Jane added.

"What can I say?" a voice called out from off to our right. "Our kind does Old New York well."

I turned and looked over at Aidan Christos as he walked toward us. The forty-year-old vampire looked all of eighteen in his skull and bones Hot Topic hoodie, his emo swoop of black hair hanging down into his eyes.

"I appreciate you stopping by," he said, walking past us and off across the empty mall. When he moved, the steps from his Doc Martens didn't even make a sound.

"Can you at least pretend to make footsteps?" I asked. "It's creepy."

Aidan sighed and clomped around in a slow, deliberate circle. "Better?" he asked, but before I could answer he stopped and stared at us. "You're wet. Why are you two wet?"

I looked over at Jane and smiled. "That must be those keen vampiric powers of observation I keep hearing about."

The vampire smiled from within the darkness of the hoodie he wore, the tips of his fangs the only thing visible on the teenage boy's face. He stood there, glaring at me, and I felt a wave of terror project over me directly coming from him—an oldie but goodie that I was already familiar with in the vampire's bag of tricks.

"Cut the crap," I said, pushing past him into the darkened atrium of the Gibson-Case Center, the secret home of New York City's greatest concentration of vampires. "I'm not in the mood, Aidan."

Aidan grabbed my arm and stopped me. It was like being grabbed by a stone statue.

"So, how did it go?" he asked. "Did you take care of her? And again, why *are* you all wet?"

"Oh, we saw her all right," Jane said. "That's one creepy bitch."

"We might be talking some property damage in there," I said. Aidan looked concerned and I sighed. "Okay, fine. We're probably talking a *lot* of property damage in there. There was a small fire and the sprinklers went all *Singin' in the Rain* on us, not to mention all the broken lamps . . ."

"There was a fire?" he asked.

I nodded.

"Well, good to see the fire-suppression system works, anyway," he said. "I'd hate to think of Vampire Central going up in flames."

I shivered as the images of Cassie taking the needles to her eyes came back to me. "That spirit was messed up," I said. "You're going to get a lot of property damage with something like that."

Jane walked over to Aidan. "You really didn't have any way of dealing with her?"

"We're biters and fighters," Aidan said. "Hard to drain the blood from something you can't touch. So, as you might have figured out, we're not really fans of haunting."

Jane laughed. Aidan and I looked at her.

"Sorry," she said. "It's just . . . well, technically, I haunted this place once."

Aidan shook his head. "We're not talking about a ghost in the machine here, technomancer. You saw that woman. My master, Brandon, tasked me with checking it out after shoppers started complaining, but, well, there's really nothing one of my kind can do to something of her kind, you know?"

"Which is why you called in the experts," I said.

Aidan nodded, and then started walking again. "Believe me, Brandon considers this a huge favor, stopping to check it out."

"So, why didn't Brandon ask us himself, I wonder?" I asked.

"Maybe there's a *90210* marathon on?" Jane offered. "I mean, the great vampire lord did take his name from it, after all."

Aidan jammed his hands into the pockets of his hoodie and shrugged. "He's a private guy," he said. "King of the castle and all that."

"Literally," Jane said. "Speaking of which, you never invite us to pop over to your little Epcot Castle anymore."

Aidan stopped walking once again, looking like a pissed-off teenager despite his fortysomething years. "First of all, it's far more real than anything at Epcot. Castle Bran is authentic. They moved it here long before I was turned, building this arcology around it to hide it. Secondly, I don't think just dropping in is all that great an idea nowadays."

I shook my head and started walking again. Jane followed. "Geez," I said. "Stop the great vampire/human war and I can't even get a visitor's pass? I'm hurt."

"Give it time," Aidan said, coming up soundlessly next to us. "You know how it flows differently for us."

"It's all right," I said. "We've already got a more pressing date. Business down at the Lovecraft Café."

The massive glass doors leading out of the atrium to Columbus Circle came into view up ahead. Aidan cocked his head. "I know the night is just starting off for me, but isn't it a little late for you guys to be calling meetings?"

"No rest for the wicked, or government employees," Jane said with an enthusiastic smile. As wet and damaged as she was, I don't know where she found the energy to be so chipper.

"I'm sure something sinister is going down for them to be calling us in now," I said.

"Brandon may have us under orders to stay out of most human affairs right now, but you *did* do us this favor," Aidan said. "So just let me know if you need me . . . you know, if things go bad."

"Then I should just ask now," I said. "Ninety percent of this job is cleaning up things that go bad."

"And the other ninety percent is filing paperwork on it," Jane said.

"That's bad math," I said.

"That may be," she said, "but we deal with impossible things all the time. You're suddenly going to start arguing about the math getting wonky now, hon?"

"Fair point," I conceded. Part of the tattooist's raw emotions were welling up again, and had me wanting to pick a fight, but I fought the urge. "Truth be told—if we're going for messed up math here—I'd probably say that my caseload paperwork takes up at least a hundred and twenty percent of my time on the clock."

Aidan cleared his throat. A ring of keys was in his hand. "Do you mind?" he asked, unlocking one of the glass doors that led out onto the rainy streets of Manhattan.

"Your gratitude is underwhelming," I said. I held my hand out and felt the rain coming down hard on it. "At least I don't have to worry about getting dry anytime soon."

"Sometime tonight, kids," Aidan said. "You don't have to go home but you can't banter here."

"Fine," I said. "Although I'll have you know that I consider banter a necessary tool in keeping from wetting myself in a lot of these situations."

Jane gave an uncomfortable laugh. "Sexy."

Aidan frowned. "Can I add that to my list of things I wish I could unhear?"

I started to respond, but Jane grabbed me by the arm and pulled me out into the streets. "Come on," she said, "before you say anything else that makes me question our relationship further."

As we exited the building, the Columbus Circle wind at the southwest corner of Central Park whipped Jane's long wet hair around like she had gone all Medusa. I turned around as something struck me odd.

"I'm surprised you didn't call Connor first," I said. "My

partner is the resident ghost whisperer in Other Division with the Department, you know . . . *and* your brother."

"Oh, believe me, I did call him first," Aidan said, "but he was busy."

"So nice to be considered second choice," I said. "It's like my prom all over again."

"Connor's too busy for his own brother?" Jane asked. She ran her fingers through her already windblown hair as she tried in vain to make it settle down. "You'd think after a twenty-year absence . . ."

Aidan pulled his hood up to avoid the water. Whether it was vanity or some vampiric aversion to it, I didn't know.

"That's kinda the problem," he said. "Not every day can be a happy family reunion . . . especially with the workload your boss heaps on him. Plus there's all the work Brandon has Connor doing for our cause. Apparently vampires going bye-bye the past few years, and then just showing up again all friendly like, has caused a lot of meetings between our people."

"Lucky Connor," I said, "playing liaison to the undead . . ."

Aidan smiled as the two of us walked off to the curb, his fangs showing once again. "I guess having a vamp in the family means he gets the short straw."

"We've got to get to our own meeting," I said, not wanting to delay any longer. "Hopefully ours doesn't involve your meetings. They might meet to make little baby meetings."

"Let's hope not," Jane said, hailing a cab that was rounding Columbus Circle. It slowed for her, even as disheveled as she was. "I hope the meeting goes quickly either way. I still need to wash all the glass out of my hair. Ick."

"Better glass than blood," I said.

"Agreed," Aidan added from over by the great glass doors of the Gibson-Case Center, and then gave me a dark smile as his eyes moved to Jane. "Would be a waste of perfectly good blood."

I ignored his words, but the residual anger I was experiencing rose up inside me and wanted me to go back and see how large a pile of dust I could leave him in. I didn't need to reawaken the vampire/human war simply because I had an all-too-intense reading with my power.

3

As our cab shot down Broadway to the East Village, the two of us jostled around in the back of the vehicle. Still distracted by the intense jealousy of the tattooist coursing through me, I almost jumped out of my skin when Jane's hand brushed up against the back of mine.

"Brandon's going to be pretty cheesed off by the amount of damage we did in there," Jane added.

"*We* didn't do the damage," I said. "That creepy tattooist lady did it all. Granted, she was tossing stuff at us left and right, but we didn't do anything except try to stay alive through all that."

"We'll see," she said.

"Let the Big Biter on Campus try to collect damages," I said. "Ha! Compensation from the Department of Extraordinary Affairs during a budget crisis? Good luck with that. Don't worry. Aidan's just worried what his boss will think of all the damage done under his instruction like a good little vampire lapdog."

"Fangs and all," Jane said. "You're right. Connor will probably talk some sense into them."

"Let's hope so," I said. "Hopefully a little brotherly love should calm Captain Emo and his master down."

I laid my head back against the seat and remained silent for the rest of our cab ride. When it dropped us off at our East Village coffee shop cover operation on Eleventh Street, we hit the sidewalk right outside of the large red doors that led into the Lovecraft. We raced out of the rain and into the café, embracing its warmth and its dark wood floors and exposed brick walls that were adorned with movie posters on both sides of the long, open space. Most of the décor was a clutter of mismatched furniture—comfy chairs, low café tables—and a long, wooden counter ran along the entire right side of room. The coffeehouse wasn't full, but the faces I did see gathered around in the café area were all people I knew from the Department hidden beyond the cover operation.

"Looks like half the Department is on a coffee break," I said, acknowledging the throng of coworkers that had assembled in the public café area.

"What's going on?" Jane asked. "Why is everyone up here in the coffeehouse?"

"I have no idea," I said. "Maybe they're fumigating the Department again. Don't tell me . . . they can't get the smell of rotting zombies out of the curtains in the hidden office area."

An especially familiar face came into view as my partner, Connor Christos, came walking over to us. "Not quite, kid," Connor said, his hands jammed down into the pockets of his beaten old trench coat. His clothes underneath it

were a bit dressier than my usual jeans and T-shirt but my
partner always looked a little wrinkled around the edges.
His simple black tie was loose and skewed to one side. As
if the thick white streaks in his sandy brown hair weren't
enough, the grim look on his face made him look older
than his midthirties. "We were in the middle of one of our
all-night financial meetings, when the Inspectre took a call
from Dave Davidson downtown. Quimbley's got the details. Wouldn't tell me a thing except I needed to get you
down here."

Ever since a set of even more draconian Departmental
cuts than usual a few weeks ago, and the loss of lots of an-
cillary staff members, I knew things had been rough, but I
hadn't realized it was so bad they had to be going over the
books in the midnight hours. I switched my focus to farther
back in the coffeehouse over by the service counter where
Inspectre Argyle Quimbley was surrounded by a few other
people. The old Brit leader of Other Division was in his
usual tweed, twirling the ends of his walrus-like mustache
as he looked over a folder. Next to him was a dark-skinned
woman whose hair was pulled back off her shoulders in
a no-nonsense ponytail—Allorah Daniels, doing double
duty as a member of our governing Enchancellors as well
as our resident vampire hunter. She held a folder identical
to the one in the Inspectre's hands.

I headed across the room to them, addressing my boss.
Connor and Jane followed. "Inspectre . . . ?"

Despite the concern on the old man's face, he smiled
when he saw me. "Hello, my boy," he said.

"What's going on?" I asked as a horrible thought dawned
on me. "We're not . . . *fired*, are we?" I could barely say the
words, and when I did, a panic rose in my chest. The last
thing I wanted was to be forced back into a life of thiev-

ing to survive in the skyrocketing real estate market that was Manhattan. My apartment down in SoHo was my last holdover from those days, the one thing I had kept to ease into the transition to using my powers for good.

The Inspectre sighed. "I won't lie," he said. "The budget doesn't look good."

"*That's* an understatement," snorted Allorah from next to him. "We'll be lucky if the Enchancellorship keep their jobs."

Something in me snapped. "No offense, *Enchancellor*, but I'm not worried so much about the upper management," I said. "Most of them are retirement age, anyway. I'm worried about me and my fellow agents."

Allorah gave me a dark look. "Your compassion is underwhelming, Mr. Canderous," she said.

"Hey, I'm just saying that since you got the order a few weeks back to trim the fat, I think it would make sense to keep the agents out in the field. If we're going to clean house, start at the top. Mediocrity rises, after all."

"Don't worry," Allorah said, looking through her folder. "You Other Division people are always safe when it comes to the budget."

Connor laughed. "Of course we are," he said. "Us Other Division folk are such multitaskers by designation that we can be set to any task. We've had to kiss any downtime good-bye these past few weeks."

"We *had* downtime?" I asked. When no one answered, I felt my blood rising. "I thought all this would have changed when we became the heroes of the city. Money should be raining down on us, right? Didn't the Mayor hear that we saved the city from a bloodbath of vampiric proportions?"

Connor walked past me and threw himself down into

one of the lounge chairs nearby. "That's the problem, kid. There *wasn't* a bloodbath."

I looked at him, frustrated. I tossed up my hands. "And that's a problem *how*?"

"Not enough of a body count," he said. I went to speak, but Connor held his hand up to silence me. "Think about it, kid. If you have a regular-world shooting in this city, suddenly there are all these extra resources to go around . . . more cops and cars on the street. Puts on a big show, sends a message out to the general public: *Bad guys beware!* But what we do, well, it's secretive. Everything we do is masked in seclusion. And let's face it. To the power brokers down at City Hall, nothing bad happened, technically. No one died, so how are they going to justify putting a lot of money toward the Department? There wasn't enough of a bloodbath to justify more money coming toward us."

"That's insane," Jane said. She grabbed onto my arm and squeezed like she was trying to hold herself up.

"Insane?" the Inspectre asked, sadness filling his face. "No. That, my dear, is simply bureaucracy."

"So, now what?" I asked. "Do we hope for a high body count or something so we can reappropriate some funds?"

Allorah gave a grim smile at that and sighed. "I'll talk to the Enchancellorship," she offered. "They have some pull when it comes to dealing with City Hall. I think we may know where a skeleton or two of theirs may be buried."

"And if not," Jane offered, "I'm sure someone over in Greater and Lesser Arcana can always reanimate a few . . ."

Allorah fixed Jane with a look of disdain that I knew well, as it had been directed at me a few months ago when I had been hiding knowledge of New York–based vampires from her. It had been an uncomfortable look to have directed at me, but seeing it focused on my Jane hurt even more.

She was clearly going to let loose on Jane, but the Inspectre cut her off. "Enough," he said, stern. "The both of you. We shouldn't fight among ourselves. To answer your question, Simon, before you jumped down Miss Daniels's throat, no. None of you are being fired. We're already reduced to a skeleton crew as is. That is not why I called you in tonight. You were requested by Mr. Davidson from the Mayor's Office of Plausible Deniability. We're waiting on him to arrive, I'm afraid."

Jane looked concerned. "Begging your pardon, Inspectre, but I have to ask. Is that just an expression, or are we talking *actual* skeletons?"

"A fair question, but no," he said, taking it seriously. "In this case, it is just an expression, my dear girl."

The main doors to the Lovecraft Café opened behind me, causing a sudden hush in my circle of people. Connor looked past me and his face turned dark, his hands digging into the arms of the chair, but he didn't move to get up. I turned around with caution while discreetly slipping one hand inside my coat and unlatching the safety loop on my retractable bat hanging there.

Mayoral liaison David Davidson had just entered the bar, a dripping wet umbrella in hand. I relaxed my hand. Davidson was a bureaucrat through and through, but he wasn't enough of an evil entity for me to go all Babe Ruth on his ass. Politicians walked a dangerous line awfully close to it, though.

The few coffee shop customers who weren't employees of the Department of Extraordinary Affairs took no notice, but the rest of us eyed him. He slowly lowered his umbrella and shook it out over the floor mats before sliding it into the umbrella stand off to the left of the door. Once Davidson spotted us, he walked back to our group with slow, deliberate steps, taking his time. He wore all the trappings of his political office—a dark gray suit, a red splash of color from his power tie, and a much nicer trench coat than the one Connor was wearing. His tie was, as usual, knotted perfectly and his graying black hair parted and all in place despite the stormy weather he had just walked in from.

As he approached us, his eyes were wary.

"How's the mayor?" Connor asked from his chair with a little venom to his words. "Busy with support groups for the zombie hordes that pop up every now and then? Let me guess . . . they're probably lobbying to be called the Formerly Living."

Davidson gave Connor a dismissive look. "His Honor is fine," Davidson said. "Thank you for asking." He turned his attention away from Connor and looked to the Inspectre and Allorah.

The Inspectre fixed Davidson with a fake smile that beamed out from beneath his walrus-like mustache. "Your call sounded urgent earlier, so what can we do for the Office of Plausible Deniability this rainy evening?" the Inspectre asked.

Davidson pointed at me and Connor. "I was hoping to wrangle up those Other Division troops of yours I called about earlier to check something out for me tonight," he said.

I laughed. "I don't know," I said, bitterness in my words. "I mean, with all the recent cuts and layoffs, we're already looking pretty swamped. I've probably at least doubled my caseload lately. You can thank the mayor for me personally."

Davidson narrowed his eyes at me, but kept his politician's smile. "There can always be more," he said, unflappable as always.

"Wow," I said, spitting my words out in his face. "An idle threat."

"Simon," the Inspectre interrupted. There was a warning in his tone. "That is conduct unbecoming a member of the Department, not to mention one from the Fraternal Order of Goodness."

I felt my anger twist into embarrassment, wishing it wasn't all happening in front of Jane. She must have sensed it because she squeezed my hand and gave me a thin smile. "Sorry, sir," I said.

Davidson looked around the group of us like he was king of the hill. "May I continue?"

"By all means," the Inspectre said.

Davidson jerked his thumb toward Jane and looked at Inspectre Quimbley. "You mind if I grab her as well?" I felt a weird flare of jealousy, and tried to damp it down. I still couldn't shake Cassie's feelings.

"Jane?" the Inspectre asked, his eyebrows rising. "Whatever for?"

Davidson ran his eyes up and down her. Despite his usual politician's polish, he almost looked lascivious when he did it, or at least that was what the twinge of jealousy I felt from the tattooist was telling me. I pushed it down.

"We could use a woman's touch on this case," Davidson said.

Jane squeezed my hand. Hard. "Wow," Jane said. "Sexist much?"

"No kidding," I said. I put myself between the two of them, as protective jealousy rose up in me. "And why's that exactly?"

Davidson held his arms up, hands open and empty.

"Easy, Mr. Canderous," he said. "I'm just saying we might need someone with her particular assets."

I turned to the Inspectre. "Sir?"

The Inspectre hesitated, and then gave a slow, stern nod.

"You want to tell us what's up?" Connor said, still seated.

Davidson's smile faltered. "I'm not really sure yet," he said. "We've got a crime scene. The regular cops who showed up on the scene wouldn't say. They just called it in to my department and left it at that. Whatever it is, though, they want nothing to do with it and when a call comes in on something like that, well . . . it's usually something in your realm of expertise. We've got a dead teacher on our hands." Davidson pulled out a small notebook and flipped it open. "A Professor Mason Redfield."

"Mason?" the Inspectre asked. The color drained from his face as if he was seeing a ghost. "A gentleman around my age?"

"I'd say so," Davidson said. "Not nearly as lively as you, clearly. You know him?"

The Inspectre stared off across the room, lost in thought, and gave a slight nod. "I did," he said. "Long ago."

"So, I can have a few of your people?" he asked.

The Inspectre nodded again, his face sad and distracted. "Take whoever you need," the Inspectre said, and then turned to me. "You take point on this."

I looked over at Connor, but he didn't seem to mind. "Are you sure, Inspectre?" I asked.

"Very," he said, his face dead serious now.

"Great," Davidson said, trying to speed things along. He gestured toward the exit. "I think Simon, Connor, and Jane should cover it. Shall we?"

My eyes stayed on the Inspectre. I had never seen him so unnerved before.

"Go," the Inspectre said, closing the folders in his hands. "I'll let Director Wesker know that Jane went with you. He won't be too pleased that I allocated one of his people to Davidson, but there are *some* perks to being the senior ranking officer around here, I suppose."

"I'll try to return them in one piece," Davidson said, the sparkle returning to his smile. "Promise. I have a police van waiting outside. It will spare you having to cab it back uptown. I know how tight you folks are for cash around here."

Connor stood up and brushed past Davidson, heading for the front door of the café. "Don't get too toothy there, smiley," he said to me. "I call shotgun." Davidson started after him.

"Dammit!" I said. "I wanted shotgun."

"Fine by me," Jane said. She took my hand and ran off after them, practically dragging me. "I call flamethrower."

4

Davidson drove while the rest of us rode in the back of the police van in silence. Jane leaned her head against my shoulder as we listened to the sound of the rain beating down on the roof of the van as it raced up through the concrete canyons of Manhattan.

The going got slower as we headed farther up to the East Side. Rain that lasted more than a few hours in Manhattan could bring the city to a dead stop, but at the moment we were at least maintaining a slow crawl through an ocean of traffic. Somewhere in the east Forties we turned right off of First Avenue and headed farther east than I usually traveled. I thought we might be heading into the East River itself, but then I noticed several large buildings filling the skyline.

All of them were towering—about ten in all—and looked like they all belonged to the same construction project, with each of them in various states of completion. Large straight towers of steel fit with bare construction bulbs rose above the slick black glass and modern steel architecture of the finished floors below. Only the center grouping of buildings looked finished and lit up from habitation.

Davidson pulled into the only finished arc of a drive that I could see, running through a small patch of unfinished landscaping that still managed to block the entrance view from the street. Several empty cop cars were already parked along the drive.

We stepped out of the police van and I held an umbrella out for Jane as she crawled under it with me. Davidson came around to our side with his own umbrella and looked up at the impressive size and design of the building.

"You sure this place is habitable?" I asked.

Davidson nodded. "Some of it," he said. "There are several buildings going up for this whole development. About three of them are finished and already have occupants."

Connor whistled as he joined us and took it all in. "How much is rent on this place?"

"Trust me, you don't want to know," Davidson said and started toward the entrance to the lobby. "Let's just say I don't think anyone with our government paychecks will be moving on up to the East Side to a deluxe apartment in the sky anytime soon."

"Funny," I said. "I figure with the kickbacks you see from helping out Sectarians and vampires, you'd be set up for life."

Davidson stopped and turned on me. With the look on his face, I braced for him to launch into me. Instead, he pursed his lips and shook his head. "Not tonight, Simon," he said. "We're about to enter a building where some of the most prestigious people in Manhattan live and we're going to be trying to investigate something discreetly. My interests are the Mayor's, not my own. If you want to cut into someone, why don't you write him a letter?"

"Like I need more paperwork?"

Davidson walked over to Connor. "I liked him better when he was still new," he said. "At least then he followed your lead a bit before becoming irreverent."

Connor shrugged. "What can I say? I trained him right."

Davidson turned away from us all and headed into the building without waiting.

I turned to Connor. "Thanks, Dad," I said. "Can I borrow the car?"

Connor headed for the building as well. "Don't start that with me," he said. "I get enough of that from Aidan. He acts like he's actually eighteen sometimes."

"But he *is* your older brother, right?" Jane asked.

"Vampires seem to have a very distorted sense of age and maturity," Connor said, "because time doesn't affect them quite the same. I think they get a really bad case of arrested development. How does one act their age when one is technically ageless?"

We hurried after Davidson and headed into the most finished of the buildings. The lobby was swanky with fresh leather furniture and a few choice art pieces that were actually tasteful. Davidson flashed an ID and our group hit the elevators, riding up until we got off on the twenty-seventh floor. A large assembly of police officers was gathered in the hallway nearby and we had to push past them before we found someone in charge. A uniformed officer in his forties with a little paunch nodded at Davidson. He eyed the three of us with the usual disdain that we were used to from the regular cops.

Davidson reached out and shook the officer's hand. "What's got your men so spooked, Sergeant?" he asked.

The head officer hesitated, a look of frustration crossing his face. None of his men made a move to offer up
anything.

"You know what, Mr. Davidson?" he said. "Why don't
you just take your Monster Squad inside and see for yourself?"

"Nice," I said. "Why don't you clear out some of your
boys, then? Or is the NYPD afraid of a little rain outside?"

The officer's eyes widened. He looked like he might be
on the verge of pulling his gun on me.

Davidson raised one hand to the officer and the other to
me. "Gentlemen, please," he said. "Let's just do our jobs."

The officer nodded, and then started ordering his men
off the floor of the apartment building. Once they cleared
the area, Davidson threw open the door to the apartment
in front of us.

The space itself wasn't the first thing my eyes landed on.
A magnificent view of the East River and the Queens skyline filled up an entire wall of sliding glass doors at the far
end of the room. The shadows of gargoyles stood out along a
patio beyond the windows, lit up occasionally by a reflection
of city lights coming off of a full-sized pool. Already I had a
bit of apartment envy and I hadn't even stepped in yet.

"Welcome to the home of Mason Redfield," Davidson
said. "Deceased."

The four of us entered the apartment and the first thing
I noticed was that the main room was several times larger
than my entire apartment and almost as tastefully decorated. The owner of the apartment was lying dead and face-
up in the middle of the living room.

"Nice place," Jane said, nervously looking around the
space and avoiding looking at the guy. "Bet there's a lot of
drawer space."

I tensed as a surprise twinge of the tattooist's raw emotional anger flared up for just a second, and I shot Jane a look as I pushed it down as best I could. "Not now, Jane. Not here."

Connor circled around the dead man in the center of the room, barely paying attention to the body. "You know, for a crime scene, it looks remarkably tidy," he said.

I walked over to where the body lay. He was an older gentleman in his late fifties with gray hair pulled back in a widow's peak like an aging Eddie Munster.

"His eyes are open," Jane said from where she stood farther away. His cold blue eyes were staring up at the ceiling, blank. "Creepy."

Connor knelt down and closed them.

"Thanks," she said.

"No problem," Connor said, and then began looking over the body without disturbing it. "It's the least I could do for an old acquaintance of the Inspectre." He studied the corpse for a few moments more before speaking. "I don't see a mark on him."

Connor looked around the room, and then pulled out one of the vials of ghost bait he always had on him. He uncorked it and the smell of patchouli hit my nostrils. After several moments of nothing happening, he corked it and slid it back inside his coat.

"If his ghost is around here somewhere," Connor continued, "I'm not picking it up."

Jane moved a little closer. She cocked her head down to look at the corpse more closely. "Look at his mouth," she said. "His lips are parted and there's some kind of sheen just behind them."

"Let me," I said, kneeling down on the other side of the body. "I've already got my gloves on."

I grabbed the side of his jaw and eased the corpse's mouth open. "What the hell . . . ?"

I turned his head to the side. A clear liquid poured out of the man's mouth onto the fancy wood floors.

"Water," I said. "Or at least it looks like it."

By now, Connor had slipped on a pair of gloves as well. He moved the man's head back to the way we had found him. He pulled out a Maglite, twisted it on, and held it up to the man's mouth. "There's more." He compressed the man's chest and water poured out of his mouth again, this time to both sides of his face. "His lungs are full of it."

Davidson stepped back. "Are you telling me he drowned?"

"From the inside," Connor said. "Yes."

"But his clothes and hair are dry," Jane said.

Davidson jerked his thumb at her. "What she said. Maybe someone forced a hose down his throat?"

"I don't think so," Jane said. "Look at the floor. Until Simon tilted his head, there wasn't a drop of water anywhere. If there had been a struggle or something like that, you'd think there would be water all over the place."

I stood up. "She's right. No wonder the regular cops are spooked. No signs of struggle . . . nothing that makes sense."

Davidson crossed his arms and stood in silence for a minute. When he looked up again, he was staring at me. "You want to do your little magic-fingers thing you do?"

"Magic fingers," I said, standing. I stripped off my gloves. "You make me feel like a coin-op bed in a sleazy motel."

"Hey, if that's what works for you . . ."

"Quiet," I said, and then set to work passing my hands

over all the objects, antiques, and decorations around the room.

"Well?" Davidson said, sounding rather annoyed.

"Nothing," I said and shrugged.

"Did you forget to charge your psychometry or something?" he asked.

I stared at him, shaking my head. "Do you have the first clue how this works with me? The building is new, and I think a lot of the stuff this guy has here is new, too. All of these quality-looking antiques? Fakes."

"So?"

"I can read a lot of objects—old, new—but it helps if they have some significance for there to be a psychometric charge. Either everything is too new to have a lick of a charge or something is blocking it somehow. Not everything in this world carries a charge to it."

Davidson looked more confused than ever. He turned to Connor. "Is there a chart of some kind that I could use to follow all this?"

"This isn't science," I said. "It's parascience. The research, even in our records down in the Gauntlet, is a bit sketchy on the how and why of it all. I'm sorry if it doesn't fit your investigative needs."

Davidson unfolded his arms and pointed at the corpse in the center of the room. "What about reading the body?"

"Thanks, but no, thanks," I said. "I don't do the dead."

"Eww," Jane said, flailing her hands like she was trying to shake the mental image off of her.

I scrunched my face up. "I didn't mean it like that," I said. "I just meant Connor's the guy who deals with the dead."

Connor stood up from the body. "Don't look at me," he

said. "Like I mentioned a minute ago, this guy's soul ain't around here."

Davidson's lips were pursed in agitation. He closed his eyes, and when he opened them, his usual mask of composure was back in place. He walked over to Jane and put his hand on her shoulder.

"Listen, Jane," Davidson said. "I need you to go around to the rest of the apartments on this floor and ask some questions. See if anyone heard anything."

"That's why you brought me along?" she said, looking a little miffed. "Couldn't your cops have done that for you?"

David Davidson shook his head. "Did you see them in the hallway before?" he asked. "They were freaked-out enough that they didn't even want to come back into the apartment. You want me to send those guys knocking on all the doors? I think you'd be a far more welcome sight to the residents. The people who can afford to live in a building like this are either cultured or rich beyond the beyond. Probably both. They're going to be more receptive—more forthcoming—to a pretty young woman than to creeped-out cops."

"Oh," Jane said, crossing her arms. "How sexist of you. And here I thought you might actually need me for my technomancy." She made no effort to move.

Davidson looked over at me. "Are all ex-cultists this stubborn?"

Jane's eyes flared with anger, so I spoke up quickly.

"Pretty much," I said. "Be lucky she's an *ex*-cultist. Otherwise, I wouldn't want to be standing that close to her if I were you."

Jane gave him an evil grin. "A girl can learn a lot from cultists. Like how to fillet a man using a kukri . . ."

Davidson smiled back at her, not missing a beat. "Maybe

we can save that as our second option . . . you know, after asking questions of the nice people who live here."

Jane looked over to me. Her eyes smoldered. I nodded. "Go," I said. "There's nothing to be done in here yet. Talk to the neighbors. Then check their security system records."

"Security systems don't ever want to cooperate with my technomancy," she said, "locks or otherwise. It's like they've purposely been trained to not talk to me."

"Still, there's nothing for you to do in here. I think this crime scene is technically going to get classified as Other Division anyway, so that means Connor and I will get stuck with all the paperwork on this one."

"I'll go talk to all the neighbors, then," Jane said, still somewhat cheesed off, "but if anything Arcana related comes up, call me."

Connor let out a single laugh. "You mean other than Professor Redfield drowning from the inside without any signs of struggle, forced entry, or water spilled?"

Jane shivered and her face lost its look of anger. "Yeah, other than that."

She turned around, shaking off the darkness that had crossed her face, and headed back to the front door of the apartment.

"All right," Connor said. "Let's see what we can see."

I set to work once again trying to run the psychometric histories in the room, but whether they were devoid of them or I was simply thrown by Jane's comment about drawer space earlier and afraid to use them since the incident with the tattooist and its weird aftereffects, I wasn't sure.

All I knew was that my emotions were still stuck on high and it was hard enough to fight off that woman's urges without having them mess around with my own emotions.

My mind kept superimposing Jane meeting a sexy stranger while knocking on doors for the investigation.

I tried to focus on the crime scene but it was little use. The tattooist's jealous rage kept me haunted by thoughts of gouging my own eyes out, but without the needle of a tattoo gun at my disposal, the best I could hope for was getting a black eye from trying to use my bat instead. I fought the urge, but only barely.

5

Without a lingering spirit to be found, Connor was more than willing to call it a night fairly early, which meant that the two of us headed back to the Lovecraft Café. Following up on the case could wait until we broke a lead on it, but given the budget cuts, the preliminary paperwork could not.

We headed back through the coffeehouse and behind the dark curtain that led into the theater hidden behind it. The eighties version of *Clash of the Titans* played on the movie screen. Laurence Olivier was chewing up the scenery as Zeus as we made our way down the right-hand aisle past the crowd of thirty or so watchers. At the back corner of the theater, I swiped a plastic keycard against a metal plate next to a door marked H.P. The door swung into the open bull pen of the Department of Extraordinary Affairs with its carved in runes ringing the tops of the walls. We headed back past the cubicle farms and doors heading off in every direction until we hit the long red curtains that sectioned off Other Division from the rest. Connor and I settled in at our partners desk, which sat in a space that was larger than the cubicles and partially walled higher. Each of us worked in silence drafting our own accounts of what we both found and didn't find. I was almost falling asleep in one of my case folders when Connor spoke up.

"What was that crack Jane made earlier?" Connor asked. "The one about Professor Redfield having a lot of drawer space . . . Seemed to rile you."

"It was nothing," I said, feeling the tattooist's residual anger rising up once again at the mention of it. "Let it go." I fell back into work and silence for a few more minutes, forcing the emotions down again, but when I looked up at Connor for a second, he was watching me.

"Yes?" I asked.

"Any wedding bells in the future?"

"Whoa," I said, throwing my pen at him. I tried to hide the unbidden anger as it rose again, tried to play it off. "Are you proposing?"

"Funny," Connor said. "You know who I mean. You and Jane."

"Slow down," I said, sharp. "Right now we're just fine as is, thanks." I fished another pen out of the D.E.A. mug on my desk and went back to my file.

"Really?" Connor asked, skepticism thick in the single word.

"Really," I assured him, hoping to end the discussion.

"Well, maybe you could try not sounding so pissed off when you say it, then," he said.

I looked up from my desk, sighing. I pushed the anger down. "I thought I was doing a fairly good job at hiding it. I'm that transparent, am I?"

"Not to most people," Connor said. "No. Probably not. But to your partner in slime? Yeah, it's pretty obvious."

I swore under my breath. "Remind me to sign up for No, You Can't Read My Poker Face when they offer it up next time."

Connor settled back into his chair. "Will do," he said. "Am I detecting trouble in young hipster paradise?"

"Something like that," I said, attempting to dodge the question by delving back into my paperwork.

Connor shifted a stack of case files from his in-box to right in front of him. "I'm all ears, at least for the next few hours," he said, then looked at the rest of the stack still sitting there. "Maybe even a few more than that."

"Fine," I said, rubbing my eyes. I put down my pen. "I had a little psychometric episode earlier unlike any I've ever had before. The two of us were helping your brother with that ghost problem they've been having over at the Gibson-Case Center."

"The tattooist?" Connor asked. I nodded. "Aidan told me about her before. Seems like he was a bit frustrated to be dealing with something he couldn't punch, kick, or bite."

"Yeah, that's about right," I said. "Anyway, I psychometried my way into the woman's past and . . . I don't know. It felt different. She was all *Fatal Attraction* over this guy who was cheating on her and I just got caught up in her whirlwind of emotions. She was passionate, angry, outraged, all at once . . . and when I pulled out of it, I couldn't shake her severe emotional state. I still can't. It flared up at Professor Redfield's apartment when Jane teased me about the drawer space."

"And this hasn't happened before?" Connor asked. "The emotion of someone's past lingering like that?"

I shook my head. "I've always had trouble with using my powers," I said. "You know that, but nothing quite like this, not since before I joined the Department and started working with you on controlling them. The emotion was so . . . *raw* that I couldn't ignore it. When I first came out of the vision, I was so caught up in it still I ended up snapping at Jane."

"About . . . ?"

"Something stupid," I said, avoiding looking over at him. "A piece of furniture."

"All great fights are over stupid things when it comes to building a relationship," he said.

"Thanks, Master Yoda, but I don't think a chest of drawers is something to get all worked up about."

Connor shrugged and started in on his paperwork. "Depends on the chest of drawers, I suppose."

"That's just it," I said. "One second we're fighting ghosts; the next I'm snapping at her about the dresser she liked there."

Connor looked up at me. "And that's an issue . . . why?"

"I don't know," I said. "Because right now she only has a single drawer in my apartment and wants something more, I suppose."

"And you think this was all due to your interaction with the tattooist, kid? You sure you just don't have commitment issues?"

"I'm not sure," I said. "I know I have my issues when it comes to women. I've never gotten as close to someone as I have with Jane. I'm in untested waters there. Plus, you know how particular I am when it comes to antique furniture and all that. I spent years making money off of pieces here and there. Let's face it, Connor . . . there's an importance to assigning a piece of furniture to someone, a charge of emotional attachment that comes from taking a big step like that. Don't you think?"

Connor rolled his eyes at me. "Yeah, I can see how her wanting more than your old underwear drawer to keep her stuff in is totally unreasonable," he said. "Oh, wait. No, I *can't*. It's not like she asked to move in."

"You think she wants to move in?" I asked, a strange panic rising in my chest.

"Did *she* say that?"

"Well . . . no."

Connor rolled his eyes at me. "Relax."

"Forget it," I said, trying to calm myself. "If you had been through all that raw pain like I had, you might stand a chance of seeing where I'm coming from."

I grabbed my pen and started up with my paperwork again. Compared to getting advice from Connor, it was almost enjoyable, and the panic fell away.

"Tell me this, kid," he said. "How many nights does she stay over?"

"In a week?"

"Yeah," Connor said. "How many?"

I calculated it in my head. "Five or six, I guess."

Connor threw up his arms. "Jesus, kid. Whether you want to admit it or not, you are living together already. If that's the way it is, give the girl some more storage space."

Doubt crept into my mind. If Connor was this exasperated with me, maybe I was overreacting. "You think?"

Connor leaned forward over his desk, lowering his voice. "Listen, I know you're still new at relationships and all, let alone having one that works, and it hasn't been that long. But trust me on this. As much as I frown on office romances, I like Jane, and though it pains me to say it, I think you two kind of work well together. You push her away on something as trivial as this and it's going to build, fester. You'll ask her to pass the creamer one morning and next thing you know, it will be smashing on the wall next to your head from her throwing it at you. Give the girl more space and man up."

"You're right," I said, finally conceding. "I hear you. I just wish I didn't have this damn ghost's emotional baggage sitting so deep in me. I can't shake it."

"Shake what?" Jane's voice came out of the blue from behind me. I jumped in my seat.

"God," I said, trying to check my nerves as best as I could. "Don't sneak up on me like that."

Jane looked at me with a curious smile. "O . . . kay," she said. "Sorry. So, what can't you shake?"

I really didn't want to reveal what Connor and I had just been talking about. There was stuff you said to your male friends that should never come to the ears of your significant other. Even *I* knew that.

Connor laughed and spoke instead. "The kid was just saying he couldn't shake this sense of dread from all the new paperwork coming our way."

Jane nodded and relaxed. "Tell me about it," she said. "When I went over to Greater and Lesser Arcana, I thought they took away my desk and turned my area into a storage room, but apparently that's just all the work piling up for me."

I spread my hand out over our office space. "Welcome to the club," I said.

"Thanks," she said. She looked around, and then lowered her voice. "Do you think this Professor Redfield thing is going to take long? I don't mind helping out the Inspectre, but I'm not part of your Other Division and Wesker will be all over me if I don't get back to all my Arcana stuff soon."

"I don't know how long it's going to take," Connor said. "I guess some of it depends on you. Did you bring back any good news after questioning all of the professor's neighbors?"

Jane's face turned sour. "Remind me to thank Davidson for that later. I've got a nice cantrip I've been dying to try out and he's earned a nice Pinocchio nose for a few days, if you ask me."

"Hell hath no fury . . ." Connor said, trailing off and shaking his finger at me. "Remember that kid."

I nodded but didn't respond. If Connor was making a crack related to our previous conversation about the cuck-olded tattooist, I wasn't sure, and now was not the time to ask him. Instead, I looked up at Jane. "What did you find?"

Jane leaned back against the wall of our sectioned-off area. "Well, for starters," Jane said. "The neighbors are saying that the place is haunted."

"The whole high-rise?" I asked.

"No, just the area by Professor Redfield's apartment."

Connor gave a dismissive laugh. "Sorry to burst your investigative bubble, but I seriously doubt the place is haunted," he said. "I didn't sense a Casper in sight. That building is practically new. It hasn't had enough time or tenants to get haunted."

Jane threw her notebook down on my desk and let out a deep sigh. "Look," she said. "It's bad enough that I got relegated to patrolling the halls of that high-rise. Between the ogling from the male tenants and the general reluctance of most of them to give up anything useful, it was a real blast, let me tell you. But! Please don't belittle the mes-senger, okay? I questioned all of them separately and didn't lead the conversations. Everyone gave up variations of the same story. Gorgeous lady in a blue-green dress, long dark hair past her shoulders. When they approached, she would vanish. Happy?"

Jane turned in a huff and headed out of our space and back up the aisle toward the main bull pen. Connor got up from his desk first, grabbed his still-wet trench coat off our makeshift coatrack, and ran after her. I took longer, grabbing my own coat and gathering up my umbrella and retractable bat before heading after them. I caught up with them when I entered the café area of our cover operation and found them over by the condiment station by the curtained-off door to the theater.

Connor held up his hands. "Sorry, Jane," he said. "I'm not saying I don't believe you. I'm just saying that I didn't catch a hint of anything ghostly when we were there."

"Maybe we need to go over the place again," I offered. "Not that I'm looking to head back out in this weather."

A dark look crossed Connor's face. "Dammit," he said. "We can't let it wait. The longer we put it off, the exponentially colder the trail will get. Whatever's going on, we have to attend to it sooner than later."

I looked toward the front windows of the Lovecraft Café. The storm was still pouring down sheets of rain outside. "You don't need Jane and me for that, do you? I mean, I was kinda hoping for a little bit of warmth indoors tonight."

"Sorry, kid," Connor said. "Like it or not, the two of you both qualify as investigators on this case. Everybody gets to return to the scene of the crime."

"Great," Jane said. "I *still* have to write up all the paperwork on my going door to door, but I guess that will have to wait." She looked at me, tired. "Next time, remind me to come back with less investigation-stirring data, will you?"

"Let's get going, then," Connor said. "The sooner we

wrap this up for the Inspectre, the sooner we all get back to our regular office drudgery."

Jane gave an enthusiastic thumbs-up. "Awesome," she said. "Let me go tell Director Wesker I'm heading back out and grab my coat. My boss won't be too pleased, but then again, when is he ever?"

She gave us a quick smile before I could even agree with her, and then ran off through the black curtains that led back into the theater and our offices.

"Making us work as a couple," I mused. "Do I get time and a half for that or something?"

Connor shook his head. "Not in this economy," he said, pulling his coat on.

"Then it sucks to be working in this economy," I said. "And in this weather."

"Can't control either," Connor said, "but don't sweat it, kid. You need to worry about the things you *can* control."

"Thanks for covering for me back at our desks," I said. "When she asked about what I couldn't shake."

Connor smiled. "No problem," he said. "Don't worry about that, either. The older you get, the more practiced you get at lying on the fly. You go through enough relationships and it just gets easier."

"Such a romantic," I said. "Well, I've got that to look forward to, I suppose."

"I wouldn't worry about the future too much," he said, turning away from me and walking off.

"Oh, no?" I asked.

"Nope," he said, heading for the coffee counter. "Probably won't live long enough."

6

Professor Mason Redfield's apartment was the way we had left it hours earlier—minus the professor's body from the middle of his living room, of course.

"Nice to see the regular cops can still act as a cleanup crew," Connor said.

"I prefer to think of them as our janitors," I said, leaving the spot where the body had lain and heading off to a set of bookcases on my right.

"Tsk-tsk," Jane said. "Now, boys, be nice. They were perfectly fine when I was roaming the halls here."

"Of course they were," I said, starting to look through the volumes of theater and film books stacked neatly along them. "You've got girly bits and all the stuff that guys want to be nice to."

Jane shrugged and fixed me with a wicked grin from across the room. "I wonder if one of *them* would let me have more storage space in their apartment," she said.

My face flushed as a jealousy far more potent than my own would have been gurgled up. "Maybe," I said, a little tweaked that she was bringing it up in front of Connor. "You want to try your luck with one of them? Go for it."

Connor stepped between us and spoke before Jane had a chance to respond. "Can we please focus on the casework here?" he asked. "This is a murder scene, not *The Dating Game*. Show some respect for the departed professor *and* the Inspectre. Now focus. Do you think he'd entrust this particular investigation to just anybody?"

"You're right," Jane said. "Sorry."

"Me, too," I said, willing myself to calm down. The flare subsided.

The three of us set about exploring the apartment. Despite nothing triggering my power earlier, I pressed my power into a few of the books on the shelves, bringing up nothing but a variety of images of the still-living Professor Redfield lecturing students down at New York University.

"Anything?" Connor asked. "We need some kind of motivation for this murder."

"Maybe he failed the wrong film student," I suggested.

Connor shook his head. "Still wouldn't explain this ghost woman in green Jane was told about," he said.

"Okay, fine," I said. "Then maybe they're building this place on an Indian burial ground . . . ?"

Jane gave me a weak smile, one side of her mouth curling up all cute-like. "Let's not get all *Poltergeist* now."

I looked back to Connor.

He shrugged and scanned the apartment. "What she said. I wouldn't go with *Poltergeist*. I'm still not picking up any displaced spirits here."

I went back to scanning the bookshelves. "Just throwing

out suggestions in the face of nothing here," I said. "Trying to keep my thinking outside of the box."

"Could you try to keep it in a nearby box at least?" Connor said, agitated.

"Hey," I said, spinning around, his agitation causing my tattooist's anger to spike. "I'm trying here."

"Guys," Jane said, but the two of us were too busy sniping at each other to give her our attention.

"Try harder, then," Connor said.

"Guys," Jane whispered, with urgency this time. Connor and I turned to look at her. She was staring past us at the wall of windows behind us. I turned back to it with caution. Beyond the glass, a lone female figure stood in the darkness and pouring rain on the patio out by the swimming pool. Long black hair rolled in loose curls over her shoulders and a green drape of a gown that covered her body. She stood there motionless, staring.

Jane whispered, "What do we do?"

"We establish contact," Connor said, creeping toward the glass doors. He reached into the outer pocket of his trench coat and pulled out a corked vial. "Or trap her and make her talk."

"Lead on, ghost whisperer," I said and fell in step behind him. When he got to the glass doors, he slid one of them open and the three of us stepped out onto the patio. The rain came down hard, making countless circular ripples along the surface of the pool as it fell. Connor stepped out into the rain. The woman's eyes followed him, yet she remained poised and stock-still.

Connor thumbed the stopper off the vial in his hand. Its contents rose up into the air in a twist of brown smoke and drifted off toward her, but the tendrils failed to wind their way around her, instead dissipating. Connor looked back over his shoulder at us. "Not a ghost," he said and slipped the empty vial back into his coat pocket. "Never trust neighbors to classify something right."

I stepped forward. "Excuse me," I shouted out to her. "You want to tell us what you're doing out here?"

The woman shifted her focus over to me. She was striking, with high cheekbones, but when her eyes met mine, a chill cut into my soul.

"Hey!" Connor said, snapping his fingers to get her attention once more. "The kid asked you a question. Did you know the professor . . . and how did you get out here?"

"She's not talking," Jane said.

"I noticed that," Connor said.

"We can take care of that downtown," I said. I pulled out my bat and extended it even though the woman definitely wasn't hiding anything on her—not in that dress, anyway.

Her eyes went to my hands. I walked toward her through the downfall of rain, but for every step I took, the woman backed away one.

"Easy, now," I said. "We're going to get answers from you, one way or the other."

I kept advancing as she retreated until her back was pressed up against the railing between two of the gargoyles at the far edge of the patio. I paused as I gave the stone statues the once-over. If they came to life or anything like that, I was not going to be happy.

The farther away from the building I stepped, the worse the storm got, wind whipping all around us. Behind the woman, I could see the East River and the skyline of Queens off in the distance, giving me a bout of vertigo from the perspective.

After a moment of inspecting the gargoyles, I decided they looked inanimate enough and started closing with the

woman once more. I stepped around the pool to avoid it
and kept moving with caution toward the woman, fishing
a pair of handcuffs out of my coat's inside pocket. It was
exciting to have someone cuffable for a change. "Don't do
anything stupid," I said. "We're authorized by the Department of Extraordinary Affairs to take you into custody for
the possible murder of Professor Mason Redfield."

The woman locked her eyes with mine and stepped toward me. She placed her hands out in front of her as if
prepared to be arrested, and I tucked my bat under my arm
as I closed the distance to cuff her, but then I realized her
arms kept moving. The woman brought them straight out
in front of her, then spread them out to her sides like she
was about to be crucified. When she bent her knees a second later, I realized what she was about to do.

"Jumper!" I shouted. Connor ran around the other side
of the pool toward her, but I was closer. Falling rain stung
my eyes as I stumbled forward, and it took all I had not to
slip into the pool as I lunged to grab the woman, but I was
too late.

With very little effort, the woman leapt up into the air
and fell back over the railing in a graceful arc, sliding
out through the pouring rain like she was doing a back
handspring. She disappeared out of sight like a shot as
I slammed into the spot along the railing where she had
stood just seconds ago.

"No!" I shouted. Connor and Jane arrived next to me a
second later and the three of us watched in horror as the
woman fell through the open air. Like an Olympic diver,
her form was spot-on—arms high over her head and legs
pulled tightly together in perfect form. I waited for the
gruesome result of it all as she plummeted to the roof way
down below, but my eyes caught something promising

there—another pool. The woman hit the water with professional diving precision, but despite the beauty of it, a large plume of spray rose up as she entered the water.

I took my satchel from over my shoulder and threw it toward Jane. I pulled off my jacket and tossed it to Connor, the rain immediately soaking through the black T-shirt I had on underneath it.

"Kid . . ." Connor started, but I didn't give him a chance to say much more.

I threw my legs over the railing and judged the distance out from the side of the building to the pool down below. "Can't let her get away," I said. "For the Inspectre."

"Simon," Jane called out as she grabbed for me. "Don't."

It was too late. I caught the last of her words seconds after I let go and pushed off the ledge of the building. The rain whipped at me as I fell and I squeezed my eyes shut, leaving them open just enough to calculate if I had aimed for the pool correctly or if I should prepare to have my feet driven all the way up into my skull. I balled myself up, tucking my legs to my chest in cannonball position as best I could. My already soaked-through jeans made it difficult to do, but I didn't want to survive the fall only to break my legs on the pool bottom or by landing on the woman I was chasing.

I hit the water hard, the shock of its coldness driving the air from my lungs. My ass hit the bottom of the pool, my tailbone slamming into it. I struggled to get my legs underneath me. The fire in my chest from lack of oxygen burned. I pushed off the bottom of the pool, the weight of my clothes making my struggle sluggish. When I couldn't hold my breath anymore, I gasped in, praying I was near the surface. My initial intake, however, was water, which set me in a deeper panic, but thankfully I broke the surface and my next breath was sweet, delicious air. I gagged, fighting to keep my head above water, and gasped for my next breath. My elbow came down hard against the edge of the pool as I flailed for something to grab onto, adding a new pain to the one already burning in my lungs. I slid down, but my left hand caught the edge of the pool and I dug my fingertips in. With my other arm, I hoisted myself above the water to shoulder level and turned to scan the pool for the woman as I cleared my lungs in a fit of hacking coughs.

Between the pouring rain and the waves from my impact, I couldn't make out anyone in the pool with me above or below the surface. I searched the murky darkness as I waited for the water to calm, but I didn't see anything until a female form pulled itself out of the shadowy water across the pool.

"Crazy bitch," I muttered to myself, my heart still pounding from the fall. "I'll see your crazy and raise you."

In my soaked clothes, I felt like I weighed a million pounds, but there was no time to waste. My suspect was already turning, and once she noticed me there, the chase would be on again. Keeping my eyes on her, I pressed the palms of both hands onto the pool's edge and hoisted myself up and out of the water.

Or tried to, at any rate.

Before I could get all the way out, a wave of water rose up in front of the woman and rolled across the top of the pool, washing over my legs. Pressure wrapped around my calves, becoming solid as if it were hands pulling at my lower half. It tugged at me and I fell onto the expensive-looking tile work along the pool's edge. My ribs screamed in pain from the impact, but I didn't have time to concern myself with it—I was being dragged back into the pool against my will.

I fought whatever strange riptide had me as something about the feel of the water changed. The pressure of it was increasing, making it more and more difficult to breathe. I made for the shallow end, but it was like trying to swim through molasses. As spots of light started to fill my vision from lack of oxygen, I caught sight of the woman once again. One of her arms was extended out from her, taut and muscular. She closed her fist slowly and the pressure increased. I would have loved to marvel with Other Division curiosity at how she was controlling the water, but right now all I could think about was how nice it would be to not die this way.

Movement from above the woman caught my eye. Another figure was plummeting down from above. Between the dark, the rain, and the figure's growing speed, I couldn't tell if it was Connor or Jane, but whichever one of them it was, they were *not* going to make it into the pool, a fact that caused my heart to leap out of my chest. Before I could even think to look away, the figure landed square on top of the woman. The sound of them impacting against each other was not as meaty as I had expected. The collision was more like stone grinding against stone—one of the gargoyles from up above. It shattered, crumbling on the spot into a million broken pieces in a pile of rubble.

The woman, however, didn't crumble like the gargoyle did. She exploded, not into a geyser of bloody, fleshy bits, but into *water*. The spray flew in every direction like an ocean wave hitting an outcropping of rocks, leaving no trace of the woman whatsoever. The pressure in the water faded and in a flash I was across the pool to where I could finally stand and wade my way out of it. I ran over to the spot where the broken gargoyle lay.

As I shifted the rubble around with my boot, Jane came

barreling out of a set of exit doors onto the patio, her hair wet and my satchel still in her hands. Her face washed with relief when she saw I was alive. As she walked over to me, she looked to the pile of stone, and then up into the rain toward Professor Redfield's patio.

"What the hell happened?" she asked.

"*I* happened," a voice called out from behind her. Connor stood in the doorway Jane had just come through, panting and rolling his left shoulder. "Jesus, those gargoyles weigh as much as a kraken."

Jane hugged me and handed my satchel over. "What happened?" she repeated. "The second you threw yourself over the railing, I took off down the stairs and missed everything."

"It looked like that woman was doing something to you in the pool, kid," Connor said, walking over to us. He handed me my jacket, looked down at the pile of stone, and kicked a few pieces around, too. "Interesting. No body."

"Oh, you noticed?" I said, still catching my breath. "I don't know what the hell she really is, but basically she was using the pool water to crush me. Maybe she's some kind of water elemental . . . ?"

Connor shook his head at me. "And this is why we don't go jumping over high-rise railings after strange women," he said. His chiding was probably the closest I was going to get to hearing him say that he was glad I was okay.

"Well, *I* thought it was heroic," Jane said, smiling. "Stupid, but heroic."

"Thanks," I said. I brushed her wet hair out of the way and kissed her forehead. "Next time, you get to jump first."

She hugged me and I hissed as pain flared up my side.

"Careful," I said.

Jane stepped back quickly, concern on her face. "Are you hurt?"

I pressed along my bruised ribs gently, testing them. "Not too badly," I said. "More my pride than anything. Drowning in someone's pool isn't the way I really pictured myself dying. A vampire, werewolves, maybe, but not this."

Connor tsk-tsked me.

"What?"

"Let's get out of here," he said, heading back toward the door, "before I nominate you for the Departmental Medal of Stupidity."

I wasn't sure if that was a real thing or not. I wouldn't put it past the Department to issue something like that, maybe a dunce cap to make an object lesson out of foolhardy agents. Connor walked off before I had a chance to ask him. All I could do was let Jane help me hobble my way off the patio. Given all our cuts recently, I wondered whose paycheck was going to cover the damage the falling gargoyle had made. I doubted we could expense it.

7

I wasn't normally one to strip in the partially walled office cube that comprised the space Connor and I shared, but by the time we got back to the Department of Extraordinary Affairs, I hadn't dried off at all and was shivering from my jump into the pool. Jane left me with Connor and ran off to report to Director Wesker over in Greater & Lesser Arcana as I hung up my satchel to dry out, and then peeled off my suede leather jacket before dropping it into a plastic-lined bin I now kept next to my desk.

Connor looked down at it. "Nice idea, kid. When did you put that there?"

I leaned against our partners desk as I struggled out of my wet Doc Martens, which were now clinging to my feet like they were glued on. "After that ectoplasm in the popcorn-machine incident in that off-Broadway theater," I said. "My cleaning bills are through the roof, and even before these cuts, the Inspectre stopped letting me expense them. You'd think damage done in the line of duty would be covered . . ."

"I wouldn't press him, kid."

"No?" My Docs didn't want to come off. I undid the laces even more and wiggled off the first one, tossing it in the bin.

"No," Connor said. "It could be worse."

"Worse than bagging my clothes up here on a weekly basis and then dragging them to the cleaners on my own dime? How could it be worse?"

"You press the Inspectre on it, and they might start issuing us uniforms. You want to wear a tan jumpsuit with your name stitched over the pocket?"

"Depends," I said. "Do I get to be Egon? Do I get a Proton Pack?" My other boot came free and I put it with the other one.

"I don't think so." Connor pointed to the mountains of files and paperwork piled on both of our desks. It had grown several inches in the few hours we had been gone. "Think of what it takes to even get ballpoint pens from supply. You rip a field-issued jumpsuit and try to requisition a new one? You'll be roaming the halls in your boxers at least a week waiting."

"Speaking of which, can you watch our cubicle door? I need to finish getting out of the rest of this stuff."

Connor turned away. "Gladly. Although why you need to do it here . . ."

"It's just easier," I said. I walked around to the work side of my desk, slid the lower-left-hand drawer open, and fished out a dry T-shirt. I pulled off the wet one, threw it on top of my boots, and slid the new one over my head. The front of it read: I BRAKE FOR IMAGINARY CREATURES. "I'm living out of my drawer here."

Connor laughed. "Now you know how Jane feels at your place."

His comment stung. I tried to ignore it, but another flare of the tattooist's way over-the-top emotions hit me. I bit my lip and fought the urge to say something, instead focusing on putting on a dry pair of jeans that were also sitting in the drawer. I slid them on, thankful to be dry once again and forcing the emotions down. "Okay," I said. "Done."

Connor turned and gave me a skeptical look.

"What?" I asked.

"Your face, kid. What's the matter? Did I strike a raw nerve with my Jane comment?"

I sighed. "Yeah, I guess," I admitted. "That tattooist emotional-baggage thing flared up again."

I sat down at my desk and Connor walked over to his.

"Look at the bright side," he said, sitting down. "You probably won't have to worry about Jane getting the itch to marry you."

"I won't?"

"You jumping to conclusions that Jane wanting more drawer space means she wants to move in should land you in a padded room long before that."

"Comforting," I said. I set to work writing out the details of the events of the past few hours, almost enjoying the silence while doing it. At least Connor wasn't jabbing me about my newfound domestic issues with Jane. When my eyes started to blur from all the paperwork, I stopped and gathered my papers. I stood up. "I'm going to run this up to the Inspectre."

"Go crazy, kid," Connor said, looking up from his own chaos of paper across from me, "but aren't you forgetting something?"

I thought for a moment, and then shrugged.

Connor pointed at my bare feet. "No socks, no shoes," he said. "No service."

I opened my lower-left-hand drawer once more. "Thanks for the reminder," I said. "I don't know where my head's at. Maybe that water woman squeezed some of my brains out when she was trying to drown me." Fresh socks and dry boots, and under that, nothing more. I pulled them out and put them on. "Time to restock my wardrobe. Looks like this is all that's left."

"Then you better hope you don't run into anything heading up to the Inspectre's office," Connor said.

I stood up, feeling almost human again, the leather of the new boots stiff against my feet. "A wandering monster encounter is highly unlikely. I think I can manage."

I turned and headed away from our desks, walking off toward the stairs that led to the Inspectre's office up on the second floor.

"Oh, you say that now," Connor shouted after me, "but don't forget where we work."

I slowed my pace as I walked. Connor had a point. A healthy amount of paranoia about danger lurking around every corner had kept my older partner alive so far, and if there was ever a place full of potentially menacing corners, it was the Department of Extraordinary Affairs.

I found the Inspectre buried in a paperwork mountain all his own when I got to his office. The usually neat and orderly British gentleman's office was littered with more casework and files than I had ever seen, little piles of manila folders dotting the rich cherrywood finish of the room.

"Sir?" I called out as I stepped into his office. He finished what he was writing before looking up at me, a bit agitated. "I've prepared a file on Mason Redfield . . ."

"Dammit, boy," the Inspectre blustered, standing up. He came out from behind his desk, crossed over to me, and snatched the folder from my hand. "You mean to tell me you've been back long enough to write out a case file and didn't think to come see me first?"

I stepped back, a little surprised by the anger in the Inspectre's voice. "I'm sorry," I said. "I just thought . . ."

The Inspectre turned away from me and went back to his desk. He threw the folder down, not even bothering to look at it. He breathed in like he was getting ready to yell, but stopped himself. He slid his thumb and index finger under his glasses and rubbed his eyes.

"Forgive me," he said, softening. "Perhaps I didn't make my request clear enough for urgency in this matter."

"I was just following standard protocol . . ."

"Of course you were," he said, waving my words away with his hand. "Bully for you. I trust you have something to report . . . ?"

"Yes," I said. "My report is . . . in my report." I pointed at the folder on the desk.

The Inspectre put his hand on it, but made no effort to open it. "I think I would prefer to hear it from you, my boy."

For the first time I noticed the deep weariness on his face. His eyes were heavier than usual, full of exhaustion.

"Absolutely," I said. "Of course. When we found Professor Redfield's body . . ."

The Inspectre raised his hand off the folder in front of him. "Spare me the more gruesome details, my boy. Friends from long ago haunt you the most if you know too many particulars about their passing."

"Sorry," I said, picking up the folder and searching my papers for what should and shouldn't be said.

"No need for apologies," the Inspectre said, sounding sad this time. "It's something they simply don't prepare you for in what passes for training around here."

I had written so much down, I didn't know where to start editing, so I closed the folder. "One thing is for sure, sir. Mason Redfield's death was not of natural causes." I tried to imagine what it would be like to drown from the inside out like that, but couldn't. "There were no signs that he struggled. He looked almost . . . peaceful."

"Good," the Inspectre said, solemn. He took off his glasses. "That is something. It may seem like a small thing to you, Simon, but when you get to be my age, there is a . . . comfort, I suppose, in the thought of dying peacefully. Truth be told, I never expected to make it past fifty. Then again, neither did Mason."

Curiosity got the better of me. "You mentioned earlier tonight that the professor was a friend of yours . . . ?"

The Inspectre stood and turned to the display case behind him that took up most of the wall. It was filled with books as well as a few ornamental museum pieces scattered among the shelves. His hand rose, gently gliding along the edge of the top of it. It came to rest on a length of dark polished wood with a thin band of tarnished copper near one end of it. A walking stick. He pulled it down, held it carefully in both hands, and stared down at it, fixated.

"He was more than just a friend," the Inspectre said. "He was my first partner in the Fraternal Order of Goodness, our older brotherhood of investigators which predates the government-run Department of Extraordinary Affairs by several hundred years." He tossed the cane to me. "See for yourself, my boy."

I caught it with both hands and sat myself down in one of the chairs on the other side of the Inspectre's desk, inspecting the cane as I did so. Along the metal band read the word DAMOCLES. The object crackled with energy in my hands, almost eager to reveal itself to my power like a child wanting to tell about his day at school. There was rich history in this object. With that much power ready to release, sinking into the chair was my best option. I wanted to use my psychometry on the cane, but I didn't want to fall over from blood-sugar depletion from such a heavily charged object.

I pressed my power into the cane and my mind flashed back through time. It was nighttime in an old graveyard somewhere along the East River. A large jagged fissure in the earth gaped open where grass met the rise of a short, rocky slope where a young Argyle Quimbley was busy fighting his way through a steady stream of pale, ghoulish creatures crawling up out of it. Riding the vision out behind his eyes, I was surprised at how good he was doing—my Other Division boss was kicking ass like it was going out of style, cutting quite a striking and dashing figure. I felt his youth and prowess as a young agent. He was a far cry from the man I knew—muscular and dressed for combat action in khakis and a leather bomber jacket.

Argyle Quimbley slammed the butt of the cane into the gut of one charging creature, and then slid a hidden blade out of its other end and plunged it into the chest of another. The ghoul roared in pain and Argyle Quimbley raised his boot and kicked it free from his sword. He was a swash-buckling dynamo, but as I watched, I realized the Inspectre had a bigger problem than simply cutting them down. The creature that Quimbley had just stabbed in the heart got back on its feet and started after him once again.

"Could you research a little faster, Mason?" Quimbley shouted as he continued to fend off the swarm. "These ghouls don't seem to be staying down and it would be advantageous to know their weak points. Judging from that last one, I'd say we can rule out the heart."

Having just been thrust into the mind and body of a young Argyle Quimbley, I had barely taken notice of Mason Redfield standing there. He stood only a few feet away, flipping through a dark green file folder, but looked far less fashionable than Quimbley did. With elbow pads on his tweed jacket, Mason Redfield almost looked like the modern-day version of the Inspectre. A tiny flashlight floated above his head as he pored over the file. His hair hung down across his forehead in a wild mess and he pushed it out of the way as he thumbed through the file.

"I'm reading as fast as I can, Argyle," he shouted, "but these damn files are out of order." Mason's accent was pure American next to the Inspectre's English tones, although he sounded as if he were trying to affect a passable Clark Gable. Even so, the man sounded flustered and nervous. "It's like trying to read an encyclopedia in the dark. By the time I assess the proper ecology of ghouls, I suspect we may be good and dead."

"Now, now," Argyle said, slashing at two more off to their right. "We'll have none of that talk while we're still breathing. You keep reading and I'll keep fending."

"Who has the time for all this paperwork these days, I ask you?" Mason sniped. "If the Fraternal Order of Goodness doesn't watch out, they're going to kill their membership by sheer weight of paperwork alone."

Despite the peril of constant fighting all around them, I couldn't help but smile at that. It was oddly comforting to hear how little that had changed in the past forty years.

Mason continued thumbing through the contents of the folder.

"Hurry up," Argyle said. "There are more scrabbling about down below. I can hear the nasty buggers."

Mason looked up, his face going white. "We're not venturing down there as well, are we?"

Argyle leaned back to dodge a series of claws slashing at his face before he could answer. He stabbed at the ghoul, driving it back but not killing it. "Are we going into the fissure?" he asked, looking around for the next incoming ghoul. "No. Not intentionally, anyway."

"Good," Mason said. "For a second I—"

Argyle watched as a dark shadow flew up and out of the fissure. The creature was heading straight for Mason at breakneck speed. Quimbley sidestepped one of the other creatures already engaging him, slicing it in two across its waist as he went, sending both halves of it tumbling back into the fissure. Now free, he ran to help Mason, but judging from his distance, he wouldn't make it in time. The charging creature blindsided Mason, wrapping its arms around him and tumbling Argyle's partner to the ground. The tiny hovering flashlight over Mason's head fell with him, skittering across the ground. As Mason started to struggle, Argyle finally closed the distance and kicked the creature off his partner. With a flick of his wrist, Argyle's nimble blade slid out into the night, lashing off the creature's head. Its body dropped in a writhing heap to the ground and, much to Argyle's happiness, stayed down.

Mason flexed his hand as he stood back up, calling his flashlight back over to him like he had Jedi powers. It swirled back into place above him, the light once more falling on the folder still in his hands. He pulled one of the papers from the folder, held it up, and shouted. "The head," he said with excitement. "It seems to be the only way noted in the file."

"Yes," Quimbley said, quite pleased. "It appears so. Of course the head. Tends to work for most creatures, really. Why didn't I think of that sooner?"

I felt the sparkle in his eye, the way his adrenaline pumped him up with hope. Just knowing how to take them down was enough to turn the tide of this battle. With renewed vigor, he swung his sword into action, beheading the creatures left and right like he was the Tasmanian devil on steroids.

Mason joined him in the fray, pummeling the creatures with an impressive type of telekinetic arcane, using nearby stones as his projectiles. The rocks alone weren't enough to stop the monstrosities, but they were enough to hinder and distract them while Argyle Quimbley moved in to deal the deathblows. The dispatching of the remaining ghouls went quickly, and in the end, there were only the two agents from the Fraternal Order of Goodness left standing in a sea of headless ghouls.

"Are you all right?" Argyle asked, huffing and puffing. He dropped his sword to the ground and bent over with his hands on his knees as he tried to catch his breath.

"I believe so," Mason said. He held his hand out under the flashlight and it dropped out of the air, slipping through his fingers. It clattered to the ground and the light went dead. "Can't say as much for my light source." He bent down to retrieve it, giving a groan. Young as they were, the pains of combat were still on them. They might bounce back quicker, but peril still took its toll.

The graveyard along the fissure was a little darker for the lack of light, but there was still enough ambient city light that I could make out Mason's movements, even though they were far more shadowy. Despite that, I sensed another shift among the shadows and I felt Quimbley's muscles tense.

"Mason!" Quimbley shouted. "Behind you!"

Mason stood up with his dead flashlight and spun about, but his focus was too high. The threat was at his feet. The upper half of the ghoul that Argyle had cut in two moments ago had clawed its way back up to the lip of the fissure. One of its arms lashed out, its sharpened talons catching the fabric of Mason's pant leg. Using its other hand for leverage, the monster grabbed onto one of the jutting rocks down in the fissure and started pulling Mason toward him. That split second Mason wasn't looking down undid everything, and as the creature tugged, Mason lost his balance. He fell down, wincing as several of the pointier rocks dug into his back.

Argyle Quimbley dove for his friend, his heart racing. Mason flailed on the ground, trying to flip himself over while kicking at the ghoul, but each move he made only drove him farther toward the fissure. Argyle caught Mason's hand in his, rolling his partner over. Mason grabbed at anything he could with his free hand.

"Pull!" Mason screamed out, his face pure panic. Terror filled his eyes, the widened whites of them standing out in the dark graveyard.

Argyle pulled, but it was having little effect. "I am, blast it!" he shouted. "Just mind your feet! Don't let that thing bite you."

While sound advice by my reckoning, the thought of being bitten only caused Mason to panic more. He started lashing out with both of his feet over and over, catching the ghoul in its maw of decaying teeth every time. The creature cackled as if it were relishing the pain of it all. What was worse was the fact that with every kick, I could feel Argyle's grip on Mason Redfield slipping.

The creature bit down on Mason's boot with its gnarl of teeth, tugging hard on it. A chunk of it tore free in its mouth, taking a bit of sock with it and exposing the pale white flesh of his ankle. Time was running out. Mason was either going into the abyss or was about to become a ghoul thanks to a leg chomp.

Argyle let go of Mason with one of his hands and felt around on the ground. His fingers found the edge of his blade and he grabbed at it with care until he grasped the wooden tip that acted as its pommel. He wrapped his hand around it, slashing through the air as he turned back toward the fight. He lunged the sharpened steel tip toward Mason.

A new terror sprung up in Mason's eyes as he saw the blade coming toward him. The blade flashed inches from his face, continued past it, and slid along the backs of his shoulders until it tore straight into the mouth of the ghoul, breaking off two of its teeth. It lodged there, keeping its maw from closing on Mason's ankle. Argyle pushed forward until the blade came out of the back of the creature's head and then twisted it.

The creature howled, letting go of Mason. The agent scrabbled back from the fissure while Argyle Quimbley kept the skewered monster at bay. He yanked the blade upward and it was too much for the creature. A horrid *pop* came from within its head before the bones of its jaw shifted, floating loosely under its rotting skin. Once Mason was clear, Argyle stepped forward, raised his boot to the creature's head, and pushed it away to dislodge it from the sword. Broken, the creature fell back into the fissure, howling all the way as it fell.

Argyle backed away from the hole in the ground, not daring to turn his back on it. The tip of the blade hissed and bubbled underneath a thick slime of the creature's innards. The ichor continued to eat away at the metal until the end of the blade fell off, bluntly hitting Argyle's foot. Once he put some distance between himself and the opening in the ground, he turned his attention to his still-prone partner.

"Mason, are you all right?" he asked.

Mason scrabbled across the ground like a crab as he moved away from the edge of the fissure. He crawled toward Argyle Quimbley and rolled on his back, still shaking. His deep breaths of exhaustion turned to hysterical laughter as he sat up, brushing himself off.

"When you went for your sword, Argyle, I thought you were simply going to put me out of my misery." Mason's nerves were thick in his voice, the look on his face pained. "I thank you for being more levelheaded than that."

Mason raised his hand out to Quimbley for a hand up, but the broken blade of Quimbley's sword stayed in place between the two of them. Argyle made no move to lower it, keeping it leveled at his partner.

"Argyle . . ." Mason started, suspicion in his eyes.

"Now, now," Quimbley said, sounding disarming. "Surely you recall Fraternal Order protocol. You show me your boot there, the one with the nice chunk out of it. If the skin's not broken, then we can talk."

Mason looked hurt, but offered up his foot with the torn boot over it. Argyle used the jagged tip of the sword to inspect the area, causing Mason to flinch in response.

"Oh, for heaven's sake, Argyle. Be careful with your damned sword, won't you? You're just as likely to break the skin and let ghoul contagion in as if they *had* bitten me."

Argyle ignored him and continued inspecting the hole

in Mason's boot until he was satisfied. He lowered the sword and offered his free hand to Mason. His partner took it, but there was a bit of fire in his eyes now.

"So very trusting of you, Argyle," he spat out.

Quimbley remained calm and moved to pick up the broken end of the blade using a handkerchief, wiping it down.

"Nothing personal," he said, "but you can never be too careful. You know that. Sentimentality can't enter into things if we're to survive in this world."

"Such times," Mason said, brushing himself off, "when friends may turn on friends."

Without another word, Mason began hefting the corpses of the dead ghouls back into the fissure. Argyle's tension in the silence weighed heavily on his heart, and I felt every ounce of it. There was nothing to say right now that would make the situation any less awkward, so instead he joined Mason in the task of body disposal.

When it was done, Mason stared down into the fissure, unmoving with a face that was a mask of dark seriousness.

"Come, now, Mason," Argyle said. "We'd best be going. I doubt we'll see any more activity here. The sun should be up soon. I'll see if anyone at F.O.G. knows of a good contractor to come fill this fissure in with concrete. You can go about carving protective runes in it later . . ." Argyle started along a path leading back through the cemetery, and then turned back when he realized Mason wasn't following along with him. Quimbley turned to look back. Mason Redfield remained by the lip of fissure, staring down into the abyss. "Perhaps you would prefer to stay in the graveyard?"

This seemed to snap Mason out of his trance. "No, I would not," he said, agitated. He turned and pushed past Argyle Quimbley as he headed up the main path leading out. "In fact, not only do I want out of this graveyard; I think I want out of this *life*."

Argyle ran to catch up with him, using his cane to stop him. "Surely you don't mean suicide?"

Mason looked horrified. "Good God, no," he said. He pushed the cane out of his way and continued up the path. "I meant the Fraternal Order of Goodness."

"You can't be serious. We can't afford to lose someone as promising as you. Think of what your leaving would mean. Who's going to fight things like *that*?"

"I don't know," he said, weary, "but it won't be me. I am sure there is a surplus of eager young men out there willing to die for a good cause, but after almost falling into that hole, I'm not so sure anymore. I would like to see thirty, forty, and, God willing, eighty."

"Nonsense," Argyle said, a bit dismissive in a cheering sort of way. "You're just shaken, is all. Come. We'll have a few drinks down at Eccentric Circles. In a few hours, you'll feel fine."

The look on Mason's face was a distant one. "No," he said, shaking his head. "I don't suppose I will ever feel fine leading a life like this."

Quimbley clapped his partner on the back. "Save any decisions for the light of day," he said. The two men started up the graveyard path together, but only one of them looked certain in his steps.

I pulled myself out of the vision, feeling a bit shaky from how long I had been in it. The Inspectre had his head down in one of the files on his desk, but looked up when I took in a deep breath. He reached into his desk drawer, pulled out a small covered dish, and slid it across to me.

I pulled off the lid and looked inside. "Sugar cubes?" I asked.

"I *am* English," he said. "I keep the sugar cubes around because I'm required by British law to take teatime. What did you see?"

I took turns between scarfing down the much-needed sugar like a show pony and explaining to the professor just what I had seen. He listened without interruption, giving a wan smile when I finished.

"I was probably around your age then," the Inspectre said. "Thought a sword cane would be the most inconspicuous weapon, but I don't think many young men of my time were seen with them."

I looked down where it lay in my lap still and pulled the blade free from the cane. The metal was worn with age now and well corroded at the end where it had broken off. I rattled the hollow section of cane and the remaining piece of the sword slid out onto my lap. "You never fixed it."

The Inspectre shook his head, solemn. "Some things are better left as a reminder of what can be broken," he said. "My friendship with Mason, for one. He was my first partner in the field." The Inspectre held his hands out. I set the pieces of sword in them, careful to lay the blades down flat. With care, the Inspectre slid them back into the cane, and then placed it back on the rim of the top shelf again. For several moments, he stood there with his back to me until I couldn't take it anymore.

"What happened?" I asked. "After that night."

The Inspectre turned around, looking a little older. He sat back down in his chair. "Mason simply didn't come in the next day. Or the day after that. I heard from a colleague who ran into him in the street that he looked different. Happy, if I remember it correctly."

"So he just walked away from the Order?" I asked, anger creeping into my voice.

"Now, now," the Inspectre said. "Don't judge so hastily. Mason simply chose to live his life . . . differently."

"What does that mean, exactly?" I asked. "Did one of those ghouls actually bite him? He went evil?"

"Oh, heavens no! Surely you saw the look on his face when I pulled him out of that fissure. Mason was stone-cold scared and all too willing to walk away from this life."

"But why?" I asked. "I mean, if I had seen all that he had seen, I don't think I could turn away from a life of fighting the dark horrors that haunt this city."

The Inspectre looked at me over the top of his glasses, his face fixed in a very serious expression. "The Fraternal Order of Goodness is not for everyone, Simon. You have to remember that in the old days, there was barely even a Department of Extraordinary Affairs. Life within F.O.G. is thankless work with long hours and few benefits, even fewer now with these recent budget cuts from downtown. An agent of the Order has to love what they do, I suppose, in some perverse, masochistic way."

Who was I to try to second-guess Mason Redfield? He was a man I had met only twice—once through a psychometric flash and once as a corpse. "I guess I understand."

The Inspectre gave me a surprised smile. "Do you, now?"

I nodded. "When I came to the D.E.A., I was searching for something, something greater than a paycheck. Up until that moment, I would have gone on using my psychometry for heists and low-level thieving forever . . ."

"You would have eventually been caught," the Inspectre corrected.

"That's my point," I said. "I chose the D.E.A. and becoming a F.O.G.gie because I almost *was* caught—caught up in betrayal by the old crowd I ran with. You *do* recall Mina Saria, don't you?"

The Inspectre nodded. "That psychotic redhead, yes? Currently missing and in possession of Edvard Munch's *The Scream*, I believe."

"Correct," I said, shuddering at the thought of her. My encounters with her were harrowing enough to fill a book. "Surviving those near misses in my old criminal life with her woke me up. I wanted control of my life, a sense of purpose. Doing good, as simplistic as it sounds, is a far more rewarding fit. It gave me a better purpose."

The Inspectre steepled his fingers against his chin as he considered what I said. "That's what I meant about the Order not being for everyone," he said. "Mason Redfield had his sense of purpose scared out of him that night. He turned to another purpose that had caught his eye prior to joining the Order—his love of cinema and a desire to teach. Ironically, it was his love of horror films that drove him to the Fraternal Order of Goodness in the first place."

It was hard to imagine the semifailed swashbuckler at the head of a classroom, but hey, it worked for Indiana Jones. "Turned to teaching film," I said. "Makes sense. There, the monsters can't really get you."

The Inspectre's face sobered. "I hadn't really considered that when it happened," he said. "I was too angry at him. You see, at the time I was new to the game myself. I hated Mason for abandoning what I thought was his true calling. I handled myself . . . poorly."

"How so?" I asked.

The Inspectre's face turned red and he shifted in his chair, unable to find comfort in it. "I took his leaving as a personal affront. All I knew was that I was left on my own within the Order. I hated him for abandoning me like that, selfish as I was. Stubbornly, I refused to break in a new partner, insisting on doing everything on my own from then on. Some called me foolish, reckless . . . but to me it only meant I had to work harder and be more careful. I kept myself busy and it made it easy not to get in touch with Mason much once he left the Order. By the time I worked through my foolish anger, too much time had passed. Any thoughts I had of reconciling the situation would only have been too little, too late."

The Inspectre fell silent.

"So you *never* talked to him again?"

The Inspectre shook his head. "To what end?" he asked. "To give *me* closure? Mason walked away from it all, and who was I to come back into his life as a constant reminder of all the evils waiting to be confronted in the world? I kept tabs on him at first, naturally, making sure he was adjusting to the mundane world once again. He settled into the world of academia, and all I had to do was let things lie at that point."

"I don't understand," I said. "I felt part of what you felt when I was in my vision. I saw the friendship you had with him. You could have still had that—"

"Don't you think I *know* that?" the Inspectre snapped, barking at me. "Don't you think I know what I lost that day?"

I jumped in my seat. Seeing the Inspectre this unnerved rattled me more than I expected.

"It kills me," he continued, angrier with each word that flew from his lips, "that I should go so many years only to hear about the man's death and worse, in a paranormal fashion on top of it. Do you know how much that guts me, how asleep on the watch it makes me feel?"

"Sorry," I said. There was little healing power in the word, but maybe the Inspectre wasn't looking to heal. Maybe he didn't want someone to fix it. It had been broken too long for me to think anything I said would actually help. It was like trying to put a Band-Aid on a shark bite. Sometimes people just needed to vent and get it out of their system. I decided on another tack—getting back to business.

"So he was a teacher," I said. "That's as good a place to start as any. I should probably ask around and see if any of his students or other faculty noticed anything strange about him over the past few weeks."

The talk of the Inspectre's dead friend in an investigative capacity seemed to help him compose himself. His anger faded from his face and he nodded.

"Yes," he said. "I would check his offices over at New York University. Take Connor with you. Mind you, use discretion."

"Don't we always?"

"Yes, my boy, but now more than ever, given our precarious state of affairs with the city. I would hate to give Director Wesker or Dave Davidson any reason to suggest any sort of impropriety when it came to handling this personal case over others. For instance, some might see this as me exploiting Departmental resources."

"But Davidson brought us this case," I said.

"True," the Inspectre said, returning to the pile of papers scattered in front of him. "Nonetheless, exercise extreme prudence in your investigation."

"Got it," I said. I stood up and headed for the door.

"And, Simon," the Inspectre said, lifting his head up out of his paperwork. "Please be careful. Given the supernatural nature of his death, maybe the good college professor wasn't as out of the arcana business as much as I previously thought."

8

New York University was big on film and theater, but thankfully not so much on security measures. At least, not for someone who looked like a student still and practiced psychometry. This late at night Connor and I didn't have to worry about many students in the academic buildings, but every other lock getting to the professor's office required either a quick psychometric blast to read the electronic ones or my skills with my lock picks for the rest of them. By the time we hit the professor's office door, the repetition of picking the older locks had become easy. The professor's door practically opened the second I inserted my torsion wrench and one of my half-diamond picks into the lock, swinging inward and revealing darkness in the office behind it.

"Jesus, kid," Connor said. "You sure that one wasn't already open?"

"Yup," I said, shoving my picks back up my left sleeve. "I'm just that good."

Connor pushed past me into the dark office, annoyed. "Nice to see you keeping it humble."

"Hey, I don't take pride in much, but let me have this, okay?"

I slipped into the office after him and flicked on the light just inside the door, then closed the door behind me. A pile of unopened mail sat underneath a mail slot on the floor to the right of the door. "Looks like no one's taken notice of the professor's absence yet." I turned my attention to the rest of the room.

For a college professor, the office was pretty posh. The furniture was of the old-school drawing room variety, Gothic pieces rich with carved foliage, huge and chunky like they could withstand a hurricane. The walls were lined with academic texts and film memorabilia—books, statues, movie-related knickknacks, and artwork everywhere.

"Wow," I said. "This guy had really been working his tenure here."

Connor gave a low whistle. "I think we might have stumbled into the Museum of Television and Radio by mistake."

I knew Professor Redfield had left the Fraternal Order of Goodness to return to his love of film and teaching, but there was more of an overabundance of film-related memorabilia mixed throughout the academic trappings than I had expected.

"Notice anything strange?" Connor asked.

I looked around the darkened office, trying to look for anything out of place.

"It's very tidy," I said.

Connor nodded, leaning over to run his hands along the smooth surface of the professor's desk. "A little too, wouldn't you say?" Outside of a few neat piles of paper on it, the desk was relatively clear. Compared to mine back at the Department of Extraordinary Affairs, it was practically empty.

Looking around, I noticed it was true. "For a guy who was murdered so suddenly, this place looks like it was taken care of beforehand. Either he was knew he was going to die, or he was a neat freak, or someone cleaned this place up after killing him."

"I've never known a professor who kept a tidy office," Connor said. He leaned farther over on the top of the desk, his face practically touching it. He inhaled deeply. "The smell of polish is relatively fresh."

I stepped to the display case along the wall behind the late professor's desk and pulled on my gloves. It was covered in an array of figurines that all looked like they were monsters or characters from ancient Greece. I grabbed one of the figures off the shelf behind the desk. The thing looked something like a cross between the classic Godzilla and a Tyrannosaurus rex. "Well, they're not Zuni fetish dolls or anything, but some of these pug uglies sure look evil enough, not that the professor was supposed to be dabbling in arcana these days. Check this out." I threw the figurine over to Connor. He caught it and turned it over. His eyes went wide after marveling at it for a moment.

"What is it?"

"Careful," he said, holding the figurine up gently. "This is an original Harryhausen."

My blank stare was enough to garner a disappointed look from Connor. He shook his head at me. "You're in my territory now, kid. Movie paraphernalia." He held the mechanical beastie up, almost like a ventriloquist dummy.

"This little ugly guy here is from *The Beast from 20,000 Fathoms*. Ray Harryhausen was the special-effects wizard who created all the old-school stop-motion monsters. The man did *King Kong*, for goodness' sake."

"I thought Hepburn and Bogie were your thing," I said, looking over the other figures on the shelf. Now that Connor had pointed it out, some of the creatures looked vaguely familiar from movies I had seen, but I felt a little bit ashamed I hadn't figured it out for myself. That was what I got for relying so heavily on my psychometry over the years—instant expertise without becoming an expert on anything.

"Sure," he continued. "I have my favorites, but these are a classic of a different kind. I bet these are worth a mint."

Connor held the figure out to me, but I didn't take it, instead moving away from the display.

"You put it away," I said.

Connor gave me a suspicious look, but did as I said and put the figure back on the shelf. "You okay, kid?"

"It's probably best not to give the priceless shiny to the ex-thief psychometrist who still needs to make his hefty SoHo maintenance fees this month."

"Can't understand why you went for a fringe government job," he said. "No way you're going to be able to finance that apartment forever."

"Either way," I said, "no need to tempt me. I'll find a way."

"You could sell the place," Connor said, turning to look over the professor's desk.

A small ball of panic bunched up in my chest. "No way," I said, defensive. "It was my last hurrah when I gave up my old life. My past crimes paid the way for my future, for my freedom."

"Still," he said. "Ill-gotten goods funded it. Maybe it's time to give the place up. Unless you're expecting some kind of year-end bonus that I'm not aware of . . . ?"

I stopped looking around the room and turned to Connor, a hint of anger in my voice. "I'm not giving the place up. It's just a lot harder trying to live honestly than I thought, okay?"

Connor flipped open a teacher's planner on the desk and looked through it. "There's one way you could make your life easier financially, kid."

"Oh?" I said.

"You could have Jane move in," Connor suggested. "That halves all your bills instantly."

The residual emotions of the tattooist pressed their way to the surface and I snapped in anger. "Has Jane talked to you about this, too?" I asked. I stared into his eyes, searching them.

"Nope," he said, "but would her moving in be such a bad idea?"

"I don't know," I said, shaking my head to clear it and get rid of the growing sensation. "I don't want to jinx it. Things are good as they stand."

"What's to jinx, kid?"

"I don't think I do relationships well," I said, the anger turning to rampant insecurity. "Let's look at my track record. My last girlfriend was a high-priced art thief."

Connor laughed. "I take it *The Scream* is still missing?"

I nodded. "I bet she's got it hanging on the wall in her lair somewhere. Mina was messed up—abusive, demeaning, everything a wannabe badass thief should want in a girl. When I smartened up, we went our separate ways, which left her vacillating between stalking me, killing me, or handing me over to cultists. I can't help but wonder . . .

what did I really do to bring that out in someone? I mean, yeah, I used to be a dick when I was dating her, but I'd like to think I grew past that."

Connor scrunched his face and held his hand up, rolling it back and forth in the air. "More or less."

"Thanks," I said. "I guess I just don't trust myself after that and now I keep getting these flare-ups of anger and jealousy from the tattooist."

"I thought so," he said. "You don't snap on me all that often."

"Sorry," I said, concentrating on relaxing. I felt almost normal again.

"Kid, you've got a good woman now. Don't drive yourself crazy overthinking it. If you're happy, you're happy, but don't let your past control you on this. Sure, be mindful of it, but don't *live* in it."

"It's just hard to change my thinking. I need to rewire my brain or something."

"At the very least, you should limber it up," Connor said, crossing back to the professor's desk. He grabbed a Lucite block from the corner of it and handed it to me. "Try this for a little psychometric gymnastics."

The clear, heavy piece was an award of some kind. Etched into it was a film reel that ran around the entire base of the piece. "I'd like to thank the Academy," I said. "Looks like the professor had a little bit of vanity in displaying his accolades."

"Just check it out," Connor said. "I'm going to Knock and see if there's any way to draw the late professor's spirit out if it's lingering."

"Careful," I said, shuddering. "Last time I saw you Knocking, you were half out of your mind and raising most of the graveyard at Trinity Church."

"Don't remind me," he said. "I still feel the Spirit of Concussions Past when I think of that night."

Connor went around the desk and sat down in the professor's chair, taking a moment to focus himself before getting down to business. I sat myself down in one of the chairs opposite him, cradling the Lucite award in my arms like a newborn. Without another thought, I pressed my powers into it.

As my psychometric vision kicked in, the image of Connor sitting at the desk morphed into one of Professor Redfield. At the moment he was old but quite alive and doing the exciting task of grading papers while drinking what amounted to a small fishbowl of scotch.

It was strange seeing the professor alive again in one of my visions, this time old. Before, he had been young and lively, nervous in the face of battle; now he was simply an old man in professor mode.

I rewound through images of the events that had taken place in his office like searching through old newspaper records in a library. A variety of people came and went, and I ignored most of them. The bulk looked like the odd student here or there simply coming to their professor during office hours. I kept going through them until I caught sight of a group of lingering students in one long section of the vision. I drew my focus in on them and pulled my mind into those specific moments. The old man sat at his desk, holding court. Five students sat around his office, intent on every word he was saying. The last and most attentive was an eager young blond girl named Elyse who hung on his every word. A tall, black muscular guy with ear gauging, Darryl, took notes on a laptop while a chunky kid with a video camera and the unfortunate nickname Heavy Mike listened intently with a couple of other film school hopefuls—a punked-out blond Hispanic kid name George and a skinny brown-haired kid, Trent. Professor Redfield was busy regaling them with stories of the glory days or horror cinema, hearkening back to the extreme makeup that Lon Chaney used to wear.

The sway he held these students under was a bit creepy, but I watched as long as I could before I felt my blood sugar depleting itself.

When I came out of the vision, Connor was still seated at the professor's desk. "Well?" he asked. "No luck on my end. If the professor's spirit is lingering around here, there isn't anything earthly that he's attached to. What about you? Anything, kid?"

"Maybe," I said. "From what I saw, it looked like Mason had a little posse. Film geeks doting on his every word, laughing at his every story. Whether it was grade grubbing or not, I'm not quite sure. The adoration bordered on cultish."

"We should check it out," Connor said. "Someone has to know something more about the professor. Who he hung with, who might have had it out for him. Did you catch names?"

"Only a couple of them," I said. "There was an Elyse, Darryl, Trent . . . a big guy they called Heavy Mike. Subtle, right?"

"Anything more than first names, kid?" Connor asked. "It's going to take a lot of wandering Manhattan going on just that."

"Sorry," I said. "That's the problem with reading Professor Redfield's belongings. They're his stuff. It shows me some stuff about *him*, but I can't really dive into the past of the others unless they've handled his objects, too. Even then, it's not a sure thing."

"Looks like we've got our work cut out for us, then," Connor said, getting up from the desk, "but not tonight. Despite this being the city that never sleeps, I doubt we're going to get anything but drunken stragglers to question this time of night."

"I can start asking around tomorrow," I said, heading for the door. "Maybe I should hit that solo."

Connor gave me a look. "You sure? Why?"

We stepped out of the professor's office and headed through the deserted halls of the university. "If I bring you along all old looking with that white stripe in your hair, everyone's going to think I brought a cop with me. No one's going to talk."

"Jesus, kid," Connor said, stopping in the hall. "You make me sound like I'm a hundred."

"Sorry," I said. "Didn't mean that. It's just . . . look at you in your Bogie trench coat. You aren't exactly college-age looking. I'd peg you for a cop."

"Fine," Connor said, heading for the doors to the outside world coming up ahead of us. "Have it your way. I can sleep in, then."

"Now, Grandpa . . ." I said, starting after him.

Connor looked over his shoulder at me, shooting me with a look of pure hatred as he pushed out onto the streets of New York City once more. "I'm meeting up with Aidan over at Eccentric Circles," he continued. "Having a day job and spending time with my brother on a vampiric schedule is leaving me sorely lacking in the sleep department. You're welcome to come with."

Part of me was instantly jonesing for the decadent disco fries they served at our Departmental hang out, but I shook my head.

"I should probably head home," I said. "I think there's a few things I need to iron out with Jane still."

Connor shrugged. "Your funeral. Suit yourself."

"You know," I said, turning to head off toward my apartment, "you used to be a lot less sassy about things when you thought Aidan was dead."

Connor smiled. "Sorry, kid."

9

Jane was out cold when I got home, and rather than risk waking her by trying to slip silently into bed, I crashed out on my couch in the living room. I had fallen asleep there plenty of times when I was single and I convinced myself it would just be easier, but when I woke in the morning, I just felt lame for doing it. I scribbled a quick note telling Jane that I loved her, left it on the pillow next to her in my bedroom, and hurried out of my apartment as I slipped my satchel over my shoulder before she could wake. If I was lucky, I could catch the early-morning rush of students bustling around New York University.

I hit up Bagels on the Square for one with everything and enough coffee to wake the dead before skulking around the empty fountain in the center of Washington Square Park. I hoped to find someone who could tell me more about Professor Redfield, but other than a few students calling him a whack job or a lovable eccentric, I spent more time fending off the weed dealers than getting anything accomplished. Frustrated, I moved out of the park and made my way up University Place a few blocks in search of a more productive venue.

Stuck somewhere between my guilt from avoiding Jane this morning and still asking around campus about the professor, I found that I had wandered into one of the antiques stores around Tenth Street. The store was long and narrow, but packed with an eclectic mix of furniture, none of it looking more than sixty or seventy years old. Just seeing the type of stuff I was used to picking through as a psychometrist helped take away some of my stress, and as I worked my way back through the mostly deserted store, I thought maybe I could unstress myself a little more by contending with some of my Jane issues, too. The recent developments with my powers left me unsure about the whole Jane situation, but I was willing to try to push myself past all the angry flare-ups that had been happening. Maybe if I baby-stepped my way into pricing out some dressers with her in mind, it would at least be a step in the right direction.

Near the back of the store was a mixed collection of bedroom pieces, almost all of it having seen better days. Still, a few bits of furniture showed some promise. One was a dark brown art deco–looking unit with brushed brass pulls on the front of it. I went over to it, stripping off my gloves. If I was going to find something special enough for Jane to have after all my ridiculousness, it had to be the right piece but also one that wasn't too psychometrically charged that I might trigger off it once it was in my home. I lay my hands down on top of the polished-smooth top of it and pressed my power into it.

My mind's eye pushed back through the history of the object, searching its past. The image forming in my mind

resolved into that of an empty and unfamiliar bedroom.
The whole place was tastefully done up in the same mid-
Century style of the dresser with the focus of the room
being a king-sized bed, which I sat upon, that took up a
large portion of the space. I pressed myself into the mind
of whoever I was, trying to gather what information I could
about the dresser's previous owners.

Nothing. The mind was a complete blank. I fished
around in the emptiness for the thoughts of another, but
still nothing.

"What the hell . . . ?" I asked, out loud. Nothing like this
had ever happened to me before, but something odd struck
me when I spoke. *My voice.* What usually happened in one
of my visions was that I always sounded like someone else,
but not this time. I sounded like me.

I looked down at the person's hands in his lap. They
were my own, settled on top of my satchel. How I was myself in this vision, I didn't know, but before I could give it
much more thought, I noticed movement in the sheets of
the bed I was sitting on.

I bolted up and spun around. Something was rising up in
the middle of the bed, as if a line was drawing up the bed-
spread from its center point. I backed away from it, feeling for
my bat at my side and relaxing a little when my hand found it
in my holster. I pulled it free, extended it, and waited.

The sheet fell away, revealing a haunting and familiar
face—Cassie, the ghost tattooist from the antiques store at
the Gibson-Case Center. Her dead eyes were covered by
her dark, giant hipster sunglasses, with a hint of a blood
trickling out from behind them. Her tattoo gun was in her
hand and she revved its motor. The dangling cord of the
device dissolved off into a swirl of mist trailing behind her
as she stepped through the bed toward me.

"No," I said to myself, as firm as I could to control my panic. I swung my bat at her, but it passed right through, her solid form twirling into a cloud of mist before re-forming in my bat's wake. She revved the needle gun again and kept advancing. I couldn't hit her, but I wasn't going to wait to find out if she could attack me, not with that needle gun in her hand.

The backs of my legs hit the dresser behind me. I had every plan to dash left, then forward toward a closed door that hopefully led out of the room, but before I could run, the sound of sliding drawers hit my ears.

The dresser drawers on either side of my legs fell to the floor and a pair of human arms reached out from within, wrapping around my body. I recognized the tweed sleeves of the jacket; Mason Redfield's arms wrapped tight around my legs, immobilizing me.

Trapped. Screw this, I thought. Time to pull myself out of the vision. I closed my mind's eye, only to have it slam back open on me. I willed it closed again, but again, it came flying open. All the while the tattooist kept advancing on me. I had never personally taken a beating as myself in a vision before, and I didn't plan on starting now.

The tattooist crept closer, which meant only one thing: I had to free myself from the professor's arms. *Now.* I slammed my bat down along the side of my left leg as the two arms wrapped around me. The blow stung my leg, but it hurt the professor's arm more than it did me.

The arms let go of my legs, and I ran for the door across the room. The blind tattooist cocked her head, listening for my steps, correcting her course. I pulled at the doorknob.
Locked.

I spun and pressed my back against the door. Across the room, the younger Mason Redfield I had seen in my psychometric vision pulled himself out of the dresser, shattering it apart into a pile of wreckage. My brain filled with their raw emotional states from when I had first experienced both of them—the woman's jealous rage and Mason Redfield's fear from the night I had seen him fighting ghouls with the Inspectre. I started to sweat, slamming my head back against the door as all the emotions took over.

I hefted up my bat as the two of them closed with me. Maybe my bat would affect them or maybe it wouldn't. Either way, I'd find out, going down swinging as best I could.

The pain in my leg still throbbed from where I had hit it with the bat. No, that wasn't quite right . . . not where I had hit it. This was something else, a strange pulsing sensation on my *other* leg, higher and closer to my hip—my phone on vibrate. I reached into my pocket and pulled it out, flipping it open.

"Hello?"

Static came through on the line, but I could hear the faint sound of a voice behind it all.

"Hello?" I shouted into it.

It crackled again, and then through it all, ". . . kid?"

"Connor!" I shouted.

The psychometric vision rushed away from me and the real world snapped back to the inside of the store on University Place, where I fell face-first into the dresser I had been reading. My head slammed down onto it, and I fell to the floor, dropping my phone. The cool tile pressed against me and I scrabbled for my cell, my hand closing over it.

"I'm here," I shouted. The sound of footsteps came toward me from the front of the store. I held my phone back up to my ear.

"You okay, kid?" Connor asked. "Took you long enough to answer."

"Yeah," I said, using the dresser to steady myself as I helped myself up. "I was just dealing with something." I didn't dare tell him about the episode for fear that he might take me off active. For now, I simply had to resist using my powers.

The owner of the shop I had heard coming in came around the end of the aisle, a look of concern on her face. I smiled and gave her a thumbs-up. She gave me a nervous smile back and retreated.

"Any luck tracking down leads on the professor?" Connor asked.

"Not much. Got a bunch of people saying he was a bit eccentric, as you might imagine, but I could have told you that before wandering around down here. Seemed mostly positive from what I was able to gather so far."

"You think maybe you could head on up to the offices?" he asked. "Things are backing up here and I'm afraid for our partners desk under this level of paperwork."

"Yeah," I said without hesitation, starting off east through the Village. "Not a problem." The thought of sitting down at my desk and not using an ounce of psychometry for a little while felt like the best idea in the world right now.

I slipped my phone back into my pocket and pulled my gloves back on. To double ensure I didn't trigger a blessed thing, I jammed my hands down into my jacket pockets. My brain and emotions needed to settle. It saddened me that sometimes shopping was far more perilous that dealing with zombies and vampires.

10

Hours of paperwork back at the office kept me nice and distracted from the mental confusion of earlier in the day. When Jane texted me hours later saying she was at Mason Redfield's apartment working, I felt settled enough that I headed out into the dark and the rain to meet up with her.

I opened the door to Professor Redfield's high-rise apartment before ducking underneath the police tape and stepping in. Outside the patio doors rain poured down, giving the low light of the apartment a creepy look. Jane was sitting in one of the professor's giant wing chairs with a bunch of books on her lap and a satchel lying at her feet. A variety of candles, charms, and chalk bits were scattered on the floor in front of her. She was engrossed in one of the books and looked up only when I closed the door behind me. She let out a tiny yelp.

"Sorry," I said. I craned my head, looking around the quiet, empty apartment. "You said they had you working . . . Did they leave you alone here?"

Jane nodded. I went over to her and started picking up the bits and pieces scattered by her feet.

"Unbelievable," I said.

"It's okay," she said, grabbing my wrist to stop me. "I haven't seen any sign of Aqua-Woman. I'm just wrapping up warding the place. Sorry I screamed. When you came through the door, I thought you might have been the ghost of the professor."

"Do I look like I'm a ghost in my late fifties?" I said. "I know working for the Department is probably aging me prematurely, but come on."

Jane stood, wrapped her arms around me, and kissed me. After a moment she stepped back and looked up at me. "Better?"

"Much," I said, smiling. "How's it going?"

"I *think* it's going good," she said.

"Think?"

Jane let out an exasperated sigh. "Look, I've never done this before." She grabbed up the book she had been reading. "Director Wesker came through here and spent about seven seconds instructing me on how to properly ward a place before he had to run off on another case. This skeleton-staff work schedule is killing me. I think I've protected the place with the symbols on the walls and even laid down a few traps if anything paranormal returns to the scene."

I walked around the main living room area looking at the variety of symbols drawn on the wall in Jane's handwriting. There were all kinds that looked vaguely runic to my eye, but what did I know? I was out of my element.

"So what do you think?" I asked. "You think this woman in green was bound to the professor somehow?"

"I don't know," Jane said. She started packing up her

stuff, handing me a small pile of books. "Here. I thought these looked promising for you."

"I already tried to get a read on the stuff in here," I said.

"I figured maybe with all the distractions your powers have been giving you lately, you might want to chance it again."

"Sure," I said. I stuffed the books into the messenger bag hanging at my side, not even getting into why I had zero plans to read anything with my powers right now. "But getting back to my question . . . what do you think? Was that woman bound to the professor?"

Jane shrugged as she filled up her own bag with the materials on the floor. "Maybe," she said. "Part of me wonders if she lived here. If she did, I bet she had more than a drawer."

Although Jane sounded playful enough when she said it, the angry twinge rose up in my heart unbidden and I couldn't hide it in my voice. "Jane . . ."

"I'm fine," she said. By the tone in her voice, it didn't sound like it.

"About the other night," I said, swallowing it down. "I'm sorry I hesitated when you asked about me about the set of drawers. These emotional flairs from the tattooist have really been messing with me. Connor had to remind me you were asking for more space, not anything big like moving in."

"Exactly," she said. "I wasn't asking that. I just wanted somewhere to put my things." The look on her face faded, replaced with one of shy concern. "But since you went there, would it be so horrible?"

The tattooist's emotions tried to press themselves forward, but I tried to be rational. "I just don't want to mess this up," I said. "I don't want to rush anything. I've rushed things before, and you *know* my history. I've a lot to think about . . ."

"Like what?" Jane asked, snapping a little. "Seems pretty simple to me. Either you want to be with me or you don't, right?"

I sighed. "Let's not fight," I said. "It's late. We're both exhausted and touchy. I just came to pick you up, maybe take you to dinner."

Jane softened a little and nodded. "That, I can get behind."

The half-built driveway loop in front of the high-rise was half-flooded from the downpour of rain, but thankfully one fully built sidewalk was in place and led down to First Avenue. Once my arm was around Jane under the protection of my umbrella, we huddled under it and I finally felt myself relaxing. I didn't want to worry about our domestic problems all night, and in that regard, I needn't have worried.

As we came off of First Avenue onto the side street, we were met by a lack of late-night traffic and a now-familiar figure. The green woman Jane had been warding the apartment against was standing out in the downpour in the middle of the empty street.

"Holy hell," I said. "Guess that answers the question of if we finished her off when Connor dropped the statue on her."

Jane looked uneasy. "Should we call in the troops?" she asked.

"We *are* the troops," I said, taking out my bat. "Budget cuts, remember?"

"Oh, right." Jane looked disappointed. "Crap."

"You okay with this?"

Jane nodded. "I just hate fighting in the rain," she said. "More so when it's some aquatic bitch who tried to drown my boyfriend."

I squeezed her shoulder. "Feel free to work with that. A little vengeful thinking can go a long way when it comes to a fight."

I collapsed my umbrella, pulled my bat out of its holster, and slid the umbrella into it.

"Gotcha," Jane said and the two of us headed off for the green woman. When the woman saw us in motion, she strode toward us in great, deliberate strides, Terminator-style. She stopped thirty feet away in the middle of the deserted street, and I hesitated. Jane kept moving forward, but the woman raised her arms out to her sides and turned her head up to the heavens. I wasn't sure what she was doing, but I had a bad feeling about it. I reached for Jane, catching her arm.

"Wait," I said, tugging her back.

The words were barely out of my mouth when I heard the sound of rushing water explode somewhere off to my right. I turned, and water was shooting toward me from the remains of a fire hydrant along the curb. It slammed into me full force, causing me to fling Jane off in the opposite direction as its pressure catapulted me into a row of parked cars. I landed hard on one of the roofs of a gypsy cab, leaving one hell of a body print in it and absorbing a ton of pain that screamed across my back.

Jane was luckier. My spin had sent her stumbling across the street, but now she was running in the direction of her momentum, diving for the cover of a van parked on the opposite side of the street.

I rolled off the top of the cab toward the safety of the

sidewalk area. Water was now filling the street at a rapid flow. The direct approach wasn't going to work with this creature. As I tried to come up with a next move, the sound of crumbling stone rose up behind me. I looked down. I was standing next to another fire hydrant . . . and it was shaking violently, crumbling the sidewalk beneath it.

Pained as my back was, I found the strength to scrabble back over the crumpled roof of the car and fell off it onto the flooding street. I came down with a splash in ankle-deep water and took cover against the side of the car. The hydrant erupted, shoving the entire car toward me. It slammed into me, knocking me face-first into the water. I held my breath until I got my hands under me, then pushed myself back up. I looked at my enemy, and all her focus was on me, her arms still outstretched. I had no idea where the hell all the hydrants were on this street, but I had a feeling I was about to find out the extremely hard way.

A familiar sound rose over the rush of water. The crackle and hiss of electronic connection. I knew it well. It was easy since it was the telltale sign of Jane ramping up her powers. I looked off to my right. Jane was still hidden by the van, but her hands were laid out on its hood. Her eyes were lit with energy as she chanted her technomancy into the vehicle and it started up with a roar, the engine revving up to a near-impossible whine. Its lights flashed on, burning bright. Seconds later the glass exploded out of the headlights themselves. Arcs of electric blue fire shot out of the empty sockets and crackled over the distance before shooting into the green woman. Her body crumpled as she doubled over in pain, but Jane didn't let up with her attack.

I stood up, running over to Jane, taking a wide arc to make sure I was well behind her as she electrocuted the woman. As power poured out of the van, the vehicle shook, smoke rising from it in thick, noxious clouds. The pop of something at the front of it rang out, and the hood flapped up with the explosion. The battery was on fire, covered in flame, and the last of its power shot from Jane's hand into the green woman in a final tail of energy.

I grabbed Jane and pulled her away from the vehicle. She looked spent, like she had pulled an all-nighter, but I had to make sure she didn't take any damage from the rapidly burning van. I dragged her into the street with me to see the results of her handiwork.

The green woman was down on one knee now, but she pushed off of the ground and stood back up. The dark serenity was gone from her face, replace by uncertainty and fear.

"I think you hurt her."

The news seemed to put a little wind back in my girl-friend's sails and she smiled. "Good," she said.

The green woman turned and ran. Cars were coming up the street now and she ran over the tops of them as they came, always landing on her feet and keeping her brisk pace. The falling rain drew into her as she ran, reconstructing bits and pieces of her that the passing cars tore away when she failed to dodge one completely.

Jane and I weren't as pliable against the oncoming traffic and took to the sidewalks, avoiding the steady flood of water filling the streets from the broken hydrants.

"What do we do if we catch her?" Jane shouted over the sound of rushing water.

"Hell if I know," I said. "Improvise."

The farther we chased the woman, the more destruction seemed to rise up all around us. Fire hydrants erupted left and right as the woman passed them. They lacked the aim of the ones she had taken her time to direct at us, but they were just as harmful, water shooting every which way into the air. Several shop windows either cracked or completely shattered under their concussive force. Glass rained down into our hair as Jane and I covered our eyes, still giving chase.

The woman looked back to assess her situation. Hate was in her eyes now. Despite all her attempts and distractions that she was throwing at us, Jane and I were still gaining on her. Desperate, she changed direction and darted off to her right and into an alley.

Jane and I ran down into its darkness after her. The staccato beat of the rain was louder, drumming off the rows of trash cans and Dumpsters lining both sides of the narrow space. The splash of our footfalls added to the eeriness among the cold, wet shadows here. The woman was in a full-on run, but I saw a glimmer of hope up ahead. The alley dead-ended a couple of hundred feet ahead of us.

The green woman hadn't noticed it yet and kept on trucking at full speed. Her attention was turned on us as she ran, and only at the last second did she notice the wall in front of her. She hit it at a full run, a large wash of water spreading out and up the wall, yet she remained solid. She was dazed and it took her a second to regain her focus, but by that time we had stopped a few feet behind her. She spun around to confront us, a look of panic on her face.

"All right, lady," I said, raising my bat, winded. "I don't know *what* you are, but I know this—you're coming with us."

The look of panic on her face dissolved and in its place rose an unexpected look of calm that unnerved me. I stepped forward using caution, but the woman just shook her head at me in slow motion. A dark smile crossed her lips.

"No?" I asked, tightening the grip on my bat. I let uncertainty get the better of me and stopped advancing on her.

The woman shook her head again, and then cocked her eyes over to Jane on my right. I wasn't sure what the woman was up to, but I didn't like that she was shifting her focus to Jane now. From the uncomfortable look on Jane's face, she wasn't too keen on the attention, either.

"Hey!" I shouted, slapping the bat down in my gloved hand with a wet smack that sent up a small splash of water. "Eyes over here!"

My words had no effect on her and she just continued staring at Jane. I had to do something. I stepped forward, closing the gap.

The woman pressed herself back against the bricks of the wall behind her. Her hands spread out along it, her fingers digging into the wall while her eyes remained on my girlfriend.

"Easy," I said, drawing out the word as long as I could.

I reached for the woman's right arm, but it was already too late. She pushed herself away from the bricks, launching herself directly at Jane. I expected the woman to raise her arms, to try to grapple with Jane, but instead she dropped them to her sides. The woman's body slammed into Jane, but didn't knock her over. Jane staggered for a moment, reeling as the woman transformed, losing all solidity and washing over her.

There wasn't even a chance for Jane to scream. Her mouth filled with water as the green woman passed both over *and* through her. Jane's eyes went wide as she struggled to catch a breath, but it was over before full-on panic could set in. The wave rolled beyond Jane, forming once again into the woman when it was past us. She didn't miss a step as she hit the ground running and took off splashing her way back up the alley toward freedom. All of a sudden I felt pretty sure I knew how Mason Redfield had died.

Jane staggered and I dropped my bat to catch her before she fell into my arms, coughing. She took several choking breaths of air as she spit up a small fountain of the greenish water. I patted her back, helping her as best I could to return her to her regular breath. After a moment, her chest stopped heaving and she laid her forehead calmly against my chin.

"Well," I said. "That could have gone worse."

Jane looked up at me. "Oh, really?" she said, her voice weak. "How exactly?"

"You're still breathing, aren't you? Consider yourself luckier than Mason Redfield when she tried to drown him."

Jane narrowed her eyes at me like she was going to say something snippy, but the look vanished almost as soon as it had appeared. "True."

"I know Wesker probably sets a different bar for success than the Inspectre does for Other Division, but we consider 'Still Breathing' a good benchmark."

Jane looked back up the now-deserted alley, her eyes barely open against the downpour of rain. "You want to go after her?"

I shook my head as I reached down and picked up my bat. "I'm afraid it's too late for that. She's long gone by now."

Jane looked sad, like she might even be crying, but with all the rain it was hard to tell. "I'm sorry," she said.

"What do you have to be sorry about? That a psychotic water woman chose to give you a bath in the middle of a rainstorm?"

Jane gave me a sad smile.

"You should be happy," I continued, squeezing her in my arms. "After an attack like that, we have pretty solid confirmation now of who drowned Professor Redfield from the inside out. Now what we need to do is figure out who she is, why she would want the good professor dead, and how we can stop her from drowning anyone else alive."

Jane nodded, but still looked quite shaken.

"Cheer up," I said, hugging her.

She squeezed me tight, her head buried in my neck. "Why?" she asked with weak hope in her voice.

I pushed her back from me, looked her in the eye, and nodded. "You seemed to actually hurt her," I said. "That's promising. All I managed to do was menace her with a bat, and not very effectively. Back at the van, you scorched her pretty good."

Jane looked uncertain. "Blowing up a van. I'm going to catch holy hell for that, aren't I?"

"We can check it with Ghoulateral Damage Division, if there's anyone left there these days."

I spun Jane around and headed her back down the alley. I traded my bat for my umbrella and slid the bat into its holster. I opened the umbrella and the two of us huddled under it despite the fact that we were both already soaked through. There was a comfort in it nonetheless. Now if I could only fine some answers about the crazy woman in green that comforted me . . .

11

Jane looked over at me across the wrought-iron elevator cage we rode up to my apartment. She gave me a weak smile, which warmed my heart even though she looked as much like a drowned rat as I did. The old-world elevator rose up through my building, clattering its way up past floor after floor, the low hum of its motor a soothing sound after a night of chaos.

Jane moaned, followed by a piteous trail of laughter. "You know you're in trouble when just riding in an elevator hurts," she said.

I would have nodded in agreement, but I couldn't lift my head forward from where it rested against the side of the elevator. Tonight's pursuit had been a brutal one, but only when it was over did our bodies truly start to feel the toll of our exertion. The only good thing to happen since hobbling our way out of the alley near the professor's high-rise was that the rain and broken hydrants had taken care of dousing the flames of the van Jane had exploded with her technomancy. Other than that, our bodies had slowly given in to the aches and pains that followed our fruitless chase.

When the elevator hit my floor, I rolled back the black iron accordion gate and the two of us hobbled our way to my apartment door at the end of the hall. I fished out my keys and managed to get my door open despite my feeble state. I didn't even bother to flick on the lights and instead took in the welcoming silence of my home. The quiet majesty of my living room was dark, but the wall of windows along the left side of it let in enough light to show off my old-world gentleman's club motif—rich leather sofas and an entire wall of shelves that housed various antique finds of mine. I pulled off my waterlogged coat and hung it by the door before going any farther.

I helped Jane squirm out of her coat and hung it next to mine. "You really ought to have a chute installed that drops straight down to the incinerator."

"I don't think that would be such a great idea," I said, crossing over to my sofa. "I'd be half tempted to throw myself down there, if only to dry off."

I started off down the main hall that led back to the other rooms of the apartment. "I'm going to change."

"I'm going to shower," Jane said. She kicked off her shoes and squelched down the hallway behind me in her wet socks on her way to the bathroom. "If you could just pull something out for me to wear, that would be great."

"Sure," I said.

I continued down the hall to my bedroom and changed into something less soaking wet. One Ramones T-shirt and a fresh pair of jeans later, I hit my couch out in the living room, opening up my satchel and pulling out the now-soaked books that Jane had picked for me from Redfield's place. The distraction of trying to read them with my powers if only to identify students from his lectures was a welcome one after the night we had been through, and I was thrilled to see that exhaustion seemed to be keeping any untoward flare-ups at bay. NYU lecture halls filled my mind's eye as I pushed into the visions of the professor educating his students on the history of film. While engaging, it hardly was anything I imagined someone killing him over. Eventually the drone of his voice and the subject matter became too much and I decided to switch up books.

When I pulled out of the vision, it was to a different sound entirely. Jane was screaming from the other room.

"Jane . . . ?" I said, my voice and body both weak from the hit my blood sugar took with the vision. I grabbed a pack of Life Savers from a tray of them on one of my end tables and opened it, popping them in my mouth and swallowing them whole.

"Simon!" Jane called out from the bathroom.

I rose from the couch and ran on unsteady legs down my hallway toward the back of the apartment. I threw open the bathroom door, startling her. Her hair was hanging down, wet, and Jane was wrapped in a white towel. Her eyes were so bugged out I thought they might pop.

"What is it?" I asked. I looked around the bathroom for any sign of trouble.

"I just got all the ick off me from tonight," she said, "and when I was drying off, I found *this*."

Jane pulled aside her hair and spun around, facing her back to the bathroom mirror. She lowered the towel so it exposed just below her shoulder blades. Set between them was what looked like a tattoo of a dark green swirl of symbols with words circling them in a language I didn't know. The outer edge of the swirl was a ring that was composed of what looked like writhing snakes that were, in fact, writhing.

"What the hell *is* that?" Jane asked, her voice on the verge of slipping into full-blown hysteria. I had to calm her, and quick.

I walked over to her and put my hand over the mark. It was below the skin, but the snakes were definitely moving within the pattern itself. I pressed my hand down harder, trying to feel for them, but it was like trying to touch a projection on a movie screen.

"Odd," I said, feeling the rise and fall of her chest as she panicked. I traced it with a gentle touch. "Does it hurt at all?"

"No," she said. "Does that really matter? It's *on* me. Isn't that enough?"

"Calm down until we have something to panic about, okay?" I asked. Jane nodded. "Good. Now, do you feel any different?"

"You mean other than freaked-out?" Jane asked, sharp.

"Yes," I said. "Other than that."

"Nope. Just freaked-out."

I looked her in the eye and gave her a smile. "So I take it you didn't get this from a wild night out with the girls, then?"

"What?" she said, missing my attempt at humor and snapping at me instead. "No, Simon! Get it off of me!"

"Hold on," I said. I grabbed the edge of the towel, lifted it, and rubbed at the spot. After a minute of vigorous scrubbing, I pulled the towel away.

"Well?" Jane asked.

"No use," I said. "It's still there." I looked at the towel. It was still clean. "Whatever it is, it's not like an ink stamp. None of it came off."

"Oh, hell," she said. "This is it. That bitch marked me, didn't she? I *knew* something felt off. I got in the damn shower and I just stood there for, like, an hour letting the water run over me, but look at my skin and hands. They didn't even prune. I'm telling you, she did something to me. I'm going to go to bed and when you wake up, you'll be lying next to a giant water snake or a puddle or something—"

"Calm down," I repeated, saying it for my benefit as well as hers.

"That's easy for you to say," she said. "You're not marked. That woman didn't dive through you!"

"We don't know anything yet, so don't panic," I said. "When you went through D.E.A. orientation, didn't they teach you that panic is for the norms?"

"*What* orientation?" she asked. "The day I started, they sent me to HR and they barely handed me my welcome kit before Director Wesker pulled me out of there and dragged me off to Tome, Sweet Tome to start cataloging the Black Stacks. I think the only real orientation I ever received was being instructed not to cry while working for Thaddeus Wesker."

"A valuable lesson, mind you," I pointed out.

Jane craned her head to look around into the mirror at herself. "That doesn't really help me now, Simon."

I grabbed Jane and eased her out into the hall so she couldn't look at the tattoo anymore. "I know," I said, guiding her down the hall toward the bedroom, "but we don't really have an emergency room for something like this, you know? I don't think anyone from the graveyard shift is up on this type of thing, but I think I know who might be able to tell us something in the morning."

"You do?" Jane said, looking hopeful for the first time tonight.

"Yup," I said, leading her over to her side of the bed. "Allorah Daniels."

Jane's face was a mask of skepticism. "Won't she be busy Enchancelloring?"

"We're all working hard to cover each other's asses these days," I said. "I'm sure she won't mind taking a break from old men and paperwork to get in some lab time. Science *was* her first love, after all. But first, you need to rest tonight. If there's no pain or symptoms from it, we'll defer to her expertise in the morning first thing. I promise."

Jane lay back against her pillow and slid underneath the sheets, leaving her towel lying in a pile on the floor right next to the bed. "I don't see how I'm supposed to get any sleep," she said, worry returning to her face.

I tucked her in, and then went over to the night table on my side of the bed.

"I have just the thing for that," I said, fishing a small vial out from a jumble of miscellaneous junk in the drawer. I held it up. Down one side were the letters *RVW*.

"What is that?" she asked.

I held it out to her and dropped it in her hand. "Wow," I said. "They really did rush you through your orientation. You have this in that welcome kit you still carry around as a purse. It's a sleeping potion of sorts."

"RVW," she said, reading the side of it before twisting off its top. "Rip Van Winkle. Not very clever."

"I'm pretty sure the Enchancellors came up with the name," I said. "Leave it to the bureaucrats to lack any artistic finesse."

She raised it to her lips.

"Careful," I said. "Just a drop should do it. Otherwise, who knows when you might wake up."

"Don't worry," she said, taking a tiny swallow from it.

"If I slept for twenty years, I'm sure that this *thing* on my back would have killed me by then."

"Comforting," I said, and crawled into bed on my side.

"I thought so," Jane said, already yawning. Her eyes slipped shut.

"Sweet dreams, my love," I said, putting my hand on her forehead. I ran my fingers through her still-damp hair.

"Only if you visit . . ." she said with a sleepy smile and was out like a light. I took the vial from her hand and stared at her for a few moments, wondering about the mark. How was I going to get to sleep thinking about it?

What the hell, I thought, and took a hit of the stuff myself. I only hoped the woman in green wouldn't visit me in my dreams. With my luck, I'd be naked without my bat, and I really didn't want to look *that* up in any of the dream interpretation books.

12

The next morning we were up and out of the house like the devil was chasing us. For all we knew about that mark on Jane's back, maybe he was. I reported the discovery of Mason Redfield's killer to the Inspectre before dragging a worried Jane down to Allorah Daniels's office/lab and calling her in. She was more than happy to get away from her Tuesday-morning breakfast meeting with the rest of the Enchancellors, most of whom looked like they might be asleep at the meeting table when I pulled her away.

Allorah guided Jane over to a bare, brushed-steel table that stood at the lab end of her office and had Jane lie down on it.

"Gah!" Jane cried out. "Cold!"

"Sorry," Allorah said and set about examining the mark on Jane's back by pulling up Jane's plain black tank top until the writhing symbol was fully in sight.

I leaned over to look closer myself. "Don't you have any

of that giant tissue paper doctors use on their examination beds?" I asked.

Allorah turned her head and gave me a silencing look with cold eyes. "My apologies," she said. "The creatures that I poke and prod at usually don't complain."

"Oh no?"

"No," she said, turning back to her examination. "They're usually dead or, at the very least, rotting."

I was starting to think I had made a bad call bringing Jane to her. "Maybe we should take Jane to a regular doctor," I said.

Allorah turned to me, standing up straight. "And say what exactly? That a mysterious woman dove through Agent Clayton-Forrester? I didn't know that traditional medicine could cure that these days."

"It's okay," Jane said, still facedown on the table. "Really. I just wasn't ready. The cold of the table took me by surprise, that's all."

Allorah went back to examining the spot between Jane's shoulder blades. She grabbed a digital camera off one of her nearby laboratory shelves and took several close-ups before setting the camera aside once again. She bent over Jane, so close she could have licked the spot.

"Strange," she said.

"What is?" I asked, moving even closer to try to see what she was seeing.

Allorah reached inside her lab coat and pulled out a large circular necklace hiding within her own shirt. I was familiar with it. My psychometry had shown me Allorah in her younger days as a high school science teacher defending herself against Damaris, Brandon's vampire consort. Just remembering the damage the circular blade had done sent a chill up my spine upon seeing it once again.

"Look at the designs in the mark on her back," she said, showing me her necklace at the same time. "They remind me of the ones on my apotropaic eye. They look Greek in origin."

"You sure about that?" I asked, studying the necklace against the symbol.

"Pretty sure," Allorah said, twirling the necklace on its chain. "I got this in Greece."

Jane propped herself up on her elbows. "I don't care what it is," she said. "I just want to know if you can get it off of me."

Allorah looked down at her, meeting Jane's eyes. "Like, cut it off? I could try."

The color left Jane's face and she put her head back down onto the surface of the table. I gave Allorah a look of disbelief. "You people skills still leave a lot to be desired, Ms. Daniels."

Allorah's face softened. "Don't worry," she said, putting a reassuring hand on Jane's shoulder, smoothing her tank top back down. "I wouldn't do that to you."

Jane turned to her, glancing up with hope on her face. "You wouldn't?"

"No," Allorah said. "I don't know how it's bonded to you quite yet. We could *try* to remove it, but whatever may be protecting it might kill you in the process."

Jane flinched at her words.

Allorah looked over at me. "What?" she said, defensive. "I'm much better at dissecting and dismembering."

"Don't we have—I don't know—a witch doctor or something?" I asked.

Allorah looked pissed. She stormed off with her arms widespread, showing off the expanse of her extensive open office space. "Do you see what I'm working with here? High school classroom leftovers . . . I'm pretty resourceful, but I'm quite a bit short of being a medical MacGyver."

Jane sat up, pulling her tank top back into place. "So, what do you suggest we do?" she asked. "I'm beginning to think I was safer when I was still temping for cultists."

Allorah sighed. "For starters," she said, "you can go home and relax."

"That's *it*?" I asked, exploding.

Allorah remained calm and cool. "That's it."

I looked at her in frustration, then walked off across the open loft toward her office area. "You're as useful as going to the school nurse."

"Simon," Allorah said in a sharp tone. "Please understand. Jane's been marked. Of that, there's no doubt. The real question is: for what reason? She's not in pain or visibly hurt. Until Jane exhibits some kind of symptom because of it—and she may not—there's very little we can do."

"Shouldn't I be quarantined or something?" Jane asked, hopping down from the table. "I could barely pull myself out of the shower last night."

Allorah smiled. "Maybe you just like showers," she said. "There are some mornings I can't get out of them, either. For now, you're fine. I'll research this. There's no sign of anything wrong with you, other than the mark. Nothing viral, no wounds or sores . . ."

"I feel sore," Jane said.

"You and me both," I added.

Allorah put both her hands to her ears, covering them. "I don't need to hear about your sexual exploits, I assure you."

"It's nothing like that," I said, shaking my head at her.

"We both just took a pretty brutal beating at the hand of that aqua-woman."

"Hold on," Allorah said, running over to her desk. She shuffled through several of the folders on it until she pulled one to the top, flipping through it. "Argyle told me about this. This is the same woman you dove off the roof after, yes? The one that tried to drown you?"

"One and the same," I said.

"And you're telling me you saw her again?" she asked. She flipped through the folder, and then stopped. "I don't seem to have a report on that."

"It just happened last night," I said. "I haven't had time to file anything yet. There were fire hydrants going off at us left and right using some form of water manipulation. I think it's safe to assume she's the one who drowned Mason Redfield from the inside out."

Allorah closed the folder and came back over to the lab area. "Do you have a sample?"

I was about to say no, and then remembered my jacket, which was still damp. I went over to where it was hanging on the back of one of the chairs across the lab. It weighed a ton still. In my haste to get Jane to the Department for an exam early this morning, I hadn't even thought to grab something dry.

I walked over to one of the lab tables covered with supplies and grabbed an empty glass container off of it. I lifted my coat up over it and twisted it until water trickled out of it.

Allorah set to work with different pieces of her chemistry set. "This is a pure sample?" she asked.

"Mostly," I said. "We *were* fighting in the rain, after all."

Allorah continued working in silence for several more minutes like Dr. Frankenstein in his secret lab, running tests and recording results. She was at one of her micro-scopes when she stood up from it and frowned.

"And you were where again?" she asked.

"Outside the high-rise where we found the professor," I said, "way over on the East Side by the river."

"Odd," she said.

"What is?" Jane asked from the chair she had settled into.

"The water from all those exploding hydrants is *still* city water. It's all processed and therefore should be drink-able. In theory, anyway."

"So?" I asked. "It was raining. We weren't all that thirsty."

"That's the thing," Allorah said, pointing at the glass slide on the microscope. "You couldn't have drunk this sample if you wanted to."

Jane stood and wrapped her arms around my left one. "Why not?"

Allorah tapped at the slide. "Because this sample that this water woman attacked you with? It's salt water. Sea-water . . . as in, from the ocean."

"But we weren't even near seawater," I said.

Allorah cocked her head, and then looked off toward a refrigerated glass case farther along the lab setup. "Hold on a second." She walked over to the case and searched through it, pulling out three or four other slides. She slid one of them under the microscope.

"What are those?" Jane asked.

"The other water samples," Allorah said. "These are all from what we found when they emptied the professor's lungs. He was also drowned with seawater, so there's con-firmation of your killer."

"I'm not sure what that means for the case," Jane said.

"I am," I said. "It means we need to expand our search area for this woman. The closest ocean water is much farther downtown, where the East River meets up with New York Harbor." I was already heading for the door out of Allorah Daniels's office. "Time to see the Inspectre for a boat."

13

I nearly wept in thanks for the sturdiness of the railing leading up the stairs to the Inspectre's office. Without it, I doubt I would have made it past step one. The burn in my legs from chasing the green woman was less than last night, but stairs were a whole different torture device after all that running. By the time I reached the top step and turned right heading for the Inspectre's office, I had a nice, slow mummy shuffle going on.

The sounds of struggle came from behind the Inspectre's office door. I went for my bat and pushed the door open only to find Argyle Quimbley all by himself. To my surprise he wasn't in one of his usual hundred tweed coats today, nor was he sitting at his desk. The Inspectre was in *jeans* and a black turtleneck, his broken sword from the cane in hand as he advanced back and forth across his office floor. His face was red with the effort, but he swung the sword with slow, practiced patterns. Impressive as the moves were overall, I had the feeling that I could have easily dodged them had they been aimed at me. Regardless, I hoped that I had half the skill he showed at his age. I watched in silence for several minutes more until he ended his practice with one final enveloping flourish in the air. He still hadn't noticed me standing at the door.

"Is it Casual Friday already?" I asked.

The Inspectre started, fumbling the sword cane. It spun out of control in his hand, but he had the quick thinking to pull back from it rather than grab for it, probably saving a few fingers. The blade clattered to the floor, taking a chip out of his desk with its broken tip on the way down. The Inspectre bent down and picked it up, then stood up slowly, his breath coming in short, winded gasps.

"Inspectre?" I said, stepping to him, arms ready to catch him if he fell.

Argyle Quimbley waved me away with his free hand. "It's nothing, my boy, I assure you. Merely an old man feeling the full effects of his years."

I nodded silently. I couldn't argue with him. My psychometry had shown me what he was like in his prime, and he was far past those days.

"I'm dressed down today because I have the sneaking suspicion I'll be back in the field soon enough the way the budget seems to be dwindling," he said. "I still haven't read through all the cuts yet. Thought I'd brush up on some of my old moves, but I fear my hinges need oiling before this Tin Man goes active again."

"Not bad form, though," I said, hoping to give some encouragement.

The Inspectre gave me a polite smile before walking back to his desk, where he grabbed up the empty cane and slid the broken sword back into it. "Thank you for humoring me," he said, "but it's not necessary." He moved behind his desk and put the sword cane back up on the top shelf with care. "I trust you didn't come here to watch me spar with shadows. Any developments on what happened to Mason?"

I always hated giving bad news, but it was worse since I didn't have anything positive to tell my mentor about so personal a case to him. He listened as I went on about asking around campus about the professor, minus my in-store incident with the dresser, to the attack Jane and I had endured from the green woman.

"That's everything?" he asked when I was done.

I nodded. "The students who did talk to me about Professor Redfield spoke very highly of him," I said, going with encouragement again. "But even after that aquatic she-beast attacked and marked Jane last night, we still don't know why she killed Mason Redfield. On the plus side, Aqua-Woman did try to drown Jane as she was trying to escape us when we cornered her, so we must be getting closer to the truth."

The Inspectre slammed his fist on his desk. "People are dying and this city would rather have us worrying about how much printer paper we use and who we can live without in the Department." He shuffled through the files on his desk, snatching up a piece of paper, shaking it at me. "Do you know that we spent over ten thousand dollars last year on pens alone? How on earth did we even do that?"

"Actually," I said, "I have an answer for that one."

"Oh?" the Inspectre said, raising one of his busy eyebrows. He stroked at his mustache.

"Jane mentioned it to me. It seems the ink in them is a perfect replacement for Wyrm's Blood. Easier to find, too. Greater and Lesser Arcana have been going through them like crazy. At first I thought maybe Jane was a closet pen fetishist, but nope. Just Wesker and his crew scrounging up spell components."

Inspectre Quimbley sighed and rubbed his eyes. "Well, then! Maybe the Enchancellors should put Director Wesker in charge of everything here. I haven't the heart for all this red tape or letting people go."

"I suspect Thaddeus Wesker would take a perverse pleasure in assuming the throne," I said.

"The budget cuts," he said, angry. "The passing of old friends . . . How is one supposed to mourn let alone get anything done around here?"

"I'm sorry there hasn't been more progress," I said. "It's no excuse, but like you said, everyone is overworked these days. It's causing a lot of stress, even more so with me and Jane."

"Power still flaring up on you?" he asked.

"You've heard about it, too?"

"A good leader keeps his ears open for what may be troubling his agents," he said. "A lesson I learned far too late to help Mason with his problems years ago, I'm afraid."

"I don't want to trouble you with it, sir."

"Nonsense," the Inspectre said, gesturing toward the free chair across from him on the other side of the desk. "Clearly it's troubling you or you wouldn't have brought it up. If something's distracting you from your work, I'd like to know about it. An undistracted agent is a living agent, as it were."

"Very well," I said as I sank into the leather chair, feeling a bit like I was in therapy. "Ever since helping out our sunlight-challenged friends over at the Gibson-Case Center, I've been channeling all this jealous anger and rage. This ghost tattooist left me trying to shake off all these twisted feelings of hers from when she had been living, and it's been causing me to snap at Jane. She had been asking me about more space for her at my apartment, and I don't know. After feeling the tattooist's rage after trusting someone and being betrayed, it's just messing with me being close to someone right now. It really gives me pause."

"So, what?" the Inspectre asked.

"I'm not sure," I said. "I want to take it slow, but I found myself looking at antique dressers the other day when I should have been concentrating on fieldwork. When I was hunting around for students who knew the professor."

"Be sure to note that on your time card," the Inspectre said.

"I'm salaried, so . . ." I started to say, and then stopped myself when I saw him smiling. "See? Even my sense of humor is thrown off."

All the anger was gone from the Inspectre's face now. He looked me in the eye, his hands folded together in front of him. "My boy," he said. "I've seen a lot of things over the years that I don't understand. Things that naturally defy understanding, but there are some things I *do* understand. That girl Jane loves you. Not everyone gets that in this world, not the way I see she looks at you."

I didn't know what to say, but I could feel my face going red.

"Now, now," the Inspectre said. "I also understand this: our lives, especially in the Department and at F.O.G., are always too brief. That is always a possibility in our simple day-to-day existence. You want to make sure you do right by her. Pushing people away, well, that's something I do know a little bit about. It makes you live with regret, and regret is a monster that slowly eats away at you."

"It killed you when you heard Professor Redfield was dead, didn't it?"

The Inspectre closed his eyes and nodded. "More than you know, my boy," he said. "When Mason left the Fraternal Order of Goodness, I all but pushed him out of my life. I simply didn't have time for someone who walked away from what I considered the noblest of causes. If he didn't care enough to stand against evil, he was dead to me."

"But after hearing about his life as a teacher in my preliminary reports, you felt different."

The Inspectre nodded. "A life had happened to that man since I knew him," he said, "one that I never got to know. From what you've told me of his university life and his students, it sounds like it was a good one."

"From what I can tell so far," I said, "yes."

The Inspectre looked distant. "I should have liked to have known it, that's all." He turned to look at me. "Sometimes I envy you your power, Mr. Canderous, your ability to reach into the pasts of others and truly see it."

"It's funny," I said. "I've spent so much time trying to avoid reading anyone I was close to psychometrically because it always ruined things for me in the past. I always saw what I did as a bit of a curse or, at best, a way to score a quick buck. I never thought of it like that."

"I'm afraid that I am partly to blame for that," the Inspectre said.

"How so?"

"I've pushed you too hard with this, on top of your regular caseload," he said. "I've let my own personal involvement get in the way. For that, I am truly sorry."

"It's okay," I said. "I'm a big boy. I can handle it . . ."

The Inspectre stood and came around his desk. He patted me on the shoulder, and then started toward his office door. I stood and followed.

"Do me a favor, would you?" he asked. He stopped at the door, his hand on the knob, and turned to look at me.

"Sure. What is it?"

"Take the rest of the afternoon off."

I stepped back, shocked. Was I hearing him right? "Now?" I asked. "What about everything we just talked about? The budget cuts and the workload . . ."

"That can wait," he said. "And that wasn't all we talked about."

"This is about Jane, isn't it?"

The Inspectre opened his office door. "I want you to give it some thought," he said. "About what really matters, about *who* really matters to you. Do it without distraction, but take a little gratis downtime approved by me to do so."

Something deep inside me felt like it had just been freed and a tension I didn't even realize I had been carrying released. Maybe a few hours of downtime would do me some good after all. "Thank you," I said.

He nodded.

"A few of us are meeting up tonight after work at Eccentric Circles," he said. "Nothing formal, just getting together to celebrate the passing of one of our own."

"But Mason left the Fraternal Order of Goodness," I said.

"Nonetheless," he said. "I think the other agents are mostly humoring me. Still, I could use a few drinks to loosen my lips and wax nostalgic."

"I'll try to be there," I said, stepping out of his office. "Thanks."

As the Inspectre closed the door behind me, his face

registered a silent sadness. I wasn't sure if it was from old age having seeped into his bones or not, but I decided that after taking a little time off for myself, at least a round or two of drinks would be on me tonight. Getting the Inspectre a little drunk seemed like a fine way to respect my elders, and now that I thought of it, I never did ask him for the damned boat requisition I had come up here for in the first place. Ah, well, it could wait. That would probably go over better with a few drinks in him, too.

14

I considered spending my free afternoon going through my ever-growing catalog of antiques back at my apartment, but, afraid of triggering another messed-up vision, I instead found myself wandering alone over on Broadway in the Village. For hours I shopped up and down the stretch, with only one object in mind—a new dresser for my bedroom, without using my powers for once. My last incident hadn't gone so well, but I was determined to work through the mental gymnastics my power was putting me through. I looked through stores that had existed for decades, but after hours of poking about, nothing felt quite right. Frustrated, I checked my watch—my hunt would have to continue later. Right now I had to get over to Eccentric Circles if I was going to catch up with the Inspectre.

I entered the old bar. It looked like a T.G.I. Friday's designed with sort of a Harry Potter theme, oddities of the arcane world that would have given it an almost tourist-attraction hokeyness except for the fact that it was all real to those of us in the know.

The place was packed with an after-work crowd, but I didn't think all of them hailed from the Department of Extraordinary Affairs. I crushed through the crowd at the front by the bar and found the Inspectre seated on one side of a booth out back, several pitchers and glasses of beer spread out on the table. Some of the booths held familiar faces, but it was the faces seated with the Inspectre I was surprised to see. The brothers Christos sat there opposite him.

"Oh, look," Aidan called out, pointing at me. "Delivery!" The vampire couldn't help but laugh at his own joke. I, however, wasn't quite as amused.

"Funny," I said, slipping into the booth next to the Inspectre. I turned to him. "I didn't realize the undead were into memorial tributes, unless it's for one of their own."

Connor thwacked me on the arm. "Consider him my plus one, kid."

"Besides," Aidan said, "did you ever consider maybe that's part of the problem between our people? You keep assuming that our kind is only interested in what is best for us."

"Your leader sure seems to be looking out for his own interests," I said.

Aidan shook his head. "Not true," he said. "Don't mistake his general desire to be left alone as a single-minded attempt to break away from humanity completely."

"Gentlemen, please," the Inspectre interrupted, already sounding like he had put away a few beers. "Tonight is not a night to discuss vampiric affairs. We're here to mourn the loss of Mason Redfield."

I grabbed a glass and poured myself a beer from one

of the pitchers at the table. I raised it and the group of us toasted to the dear, departed professor. While I drank it down, I looked around the room. "Quite the turnout," I said. "I didn't realize so many people knew Redfield. Not bad for a guy who left the Fraternal Order of Goodness—what—thirty years ago?"

The Inspectre looked around the room, a bit melancholy. "Most of them don't recall him," the Inspectre said, wiping away a bit of foam that had accumulated in his mustache. "I think this crowd is mostly a mix of the usual oddities that inhabit Eccentric Circles. There are a few Departmental people here who came out on my behalf, but I really think there are few left in our ranks who actually remember Mason before he left the Order."

"You think any of them would know anything about the case?" I asked.

The Inspectre shook his head. "Doubtful," he said. "I don't know of anyone who's kept in touch." He took a long pull on his glass, and then set it down empty. "Least of all me."

"Don't worry, boss," Connor said from across the table. "We'll find that creepy water woman who killed Mason and attacked Jane."

I looked to Connor. "Maybe your brother has some kind of powers that can help," I said. "Something, you know, all vampirey."

Aidan smiled, but it was not one of confidence. "'Fraid not," he said. "I've only been a bloodsucker with them for about twenty years. They still call me fledgling back at the Gibson-Case Center, despite my high ranking among Brandon's core group of cronies. They're a bit secretive about what they will and won't teach the newer vampires about their growing powers, so I'm not even sure what will develop with me over time."

"Great," I said, feeling a bit defeated.

"But hey," Aidan continued, "I'm pretty sure I could charm the truth out of some of these people. Does my natural charisma count as a supernatural ability?"

"Looking all emo in your Hot Topic hoodie doesn't make you charismatic," I said. "It makes you look like a tool. Especially at forty."

"It not my fault that I look so much younger than my age," Aidan said. "You can blame Brandon and his people for that. I'm just dressing my part. Trying to fit the fashion of the time for someone in their late teens. Otherwise, I'd probably go with Connor's style, but I just look too fresh-faced and youthful to pull off an old man's trench coat."

"Hey," Connor said. "Watch it. I'm still your younger brother."

"You know," the Inspectre interrupted, pointing at the brothers Christos, "*that's* what I miss the most."

I looked at him. He had filled his glass again and was halfway done with it already. "Sir?" I asked.

"That camaraderie," he said. "That banter that comes so easily between people. Mason was a master of it."

"If it helps, Connor and I could bicker some more," Aidan said. "We're still making up for lost decades of it . . ."

The Inspectre answered the vampire, but I didn't quite catch what he said. My focus had just shifted, drawn to another table that caught my deep focus halfway across the back of the bar.

"Hold up," I said, continuing to stare.

"What is it, kid?" Connor said.

"Those are some of his," I said.

Connor shifted in his seat and looked off toward where I was staring. "His what?" he asked. "*Whose* what?"

"The professor," I said. "Those are some of his students sitting right over there. I'm pretty sure I saw them when I was flashing on some of Redfield's classes and lectures in one of my visions." At least, I thought they were the professor's from where we sat. It was hard to forget the cute blond actress with the short spiked cut, but the four other faces at their booth looked vaguely familiar as well. The girl might even make it as an actress, given how memorable her face was.

"So, those are Professor Redfield's little doters, eh?" Connor said, also checking them out.

"You want some answers?" Aidan said, rising up, forgetting his preternatural strength and practically flipping over the table. The rest of us struggled to save the pitchers of beer and our glasses. Aidan was eyeing the group at the other booth now with a dead-eyed stare. "I'll get you answers."

The Inspectre stood to meet him. "No, Aidan," he said. "Thank you. I appreciate your willingness, but as you've mentioned, your leader would rather your kind minimize their exposure."

"You can consider this a freebie," Aidan said.

"It's all right," I said, standing up myself. "I've got this. After all, I'm most likely to pass for college age, remember?"

"I could totally pass for a freshman," Aidan said, sitting back down.

"Relax, forty-year-old," I said. "You may look all of nineteen, but I've got this one."

The Inspectre clapped me on the shoulder. "See what you can find out," he said, looking around the bar with caution. "And remember what I told you: err on the side of discretion."

"Don't worry," Connor said from behind his beer, "Simon's a master of erring."

"Thanks, drunkie," I said, and headed off toward the table of students farther off across the room. The group of them was crammed into one of the deep booths, the table crowded with an assortment of pitchers, mugs, glasses, and book bags. There were five of them altogether and they were animatedly laughing and talking to one another as they drank. At the back of the booth was a young brown-haired kid sandwiched between a heavier one with greasy black hair to his left and a goateed Hispanic guy with blond punk hair to his right. More recognizable to me were the two people sitting at the outermost seats of the booth, both of whom stuck out from my visions. One end of the booth held the tall black guy with the ear gauging who was busying himself with a beer in one hand and a net book in the other. The other far end of the booth seat was occupied by the blond girl I had first recognized. She had perfect dimples and bright eyes that screamed actress in training. If there was an entry point to talking to them, it was going to be her. It didn't matter if I went in smooth approaching her. A lifetime of not being smooth around women had prepared me to go into this with the intent of crashing and burning.

As I walked toward the bar, I passed by their table at first, ignoring it, and then I did a double take.

"Hey," I said, stopping and turning to the blond girl, "don't I know you?"

She turned from her conversation with her friends and rolled her eyes at me. "Oh, brother," she said. "Are you for real? Is that seriously your 'A' game?"

I resisted the urge to launch into her, but it would blow my cover even before I started, so I bit my lip and gestured to everyone in the booth.

"No," I said. "I meant *all* of you."

As one unit, the entire table stiffened, which was the opposite of what I wanted.

"NYU, right?" I asked.

The only one to relax was the youngest-looking kid sandwiched in at the back of the booth. "Oh, yeah," he said, a little too eager, I thought. The tall guy with the ear gauging shot him a look that said he thought so, too.

"I graduated a year ago," I said, starting in with my lie. "You probably wouldn't remember me. I did a lot of geeky stuff for one of my mentors in the film department."

"Who?" the girl asked, still wary.

"A bit of an eccentric," I said. "Mason Redfield."

The girl raised an eye at me. "Oh, really?" she asked. "Well, I knew the professor pretty well and I don't remember you."

I kept my eyes on her. "I kept to myself mostly. I did a lot of . . . special project work for him."

"Really," she said, her voice flat. "What classes did you take?"

There were some things I could bluff my way past and some things I definitely couldn't. This was one of them. What classes? Specifically? I had no idea. My heart leapt into my throat as I thought about my options. I had to come up with something or they were about to learn how full of shit I was. I pointed at an extra seat at the end of their booth where most of the book bags were gathered on the table.

"May I?"

"Be our guest," the girl said. I took my time sitting, but she didn't stop staring at me. "So . . . what did you say you took with Professor Redfield?"

As I sat, I pulled off my gloves and set my hands down on the table, purposefully brushing my left one against her shoulder bag lying there. I had avoided using my powers, but I had to chance a flare-up now to get a quick reading. I pushed those worries to the side and pressed my power into the shoulder bag with one thought in my mind.

Schedule.

My mind's eye opened up on Elyse taking out her print-out of classes. I watched her as she programmed it into the calendar on her iPhone. I scanned them quickly, looking for signs in the class codes for something with a three or higher in it. Some of these students might have taken the advanced course load that a graduate like I was pretending to be had already, but I doubted all of them had. I needed enough information to sound credible.

Finding what I needed gave me an ounce of hope and I let down the guard I had put up against my worries of another flare-up. The second I did, the screen of the iPhone in the vision flickered like old-time television static, the face of the tattooist pressing forward out of it. My heart froze for a second, but rather than get caught up in the building rush of anger and jealousy that always accompanied her, I remained calm. I pulled out of the vision before it could fully take hold and shook off the disorientation. When I opened my eyes, the entire group of students was staring at me.

"You okay?" the heavy guy asked me.

I nodded, brushing it off. "Just a little drunk," I said. "No worries."

This seemed to satisfy everyone except the girl. "Your classes . . . ?" she asked, waiting.

"Let's see," I said. "Mason gave me a pass on the remedial levels of Monster Craft and bumped me up to his Harryhausen and Hollywood. Still made me take Bela, Lon, and Boris, though. Said I had a lot to learn about makeup still."

The girl stared at me a moment longer before her face shifted to a welcoming smile. "Yeah, BL and B is a real bitch," she said. "I was ready to give myself *real* facial scars instead of makeup by the time we got to finals."

"I hear that," I said, signaling for the guy working the bar. "You mind if I buy a round for the table?"

Elyse smiled. "We don't mind at all, do we, boys?" she asked, offering me her hand. "I'm Elyse. Acting track." As I expected, she had a strong, firm handshake but still kept it dainty enough. "Mr. Tall across from me there is Darryl. He edits things to make me look good in front of the camera. Chunky Monkey back there is Mike, who *is* the camera on the cinematography track. The chatty one at the back is Trent, and his fellow frosh with the soul patch and bleached-blond hair is George, the one crowding Darryl. We're trying to paper-train those two. They're undeclared still."

I waved to the group of them, nodding as I looked them over. "I'm Simon," I said.

Darryl was clacking away on his netbook in front of him on the table. "Do you have a last name?" he asked.

"Why? Are you taking notes?"

The big guy stopped typing and lowered the screen until it closed shut against the keyboard. "No," he said, folding his hands over it.

"I thought maybe you were the party stenographer," I said.

"Don't mind Darryl," Elyse said. "He's our resident tech geek–slash–editing maven. A bit OCD, but otherwise socially functional."

"Barely," Mike said.

Darryl flipped him the bird in retaliation, and then turned to me. "I just wondered what your full name was, to see if I could recall you."

"Oh, right," I said, not really ready for the question. My brain froze and I went with the first thing that came to mind. "It's Vanderous. Simon Vanderous."

"Is that Dutch?" George asked, running one hand through his blond shock of punked-out hair.

"Only half," I said, wondering if I was turning red. "Don't ask me what the other half is. I'm a bit of a mutt."

"Could you say that again for the camera?" Mike asked, and I looked over at him. Sure enough, his enormous hands were cradling a digital video camera.

"Are you . . . taping me?"

Mike looked at me from behind the camera like I was stupid. "We *are* film students," he said, "and what better way to pay tribute to our recently deceased prof than by taping our mourning?"

"So, you're here for the memorial?" I asked, wondering how they had gotten wind of it.

Elyse scrunched her face up. "Huh?" she asked. "What, now?"

"Never mind," I said as the beer arrived. I set to pouring their five glasses before filling one of my own. "I just meant we're all in mourning for Professor Redfield, aren't we? I was wondering: why *are* you here, though?"

"Eccentric Circles?" Elyse asked. I nodded. "The professor used to wax nostalgic about this place, when he wasn't waxing nostalgic about the gory glory days of monster movies and the film industry, that is. Said this bar used to remind him of his misspent youth, so I dunno. Seemed like an appropriate place for a send-off."

Maybe Professor Redfield had been just as nostalgic for the old days as the Inspectre was. For a man who had supposedly turned his back on the Fraternal Order of Goodness and the D.E.A., he certainly spent enough time hitting their favorite watering hole. And for what?

A glimpse of the world usually unseen by the average New Yorker? A world he knew existed, but had turned away from when his own life had almost been cut short at the edge of a ghoul-filled fissure? The temptation of the paranormal must have been too great to turn away from it completely. That which had been seen could not be unseen and all that.

Mike panned his camera around the bar, taking it in. "I dunno," he said. "I think the place is kind of creepy."

"True," I said.

"Well," Darryl said with a chuckle, "that's Professor Redfield for you."

"I have to ask," I said. "Do you think the university is going to throw any kind of memorial service?"

"Doubtful," Elyse said. "I don't think a lot of the other professors really understood Redfield, you know?"

"How do you mean?"

She gave a dark smile. "He's an acquired taste, now, isn't he?" she said. "Not everyone got his fascination with his particular brand of cinema. Most people look down on the horror genre with elitist disdain. It doesn't usually win awards; the *Times* won't touch them with reviews . . . If you ask me, it's snobbery in its basest form."

The entire table nodded in agreement and took a few angry swigs of their drinks. I joined them, admiring their passion for the professor's type of films and his enthusiasm for them. He had already won high regard in my mind due to the Inspectre's memories of their long-past friendship, but to see these young people so jacked up about his field of study was doubly encouraging.

"Does anyone know how he died?" I asked, doing my best to seem like I had no idea about it.

The group fell silent, either looking down at their drinks in discomfort or looking to Elyse for an answer.

"I read somewhere he was found in his new apartment," Elyse said. "I hadn't even known he was moving."

I leaned in, pressing the issue a bit. "But, like, was it natural causes?"

Elyse looked at me. Her face flashed with a moment of concern, and then she went back to her somber look. "Don't know," she said. "Don't really care. I mean, the man's *dead*. Dead's dead, Simon."

Although her face didn't show it, Elyse sounded a little pissed off by the bluntness of her statement.

"Sorry," I said. "I didn't mean anything by it . . ."

"What does that even mean?" George asked, speaking up from Darryl's left. He sounded agitated, too. "Natural causes . . . as opposed to what? *Unnatural* causes . . . ?"

"Georgey," Elyse said. "Shush. Freshman are better seen than heard . . . although with that punk blond hair of yours, maybe you shouldn't be seen, either."

"Hey!" George said, running his hands up into his wild tangle of bleached blond again. He looked genuinely hurt. "Watch it, *chica* . . ."

I needed to calm them and quick. "I just meant that I hadn't heard what happened," I said. "If he had died in his sleep or maybe it was a mugging gone wrong . . ."

Elyse threw back her glass and drained it before slamming it down on the table. "Wrap it up, boys," she said.

"You're leaving?" I asked. Elyse nodded. "But I just joined you . . ."

"We'd love to chat," she said, short, "but unlike you, we've still got class stuff to attend to, Mr. Already Graduated."

The rest of the group finished up their drinks, gathered up their things, and started sliding their way out of the booth one by one.

"Maybe we could get together and swap stories about the professor sometime," I said.

Elyse gave me a smile, but her eyes were dead to me. "Thanks for the beer," she said, "but something tells me you didn't know the professor in quite the same way we did."

Mike slid out of the booth next, his camera pointing at me still. "Say good-bye to the camera, Vanderous."

I gave a wave before standing up myself and walking after Elyse, wanting to keep them here. "Wait," I said, reaching for her.

Darryl's hand came down on my shoulder, hard. He pulled me aside.

"I think my girl said all she's going to be saying to you," he said. "Maybe the beer's making you a little braver than usual, but trust me when I say you don't want to press your luck with her."

"Right," I said, not wanting to start anything in the middle of Eccentric Circles. I had the feeling it might go against the subtlety the Inspectre had asked me to go for.

"And I *know* you don't want to press your luck with me," Darryl added.

I stayed still, and after a moment, Darryl slapped me hard on the shoulder, and then turned with his computer bag over his shoulder and headed up to the front of the bar toward the doors. I waited until all of them were gone before I headed back across the bar toward the Inspectre, Aidan, and Connor.

Aidan grinned at me from where he sat. "How'd it go, boy detective?"

"Shush," I said, sitting back down.

"Well, kid?" Connor asked. "What did you find out?"

"They loved Mason Redfield," I said. "They were gaga over him."

The Inspectre smiled. "That is of some comfort to hear."

"Great," Connor said, perturbed. "So he was well loved. That really doesn't help narrow or expand our field of investigation into his murder, now, does it? At least if he had made some enemies . . ."

"The only enemies he seems to have had outside of the water woman are all those fake movie monsters in his office," I said, "and I doubt they could do anything other than fetch a nice price on eBay. We'll keep on it, Inspectre, but that group was a creepy little Mason Redfield cheer squad. Still, I think they may not be giving me the whole picture yet."

"Really?" the Inspectre asked. "Why not, my boy?"

"When I tried to head the conversation into the paranormal, they didn't pick up on any of my cues. Then when the guy with the blond punk hair made a joke that might have suggested something paranormal, Elyse clammed him up . . . *fast*. They left before I could press them any further, but I bet they know something about the professor and the water woman who killed him."

"Maybe we should work on that kid, then," Connor suggested. "The punk one. I'm sure if we press hard enough, we can find the weak link in their chain."

"Carefully," the Inspectre added. "We don't want them to bolt."

"Understood," I said, nodding. "I'll track them down on campus tomorrow. Maybe they'll feel less threatened there during the daytime. If I'm lucky, I can single one of them out."

"Daytime," Aidan said, drawing it out like it was a dirty word. "Well, that leaves me out, then."

"It'll leave *all* of you out," I said. "I'll handle this myself."

"Excellent," the Inspectre said, raising his glass with a bit of drunken unsteadiness, "but for now, we drink."

"Fine by me," I said, reaching for my glass. "As long as the Department lets me expense it."

The Inspectre cleared his throat. "Actually, about that . . ."

I held my hand up to stop him. I raised my glass to my lips and pounded it. "Don't tell me," I said. "Save it for the office tomorrow. Tonight, like you said, we drink."

15

There was nothing I hated more than the sound of construction in New York City, but it was even worse when it was happening in my own damned head thanks to a hangover the next morning. Somehow I managed to get myself up to the Department, but made sure I loaded up on four cups of high-octane caffeine in the Lovecraft Café first.

My blurriness began to fade about two cups in, but even then, I found myself just staring at piles of paperwork for at least the first forty minutes I was in without having actually done anything with them. As I rallied my brain back to functionality, the sneaking suspicion I was forgetting something important began to creep over me. I almost had it when a shadow at the entrance to my cube reminded me what it was.

"Jane," I muttered. "Good morning."

"Is it?" she said, and by the tone of her voice, she wasn't pleased. A bunch of books and papers were cradled in her arms.

"Honestly?" I asked. "No. My ass is dragging. The 'memorial' got a little more indulgent as the night went on."

"I've seen the results already," she said. "Connor and the Inspectre both look a little rough around the edges."

"Were you awake when I came in last night?"

"You aren't sure?" Jane asked, setting down the pile of books and papers in her arms.

I shook my head. "I don't recall much of anything once I got home. Where were you?"

"I stayed at my place," she said. "I figured it might be best . . . between you going out and with you having issue with all this emotion tied to using your powers."

"Sure," I said, feeling a weird energy between the two of us. "I can understand that." I patted her pile of books. "What do we have here?"

Jane looked like she was about to say something more regarding us, but turned to the books instead. "I pulled some more materials. Books on water and water-based spells and mythos. I figured they might do some double duty, helping the Inspectre out and maybe me at the same time."

"Any new developments?" I asked. "With the mark, I mean."

"My showers are getting longer," she said, and then gave me a weak smile. "I find myself craving them. I took two last night while you were out, then another one once I went home, and then I got up earlier than I usually do feeling the need to take one more. The longer I go without one, the more lethargic I feel."

"I think you should come back over to my place tonight," I said. "I don't like the idea of you being home alone in this condition."

Jane stiffened. "You didn't seem to mind last night," she said.

"That's not fair," I said. "I was mourning with the Inspectre and, well . . . things got out of hand. I'm sorry for that. I guess with all the pressure and my powers acting up, I just needed to cut loose with the guys."

"I get that," she said, putting her hand on my head and stroking my hair. "I really do, but it really seemed to freak you out with this whole drawer thing and I don't want to crowd you while you're working through your issues. Besides, I can feel this mark making me irritable."

"Don't worry about my strange flares," I said. "I'm working to repress them. I'm more concerned about keeping an eye on you until Allorah Daniels can get us some answers on that mark. I want you over."

"If you're sure . . ." Jane reached into her bag and pulled out a package covered in Spider-Man wrapping paper. She laid it down in front of me on my desk.

"What's this?"

"Open it," she said.

I grabbed the lunch-box-sized package, unwrapped it, and to my surprise it actually *was* a lunch box. The sides of it were adorned with familiar faces: Egon, Ray, Winston, Peter, and Slimer.

"Vintage Ghostbusters," I said. "Keen. But why?"

"I thought I could start making us lunch," she said. "Bringing it instead of buying it right now."

Something about the look on her face made me wary. "Okay," I said. "Sure, but what brought this on?"

"I just thought that with all the budget cuts at the Department, it might be a good idea."

"Don't worry," I said. "I can just sell off some of my psychometric finds piling up at home. I've been meaning to make the time for it somehow."

"No, really, that's okay. Just let me do lunch for now."

"Why are you being so insistent?" I asked. I grabbed both of her hands and made her look at me. "What's this really about, Jane?"

"It's just that maybe it might be better if you didn't read anything with your psychometry right now. Especially if it's going to cause another emotional flare-up."

"I have to use it," I said. "It's my *job*. Just give me some time with this. I'm working through it."

Jane looked crestfallen. "That's the thing, Simon. I don't mean to rush you, but I don't *know* how much time I have with this mark on me, do I? I'm sorry if that comes off as pushy."

"I know." I hugged her close to me. "You need to give us time to figure that out, too," I said.

Jane nodded against my chest, staying pressed up against me.

A few moments later, a cough at the edge of my cube space had us pulling apart.

Aidan stood there, looking a little paler and more gaunt than usual with a pile of folders in his hands. It was odd seeing him in our offices, especially since I had just been woken up from sunlight pouring into my bedroom not more than an hour ago.

"What are you doing here?" I asked. "Shouldn't you be in your coffin or something?"

"I wanted to make sure Connor and Argyle got back to the office safely from the bar," he said. "By the time I took care of that, the sun was coming up so I ended up trapped here for the day. Thought I'd get some vampire liaison paperwork done on behalf of Brandon while I'm here. Luckily, your secret offices have no windows."

"So, it's totally a myth you need to sleep during the day," Jane said.

Aidan nodded. "I think it's more of an attitude thing for most of the vampires," he said. "The brain needs to turn off every so often, you know? I just think a lot of my people take comfort in a bit of mental downtime."

"You look a little run-down, too," Jane said. "No offense. Hangover? Can you even get one?"

"Not really," he said. "Although I did drink enough to start feeling it before my body kicked in and metabolized it right out of me. I think I'm more run-down because of all the protective runes you guys have carved into the walls around here. I feel . . . practically human."

He said the word "human" with such distaste that I felt my blood rising at it.

"Poor you," I said. "How you must suffer feeling for a second like the rest of us mortals." Irrational anger flared up in me, the tattooist's visions still lingering in me. I even felt a twinge of jealousy that Aidan was standing too close to Jane right now, and although it tore me apart, I told myself it was all unreal, merely a figment of the residual vision.

"Don't get *too* agitated," Aidan said with a wicked grin. "I'm famished on top of it and the more you get worked up, the more I can sense your blood working its way through your body."

I wasn't sure if he was kidding or not but it helped to focus me on reality, and I calmed myself.

"You don't look too bad, Simon," Aidan continued. "I thought for sure you'd be in worse shape after all that drinking."

"He is," Jane said.

"I'll have you know that I was actually *working* for part of that night," I said.

"Yeah, he was," Aidan said. "What was the name of that hot blonde with the bob haircut again? Elaine?"

"Elyse," I corrected, cringing at Aidan's mention of her. The last thing a guy wants in front of his girlfriend is any story involving a bar that intersects with one involving another woman.

Jane looked at me sideways.

"What?" I asked. "It was for a case. They were Professor Redfield's students. I had to talk to them."

"Oh, there was more than one?" she asked with doubt in her voice.

"Not more women," I said. "Mostly guys."

"But apparently she was the only one Aidan found interesting enough to mention."

"It's not like that," I said. "She was clearly the leader of the pack among the film students. I had to soften them up, so I bought everyone a round."

Jane gathered up her pile of research. Aidan walked past her and over to Connor's side of the desks, sitting down.

"So let me get this straight," Jane said, a little of her lethargy shaking off and giving way to anger. "While I was sitting at home worrying over this mark and whatever the hell it's doing to me, you were out drinking and chatting up this blonde?"

"Technically that's true, but—"

Jane stepped out of my office area. "I don't have time to be sitting around here, then," she said. "If you can't be bothered to help me get through this, I'm going back to Enchancellor Daniels . . . or maybe even Director Wesker."

Jane stormed off before I could even process all of it. I looked over to Aidan, who was still sitting at Connor's desk. "What the hell just happened?" I asked.

"Looks like you and your girlfriend just had a fight."

"No thanks to you," I said, anger building up in me.

"Did you really think it was smart to bring Elyse up in front of her? You had to go there, didn't you?"

"Hey, I didn't know she'd go off like that," he said. "I just like to make humans sweat a little. It gives the smell in the air such a pleasant hint of blood and fear, but I didn't think it would get *that* much of a rise out of her. You must be doing something wrong at home."

"Okay, genius, then why don't you enlighten me? I mean, eternal youth has got to count for something after all, right?"

Aidan shrugged. "Don't ask me for love advice," he said. "I was the one dating the great vampire betrayer, remember?"

I was ready to jump on that given the trouble he had just stirred up for me, but the sad look on his face killed the words in my mouth.

Aidan set down the pile of papers and began rummaging through his brother's desk.

"Can I help you?" I asked.

"No," he said. "I'm good."

"What I mean is, what are you doing?" I asked. "Not cool to be rifling through Connor's stuff. I know you are brothers and all, but I believe even the undead consider privacy something of import, yes?"

Aidan stopped and laid his hands on the desk. "Well, yeah," he said, "but Connor said I could use his desk while he's in a This Week in Haunts meeting."

I checked my watch. "Running long, I see. Or maybe it's taking longer with fewer agents out there in the field."

"I guess," Aidan said. "He looked a bit frantic and pissed off when he was heading in, but that kind of seems to be his thing, you know?"

I laughed at that. "That, I do know," I said. "That I do." I grabbed a pen off my desk and tossed it to him. He caught it in perfect position for writing like it was nothing. "Use his desk, then. Just try to make human sounds and all that while you're working. When you're all silent and moving about, it creeps me out."

"I'll try," he said, "but sometimes I forget." He paused. "Sorry about earlier. With getting Jane all riled up on you."

"It's all right," I said. "By the way, if HR comes through and asks why we have a teenage boy filling in at Connor's desk, good luck explaining it to them."

Aidan leaned forward and popped his fangs. "Think this will be explanation enough?"

"Doubtful," I said. "If anything, it'll just lead to more paperwork for you."

Aidan retracted his fangs, looking a bit crestfallen. "More?"

I nodded. "For as much hitting squishy things with bats that I get to do, I end up stuck at this desk, writing out the details, an awful lot."

"Exciting," Aidan said and resumed looking through his pile of papers. He flew through them with lightning speed.

"That's one thing I envy about you vampires," I said.

"Just one thing?" Aidan asked, with a surprised laugh.

"Just one," I said. "Sorry. Not really keen on the rest of your deal."

"Fine," he said. "What is it?"

"Your kind strike me as minimalists," I said.

Aidan cocked his head. "How so?"

"You dispense with paperwork for the most part," I said. "I mean, look at the Gibson-Case Center. It's a city unto itself and yet there wasn't much of a paper trail when your people built it. Even your history . . . You've got some of it written down in that Vampinomicon or whatever it's called, but let's face it: if that thing burned up tomorrow, you'd be able to re-create it from an oral tradition because some of you who actually lived that history are still alive. I envy your lack of bureaucracy."

"I suppose you have a point," Aidan said, "but you're forgetting something."

"I am?" I asked. "What's that?"

He patted the pile of papers before him. "Time bends for us differently . . ."

"I figured that out when I met your leader and discovered he had named himself after a character from *Beverly Hills, 90210.* So?"

Aidan grabbed the stack and slowly flipped down through it, page by page. "It means that I get shafted with the mundanely human task of *your* paperwork thanks to my role as liaison between our two people. For someone whose life is already an eternity, jumping through the hoops of an organization that will most likely wither while all of us still live on makes the task of doing this paperwork a different kind of eternity all its own."

"Fair point," I said. "Sorry."

Aidan picked up a pen and started scrawling at inhuman speeds on one of the detail sheets in front of him. "It's all right," he said. "There is some consolation in all this." Aidan looked up at me, grinning. "I'll never get those bags under my eyes that you have from all this right now."

"It's not the job," I said. "These are from the hangover."

"Another thing I'm glad to not really experience," he said, and fell to his pile of paperwork without another word, blazing through it in a way I could only dream of.

16

Despite the bustling sprawl of New York University from Greenwich Village down to Houston Street, I wasn't too worried about just how the hell I was supposed to find any of the students I was looking for, thanks to the predictable and cliquish nature of film and theater people. Especially when it came to finding freshmen who were so new to the Big Apple that they latched onto one another like lost, lonely magnets. I started by hanging around Washington Square Park, and it didn't take me too long to spy Trent and George making their way across the park. George's platinum blond hair against the brown of his skin stuck out enough that I could have probably spotted him all the way from my apartment down in SoHo.

I followed the two students into one of the film studies buildings, thankful that my Department of Extraordinary Affairs ID was enough to get me in during normal school hours, unlike sneaking around the other night. I never knew

when it would or wouldn't work. It never quite held the
weight that an actual police shield did around Manhattan.
The two freshmen headed deep into the building's twist of
corridors. I kept losing them in my efforts to shadow them
as discreetly as I could, and I had to use my psychometry
a few times to flash on which way they had gone, but they
were quick hits that didn't flare up any residual anger issues. Before long, I came to a dead-end corridor with only
one door marked with a sign that read EDITING SUITE—
FILM & SOUND. I paused outside it to collect myself, trying
to decide the best approach once I stepped through it. Last
night's conversation at Eccentric Circles had gone fairly
well before they had brushed me off. Maybe the role of one
of Mason Redfield's old students would still hold up.

As I opened the door, I hoped it would, anyway. The
students seemed nice enough and I wasn't in the mood to
threaten people with my bat, not unless they were something that went bump in the night, anyway.

The editing studio beyond the door was a large, dark,
open space lit only by banks of computers along with
various decks, boom mikes, speakers, and film equipment.
Along the far side of the room was a glass-encased recording booth with a blank movie screen inside it. I thought I
might be interrupting a class in session, but then I realized
that the only students in the room were the group I had
met the other night at the bar. At one of the computer con-
soles, cameraman Heavy Mike was working on film footage along side Darryl, who, even sitting, was taller than
him. All I could see of Elyse was a shock of her blond hair
poking above a cushion-covered acoustics screen that had
a microphone hanging down into it. George had already set
to work even though he had just entered and was sitting at
a computer console near me. Trent had his back to me and

was in the process of lugging a stack of books and binders across the floor, heading toward George.

"Hey, there," I said to no one in particular.

Trent spun around, dropping the stack. George gave me a sleepy look from the computer at which he was working. He scratched his bleached shag of punk hair, and then waved. "Hey," he said, and went back to watching whatever he was working on.

Trent swore under his breath.

"Nervous much?" I asked.

"You shouldn't sneak up on people like that," Trent said. He kneeled down and started gathering up the books and binders.

"Sorry," I said, crossing to help him.

Elyse came into view from behind the acoustics screen in formfitting jeans and a *Les Miserables* T-shirt, her eyes intent on Trent and his cleanup efforts.

"Would you watch it, Trent?" she said, storming over, not even noticing me. "Some of that is all we have of the professor's notes."

Trent looked up at her. The young freshman looked worried. "Company," he said, and then nodded his head toward me.

Elyse looked up, surprised to see me there, but her face shifted in an instant to something more collegial. "Oh, hello," she said, giving me a smile. She snapped her fingers. "Simon, right?"

"Yes," I said, squatting down to help with the books on the floor.

"You don't have to do that," she said, quick and abrupt.

"I'm the reason he dropped them," I said. I didn't bother to tell her that just hearing they were some of the professor's personal notes was enough to have me wanting to get my hands on them. His office had been empty of anything personal, after all.

Elyse, however, moved faster than me, dropping down with the agility of a gymnast and scooping up the few books and notebooks Trent hadn't already reclaimed. I did get a chance to brush my hand against one of the notebooks as she stood, and I pressed my power into it for just a second before she pulled herself away and placed them next to a large piece of equipment over in the center of the room. A splash of a demonic red structure filled my mind's eye, the familiar sight of a bridge set against a dark blue blast of water. My mind focused in on a bronze nameplate attached to one of its struts.

"What's the Hell Gate Bridge?" I asked.

Elyse turned to me, suspicion in her eyes. "Excuse me?" she said.

"One of the notebooks fluttered open when they fell and the name caught my eye," I lied.

Elyse seemed to buy the story, and once she finished putting everything down, she wandered back over to me.

"It's one of the more structurally sound old-world bridges around Manhattan," she said. "Hell Gate actually refers to the strait beneath the bridge. It comes from the Dutch phrase *hellegat*, which means both 'hell gate' as well as 'bright passage,' which was the name originally given to the entire East River."

"Sure you're not a history major?" I asked. "You sure have a lot of New York knowledge."

"I should," she said. "Professor Redfield was making a documentary on the bridge. It was the project he was working on, before . . . you know."

"Gotcha," I said. My spider-sense started to tingle. Was there something more sinister to its history than just its name? Was the East River a portal to Hell or something along those lines? It seemed kind of ludicrous, but Other Division *did* deal with the ludicrous on a pretty regular basis.

"So the professor was working on a documentary?" I asked. "Seems strange, given his filmic proclivities."

"How do you mean?" Elyse said.

"You know . . . with his love of old-school horror and monster movies of the Sinbad variety," I said. "Urban architecture just seems like a strange choice, is all."

"Not really," Elyse said, stiffening a little. "Do *you* only watch one kind of movies? I mean, genre cinema was his passion, but his scope wasn't limited to *just* that. You don't teach at NYU long if you can't reach beyond your own personal passions. I mean, for instance, I dance, sing, and act, but I wouldn't define myself through just any one of those things. Neither would Professor Redfield. But if you're looking for a link to his love of all things horror film, the name of the bridge *was* Hell Gate. I think that appealed to Professor Redfield's sense of horror, the kind that exists in the real world."

"Bridges inspire a sense of horror?" I asked.

"They hold their own dark histories, don't they?" she asked, putting on a dark dramatic tone, setting a bit of spooky mood.

I still wasn't getting what she was driving at. "Such as . . . ?"

"Hell Gate was built as a commuter bridge," she said. "We're talking all kinds of potential chaos with that. Train accidents, people getting run down, jumpers . . . you name it."

Just her delivery of her little speech here was enough to give me the chills. Elyse would graduate and find herself a working actress for sure. I stepped away from her and headed over to the closest computer station, where George was working.

"So, what?" I asked. "You're going to finish the documentary for the dearly departed professor?"

Elyse danced around me with a graceful twirl, cutting me off before I could get over to George and his machine. "There are several projects of his that we're working on."

I tried looking past her at whatever George was doing, but Elyse kept her eyes locked on mine and kept in my way. "I'd love to see it sometime," I said.

Elyse's face darkened. This time she didn't look like she was acting. "I bet you would," she said, becoming short with me. "Look. We've got a lot to do here, Simon, so if you don't mind, we'd appreciate you leaving."

"I will," I said, "but I just thought—"

"I'm sure you think a lot of things," Elyse said, cutting me off, "but here's *my* thing. I've got a problem. I have to wonder how well you *really* knew the professor."

I could face zombies in the street no problem, but trying to pretend like this had my heart beating out of my chest as her suspicion rose. I only hoped I could act well enough to convince her. "I told you that the other night," I said. "I graduated a few years before most of you. He was one of my mentors."

"That's where my problem is," she said. The rest of the group all stopped what they were doing and began working their way over to me. "If you claim to be so familiar with his work, then how do you not know a damn thing about this documentary?"

Crap. Maybe I did need to enroll at NYU for acting. I felt myself tensing up, but I tried to keep my cool. "As you said, it was his latest project, and as I told you, I graduated a few years back."

Elyse snapped, darkness filling her eyes. "He'd been obsessing over Hell Gate for *decades*," she said, advancing on
me. "Who *are* you?"

Discretion was still my priority here. The girl was
small in size compared to me, but there was a lot of
power in her eyes. Years of acting training were to thank
for that, no doubt. Still, I wasn't about to pull my bat on
someone nonparanormal. I resisted the urge to back off
and held my ground. "How about you tell me what you
know?" I asked.

"How about you leave?" Elyse said with a sweet smile
over her bitter words.

"Or what?" I said. "You'll stage-combat me to death?
I'm not worried. After all, don't they train you actors how
to *miss*?"

"Funny," Elyse said.

"Just tell me what you know," I said again.

Elyse crossed her arms in defiance. "Or?"

"Just tell me," I said.

Movement caught my eye from around the room. Darryl
and Heavy Mike were walking over. Mike had his video
camera out as he came, but it was Darryl I was worried
about. He towered over me and stood protectively just over
Elyse's shoulder.

"Everything okay here, Elyse?" Darryl asked.

"Fine," she said. "Simon was just leaving."

Darryl looked at me, a bit of menace in his eyes as he
stared me down. "Good," he said.

"I was?" I asked, starting to get angry.

"Yes," she said. "You were. I don't know who you are,
but you were no friend of the professor. That's for sure."

"Aw, come on . . . fight for the camera," Mike said from
behind his video camera. "This would make excellent foot-

age. A nice scuffle . . . I bet it would even look good in court."

Trent and George moved to stand with their friends, a unified front of five against one single Simon.

"Fine," I said. "I'll go, but consider this. Someone killed the good professor and nobody seems to be as interested in that as much as I am."

"Wait," Elyse said, grabbing me by the arm. "How do *you* know he was killed? Who *are* you?"

"I can be secretive, too," I said. I pushed open the door, hoping to get out while the getting was good. To my relief, no one moved to stop me, and I was glad to get away from them. I had what I needed from them—a lead. The Hell Gate Bridge. Mason Redfield's decades-long obsession. Perhaps it would hold some answers to his death, especially with the dark, rich histories of death that bridges seemed to have.

I let the door slam shut behind me and walked away, which was probably best. If I left now, I could at least keep with my general rule about not using my bat on normal people. Not that film and theater people really counted for normal, as I was slowly learning.

17

Connor had spent his day catching up on paperwork, still nursing a hangover from last night at Eccentric Circles, and I put in a couple of hours killing some of my own paperwork after I told him about the documentary. By the time either of us had a second free and could get our asses up to the Hell Gate Bridge, it was already dark out. The best approach seemed to be coming at it from Queens through Astoria Park, but once we got there, there was still the daunting task of working our way up to the crossing. As we started up the understructure of it, I was impressed by the sheer size of it.

The Hell Gate Bridge stood against the night sky, traversing the East River where it spanned over to Wards Island. In the dark, its two stone towers rose up at either end of it and the red steel of the bridge itself stretched in a low arch across the expanse, two sets of train tracks running down the center of it. By the time we climbed all the way up to it and stood on the tracks, the September wind was whipping at Connor and me, putting a chill in my bones that was already creeping me out.

Professor Redfield had found it fascinating enough to spend great expanses of time obsessing over it. I needed to know why, and if the answers were out there, I had to find out. I stepped out onto the main section of the bridge.

Connor hesitated. I stopped and looked at him. "Coming?"

He dug his hands down into the pockets of his coat. "Probably a bad time to bring this up, but I don't really care for bridges, kid."

"No?" I asked. "Afraid of heights or something?"

"Not quite," he said. "You remember why we don't go down to Ground Zero, right?"

I nodded. "Yeah," I said. "No one from the D.E.A. dares to step foot where World Trade Center once stood. Too much sorrow. Too many ghosts."

"Pain sticks, kid. Before 9/11, bridges were the number-one source for sorrow around here. Despondent people *love* to fling themselves to their unhappy demise. A gruesome but romantically poetic way to go, if you ask me. You show me a Manhattan bridge and I'll show you at least a handful of ghosts moping around on each of them for eternity. So, like I said—not a fan of them. Just look for yourself."

I turned to look out onto the bridge, adjusting my eyes to *really* look.

I knew that most New Yorkers turned a blind eye to the stranger things they came across in Manhattan. The fragility of the human mind helped protect itself. My own mind was no exception, and even when I could focus on the hidden world around us, I was not nearly as trained as Connor at seeing the dead. I willed myself to focus on the empty spaces my conscious mind must be avoiding.

"Whoa," I said when my mind keyed in to the entire scene before me. The bridge was covered with dozens, maybe hundreds of ghostly figures. Spirits drifted directionless across the span. I turned to Connor. "Are you seeing this?"

Connor gave me a dark smile. "What do you think, kid?"

"We're not going out there, are we?" I asked. "Think about my hair."

"Way to focus on what's really important," Connor said.

I stepped closer to Connor, dropping to a whisper with the horde of apparitions so close. "I think I have a point," I said. "A very vain but accurate point."

"Jesus," Connor said, agitated. "I'm sorry you're too damn pretty to do your job." He looked out over the bridge. "You do realize that we're supposed to exhibit some sort of heroism, right? It *is* in our job description, kid."

"Right," I said, feeling somewhat dressed down. "Sorry."

"Just stay close to me," he said.

"Fine by me," I said

Connor walked off onto the bridge. The wind picked up, joined by the sound of rushing water below that I could see through the struts as we went, giving me a bit of vertigo from all the movement. The chilling bite of the wind blew at our clothes and hair. The shapes around us were like a living fog, drifting in the wind up and down the bridge. They were slow enough that we were able to move among the spirits without running the risk of passing through any of them.

"Is this something ghosts do regularly?" I asked. "I mean, get together like this? Maybe they're going to go bungee jumping off the bridge."

Connor shot me a don't-be-stupid look and continued out onto the bridge where the greater concentration of spirits were. I followed him, the ghosts drifting out of our path as we went.

Connor stopped when we were about halfway across the expanse right in the heart of the ghostly gathering. There were hundreds of them. He turned in circles, looking them over. "Interesting," he said.

Meandering spirits swirled all around me. "Popular place," I said. "I guess if you're looking to off yourself, Hell Gate is the place to go."

Connor shook his head. "I don't think these are all suicides, kid."

"Why not?"

Connor waved his hand out toward the crowd. "Look at the way they're all dressed," he said.

I studied the crowd closely, taking note of the clothes. All of them looked to be from the same era. Tall, stiff collars on some on the men in fine tailored suits, ankle-length skirts and matching jackets on many of the women. Other, more casual women had on shirtwaist dresses and sailor hats. The rest either wore broad-brimmed hats or sported the turn-of-the-century Gibson Girl hairstyle, but the wind was already playing havoc with them.

"They all look turn of the century, 1900 more or less," I said. "So?"

"That's the thing," Connor said. "If they were all suicides, they probably happened periodically through history. They should all be dressed in different styles reflecting all those times, right? But they're not. Everyone who died here is from the same era."

"So, something tragic happened all at once," I said.

Connor nodded. "That would be my guess."

"But what?" I looked down at the structure of the bridge, namely the two sets of train tracks that ran across them. "Train derailment?"

"I'm not sure," Connor said, reaching into his coat pocket and pulling out a small stoppered vial, "but we're going to find out."

He walked around in the drift of souls until he narrowed his focus in on a man in his early twenties wearing a suit two sizes too big for him. Connor flipped the stopper off the top of the vial and the air immediately filled with the smell of patchouli. Tendrils of light brown vapors rose up from it and slowly snaked their way up and around the young man. When the smoke reached his nostrils, his face fell slack.

"Hey, friend," Connor said, sounding quite collegial, "you mind telling me what you're waiting for?"

The young man gave a slow nod as he continued to stare off along the distance of the East River. "Our steamer," he said.

"You're expecting a boat?" I asked.

The man nodded again, ever so slightly.

I looked over at Connor. "Are we talking metaphorically? Like a boat to the afterlife? I don't think the East River qualifies as the River Styx, does it?"

Connor gave me a look. "Shush," he said, turning his attention back to the ghost. "Where are you going today?"

The man smiled, a grin crossing his face from ear to ear like a cartoon character. "On a picnic."

I had forgotten how exaggerated the features could get on a spirit when raw emotion came to the surface. Connor didn't react; he just nodded along with him.

"Sounds nice," he said. "When are you expecting it?"

"Soon," the man said, but his face changed. Uncertainty crept into his eyes and his mouth twisted in concern. "But, my goodness, I thought it would certainly be here by now. You do think it's coming, don't you? Mr. Carter promised us and I'd hate to think that the St. Mark's Lutherans were so unsound in their financial affairs that they had to cancel."

Connor looked at me and gave a bitter smile. "Comforting to see that budget concerns have a long and illustrious history."

"Do you think that the lady will know what the holdup is?" the young man asked, his voice barely an audible whisper on the wind.

"Lady?" Connor asked him.

The man looked around the expanse of the bridge through the crowd of his fellow ghosts, nervous. His face was pained. "I shouldn't say anything more or she'll hurt me."

"I think I know what lady," I said, stepping around to get in front of him. "A woman with dark hair, wearing a long green dress, yes?"

"Dark haired, yes," he said, "and in a green dress that I daresay is a bit of immodest on a woman."

"Figures," I said. "That dress of hers is no doubt scandalous by his standards."

"Well, at least your little water woman is a bit of a fashion plate," Connor said. "A killer, but still able to pull off the cover shot of *Paranormal Quarterly*. Nice."

I turned back to the young man. "Why are you afraid of

her?" I asked, but the look on his face was already enough to give me my answer.

The young man's fear seemed to be agitating the rest of the ghosts around him. Like a ripple in a pond, frantic energy began to radiate outward from him until we were surrounded by a sea of nervous spirits. "Foul fortunes come on foul winds," he said. "And together they blow twice as hard. She has risen, but the worst has yet to rise."

"Tell me," I begged of him, wishing I could reach out and grab him to shake him. "Who has risen? What's her name?"

"We should probably get out of here," Connor said. "As in, now."

"Tell us," I said. "Please."

"General . . . Slocum," the young man said, his fear growing. His feet left the ground as his agitation grew, swirling off into the crowd. I wasn't sure if he was gearing up to attack or not, but it was clear that Connor's ghost-wrangling mixture had worn off. I didn't want to see what happened next, but Connor was already one step ahead of me.

Already in motion, Connor bolted off across the bridge and I came running after him. Spirits dove and wove around us and I did my best to keep them from passing through me as I ran. By the time we passed beyond one of the stone towers at the end of the bridge, the swarm was well behind us and already settling down again. When the two of us stopped running, we both were panting pretty heavily.

"Dare I ask how my hair is?" I asked.

"Still perfect," Connor said, "although you could maybe use some product in all this wind."

"Smart-ass," I said. "Can you do anything to disperse them?"

Connor shook his head as he fixed the collar of his windblown trench coat. "I don't think so, kid," he said. "I don't think I've seen so many ghosts in one place since that night at the Metropolitan Museum of Art. Besides, it's hard to disperse them when I don't know why they're still here in the first place."

"So what now?" I said, adjusting my coat. I tapped my bat. "Fat lot of good this would do."

"Don't get all bent out of shape," Connor said. "I consider what we just did a win. We made it off the bridge alive, didn't we?"

I nodded. "Yeah, that's something."

"But that's not all," he added.

"No?"

"We have a name," he said. "I'm not sure who General Slocum is, but I aim to find out."

"I hope Godfrey Candella's on call, then," I said.

Connor headed off toward the lights of Queens. "With all the cuts, everybody's on call all the time."

"True," I said, yawning with fatigue, shivering, "but I think this has to wait until morning. I'm not sure if Godfrey needs his sleep, but I'm pretty sure I do."

18

Heading down to the Gauntlet always creeped me out a little. The archives were far older than the coffeehouse, movie theater, and offices above, and descending the well-worn stone stairs into the caverns that housed our gathered archival resources sometimes felt like I was going on a caving expedition. I hurried all the way down until I reached the door at the bottom and swung it open to reveal the main room where overhead lights, shelves and shelves of books, and antique wooden worktables galore gave a hint of civilization that calmed me again. As luck would have it, Godfrey Candella was rushing out of one of the aisles, heading for his office off to my right. I had to jog just to intersect with him, but when I did, I almost wished I hadn't.

"What do *you* want?" Godfrey said, continuing past me with his stack of books.

I followed him as he headed into his office. His large

wooden desk was threatening to collapse under the weight
of already accumulated books, but Godfrey seemed determined to test the limits of its structural integrity by finding
room for more.

"Nice to see you, too," I said. Godfrey shoved some papers off the top of one pile of books, letting them fall into
another one, forming one super pile of loose paper chaos.
Something didn't feel quite right. It was far too quiet down
here. The hustle and bustle of the usual staff was all but
gone at the moment.

"Where the hell is everyone?" I asked.

"*What* everyone?" Godfrey asked, snapping. "This is it.
Me. *I'm* the everyone."

I looked around for someone else down here, anyone
else. "You're kidding," I said.

Godfrey put the books down on his desk and pushed his
horn-rims back up onto his nose. "First of all," he said, "I
rarely kid. Especially when it comes to the Gauntlet."

"Right," I said, wandering to take a peek out of his office door. There was an eerie stillness to the vast book-
filled cavern. "I forgot. Of course not."

"Second of all," Godfrey said, and then fell silent for a
minute. "There is no second of all. Just me down here. So,
if you need something . . ."

"Just point me in the direction of bridges and I'll get off
your back."

Godfrey sat down at his desk and leaned back. He
folded his hands across his chest. "Let me guess," he said.
"The Hell Gate Bridge."

"Good guess," I said, impressed. "And correct. You
know it?"

"Not too well," he said, "but yeah. With a name like that,

we get a couple of requests every few months on it from agents."

"I bet," I said. "Well, listen. We found a menagerie of lingering ghosts out that way. I thought it might be a Hell Mouth or something. You know, an actual gate to hell."

Godfrey smiled and waggled a finger at me. "You've been watching too many *Buffy* reruns."

"Only for fighting techniques," I said. "I swear."

"Don't worry," Godfrey said. "It's not a Hell Mouth."

"You sure about that?"

"Pretty sure," he said, getting up. He headed for his door. "It's named from the Dutch *hellegat*, which means . . ."

" 'Bright passage,' I know."

Godfrey stopped and looked at me. "Impressive."

"Some NYU students told me," I said. "Don't worry. You're in no danger of losing your spot as head nerd around here. I just need to know about the bridge and a general who may be connected to it."

"Follow me," Godfrey said and started walking. "You said there were ghosts out there?"

"Yeah, literally hundreds of them."

"Interesting," Godfrey said. He headed off toward a section filled with large empty tables surrounded by banks of old wooden drawers.

"How's Jane?" he asked as we walked over to one of the drawers. "I haven't seen her since they announced the cuts a few weeks back. Is she . . . ?" Godfrey couldn't even finish his question.

"Yeah," I said. "She's still here."

"Good, good," he said, but he looked a little distracted.

"What about that girl you were seeing?" I asked. "The one who helped take down that bookwyrm . . . ?"

"Chloe," he reminded me. "She, like all the rest of my staff, is on a reduced schedule. She helps out with some of the work I've been bringing home on the side, but I can't show her preferential treatment, now, can I?"

"Look at the plus side—at least your girlfriend isn't infected with a mutant strain of sea slime from some aquatic she-bitch."

Godfrey looked up from the drawer he had pulled open. "That's a strange plus side," he said. "What does that even mean?"

"Oh, right," I said. "That's the more personal reason I came down here." I reached into my pocket and pulled out a few shots Allorah had taken of the mark on Jane's back. "I was wondering if you could look into this for me. This symbol is bonded onto Jane's skin and I need to know what it is." I recapped the drama of the water woman diving through my girlfriend and the strange mark she had left on Jane. When I was done, Godfrey let out a long, slow breath.

Godfrey looked it over. "Doesn't seem familiar," he said, slipping it into the inside pocket of his coat. "Sorry. I hadn't even heard about the incident yet. It's probably in my backlog of case files that are slowly taking over my entire office. I'll look into it. I just thought you were talking about your drawer incident."

My face went flush. "God! Does everyone here know about that?"

"We have to take our gossip where we can get it around here," Godfrey said, suddenly unwilling to catch my eye. He turned back to the set of drawers, closed the one he was looking in, and ran his hands farther down the case.

"Do you have a section on coping with parapsychological misadventures?" I asked. "Maybe that would help me out."

"Nope," Godfrey said, stopping his hand on the handle of another drawer. "Sorry." Godfrey pulled the drawer open and lifted out an oversized binder the size of a small suitcase. He laid it on the nearest table and flipped through it until I saw a familiar-looking sight—the Hell Gate Bridge. I slammed my hand down on the page to stop him.

"That's the one," I said, recognizing the two stone towers at either end. "You know, it looks so familiar."

"It should," Godfrey said. "It's the base design for the Sydney Harbour Bridge in Australia."

"*That's* where I've seen it before," I said. "I was starting to wonder if I was having déjà vu or some kind of past-life regression."

Godfrey looked up at me, his face serious. "Sure, we can look into past lives as a possibility."

"No, I'm good," I said. "I have enough trouble living the life I have, thanks, let alone needing to start worrying how I've screwed things up in past ones."

Godfrey nodded, and then went back to the schematics. He checked a few notes written in the margins alongside the drawing. "The Department has sent several teams out there to investigate it for an actual hell gate over the years, to insure the bridge was safe. Nothing paranormal has been reported there."

"Does that mean that something *not* paranormal has been reported? One of the spirits talked about a General Slocum. Maybe he was a commander back in the day?"

"Slocum isn't a 'he,'" Godfrey said.

"No?"

Godfrey shook his head. "No," he continued. "It's a boat, so it's technically a 'she.' A passenger ship, to be exact."

Godfrey ran his finger down the side of the schematic

until they came to rest on a set of reference numbers that didn't make a lick of sense to me. He looked off toward one of the other aisles and hurried off.

"Follow me," he said, almost as an afterthought. The head archivist was in his own little zone now. I ran after him as he headed off down an aisle that had books from floor to ceiling on either side.

While a bit of claustrophobia set in, Godfrey stopped, stood on his tiptoes to reach a book high above him, and came down with it. He flipped it open and started looking through it. I stood there in silence, waiting, letting my mind wander back to some of my personal issues, namely my situation with Jane.

"So, things are going good with Chloe?" I asked. "Other than being cut by the budget?"

Godfrey took his head out of the book and smiled. It was the first time he had truly looked neither pissed off nor businesslike the entire time I had been down here.

"Excellent," he said.

"Have you two had the 'drawer' conversation yet as well?"

"Oh, she has more than a drawer," he said. "I gave her half of my space. Gave up a good percent of my closet as well."

"So soon?" I asked. "Weren't you the one dating a supermodel just a few short months ago?"

"Actually, a string of them," he said with a blush of red spreading over his face. "Was on a bit of a lucky streak, I guess."

I bit my tongue. Half the Department knew about Godfrey's streak . . . an almost preternatural ability that was like a luck field radiating from him. We had been instructed to never talk about it directly with him, and I still felt horrible for using him once for this ability when I tracked down the cultist Cyrus Mandalay. "You poor guy," I said. "Dating models. Rough life."

"Actually," he said. "It was."

"How so?" I asked, not quite believing what I was hearing out of him. The worst I could imagine from dating a string of supermodels was that my body would cramp up from a lifetime of pleasurable delights.

"I'm not going to whine about dating a bunch of gorgeous women," Godfrey said, "but look at me. I'm pasty white, I wear glasses. I have a hard time relaxing or cutting loose. I get worried that my tie isn't always straight. I'm a poster child for book nerdery."

"You're being a bit hard on yourself, don't you think?"

"That wasn't my point," he said, continuing. "I'm just saying that I know how lucky I was that these out-of-my-league women seemed fascinated with me for a while. I relished it, but to be honest—and I don't mean to stereotype them—it was all a little vacuous. Chloe, on the other hand, she's the right mix for me. The perfect mix, I should say. I know how fortunate I am to have her in my life. I don't want to screw that up."

"You make it sound so simple," I said.

"It *is* that simple," Godfrey said. He turned back to his book, flipping through the pages once again. "The question should be why isn't it simple for *you*?"

"I don't know," I said. "I've been having these . . . flare-ups, with my powers. I've actually felt what can happen with that deep kind of love, the anger and rage it can turn into. I've been in the mind of a person crazed by that level of closeness. You got the incident report I filed on the ghost tattooist at the Gibson-Case Center, right?"

Godfrey nodded without looking up. "Last I checked,"

he said, lost in the book, "you weren't a ghost tattooist. Why should her choices affect how you react?"

I went to speak, but he had me there. I couldn't explain the intangible mental blurring of the lines between my emotions and hers to someone who hadn't experienced it himself. Instead, I shut my mouth and waited for him to find what he was looking for.

"Here we go," he said, tapping at the page. "June fifteenth, 1904. The *General Slocum* was a steamship that was chartered for a yearly church trip. More than thirteen hundred people were on that ship, and most of them went down with it."

"It sank?"

Godfrey flipped ahead in the book. "It's attributed to a fire that started on board," he said. "That, and there was little in the way of working lifeboats or flotation equipment at the time. Most everyone either burned or drowned."

"That seems like the kind of life trauma that could leave a lot of spirits roaming the material plane," I said. "Is there any mention of a woman in green?"

Godfrey read on, and then after a moment shook his head. "Nothing in here," he said. "It could be possible that she was one of the leaders of the St. Mark's Lutherans who arranged the outing, but she wasn't on board."

"I've encountered that woman," I said, "and she's no Lutheran. She struck me as something much older than that."

"Which would make sense," said Godfrey, tapping the page where he was reading. "The *Slocum* wasn't the first ship to go down there. Hundreds had sunk well into the latter half of the nineteenth century, all blamed on the harsh currents and dangerous rocks below. The U.S. Army Corps of Engineers started blasting away what lay beneath the surface in the mid–eighteen hundreds. Looks like it has clearance now, but I don't think anyone has messed with the area since the 1920s."

"A dangerous place with a dangerous name, it seems," I said.

"So it appears," Godfrey said. "But let me make this clear. This stuff I'm looking up is just regular plain ole New York history. There's nothing paranormal associated with it in our records . . ."

I turned around and started heading back through the stacks to the stairs leading up to the offices above. "Those hundreds of ghosts didn't get there themselves, Godfrey," I said. "And they're afraid of a woman in green who I think is responsible for Mason Redfield's death. There's more to the Hell Gate Bridge than what is in your history books."

"Where are you going?" Godfrey said, but I didn't hear him following. He was probably taking the time to put the book back using a little caution.

"I need to know more about what's happened at the Hell Gate Bridge, the stuff that's not in the history books, and for that I'll need to find something from one of those sunken ships," I said. I could already feel the electric tingle of my powers inside my gloves. "Something I can get my hands on. Hopefully the F.O.G.gie boat's ready, or else it's going to be a long swim."

19

From the bow of the Fraternal Order's converted cabin cruiser–turned trawler, the East River was a mix of creepy and calm, a dark canyon of water that lay between the lights of Manhattan and Queens. For once, the sky was clear, and I was thankful for the break from all the rain. Connor steered from inside the closed-off cabin, but Jane and I couldn't help but ride up front like tourists on the Circle Line. Jane's face practically lit up as she stood there, gripping the railing, eyes closed and wind flapping her ponytail back and forth.

"You look like you're feeling better," I said.

"I don't know what it is," she said. "Being on the water just makes me feel almost normal again." Jane reached up and pulled the band from her ponytail, letting her hair fly loose in the wind like a sexy blond Medusa.

"Good," I said, "but if you shout out that you're queen of the world, I may have to push you overboard."

Jane laughed out loud, her voice ringing out over the sounds of the water and the low, constant hum of the boat's engine.

"I'll try not to," she said. She leaned forward over the prow and I reached out to grab her.

"Easy," I said. The last thing I wanted was to fish her out of the East River. Her arm was freezing in the warmth of my hand and I pulled her to me, holding her. "You didn't have to come, you know."

"Yes, I did," she said, looking deep into my eyes. "You don't understand. I *had* to get out of the Department for a bit. I was getting claustrophobic in the offices. Wesker and Allorah were driving me nuts, running all these tests on my mark."

"I can certainly understand Wesker driving someone nuts," I said. "Prolonged exposure to him can also cause a rash."

The wind blew Jane's hair across her face, but it wasn't enough to hide her look of worry. "I know," she said. "I just needed a break from all the poking and prodding." She looked into the wheelhouse where Connor stood at the controls. "You sure he's okay with me tagging along on this?"

"Who cares?" I asked, smiling at her. "I'm just glad you're feeling better."

Jane spun around in my arms, putting her back against me. "I never realized how much I enjoyed the open water. Growing up in Kansas didn't exactly offer much in the way of water-based activities."

Jane let her head fall against my shoulder. I loved the mood she was in. Days of sniping at each other over the whole drawer debacle melted away, but there was still more than enough to worry about, thanks to the mark.

We rode along the river in our own mini version of the

Love Boat until I spotted the Hell Gate Bridge just past the much larger Triborough. Connor angled our boat into the waterway between the shores of Astoria Park and Wards Island. He slowed as the boat passed underneath the bridge and killed the engine entirely when we were at the sweet spot between the two stone towers that sat on either shore. Jane and I headed toward the back of the boat via the narrow walkways on either side of the cabin. Connor was already at work on the newly mounted set of winches, pulleys, and metal draggers that had been added to the back of the boat.

"Sorry to interrupt your pleasure cruise," he said when he saw us walking toward him.

"You could have at least provided some drinks or hors d'oeuvres," I said.

Connor stood and looked at me. "I'm sorry," he said. "Who captained us here again?"

"Fine," I said. "You drag something nice up to the surface with all the equipment that I can use my psychometry on out here, I'll buy the drinks. Fair enough?" I worried that I might get another visit from the rageful tattooist if I did use my power, but with Jane's spirits improved, I hoped that would help quell it. Besides, I couldn't avoid using them as much as I had been, not when there was a real chance of making headway in the case.

Jane stared at the contraption Connor was readying.

"What is that thing?" she asked.

"A dredger," Connor said.

"Oh," I said. "So it dredges."

Jane laughed, but Connor didn't. He just shook his head at me.

"You know how to use that thing?" she asked.

"Hey, ask your boyfriend about it," Connor said. "It's his boat."

"Technically it belongs to the Order. I just commandeered it. I didn't say I knew how everything worked on it."

Connor stripped off his trench coat and laid it carefully aside on the back bench of the port side. "Don't worry, kid," he said. "I'm Greek and Irish. I think I'm genetically predisposed to knowing how to operate all seafaring equipment . . . unless you want to volunteer to do a night dive out here instead?"

I looked down into the murkiness of the East River. The smell coming off it made my eyes water a little. "I'm not even sure I want to get splashed by that water, let alone immerse myself in it."

"I didn't think so," he said and threw the winch lever next to him. Its motor whined into action, the lights in the cabin flickering. As the coiled cable began to unwind, the business end of the device lowered itself into the water.

"So, what are you hoping for here?" Jane asked.

"An abnormal number of boats have gone down in these parts," I said. "Some blame it on the currents, some fires . . . but if Professor Redfield was working on a film about this location, I want to know what he discovered, because there's a connection between him, the woman in green, and those ghosts up on the bridge. If I can get my hands on any pieces of the boats down there, maybe I can get some insight into at least just what the hell really happened to those people here."

"There has to be something more to this location than the mundane," Connor added. "All those ghosts wouldn't still be here unless something terribly traumatizing had happened to them."

"So we're floating over a mass grave," Jane said, looking a little sick. "Nice." She gave me a forced smile. "You take me to the most romantic places."

"It was this or the mutant alligator cleanup in the sewers that Shadower Division got stuck with," I said.

"Good choice," she said. Jane wrapped her arm around me while we waited on the winch to unwind, leaning her head on my shoulder.

Connor killed the switch after a few minutes of running it, and an eerie silence filled the air. "This is the creepiest fishing trip ever," I said.

Jane giggled and Connor turned to her. "Why don't you two go run the engine? We'll trawl back and forth until we hook something, and then haul it up."

Jane saluted him. "Aye, aye, Captain," she said, her chipperness bordering on sickeningly sweet, before she skipped off to the cabin.

I left Connor fussing with the winch and headed to the cabin after her. I hit the engine and the boat chugged to life. I eased it up to speed, not wanting to tax the poor boat too much, not with the way the budget stacked up against us. I feared that if anything broke or needed repairs, it might have to come out of my own pocket at this point.

I worked the boat back and forth across the area underneath the bridge, the steady sound of the engine and roll of the boat luring me into a very sleepy state. Only when the boat jerked to a halt and the two of us fell to the floor of the cabin did I snap to.

I scrabbled to get back on my feet, but it was difficult to do with my flailing girlfriend trying to do the same. The boat tossing back and forth only added to the chaos in the wheelhouse.

"Kill the engine, kid!" Connor shouted from somewhere at the back of the boat.

I finally managed to get to my feet, reaching for the support of the cabin wall, but the boat lurched once more, throwing me against the opposite wall, pressing me up against the back window.

Through it I watched as Connor wrapped himself around the cable using his whole body, but his weight wasn't enough to shake the line free. It pulled against the power of the boat, the back of it sinking down from the calamitous physics of it all. I pressed away from the window, but until the boat reversed pitch, I wouldn't be able to move.

"Jane!" I shouted, but she was already working on stopping the boat. She was down on the floor once again, but she didn't need to stand to use her powers. She slammed her hand against the base of the control console and whispered her strange electronic voice to it, her technomancy killing the whining engine. The boat fell silent and settled, allowing Jane and me to get to our feet. We walked out onto the back of the boat where Connor held on to the now-slack cable.

"Well, we found something," he said.

Jane walked over and flicked at the loose cable in his hand, watching it wobble. "Did we lose it?" she asked.

Connor tugged on the cable, pulling against the slack. The line went taut in his hand. "No, I think we still got it," he said. " I'm pretty sure we freed it up. Whatever *it* is."

Connor threw the lever back on the winch, but nothing happened. The power was still off. Connor looked over to Jane. "If you wouldn't mind . . ."

"Sorry," Jane said, and touched her hand to the mechanism. Sparks flew from where the flesh of her fingers pressed against it. At her techno-whisper, the winch creaked to life once more, this time at a slow, labored crawl. No one wanted a repeat of what had just happened with almost capsizing the boat.

Connor tested the line. It was coiling up onto the reel, tension still on it.

"Whatever it is," he said, "it's heavy."

I looked at him, hopeful. "You think we're pulling up a whole boat?"

"Doubtful, kid," he said. "It's probably just caked in weeds and river bottom . . . maybe some old, dead gangsters in cement shoes, even. All of that is making the going tough."

I watched the surface of the water in fascination, waiting for our catch to unveil itself. Pockets of air rose to the surface and bubbles filled the water, increasing until the water was white with foam all along the back of the boat.

Moments later, a solid rectangular shape broke the surface, roughly the size of a man.

"A door," I said, not all that enthused with our find.

"Hey, a door *is* a part of a boat," Connor said.

I shrugged. "Just not a particularly exciting part."

Connor looked at me and shook his head. "At least it's something you can hopefully get a read on. Help me haul it in."

The two of us leaned over and began wrestling with the cable as we struggled to get a grip on the bobbing door. It was harder than I thought with the boat rising up and down as well. The door, as Connor had suggested, was covered with enough river bottom slime that I couldn't get a good grip on it. I was about to start swearing when Jane spoke up.

"Hey, guys . . ." she said.

"Hold on," I said, fighting for my grip on the cable itself as I leaned out over the water. "Trying not to go swimming here."

"I've got some swimmers for you," she said. "We've got company on the railings."

The mention of company got our interest, and the two of us forgot about the cable and door as I pulled myself back onto the boat and turned. At first I didn't notice anything, but then I saw them. Rotting, waterlogged fingers were grabbing for purchase along the edge of the boat in several spots on both sides.

Connor noticed them as well. "What the hell . . . ?" he said, and ran over to the right side of the ship.

I joined him, stopping short of the railing. I craned my neck out a little farther, looking over the side. The ancient, bloated remains of a human were recognizable as one of them pulled himself out of the river, the water soaked into it like a sponge instead of rolling off it.

"The door . . ." Connor started, but couldn't finish as he stepped back and got into a fists-raised fighting stance.

"When God closes a window, he opens up a door," I said, pulling my bat from its holster and hitting the button to extend it, "a door from the bottom of the river that releases aqua-zombies, apparently."

The rotting creatures were coming up on all sides of us now. Connor shoved at the one nearest him, and thankfully he was still wearing the work glove he had been using on the cables. His left hand sank into the creature's chest, but the force was enough to send it toppling overboard, but not before it sucked the glove clean off. Connor snatched his hand away from the next creature and stepped back.

"What's grosser than gross?" he asked. "Now I know."

The squelching sound of the glove pulling off was still fresh in my ears and I did my best to keep from vomiting from the ick factor of it all. I turned to Jane. Nothing had come up on her side, but I could see the movement of more hands clawing for purchase along the side of the boat. It was only a matter of time before they came up.

"Jane!" I shouted. "Go to the front of the boat!"

"I can help," she insisted.

"I know you can," I said, "but this isn't me being chivalrous. We've got enough baddies for *all* of us to fight. Just check and see if we're okay up there."

"On it," she said. Jane kicked into motion and dashed off toward the thin walkway that led around the wheelhouse to the bow of the ship.

Connor grabbed up his trench coat, balling it around both of his hands. "I'm gonna miss this one," he said. "A good trench is hard to find."

"Maybe it's time to trade up to a better coat," I said. The two of us moved to the center of the deck back there, positioning ourselves back to back.

"Yeah, right, kid," he said. "Soon as you give up the leather."

"It works like *armor*," I said. "Not like that dangly death trap you wear."

Connor dodged out of the way of one of the creatures. "I prefer mobility," he said. "Jesus. There're a lot coming up on my side of the boat."

"Mine, too," I said.

"Screw it," Connor said, stepping away from my back. I heard a meaty *crack* behind me followed by a splash. "We don't have to fight 'em if we just knock 'em off, kid."

I went to move, then stopped as a horrifying thought hit me.

"Wait a second," I said. "Did I just send Jane up to the front of the boat . . . *alone*?"

"Yes," Connor said. "Yes, you did. Now go!"

"Right," I said. I pulled out my bat and ran for the front. I stepped with care around the slim walkway to the left of the cabin. The head of one of the creatures came up over the side and I flashed my foot out at it, catching it square in the center of its face. The tip of my Doc Martens sank into the flesh like I was kicking a Nerf football, the sound of snapping bone cracking out from it. The body let go of the railing, but didn't fall now that my foot was holding it up by its face. I shook my leg, fighting down the urge to vomit, before the creature came free and fell back into the water.

The other aqua-zombies were still working their way up the sides, but they were no danger . . . yet. I pulled myself forward along the outside of the cabin, pausing only to grab a four-foot-long gaffing hook. I continued on, making sure my grip was secure on both that and my bat, and then jumping down onto the bow of the boat. I landed on both feet, dual wielding and ready for a fight. Jane was surrounded by a ring of rotting aquatic humanoids as she fell to her knees on the deck, her hands clawing at the back of her shoulder about where the mark was.

"Jane!" I shouted.

She looked up, her face straining as she struggled against whatever the mark was doing to her. Without pausing, I grabbed the long shaft of the hooked pole arm and tossed it to her. It clattered to the now-slime-covered deck and Jane wrapped both hands around it, using it to help her stand before menacing the creatures around her with it. Now that she was armed, I didn't hesitate. I leapt into action, slamming my bat into the closest creature. The tip of it caught up in its guts, but it crumbled the monstrosity over, leaving me struggling to regain control of my bat. When I pulled it free, I moved on to my next target, but I noticed something strange out of the corner of my eye. Jane wasn't moving. She was just standing there, stock-still, clutching the pole in both her hands like she was waiting to swing on a trapeze.

"Jane?" I shouted. "Anytime you want to join the fray, you just leap on in there . . ."

Jane still didn't move. "I . . . I can't," she stuttered out.

"What?" I said, feeling a little panic set in. Without her help, I was going to be hard-pressed to fight off all the aqua-zombies by myself.

"I want to help you, but I can't," she said, almost crying. "I think . . . I think it's the mark."

"Son of a bitch," I shouted. I cracked the next monstrosity in the head and pushed it overboard using the heel of my boot. Adrenaline kicked in and I felt a bit of a rush while I moved on to struggle against two more of the creatures. I only hoped that when I was done I wouldn't have to turn my bat on Jane as well.

"Fight it, hon," I shouted. "You're stronger than her. Are you going to let that aquatic she-bitch run the show here?"

Jane raised the gaffing pole over her head with a concerted effort, but with each inch she lifted, her face squinted with pain. After a few seconds of holding it up, she collapsed back down to her knees, dropping the pole. "I can't," she whimpered.

Connor shouted from somewhere close behind me, startling me. "Is she okay, kid?"

I turned. He had made his way to the top of the cabin, taking the higher ground in the fight and using it to his advantage in undead crowd control.

I dodged one of the swiping zombies while hitting another with my bat, squishing the flesh. I looked over at Jane again. She was still paralyzed in place. "You know what?" I called up to Connor. "I have no idea. She's powerless."

Connor looked down at me. "Well, *help* her, then."

"I'm trying," I said, wiggling my way out of one of the zombies' grip. "There's too many of them."

"*That* I can help with," Connor said and jumped down from atop the cabin. The deck shook from the impact of his landing but Connor kept his momentum and plowed himself into a whole row of the creatures on my right. Half of them spilled over the side of the boat, all of them clawing nothing but air as they tried to stop themselves.

"That worked," I said, tossing one of my remaining foes overboard. "Thanks."

"Don't thank me yet," he said. "All I've done is prolong the inevitable. I've bought us a little time."

"Right," I said and spun to help out Jane.

By the looks of her, she didn't need my help. Jane had made it back up to her feet once more and was surrounded by a ring of the creepy creatures. The odd thing was that the rotting monstrosities—outside of their simply being there—were all facing Connor and me, none of them even remotely interested in attacking my girlfriend. Jane wasn't in need of protection; the damned things were protecting *her*.

"Jane?" I asked. Her eyes were fixed in our general direction but they were unfocused. There was nobody driving the car, or if there was, Jane wasn't in the driver's seat.

"Steady," Connor said, resting a hand on my shoulder. "What's up with her new entourage?"

"I was hoping you might be able to tell me."

"I'm not sure," he said, looking for a weakness in the ring of them, "but I think we better make the first move before—"

Jane interrupted him, speaking out loud in a language I wasn't familiar with. "That's not her machine language," I said.

"No," Connor said. "It's not. It's Greek. She's ordering her undead bodyguards to attack."

"What?!" I swung my bat at the two zombies closest to her before they could even begin to move. "Oh, hell, no."

I grabbed Jane by the arm and yanked her from within their circle. Her face was still blank, but her body stumbled along willingly as I moved her toward the back of the boat.

"Not a good time to be zoning out, Janey," I said, but she remained unresponsive. I put my arm around her and guided her along the side of the cabin. Other zombies were crawling up the sides of the ship still, but paused when I moved Jane past them. "Guess there's one bright side to this."

I stepped onto the back deck first as we rounded the stern of the boat. The back was swarming with aqua-zombies, all of them keeping well away from the two of us. I lowered Jane to the deck and pressed against the wall of the wheelhouse until I got to the door and slid us both inside. I shut the door behind us and turned my attention to Jane.

Nothing had changed on her face in the past few minutes. There was no sense of recognition in her eyes, just a strange curiosity in them as she watched me. She spoke again, but none of it made a lick of sense to me. I grabbed her by the sides of her head and got right up in her face.

"Snap out of it, Janey," I said. "Come back to me."

A dark snarl rose up behind her lips, but I didn't look away.

"I know you're in there, sea witch," I said, not turning away, "but this woman is mine. If anyone gets her, it's me, got it?"

Jane fought to push me away, but I wasn't letting go.

"If you can hear me in there, Jane, don't give in to her," I said. "You're better than her."

A guttural growl rose up from Jane's chest. I wasn't sure if it was because the woman was winning or Jane was fighting her, but I let go of her face and grabbed hold of her hands. The strength in her grip was both astounding and crushing.

The door to the cabin flew open behind me and the aqua-zombies started to pour in. I let go of Jane and went to spin around, but I was too slow, unprepared. One of the creatures got its decaying hands on my arm and squeezed. They, too, had more strength to them than I had imagined. The crushing pain to my arm overwhelmed me and I screamed out. My bat clattered to the floor of the cabin.

Jane's eyes fluttered. "Simon . . . ?"

"Jane," I said. "Help me. Fight it. Fight that woman's power."

Jane's face returned to normal, which at the moment meant it was a mix of pain and confusion. She seemed to be disoriented and struggling, her arms shaking at her sides. I was so intent on trying to regain any sort of connection with her that it took me a moment to realize I was being dragged out the cabin door by the hands of the undead. "No!" I shouted, and Jane snapped to.

Jane eyed my situation, and then slapped one of her hands on the boat's control panel. The glow of raw energy being siphoned from the ship ran up her arm as she spoke to it until the power ran into her and she channeled it down her other arm. Raw energy burst forth from her hand as it shot past me and struck the zombies holding me. The jolt of electricity sent a lesser tingle of sensation into my body as well, but I pulled myself free of the mess as I started to smell the wretched burn of decaying flesh.

I fell to my knees to retrieve my bat, landing hard on my satchel and worse, digging the metal corner of the Ghost-busters lunch box inside right into my lower ribs, stinging them. Once I was down, I decided to stay there for a few moments. The idea of standing back up and catching a blast from the Jedi power battle overhead had zero appeal to me, especially with the new pain in my side. I lay there, recovering, as Jane plunged her power into zombie after zombie with what amounted to a chain of lightning that ran from one zombie to the next. The stench was awful, but the foes all along the back side of the boat blew apart like they were eggs in the microwave.

As the deck cleared, Jane's power began to falter until she stopped and collapsed on top of the control console in exhaustion. I got up off the floor to check on her. As I stood, I could see out the front of the control room once again. The bow of the boat was still covered in a monstrous swarm, and at the center of it all was Connor, fighting away. He was holding his own against the waterlogged, rotting army, but I wondered for how long. I turned away and put my hand on Jane's shoulder.

"You okay?" I asked.

Her eyes were closed and her breath was coming in short rasps, but she nodded. "Just exhausted," she said.

"Can you drive?"

She pushed herself up off the panel and looked at the wheel and the rest of the controls. "I've never driven a boat before."

"It's simple," I said. "The trick is to try and not hit any land. But you know what? In this case, I think what we need is to get the hell off the water. Aim for Wards Island, up on our left."

Jane looked nervous, but I needed to get moving if I was going to help Connor. While Jane fired up the boat and started her run at the island, I ran out of the cabin, doing my best to not slip in the slimy coating of zombie guts as I made my way back to the front of the boat. Connor had worked his way into a defensible position up against the very tip of the bow—a smart choice. The zombies could only come at him one by one due to the narrow confines of the space, but even with that advantage, more were struggling to climb up over the railing behind him.

I twirled my bat around in my hands while I raised it up into a classic batter's stance. I rested it on my shoulder for a second, focusing in on the mob, and then started swinging for the outfield as hard as I could.

It was hard work, more so thanks to the sway of the now–wildly rocking boat, but both of us kept our feet. In a matter of moments, I had worked my way closer to Connor.

"Jesus," I said, feeling the strain in my arms. "They keep coming up over the railings."

"Don't worry, kid," Connor said. "With the boat moving, I think the undead crowd is thinning."

"Good," I said. "I can barely swing anymore."

"What's the matter, kid?" he asked. "You don't want to swim for the island?"

"Not if I don't have to," I said. "I'd rather not find out whether the water of the East River would eat through me or the metal of my bat first. Or if it would make me like one of those creatures."

"I wouldn't worry about what would happen in the water," Connor said.

"No?"

"Nah," he said. "Given the workout your arms are getting, I doubt you'd have the strength to swim to shore before drowning."

"Thanks, Captain Optimism," I said.

"It would be a better way to go than having your girlfriend channel some water-based she-devil and kill you."

The numbers of our gruesome enemies were thin enough

now that I could chance a look back into the wheelhouse. Jane looked worn and half-asleep at the controls, but she still managed to shoot me a weak smile.

"She's got the mark under control," I said.

"For now," Connor added

"Yep," I said. "For now. When we find that water woman, we'll beat her into removing it. *If* we find her."

I turned back and Connor was watching me. "Don't worry," he said, as sober and sincere as I'd ever seen him. "If it comes to it, I'll take care of things if Jane turns."

I didn't say anything. I wasn't sure there was a proper way to "thank" someone for promising to beat down the woman you loved. All our training in dealing with zombies and the like was meant to prepare us to strike down our colleagues without hesitation if they turned, but I didn't think I had the courage to do it to Jane myself. Was hoping I didn't have to come to that level of difficult decision making.

At least I now understood why the appeal of the open water had put Jane in such an improved mood; the girl was just releasing her inner monstrosity.

20

We hit the shore on Wards Island, tying off the boat on the shattered wooden remains of a dock that had definitely seen better days. Thankfully we had been able to outpace the aqua-zombies in their efforts to climb back on board the boat. I was paranoid enough once we landed that I stood at the water's edge waiting for several minutes to make sure we had no hangers-on. When nothing came shambling out of the river for us, I finally retracted my bat and holstered it.

I turned around to face the darkness of the island's woods behind us. Jane was sitting on a boulder off to my right, rocking back and forth with her arms wrapped around her body. Her wind-whipped hair hung mostly over her face, giving her a crazy sea-haggish kind of look.

I walked over to her, but she didn't register my presence as I approached. I put my hand on her shoulder. "How are you feeling?"

Jane brushed her hair out of her face and looked up at me. Her cheeks were wet with tears. "Horrible," she said, "but a bit more like myself now that I'm on dry land." She continued to comb her hair down to something less Don King–like. I took her wanting to straighten herself out as a good sign that she was acting a bit less possessed now. "What came over me? What the heck happened out on the water?"

"You don't remember?"

Jane shook her head. "Snippets of it," she said. "It's all a bit cloudy for me."

"I think you had a little visit from someone," I said.

"Did I? From that woman?" she asked. I nodded and her eyes widened. "I didn't hurt you, did I?"

I knelt down in front of her and took her hands in mine. "I'm fine," I said. "You fought that woman's power and you won."

Jane shook her head and looked down on the ground. "I don't know how it happened. Being out on the open water just brought out the connection to it in me. It was overwhelming. I felt so . . . *right*. The mark started burning while you and Connor were fighting those . . . *things*. I don't remember too much else until you got me inside the cabin." Her face darkened. "I never should have come."

"Don't beat yourself up over that," I said. "You can't change the past. What's done is done. We just have to keep fighting this as it comes. We've got Allorah analyzing things from a scientific angle, and Director Wesker is looking into the arcana behind it . . ."

"But how long do I have?" Jane asked, hysteria rising to the surface in her voice. "I could feel myself losing control and no one seems to be making any progress on it."

"We'll find a way," I insisted.

"No!" Jane shouted. "We won't. I shower more and more. At this rate, soon you're going to need to buy an aquarium to hold me, Simon!"

She was over-the-top with emotion, much like I had been during my psychometric bout at the Gibson-Case Center. I know how stubborn those feelings had made me in the moment, and Jane was being just as stubborn. No matter what I was saying, she wouldn't listen to me. I stood up. "Connor," I said. "Talk to her."

I was met with silence and I looked around. At first, I couldn't see him anywhere in the darkness, but then I caught sight of his shadowy figure standing at the edge of the woods by the white of a nearby building I hadn't even noticed. He stood there stock-still, and I walked over to him with caution, my hand resting on my bat in its holster. I had already had to deal with one person under possession tonight. I was hoping I didn't have to take on another.

"Connor . . . ?" I asked, hoping I was hiding the trepidation in my voice.

I walked around in front of him. His hands were shoved deep into his pockets, and he was looking up in the air toward the building. I stepped right in front of him and caught my partner's eye.

"What's up, buddy?" I asked, unholstering my bat.

He looked over at me and his face looked normal enough. "Does anything strike you strange about where we landed?" he asked.

"Other than the undead Aqua Men off its coast? Not that I'm aware of. Why?"

Connor grabbed me by my shoulders and spun me around. "Open your eyes, kid."

I had been so concerned about Jane that I hadn't really taken in much of our environment. The three of us were standing in a cluster of trees, some kind of forest or park on Wards Island. It didn't have much in the way of lampposts or lighting of any kind, giving the area a wild and unused look, but there was one thing that stood out about the place—the building Connor had been looking at.

In front of us stood an abandoned lighthouse that rose almost as high as the bridge itself. A small rectangular room at the base of it stuck out, but other than that it looked fairly typical—a raised cylindrical structure that narrowed as it rose, ending high above in a railed balcony that surrounded the glassed-in top and its long-extinguished signal light.

Once I had taken it in, I turned back to Connor, only to find that Jane had joined us. She seemed more composed now as she stared up at the lighthouse. She looked over her shoulder at Connor.

"Doesn't look to be an active lighthouse," Connor said, "but with aqua-zombies just offshore from it and nothing else around—"

"We should probably check that out, huh?" Jane asked.

Connor looked at her. "At least one of you is paying attention," he said. "Good to have you back." He smiled, and then headed off toward the steps leading up to the entrance of the lighthouse.

I didn't move. "Excuse me for showing concern over my possessed girlfriend first," I said.

"Can we not call me 'possessed'?" Jane asked. "I haven't started hurling up pea soup or anything."

"Yet," I added. Jane shot me a hurt look. "Sorry."

Jane didn't say another word and headed off after Connor, leaving me there to feel like an insensitive cad all by my lonesome. I shook it off and followed after her, undoing the strap on my holster once again and pulling my bat free.

I hit the combination of marked buttons on the shaft of my bat that spelled out Jane's initials, which extended the custom weapon to its full size with a gentle *shikt*.

When I caught up with the two of them at the top of the steps leading up to the entrance, Jane was whispering to Connor. "Who's going first?" she asked.

Before he could respond, I pushed past the two of them. "*I'll* go," I said. I still felt caddish. The least I could do was take the lead going in. I tried the handle of the heavy door. It was solidly built, its ancient wood barded together with thick iron bars that ran across it at three separate parts. It wouldn't budge.

"Locked," I said, handing Jane my bat. She took it and I reached up the sleeve of my coat for the set of lock picks I kept there.

"Looks like you would have been going first anyway, kid," Connor said, slapping me on the back. "You sure you can pick this? Looks kind of old . . ."

I dropped to my knees and started working on the tumblers with my assortment of picks and torsion wrenches. "I should be able to," I said. "Pin locks go back almost four thousand years. The hardware has changed over the years, but not the theory or mechanics behind them. And you'd be surprised how many of the old art houses and antiques stores in Manhattan are still using those old locks. Made a lot of my old heists fairly easy."

"I keep forgetting," Jane said, mustering a false pride in her voice. "My boyfriend, the ex-thief."

"Emphasis on the *ex*," Connor added.

I went silent as I concentrated on the lock. With both my partner and my girlfriend watching, a little performance anxiety crept up on me, especially since I was using my old nefarious skills. Not being able to beat the lock would be more than embarrassing. Worse, it would give them something to bond over while picking on me.

I needn't have worried. I expected the lock to give me some difficulty given the abandoned state of the lighthouse, and I was surprised when I heard it click open under my working it seconds later.

"You make it look so easy," Jane said, giving me a silent golf clap.

"It *was* easy," I said, still examining the mechanism itself. "I expected the hardest part of opening it would be due to corrosion given its age and with it being so close to the water, but someone's been taking very good care of it."

I slid my set of picks and torsion wrenches back up my sleeve before standing and took my bat back from Jane. I put my hand against the door. "Stay sharp, people," I said and pushed it open. The door didn't make a sound.

"Well, that's disappointing," I said.

"What is?" Jane asked.

"Where's the creakiness from unoiled hinges? Maybe I watched too much *Scooby-Doo* as a kid, but I'm a bit disappointed that it didn't squeak open like they always did on the show."

"Maybe you'll get lucky and the Gator Ghoul will be waiting on the other side," Connor added.

I gave him a thumbs-up for the reference, and then turned my attention back to the lighthouse as we entered.

The interior of the circular part of the lighthouse was open and led off to another part made up of the long rectangular section we had seen from outside. The cylindrical part of the room was ringed along the far wall with a spiral staircase built into the curvature of the building. I wasn't sure what I had expected to find in here. Maybe some nautical equipment—a rain slicker that belonged to the Gorton's fisherman, perhaps. Instead, the interior of the lighthouse was littered with film equipment. Old-school cameras set up on tripods, recording equipment . . . even a table scattered with an odd assortment of different microphones and tape reels. One wall had a makeshift film screen tacked up and an old film projection machine faced it. A thick black reel of film still sat in it, threaded through the machine like a snake caught in a trap.

"What is this place?" Jane whispered.

"From the look of it, I'd say it was the good professor's home away from home," Connor said. "Unless you know of any other bridge-obsessive film teachers around town."

Jane laughed and I shushed her.

I headed for the stairs. "Let's see if we have any Goldilocks lurking around here before we get too carried away," I said.

As I started up into the lighthouse, I was thankful for the solid structural integrity of the building. Sturdy old-world stonework made up the walls, and the staircase itself was cast from black iron. I did my best to move silently, going up it without making a sound. Jane followed right behind me and Connor took the rear.

The farther I went up into it, the more my nerves were on end, but other than a shoddy old mattress on the second level up, there were no signs of habitation. It still gave me the creeps, despite the spectacular view at the top of it. I couldn't get back downstairs fast enough, Jane clutching my hand as we rushed back down.

When we reached the room full of film equipment once more, Connor spoke up, using his full voice now that we knew we were alone here. "Why the hurry, kid?"

"You don't find this place creepy?" I asked.

Connor shrugged. "Not really," he said. "I mean, nothing has tried to kill us in here yet."

"Call me crazy," I said, "but I actually take comfort when I have something tangible to deal with, something I can take a bat to. Getting a spooky feeling just gets under my skin, especially when nothing stands out."

Connor laughed. "That *is* crazy," he said.

Jane interrupted the sound of his laughter. "None of this explains why Professor Redfield was killed," she said. "Or any of those ghosts you mentioned."

"She's right," I said, "but here's a theory: maybe he set up his crazy film studio too close to her ship-sinking business. Maybe the professor awoke her ancient spirit while making his documentary or something."

"Maybe," Connor said, "but if she killed him for his knowledge of her, wouldn't she have destroyed all this, too?"

"Probably," I said, "but let's look around. There may be something here that's of use to us."

We spread out around the room, picking through the film equipment for anything that didn't look like the professor had accumulated it from the film department of NYU. I went over to a long table along the right side of the room that was cluttered with bits and pieces of broken wood. I put on my gloves as I shifted them around. Peeking out from beneath two of the boards was a white, half-rusted plate with the letters *SLO* carved into it. The rest of the piece was torn away beyond the *O*. I pulled it out from underneath everything else and held it up for Connor to see. "This looks promising, yes?" I asked.

"We're definitely taking that with us," Connor said, over by the film projector set up in the center of the room. "Make sure you bring it to the boat." He pulled out his flashlight and started examining the machine.

"What are you doing?" I said. "You want to watch movies, we've got stadium seating back in Manhattan."

"I'm trying to figure out how to unthread this film reel to pack it up and take it with us," he said. "It's the last thing the professor was working on. Maybe it will give us some insight."

"Thank God you don't want to watch it here," Jane said, nervous. She wrapped her arms around herself.

"Not here, no," Connor confirmed. "I don't want to hang out here any longer than we have to, especially if more of those river-bottom zombies come knocking. The professor was passionate about film. Let's take it out of here and see where his passions really lay."

21

The boat made it back to the docks over by Chelsea Piers even though I thought the engine and motor might have been clogged with aqua-zombie bits from earlier. Cleaning the guts and ichor off it would have to wait. After tying off, the three of us headed back and reported to the Inspectre about Mason's secret film-production lighthouse. When we showed him the film canister, he insisted on kicking all the norms out of the Lovecraft's theater as the credits on *The Picture of Dorian Gray* rolled.

A fair number of agents from a variety of divisions gathered in the theater, along with most of Other Division and some faces I recognized from some of my Fraternal Order of Goodness training sessions. The Inspectre watched the theater fill up before looking down at the film reel in his hands. Jane, looking a little more tired now that we were off the water, collapsed into one of the theater seats in the middle of a row halfway back.

"I'll take care of loading the film," the Inspectre said, lifting up the canister. "See to the girl."

I nodded. "You know how to run the projector?" I asked him as I sat down next to her.

"Can't be that hard, can it?" he scoffed. "I've solved the riddle of the cube at Astor Place, fought the Geissman Guard . . ."

"You also got lost in the Black Stacks at Tome, Sweet Tome for half an hour," Connor reminded him.

The Inspectre's face fell and he blushed. "Well, yes, you have me there, my dear boy." He tried to shake off the sudden deflation from Connor's words. "I still maintain that those occult books kept changing the layout back in the Black Stacks . . ."

"It's possible," I offered. "I mean, if a homicidal bookcase can come charging after me, surely the rest of them can move around."

"Yes," the Inspectre said, getting lost in thought. "Perhaps." He wrapped his arms around the bulk of the film canister and walked it up the aisle toward the door leading up to the projection booth.

Connor turned to look at Jane. "She okay, kid?"

I took Jane's hand in mine and squeezed it. There was little response at first, but then she squeezed back, her grip strong.

She nodded. "I'm fine," she said, her voice weak. "I just need a minute to sit and catch my breath. Everything out on the water took the wind out of me."

Connor backed down the aisle. "I'm going to sit a couple rows in front of you two lovebirds," he said. "Give you a little breathing room."

Connor settled down into the middle of the row three ahead of us. I tripped my way down ours as the credits wrapped up on *The Picture of Dorian Gray*.

Despite a small volley of swearing during the change-over of the films, the Inspectre managed to get the professor's film up and running within a few minutes. Mason Redfield's *The Gates of Hell: Water's End* came up on the screen. The footage was documentary-style, covering the long history of the location and the years of unfortunate incidents that plagued those waters. Hundreds of ships had sunk there over the years, supposedly due to treacherous currents and rock formations that took seventy years of blasting and removal to finally clear. Professor Redfield even had a touch of the horror element in its approach, given the macabre subject matter, lending the film an eerie quality that transcended most documentaries. I found myself actually enjoying it, if enjoyment could be taken in such dark subject matter. Human suffering was always fascinating, no matter what form it came in.

The film cut abruptly to a different-looking style all together. Apparently, the professor was a better film teacher than he was an editor because he had spliced in an entire section of the wrong footage. The image on the screen looked straight out of a B-grade horror flick showing a thick, billowing fog on the edge of a graveyard at night. It was so poorly done that even the gravestones looked like they might blow away if a weak wind hit during the filming. The low, guttural sound of zombies off in the darkness came over the sound system.

"How does this tie in?" Jane asked, almost as confused as I was.

"Bad splice," I said. "Guess the professor was a better teacher than doer."

"I don't think so, kid," Connor said, turning his head back to us. "Something about this seems . . . *deliberate*."

"How?"

"I'm not sure," he said. "Just a feeling." He looked up to the booth over our heads and called out, "Inspectre?"

The light from the projector flickered, almost going out as the film skipped on the screen. A churning din of metal and an unhealthy grind of the film equipment filled the theater as the light from the glow off the screen began to strobe erratically.

"That doesn't sound *or* look good," Jane said, finally perking up once more. "If we had paid to see this, I'd definitely want my money back."

"What the hell is going on?" I asked.

Connor stood. "I don't know," he said, "but I mean to find out." He looked up at the projection booth. "Inspectre, shut it down!"

"I'm trying, blast it!" the Inspectre called out.

"Try harder," Connor shouted.

A loud commotion came from the tiny open panel at the back of the theater, followed by a string of profanity that I didn't know the Inspectre had in him. "It's no use," he said. "I can't kill the power to the machine. It won't stop running, damn it all!"

Thick smoke filled the air. At first I thought it must be coming from the machine up in the projection booth, but then I realized it wasn't from there. In fact, it wasn't smoke at all.

It was fog, and it was coming out of the movie screen. Jane grabbed onto my arm, squeezing.

"Connor!" I shouted, pointing down in front. "Look!"

"I see it, kid," he said, keeping his calm. "Don't get all freaked-out marveling at it. Just be prepared."

"Prepared for what?" I asked, but I was already pulling out my bat. I had a pretty good idea forming in my head. If the fog from the movie could pour out into our world, I wondered what else could come through.

All three of us stood transfixed by what was happening on the screen. There was little we could do but watch as the movie flashed through several scenes in rapid sequence. Clips from a whole host of B-grade zombie flicks came up one after another. With each new one, creatures from each remained on the screen, pressing against it. Like swimmers coming to the surface, the figures pushed through the two-dimensional world and into ours.

"Did they—?" Jane started, but I cut her off.

"Yep," I said and started off down our row to the aisle.

As the floor in front of the screen filled with cinematically manifested undead that kept pouring off the screen, the film changed images once again, this time coming to one steady setting. This time the film had more of an amateur home-video quality.

A field of green grass stretched along a horizon against a backdrop of cloudless blue sky. A lone figure came into the frame—young, dashing, and one that I had seen before thanks to my psychometry. Mason Redfield looked a lot better this way than when I had originally met him—old, dead, and filled with water.

He turned to the screen as if noticing it, and walked toward us in the type of tweed suit he had fancied in his youth. Like all the rest of the creatures manifesting in the theater, he pushed at the screen, but met more resistance from it than the others had. Mason reeled back from it, shocked, but I could tell from the expression of determination on his face that he wasn't even close to giving up. He ran forward, slamming between film and reality like that old video for "Take on Me." Sparks flew from the screen, raining down onto the assembled zombie army below. Several agents in the theater snapped into action and charged the horde down by the screen, but Connor, Jane, and I kept watching Mason Redfield up above.

Movement off to my left caught my eye and I looked over. Inspectre Quimbley had joined us, out of breath from running down from the projection booth. His eyes were also transfixed on the screen.

"Is that *the* Mason Redfield?" I asked him.

"Back from the grave, I believe," the Inspectre said. "Trying to return to his youth, from the looks of it."

The Inspectre's old friend leapt at the screen, the screen erupting in sound and fury with a prismatic spray of color. The rejuvenated professor passed through it and landed along the tops of the front row of seats, very much alive and looking even younger than me. "Protect me, my beautiful monsters," he shouted. "At all costs." At his command, the aggression among the zombies rose, especially those who fell into a close, protective ring around the reborn professor.

The Inspectre continued down the aisle toward him. "Mason!"

Redfield was too busy staring at his own limbs to notice the Inspectre. He stood there balanced on top of the seats, flexing his arms and fingers around like they were unfamiliar to him. Eventually, he took notice of the Inspectre advancing on him and did a double take.

"Argyle?" he said with an astonished smile. "Is that you?"

"Yes, Mason."

The Inspectre's old partner's eyes widened. "You're so . . . *old* . . ."

"I think the salient point," the Inspectre said, "is the fact that you're so young."

Mason Redfield looked around. "Where are we? Where are my students? This isn't where I was supposed to be."

"We beat them to it, I guess," I said.

"They were supposed to retrieve the film," he said, angry, but then he gave a dark laugh. "Students can be so unreliable."

"What have you done, Mason?" the Inspectre asked. "What dark bargain have you struck . . . and *why*?"

Mason turned his attention back to the Inspectre. "Why?" Mason said, scoffing at him. "Have you looked in the mirror lately? Tell me, which way would you rather be? A doddering old film professor or a man in his prime? I had to die, to be reborn."

"What you are, what you have become, is *unnatural*," the Inspectre said, "and in the name of the Fraternal Order of Goodness, I—"

"The Order?" he said, laughing. "Are you telling me that there are still living members out there, other than you?"

"The Order will still be here long after you're gone, Mason, trust me." The Inspectre lunged for Mason on top of the seats, but the now-young professor batted him away with an awkward swipe of his arm. Clumsy as it was, it was enough to knock the Inspectre over onto one of the theater seats. He grunted as he went down.

"Gone?" Mason said, parroting the Inspectre's British accent. "Why, yes . . . I do believe it is time I was going." At his gestures, the circle of zombies around him pressed out into the crowd.

I came out of the row and stepped down the aisle, Jane at my heels. I pulled out my bat, extended it, and slapped it down into my hand. "You're not going anywhere," I said.

"Oh, no?" Mason said, looking amused. "I beg to differ." He gestured again at his assembled army, which was already squaring off against the rest of the agents. "Attack!"

"Good," I said, charging him. "That's what I was hoping you were going to say."

I had seen Mason Redfield's fighting techniques before, but that psychometric vision had been from years ago when he was still an active member of the Fraternal Order of Goodness. As I closed in on him, Mason must have noticed the intent in my eyes. He dropped down off the top of the seats, wobbling on his new legs like a newborn animal taking its first steps. A look of fear filled his bright young eyes and he pressed his way back into the sea of zombies, more of which fell from the screen every second.

"That's right," I said, raising my bat as I hit the first wave of the undead. "You'd better run!"

Connor fell in beside me and used the shamblers' own slow lurching to help pull them out of my way. For every one he moved, another one fell from the screen to take its place.

"I'm going try to stop the projector," Jane called out from somewhere behind me, her voice fading as she ran off. "I think that should kill the magic at work here."

The door in the lower-right corner of the theater leading off to the Department opened. Wesker came walking out of it unassumingly with a coffee mug in hand, but dropped it as he took in the chaos of the room. He looked shocked and not a little pissed off. His hands flew into a series of arcane movements directed at the zombies nearest him, but nothing happened. Panic rose up in my chest, causing me to redouble my efforts. Wesker's magic had failed against them, but I was happy to see that the blunt-force trauma my bat was delivering still worked just fine.

Connor was off holding his own nearby. Each zombie

he knocked down got a quick boot stomp to its head, filling the air with a fleshy *crunch*.

"This is the most active I've been in a movie theater since *The Rocky Horror Picture Show*," he said exuberantly.

"If you start singing 'The Time Warp,' the next notch on my bat is for you."

"Fair enough," he said, grabbing another of the zombies out of my path. "Just get over to Mason Redfield . . . and hurry."

I pressed harder through the crowd of shuffling undead mayhem, but it was no use. Mason Redfield was always a step ahead of me in the crowd as he backed away, putting more distance between us every second. Shoving through the crowd was no good. There was only one thing I could think of as an alternative.

I collapsed my bat and sheathed it before climbing up onto the front row of seats themselves, putting me half a body length higher than everyone around me. Compared to jumping off the high-rise balcony the other night, my new idea seemed only slightly less insane, but if I gave myself time to come to my senses, I'd talk myself out of it. I stopped analyzing and threw myself out over the battle.

I hadn't gone crowd surfing since they closed CBGB a few years back, but my body remembered the strange elation that came with giving yourself over to the energy of the crowd and the hands supporting you. For a moment it all felt familiar . . . until the raking claw of fingers caused me to snap to and got me moving. I rolled into motion across the sea of heads and arms, gunning for Mason Redfield.

Spinning, I kept my eyes focused on the professor. I was actually gaining on him this way and the look of panic on his face told me he knew it. He turned away from me as I closed the distance and he burst into a full run through the fighting crowd, but despite his efforts, I was still closing in on him. My hands brushed against the back collar of his suit coat, but didn't find enough to grab at. One more revolution, however, and the reborn Mason Redfield was mine.

I came out of my next roll with my hand coming down for the grab, but the professor made a swift change in direction and was no longer in my path. Before my mind could even process the thought, I saw why. I had rolled with such determination that I had lost all sense of direction and was inches away from a collision with Director Wesker. Our eyes met, surprise registering on both of our faces, but it was far too late to stop rolling. My knee came up fast on his face and smashed into his temple, knocking him back and sending him toppling to the floor of the theater. A space opened up as he fell in the fray and I aimed myself for it. I grabbed ahold of two zombies as I shot past them in the hopes of slinging myself into the space, then flipped myself into the spot, careful to avoid stepping on Wesker. Jane's boss looked like he was out cold.

Mason Redfield was already gone and making his way up the aisle toward the exit out to the café. I could maybe still nab him if I ran off after him now, but there was Wesker to think about. I couldn't just leave him there to be torn apart by zombies, even if he was a dick most of the time. Besides, Jane actually got along with her boss and would never let me hear the end of it if I left him to become all zombified.

I stood my ground protectively over the prone Wesker, knocking back zombies in whatever direction they came from. Worry set in as my arms tired, yet the hordes still came, even more of them still pouring from the screen.

"Jane!" I shouted up to the projection booth. "Any luck?"

"No," she called back.

"Can't you, I don't know, *talk* to the projector or something?"

"I tried," she said, sounding panicked. "It won't listen. I even asked politely."

"Screw politeness," I said. "The time for manners is kind of passed. Go with aggressive!"

The electric hum of Jane's technomantic voice boomed out loud over the battle sounds in the theater. The pitch of the projector changed to a metallic whine, followed by a dull, explosive *thwump*.

All of the lights went out and everything electronic went dead.

The sound of the movie died with it, leaving me in the pitch black surrounded by the sound of struggle and the low, guttural moans of the undead all around me.

"Oops," Jane said.

I spun myself around in a continuous circle, swinging blindly into the darkness to keep every last creature away from me. I didn't have a clue who might be attacking or from which direction, and I was rewarded with a few satisfying hits. I could only pray none of them were my coworkers.

The dull red glow of emergency exit lights kicking on filled the theater, giving just enough for me to make out my surroundings once more. The professor was gone from the aisle now, but his zombie horde was still scattered all around.

"Steady!" the Inspectre called out from somewhere across the theater. "Keep them contained. I want zero zombies walking out of here. Is that understood?"

His words gave me hope, especially since the screen was no longer producing any more enemies. I started swinging, thinning their ranks. The job became easier when several of them lost their shape even before I struck them, melting instead into a goo that fell from their bones and coated the floor of the theater.

Jane came down from the projection booth and walked over to me through the last bits of fighting, the reel of film held in her hands at arm's length. She clearly wanted nothing to do with it. Connor walked over to me when he finished dispatching the remaining zombies next to him. He looked down at the growing film of goo on the floor. "You think that happened to the professor, too?" he asked.

"Let's hope so," I said.

"Doubtful," the Inspectre added as he joined us, winded and huffing. "Very doubtful."

"Why do you say that?"

"The Mason I knew was resourceful, a careful thinker, and this newly reborn Mason seems to still have it. He wouldn't have planned this out only to suffer the same fate as these celluloid minions. You heard what he expected. He thought he would be with some of his students at another location, not here in our movie theater. The zombies were a mere distraction."

Director Wesker put his hand on my shoulder, squeezing down on it hard. "Speaking of distractions," Wesker said. "I want a word with Mr. Canderous and Mr. Christos in my office *now*." He reached over to Jane and snatched the film from her hands.

"Thaddeus," the Inspectre said. "There's too much to do. Redfield's on the loose and we need to keep searching for the water woman who killed him, despite the fact that he is alive once more. She may have had a hand in his rebirth. Some strange connection exists between these two incidents and we need to know what it is."

"That may be," said Director Wesker, unmoved, "but clearly your lapdogs are stirring up trouble on your behalf and I'd like a moment with them by myself."

I looked over to the Inspectre with a pained expression. "Sir . . . ?"

The Inspectre sighed. "Go, both of you," he said, still catching his breath. "I'll be along soon."

Wesker pushed Connor and me both toward the doorway to the offices, waving us toward it with the film reel.

"You'd better hurry, then," Wesker said. "I can't promise they're going to live that long."

Professor Redfield's attack had been brutal, but it was Thaddeus Wesker's string of expletives on our way back to Greater & Lesser Arcana that really stung. It might have had something to do with most of his comments being aimed directly at me more than Connor for allowing Jane to get marked.

"Do they actually teach you anything in Other Division?" Wesker asked, stomping his way toward his office in the red-lit hallways of the Department. "Or is it always free-range chaos over there?"

"That didn't fit on our business cards," I said. " 'Other Division' did."

Wesker turned to me with a hard glare in his eyes. He went to speak, stopped himself, and then threw open his office door and headed over to a workbench on the right side of the room. The lights and power flickered on both in his office and out in the hall.

Connor put his hand on my shoulder. "Not the time, kid." He walked over to Director Wesker, who was busy flicking on a magnifying work lamp on top of the workstation as he set the film reel down. "What can you tell us?"

"What I could tell you would fill up volumes," he sneered, still fuming.

"Hey," Connor snapped. "This is the first time either of us has ever been attacked by a living film, so give us a break, okay? I'd say it was a first for you, also."

Wesker turned back to the half-unspooled reel of film and set to examining it. "I've at least heard of people experimenting with this before. It's a bit of a Holy Grail among film buffs with an interest in arcana, but I've never actually heard of anyone accomplishing it." He stretched a length of the filmstrip between both of his hands and held it up under the lens. He moved it up and down to watch it as if running it through a projector. "Interesting."

I moved closer to study the strip over his shoulder, despite the aura of go-away still radiating off of him. "What is?"

He pushed the arm holding the lens over toward me, keeping the film in place underneath it. "Look closer and tell me what's missing."

I studied several of the individual frames, all of them from the end section of the film. The spliced-in section that contained bits of other horror movies was familiar with fields of grass covered with half-dug-up graves in each panel, but I realized what was missing from each and every one of them.

"The professor and the zombies," I said. "They're all gone."

"Exactly," Wesker said, lying the piece down on the reel. "This section should be filled with dozens of zombies from the film, but now they're no longer there."

"Of course they're not," Connor added. "Why should they be? All of them died in the theater, save Mason Redfield himself."

"You mean they're gone from the film completely?" I asked.

Wesker reached over to me and patted my head. "This younger generation," he said. "They catch on so quick."

Before I could say or do anything, a loud *haroom* came from the doorway and all three of us turned. Inspectre Quimbley and Jane were standing there, looking at us.

"Careful, Thaddeus," the Inspectre said, walking in. "You keep petting him like that, he's liable to follow you home."

Wesker pulled his hand away like I had grown quills. "No, thank you," he said. "You can have your lapdog back now." He wiped his hand on his pant leg, and then turned his attention back to the Inspectre. "Well? What's the damage?"

Jane stepped forward. "Actually, when I killed power to the building, I caused a bit of a problem with getting everything up and running again. I've been talking to the Department's electrical grid with my technomancy and it's starting to cooperate, but it may take a while for everything to fall in line."

Wesker changed his focus to the Inspectre, looking none too pleased. "And what about your old . . . *friend*?"

The Inspectre sighed. "I'm afraid Mason Redfield is gone. We were able to take down all of the zombies that crawled out of the film, so it wasn't a total wash."

"So you let him escape?" Wesker asked. He turned his fury on me, his finger pointing only inches from my face. "This is all your fault, Canderous."

My draw dropped. "How is this all on me?"

"I'm not sure," he said, "but every time I see a fiasco around here, you're somehow involved in it."

"Now, Thaddeus," the Inspectre chided. "No one just *let* Mason escape. He planned the whole thing perfectly, only we beat his students to the film apparently. He banked on the zombies providing enough of a distraction if his plans went wrong, thereby securing the means of his evading us. In life, Mason Redfield was quite clever, you know. And why wouldn't he be? I practically trained him when he came into the Fraternal Order of Goodness. If you want to lay blame anywhere, you had best start at my feet."

Wesker gave him a tight-lipped nod. "I'll be sure to do just that when I speak to the Enchancellors."

"Stop it!" Jane shouted, stepping between the two of them. "Our numbers in the Department are already far too few these days to start fighting among ourselves. Especially when we *all* unleashed that monster loose on the city."

The Inspectre reached for Jane's right hand, taking it in both of his. "Thank you, dear girl," he said. "It's easy to lose sight quickly in these trying times."

"Hold on," I said as something occurred to me. "Does this squash our murder investigation, then?"

Connor looked puzzled. "What do you mean, kid?"

"What I mean is that, technically speaking, Mason Redfield isn't dead. We watched him walk out of here today, alive . . . ish."

"A ritual raising like that doesn't come without a blood price," Connor added.

"Oh, I can more than guarantee that," Wesker said. He scooped up the strand of film and rubbed the nail of his thumb against it. He pulled it away and held it up, showing that it had turned a brownish red color.

"This whole spliced-in section of horror film has been soaked in blood," he said. "Something tells me it isn't his own."

"Ick," I said. "Great. So how do we stop him?"

"First things first," Wesker said. "We destroy this piece of film."

"Do you think that's going to work, Thaddeus?" the Inspectre asked.

"I'm not sure," he said, "but there is magic bound to these frames, and as far as first steps, destroying that bond is a good way to go."

"Do we have an expert on this or something?"

Wesker narrowed his eyes at me. "Did you not hear me before when I said I've never seen this done successfully before?"

"Right," I said, throwing my hands up. "Sorry."

"Can you let me do my job, then?" Wesker asked, but didn't wait for an answer. He stormed off to a tall cabinet on the other side of his office and threw it open. It was stocked with vials, tubes, and little clay pots that were full of a variety of colorful spell components. He bent down to the bottom shelf, pulled up a large, plastic jug, and carried it back to his workbench.

"Do they sell bulk bloodroot at the discount clubs now?" I asked.

"No," Wesker said, sliding on a pair of protective gloves, "and this isn't bloodroot. It's nitric acid. Movie film—more commonly, cellulose nitrate—eventually deteriorates and releases the acid naturally. Using this amount should serve as a catalyst."

"Ah," I said. "So naturally you just happen to have it around for office use."

"It also makes a fine salt substitute for spell components

when mixed," he said. "As it stands, however, it's quite toxic. You might want to step back." He picked up a set of gloves and a pair of goggles off the workbench and put them all on. "This might eat away your eyeballs if I splash any of it."

A mix of vanity and fear was enough to back me away almost before he finished his sentence.

Wesker twisted off the cap, and then poured half the container out into a large, clear petri dish. He put it down, and then scooped up the film and lowered it into the liquid, backing away from it.

In seconds the dish filled with swirling, bubbling activity. The mixture popped and hissed as sections of the film dissolved under the chemical attack. The acid turned from a clearish yellow to a dark, soupy mess. Only after a few minutes of furious activity did it begin to settle down.

Wesker walked back over to it, a satisfied smile on his face, no doubt loving the destructive display before him. When he reached it, however, the look vanished and was replaced with a disappointed one.

"Look, Simon," he said, dipping his hand into the liquid mess. "Here's something you should be familiar with—failure." He raised his hand, pinching a section of still-intact film between his fingers. Wesker kept pulling until a fair section of film came out of the sludge.

"Your chemical didn't dissolve all of it," I said.

"No," he said, walking over to a sink set off to the right of the workbench. "I suspect that what survived is the spliced-in magical part." He rinsed the section of film thoroughly before laying it down.

"So, now what?" I asked.

"I'm on it," Jane said, stepping forward with a determined look on her face despite the exhaustion in her eyes.

She grabbed up the remains of the filmstrip and brought it over to Wesker's desk. She leaned over and picked up the wastebasket next to it. On top of it were the close, sharp teeth of an electronic paper shredder.

"Jane . . ." Wesker said, but my girlfriend held up her hand, silencing him. Without another word, she slipped the film into the shredder's jagged mouth. She laid her free hand on the top of the machine as it set into action. A horrifying sound came from the machine. Jane gave a nervous look down at it, but then bent down to it, whispering an electronic string of technomantic speech at it.

In response, the power level of the machine kicked into high gear, grinding its teeth even harder into the film, but so did the earsplitting screeching coming from it. Smoke rose somewhere inside the gears of the machine and seconds later flame burst out of it. The shredder shook and sputtered as Jane continued talking to it, her eyes half-rolled back into her head as she tried in desperation to command it.

I couldn't take the sound of it or the oily haze of smoke rising from the flames licking along the top of it. I ran over and pulled the cord from the wall. Reaching for the now-melting trash can below the device, I picked it up and ran it over to the sink before dumping the whole thing in and turning on the water. Steam hissed and rose as the sound of the machine winding down faded away and the flames died. The room became as foggy as an old London evening. When the smoke cleared, I looked to Wesker, fully expecting him to explode at Jane. Even she expected it, looking ready to flinch.

But Director Wesker didn't scream or shout. Instead, he walked to the sink, turned off the water, and fished through the soaking-wet remains of the machine. "A valiant effort," he said, pulling at an end of the film splice he plucked out. It slid easily out of the nearly destroyed machine. The remaining film wasn't remotely burnt or slashed. It didn't even have a single scratch on it from where I stood. "Alas," Wesker continued.

Jane's face sank, and she looked shaken. "I don't think I've ever killed a machine before."

I gave her a weak smile. "First time for everything, hon."

She looked up at me, on the verge of tears. "I didn't know it would make me feel so . . . *sad.*"

"That's perfectly natural," Wesker said. Compared to the disdain he threw at me over the smallest of mistakes, his soothing demeanor with Jane was killing me. He rolled the filmstrip up with care and put it back down on the workbench. "Your technomancy gives you access to the machine world, an affinity for it. To you, they're more than just objects."

Jane gave a slow nod of understanding. Feeling Wesker's affinity for her, I put my arm around her shoulder, giving her a comforting squeeze.

"Please do me a favor, though," Wesker continued. His voice held the edge of his usual dark tone to it. "Next time, try to not be as impulsive as your boyfriend there."

Jane nodded again, still quiet in her newfound saddened state. Maybe now she would understand how I felt when shaking off the feelings I accumulated in my psychometric visions.

"Good," Wesker said. "Let's leave poor impulse control to those in Other Division, shall we?"

"Tsk-tsk," the Inspectre said, waggling his finger at Director Wesker. "Remember what your lovely young technomancer told you about playing nice."

"So, what now?" I asked.

Wesker pounded his fist on the workbench. "I *will* find a way to break this film, but even still, that may not be enough to stop the mad professor. For all we know, this may not even be the master print of the footage. Destroying this little section may accomplish nothing."

"I can help you figure that out," Jane said, shaking off her mood, "despite evidence to the contrary."

She gave a nervous glance over to the sink full of smoldering wreckage, and then back to Wesker.

The Inspectre nodded. "Good," he said. "See that you do." He paused and his brow furrowed as his face turned somber. "I'm truly sorry to have brought this upon all of you." He looked up at me. "I do think, however, this calls for a revisit to Mason's old haunts."

"The lighthouse?" I asked.

The Inspectre nodded once again. "He was up to something more than just making a documentary out there and we need to figure out what. Rejuvenating himself, yes, but there is something larger at hand going on at the Hell Gate Bridge."

"I'll gas up the boat," I said, heading for the door.

"I'm afraid it will have to wait until tomorrow night," the Inspectre said. "The fiscal month closed today and thanks to downtown, there aren't funds available until tomorrow to requisition it on such short notice. That said, make sure to save room for one more in the taxi before heading down to the pier tomorrow evening."

I stopped and turned to look at him. "*You're* coming?"

"I'd say it was critical at this juncture, don't you think?" He walked over to join me at the door with determination. "Mason's back in the game now. Why shouldn't I be?"

I wanted to cite his advanced age, for one, but it was

already too late. The Inspectre pushed past me and headed off down the hall toward his office. I watched him go, then looked over at Jane. I felt bad enough when I had put her in harm's way; now there was my mentor to worry about, too. I gave her a parting smile. "If you'll excuse me," I said. "I have to get the paperwork in motion for the requisition. I'll file it with the Enchancellors in the morning."

"Good luck with the bureaucrats," Wesker said with a bit of snip to it.

Jane gave him a look that shut her boss up. She turned back to me, giving a nervous smile. "No dying tomorrow night, okay?"

"I'll try not to," I said. "I'll let Connor steer the boat. That should lessen the odds a bit."

22

I filed the requisition for the boat the next morning, and once funds were released for the new fiscal month around noon, the Enchancellors approved it and the boat was ours by nightfall. All in all, a day's delay was a fairly speedy process, by Department standards anyway.

To be on the safe side, we brought the F.O.G. boat into Wards Island at a different angle, one I had hoped would be less filled with aqua-zombies. Whether it was the fact that Jane wasn't there to draw them to her or not, we got to the island without being assaulted and tied off against the broken remains of the old dock there.

From the outside, the lighthouse looked pretty much as we had left it the other night, but since we were now there looking for the freshly reborn Professor Redfield, I had my bat at the ready as Connor, the Inspectre, and I pushed our way back in through the main doors.

"Just as I suspected," I said in a whisper. "Still creepy."

"And it just got creepier," Connor added, just as quiet. "Look."

The interior of the lighthouse wasn't the way we had left it. Most of the film equipment was gone, and what little remained was trashed, broken, or knocked over amid the old, weathered furniture.

"Damned budget," the Inspectre said. "We're a day late and a professor short." He gestured toward the spiral staircase that ran along the opposite wall and the three of us started up through the lighthouse. Every floor was in the same state, but other than the destruction and damage, the place was deserted. We all came back down the stairs, me at the back of the pack with my bat flipped up casually over my shoulder as we reentered the open room on the main floor.

I slowed down as I came off the staircase, looking around the main room again.

"Does something seem a little out of whack with the perspective in here?" I asked.

"It's hard to tell among all the debris," Connor said, looking around. "What are you seeing, kid?"

"I'm not sure," I said, following the curve of the wall. "The wall by the stairs seems a bit . . . off." I raised my bat and traced it along the wall, tapping. The thick, old plaster chipped away as I went, turning to powder after so many years, but the sound was a solid one. Until I hit the area just below the stairs, that was. There the sound changed, the heft of my retractable steel bat echoing out in a tone different from the rest.

"Well, well," I said, searching along the wooden beams that ran up and down bordering the section of open wall. I stepped closer to the beam nearest me and saw the slightest hint of a break where the plaster disappeared behind the wood instead of meeting it. I pressed the section of wall and felt it give under my hand, the entire section of wall opening up into a secret room behind it.

"Nice going, kid," Connor said, patting me on the shoulder. "You want to go in first?"

I shook my head. "After you."

"How kind," Connor said, and headed in.

"Not really," I said. "I just figure if it's booby-trapped, at least I get a few more seconds of feeling good about finding the door while you trigger it instead of me."

"Nice," Connor said, slowing down as he continued into the dark behind the secret door. The Inspectre went in next and I followed, my eyes quickly adjusting to the low light. We were in a dim, windowless chamber that looked like a sinister version of the professor's NYU office, except most of the shelves here held arcane-looking relics instead of movie miniatures. Huge gaps along them led me to believe that much of the materials there had been removed. The rest of the room had the skeletal remains of film equipment—camera lenses, light rigging, an editorial deck, but it was the arcane stuff scattered throughout that gave me the creeps.

"Well, now," the Inspectre said, walking around. "This seems more like the Mason Redfield that he always feared becoming."

"I'm sorry, sir," I said.

"Nonsense, my boy," he said. "It's hardly your doing."

"That's not what I meant," I said. "It's just that I saw who he was back when I read part of your past psychometrically. I saw the promise and potential of who he could have been before he became . . . *this*."

"I never would have expected this of him and I knew the man. I haven't the faintest idea why he would become so corrupt as all this, but I must find out."

"Check this out," Connor said from where he stood in the center of the hidden room.

The Inspectre started walking over toward him, and then stopped in his tracks. I followed his gaze to a spot on a table in the center of the room. It was slick with blood.

"Whose is it?" I asked.

The Inspectre walked over to the table, looking it over. He grabbed the edge and lifted up one side of it.

"Sir?" I asked, unsure of what he was doing.

He let go of the table with one of his hands and indicated the surface where all the blood was.

"See how the blood flows when I tilt it?" he asked. "It hasn't coagulated yet. It's still fairly fresh. If this had happened before Mason's death, it would by dried by now or tacky to the touch."

"I'd say it's pretty tacky, not cleaning it up," Connor said. "It ruins the décor."

I turned and shot him a look.

"What?" he said. "Is cracking wise only your domain or something? I was just trying to ease the tension."

"Not helping," I said. "Still feeling tense, but that's probably just because we know the professor's alive again."

"Then maybe we should get to work, gentlemen," the Inspectre interrupted.

I didn't need to be told twice. "Fine," I said, not bothering to banter any further. I turned my attention to taking in as much as I could of the whole hidden room. It wasn't until I was focusing on the floor that I felt something click.

"Inspectre," I said, noting the legs of the table, "you didn't slide the table when you lifted up the one side, did you?"

He thought for a second before answering. "I don't believe so, no. Why?"

"I didn't think you had," I said. "I don't remember hearing a scraping sound." I knelt down next to the table, mindful not to kneel in the blood underneath it. "Then why are there drag marks, here . . . and here?" I pointed at two sets of marks next to each pair of legs.

"Someone must have moved it aside before," I said, and then stood back up. "Help me with this."

The three of us grabbed the dry spots along the edge of the table and lifted it, moving it away from the center of the room. No longer in the shadow of the table, a definite difference in the flooring was evident.

"A trapdoor," the Inspectre said.

Connor leaned down and felt around in the drying blood before finding a ring and pulling the door up until it was standing open resting on its hinge. The sound of running water rose up from the darkness below.

"What the hell?" I asked.

"After you, kid," Connor said, waving me toward the open hole.

"Me?" I croaked out. "Why do I have to go first?"

Connor smiled. "I walked in through the secret door first, so it's your turn now."

"Screw that," I said. "The last time I went down in something like this it was that Oubliette the Department had me test in. I nearly died when it malfunctioned. You'll excuse me if I'm a bit reluctant to go jumping into another dank, dark hole."

"Don't worry," Connor said. "You'll be fine. Besides, it builds character."

"Maybe you should try building a little character, then."

"I'm full up," he said, shrugging.

"Rock, Paper, Scissors?" I said.

"Now, why would I do that?" Connor asked. "I already don't have to go down. What's in it for me?"

"If I win," I said, "you go down there. If I lose, I'll do all your case paperwork for you for two weeks."

Connor stood there, thinking about it. He didn't look quite convinced. My partner knew he had the upper hand.

"Gentlemen," the Inspectre interrupted. "Sometime today . . ."

I had to close the deal. "I'll even file everything for you."

Connor's face lit up. "Deal," he said. "One throw, on three. One, two, three!"

I threw out my right hand, flat as could be. I looked at Connor's hand, two fingers held apart in a *V* formation.

"Scissors," I said. "Son of a bitch."

"Sorry, kid," Connor said. He clicked his fingers against my hand like he was actually cutting it.

I looked down into the hole before pulling out my flashlight. "I thought for sure you were going to throw rock."

"Not when I knew you were going to throw down paper," he said.

"You got lucky," I said. "You didn't know I was going to throw paper."

"I did too," he said. "You are such a paper. You're such a paper it hurts."

I was going to ask what Connor even meant by that, but seeing the look on the Inspectre's face shut me down. Instead, I turned my flashlight on the opening itself. An iron-rung ladder was built into the side of a stone chimney leading down to the sound of churning water far below. Without another word, I lowered myself down to the floor, slid over the edge of the trapdoor, and grabbed onto the top rung. Once I was certain I had a good grip and wasn't about to fall to my death, I began my descent, the tiny flashlight gripped in my right palm leaving my fingers free to hold on to the rungs.

"If at any moment you feel compelled to lower a basket with lotion in it," I said, making my way down the wet ladder set in the stone, "feel compelled to also drop dead."

"Don't make me get the hose, kid," Connor said and waved at me.

The Inspectre shushed him, and I turned my attention back to my descent. The well was deeper than I had imagined, but soon enough I got to the bottom of the ladder where it met the water. It rolled and splashed up the sides of the shaft, leaving me to think it must lead out to the river surrounding the island we were on.

"Anything, my boy?" the Inspectre called down.

I snaked my arm through one of the rungs and used my now-free hand to move the light around. The walls were covered with a mix of dark green slime, white foam, blood, and bits of decaying organic material I feared was human flesh.

"This isn't a well," I said. "I think it's a feeding pit."

"Feeding pit?" the Inspectre called out, puzzlement in his voice. "For what?"

"I don't know," I said, passing my light over the churning water. "Maybe that creepy green woman. Maybe Mason Redfield unearthed her from a tomb and he was taking care of her, like a twisted pet of some kind, and she eventually turned on him." My light caught something dark and solid bobbing in the churn of tiny waves. "Hold on a second. I see something."

I stuck my legs through part of the ladder, and stretched myself out over the water, reaching out. My only thought was, Please don't let it be a head. My fingers caught a bit of it for a second before it bobbed away. It was cloth, but it had some thickness to it. I leaned out a little farther and grabbed again, this time finding purchase. The electric shock of my psychometry flashed on the bag and I was whisked away into the past before I could control it or stop it from happening. The vision was dark with the sound of water all around. I couldn't see, but I was sure I was at the bottom of the pit. I pressed my mind around to figure out who I was, and in a heartbeat I knew. George, the blond-haired Hispanic punk kid who palled around with the other disciples of Mason Redfield. His mind was a confused mix, overrun by pain from having been bled out, then tossed down here. Weak and enfeebled, he struggled to get hold of the ladder but his body had not the strength. He slipped below the surface of the water as something cold and slimy wrapped around his body, crushing in. He panicked at the sensation and I did, too, forcing my mind's eye to pull itself back out of the vision.

Thankfully, my one arm was still locked in the ladder and I gasped a shocked breath from the surprise of the vision. My arm ached as I pulled the bag over to me, thankful that the water still bore much of the weight of the floating object until I could get a better grip. I fished it out of the water. George's messenger bag, the same kind I used.

I threw its strap over my shoulder and started back up the ladder. There was a bit of weight to it, making my climb a little more strained than I would have preferred, and when I reached the top of the ladder, it took both Connor and the Inspectre to hoist me up before closing the trapdoor back over the pit.

I pulled off the bag and laid it down on an empty desk off to my left along the wall. The bag was decorated with an assortment of stitched-on band names and dozens of tiny safety pins everywhere.

"What do we have here?" the Inspectre said, coming over to it.

"It was at the bottom of the well," I said. "It belonged to that blond kid George, one of Mason's students. The professor brought him here against his will. He threw him down into the pit after he got what he needed. Blood. But that's not all."

"What else?" the Inspectre asked.

"There was something down there with him," I said. "Couldn't see anything. It was too dark down there, but it was like a big fish or a snake. It . . . it finished him off."

Connor undid the short tongue holding the bag closed and flipped the flap open. Using caution, he reached in the bag and started pulled out its contents.

"Books," he said, laying them down one by one.

The Inspectre spun them so he could read them, adjusting his glasses. "*Introduction to Modern Cinema, Principles of Editing . . . The Monster Maker's Handbook.*"

Connor ran his hand over a tear in the outer material of the bag. Something solid and shiny poked through the spot. Connor stuck his hand in the hole and pushed the object out. Its metallic case was crushed in the middle, but there was no mistaking the object. "One laptop," he said. "Only partially damaged."

"It must have gotten banged up on the fall," the Inspectre said.

"No," I said, "not banged up. Crushed."

"Crushed?"

"By whatever killed George down there," I said.

"We need to be talking to living people on this one if we're going to figure this out," Connor said. "Think about what we know. The professor was working on a film. What does it take to make a movie?"

The Inspectre's face lit up. "It takes a village," he said.

"Exactly," Connor said. "It takes cast and crew. Lighting, sound, editors . . ."

"And Professor Mason Redfield certainly had some dedicated students out there," I said. "Wasn't he expecting them when he was reborn?"

I started gathering up the contents of the bag, readying them to take back to the Lovecraft Café. The Inspectre looked angry.

"Then it's time to put the screws to the professor's living students," he said. "It's time to stop wasting our resources and get some *real* answers. We need to figure out why Mason Redfield did all this and what his plans are."

"We'll find out," Connor said, "even if we have to beat it out of them."

I reached for the bat at my side, patting it in its holster. "Have bat, will travel."

23

Connor, the Inspectre, and I stopped back at the Department long enough to visit Allorah Daniels. We found the youngest Enchancellor back in her office-slash-lab, where I was surprised to also find Jane with her. I walked over to the two of them with the tattered shoulder bag held up in my right hand. Jane grabbed for it like a kid hungry for presents on Christmas morning.

"Sorry, doll," I said. "This is going on our lovely Enchancellor's dance card."

Allorah looked up from the pile of books in front of her. She did not look happy. "Oh, is it, now?" she asked. "What about Jane's health? She keeps wanting to go home and shower, but I convinced her that's not a good idea right now."

Jane nodded, then scooped up a large glass from the lab table. "I've traded up," she said. "I've switched to drinking water, which helps kill the craving to shower."

"That's good," I said.

"Not really," Allorah said. "That's her twenty-eighth glass."

"Twenty-eighth?" I repeated.

Jane put her hand on my arm. "It's okay. I feel fine."

"That's what worries me," I said. "That would kill a normal person."

Jane gave a grim smile. "As the mark indicates, I'm not normal."

A moment of awkward silence passed, before the Inspectre cleared his throat. I snapped out of my fog and held the shoulder bag out to Allorah. "This is for you," I said.

"Do I not seem busy enough trying to save your girlfriend's life here? I would think you'd show some appreciation for that."

The Inspectre stepped forward into the room. "Please, Allorah. As a personal favor to me."

Something in the seriousness of his tone softened her in an instant. "Of course, Argyle. For you, anything."

"Thank you," he said. "I owe you."

Allorah waved his words away and rose up from her desk. She took the bag from me and brought it over to her workbench, emptying its contents out onto it. "What are we looking at here?"

"We found this," I said, "in the same lighthouse that Professor Redfield converted into his impromptu workshop. It belonged to one of his students, but he bled him out to barely living and then fed him to . . . something. I'm not sure what. There was a sort of disposal-pit-well thingie underneath a hidden room where he had been keeping all this arcane paraphernalia. It was too dark for me to see when I flashed on it." I stepped over to the workbench. "Let me get one last read off of it now that I'm not at the bottom of a feed pit."

I pulled off my gloves and slapped my hands down on the bag, pressing my power into it. I feared seeing any of the gory details of Professor Redfield's actual carving up of George so instead focused my energy on pulling a location on the rest of the students from it. A dorm room at New York University and a slew of classrooms flew by my mind's eye as I went back in time. Through all the flashes, one location stood out among the more mundane ones. It was a poorly lit section of the university where George skulked along, hoping that no one was following him as he slipped into a room marked 247. When I pressed my vision for further details it blanked out and I was forced to bring myself back to reality.

Hungry from the rush of low blood sugar, I went for the Life Savers in my jacket pocket.

"Anything, kid?" Connor asked, coming over to no doubt make sure I didn't pass out on anything expensive near the lab equipment.

I nodded as I stuffed my mouth full of rainbow-colored salvation. "I think I've got an address."

"Excellent," the Inspectre said. "We should get moving."

I held up a finger. "In a minute," I said. I turned to Jane. "You might want to take a look through his computer as well."

"Me?" she said, surprised. "What for exactly?"

"We found this in the water below the lighthouse," I said. "That place may be connected to that she-bitch. It might help out with your . . . situation."

Jane's face was a little sad, but she nodded. "Okay," she said. "Can I consider that a prezzie from you, then?"

I kissed her on the cheek, then joined the Inspectre and Connor by the door leading out of Allorah's office.

"Be careful," Jane called out.

"Why start now?" Connor darkly added.

"Don't be so pessimistic," the Inspectre said, twirling his sword cane around in his hand with a bit of a flourish. "Not everyone gets to spend field time with a member of the old guard."

"No offense, boss," Connor said, heading out the door, "but I'm going to stick with my pessimism. It's served me well."

Connor walked out the door, leaving the two of us standing there. I looked over at the Inspectre and he looked hurt. Even his mustache seemed a little sadder.

"Don't worry, sir," I said, gesturing him politely to go next. "Beating up some college students should improve his mood."

I was weirdly glad to see that my powers were still keeping us on track and that the greater traumas of people dying seemed to suppress any flare-ups of the tattooist's emotion. It was a shame that it took panicked flashes of someone dying to trump my other issues, but at least my powers were focused on the case at hand now.

I found the old hallways of the unused theater space in one of the New York University buildings along the east side of Washington Square. Room 247 was exactly as I had seen it, with the exception that it had been closed off by copious amounts of yellow caution tape.

I reached for the door with one hand while unhooking my bat from its holster with the other.

Connor stopped the hand I was reaching with and used his other to point at the strip of yellow NYU caution tape across the door. It was split where the door met its frame.

"Guess they probably aren't expecting company," he whispered.

I pulled out my bat, extending it. "Too bad for them," I said.

My blood was up after what we had found earlier. On a silent count of three, Connor kicked the door in. I ran in first, bat at the ready. We were in a dark, cluttered space filled with stored bits of classrooms past. The only light in the room came from far off in the middle of it through a maze of desks, chairs, and old-style chalkboards. Three of Professor Redfield's favorite students—Elyse, Darryl, and Heavy Mike—were sitting around a circle of desks, each with a laptop open in front of them. All three heads popped up from their screens and turned our way.

"Freeze!" I shouted, waving my bat as I started working my way through the jumbled accumulation in the room.

The girl with the short shock of blond hair, Elyse, slammed her laptop shut. "Crap," she said, jumping up. She looked across the circle of desks at the tall guy with the gauged ears sitting across from her. "Darryl, I *told* you we should have booby-trapped the door."

Darryl stood up as well, cradling his laptop in his arms, still typing at it with one hand. Between him and the girl was the chunkier guy, Mike, who was already cramming books and notebooks into a large duffel bag.

"What part of 'freeze' did they not teach you at this institute of higher learning?" I shouted.

Connor and the Inspectre began picking their way through the jumble of furniture, but the going was slow. We'd never catch them at this rate. I leapt up and took to the tops of the desks in front of me and ran across them as fast as I could, hoping my precarious path held up under my feet as I went.

Heavy Mike kept stuffing his bag, looking over to the tall one. "Is it ready?" he called out.

"Almost," Darryl said, still typing away at the keyboard. "Get the hell out of here."

Heavy Mike didn't need to be told twice. He snatched up his bag, threw it over his shoulder, and disappeared into the shadows that stretched out behind him. The sounds of stuff falling over left and right rang out as he ran off. I looked around the room, searching for the blond girl again, but I couldn't see her anywhere. Then I spied her shock of blond hair lowered down inside the center of circled desks. She was knelt down in the middle of them with a sizable curved blade in her hand, and she was not alone. The other freshman from Eccentric Circles, Trent, was tied in place on the floor with several computer cables draped across his body. The open ends of them were frayed with the other ends running up to several of the laptops.

"Go for the tall one," I shouted over to Connor. My partner course-corrected through all the storage, heading for Darryl. I leapt down into the open circle in the middle of the desks, swinging my bat to disarm Elyse. I wasn't one for going full force with human foes, which threw my timing off, and Elyse ducked under my swings, nicking the prone freshman with her knife before lunging at me. It slammed into my satchel with the scrape of metal on metal ringing out—it hit against my Ghostbusters lunch box.

"Nice lunge," I said, pissed, but thankful I had avoided a wound.

"Thanks," she said with a wicked smile and a wild panic in her eyes. "The college provides excellent facilities that come in handy beyond the acting program. Helps to keep me a triple threat."

"It's not going to do you very much good with a broken arm," I said, swinging to disarm her.

Elyse feinted back and dodged the blow. "Darryl!" she called out. "Ready?"

"I think so," he said, "but the footage isn't cued up."

"Then use the office piece," she said, taking a moment to look down at the bound boy on the floor. "Anything!"

I glanced down as well. The tiny river of blood from where she had nicked Trent had flowed down over the boy's arm, pooling at the inside of his elbow joint where it touched a fray of the exposed wires from the network cable.

"Launch it!" Elyse shouted, backing to the edge of the circle.

Just as my partner arrived at Darryl's side, the tall guy fumbled his machine away from Connor's grasp. He held the laptop out of reach and then flipped it around until the screen of it was facing away from him.

At my feet, a spark rose from where wires mingled with the boy's blood, causing him to howl out in pain through the gag in his mouth. That distraction was all it took for Elyse to make a break for it. She threw herself back onto one of the surrounding desks, lifted herself into a back walk-over, and landed on her feet.

"Guess that makes me a quadruple threat," she said. "Looks like all those years of auditioning for roles as an Olympic gymnast paid off." Already Elyse was backing away across the desks.

I started after her, but stopped in my tracks by the sounds of chaos coming from Connor and Darryl struggling against each other. The laptop in Darryl's hands was sparking the same way the frayed network cable had when it touched the freshman's blood. Its screen was taken up by a full video displaying the professor's office that we had broken into the other night. The camera swept across the professor's shelves, the ones that were covered with his massive collection of movie monster miniatures, which I was upset to see were coming to life. They flew, ran, and crawled their way toward the camera, the first of them—a tiny Harpy with a considerable wingspan—flying out of the laptop screen itself. Tiny skeletal hands clawed their way along the edge of the laptop screen as bony, undead Sinbad pirates pulled their bodies out and dropped to the floor. Within seconds, dozens of foot-high creatures were swirling through the air or dashing across the floor of the unused classroom. The room quickly filled with enough of them that I started to worry about them as a real threat.

I spun back around toward Elyse. She was putting a greater distance between us with each passing second. I leapt up onto the desk to give chase but something was at my leg. I looked down at one of the Harpies dangling around my ankle, its claws tearing into the edge of my jeans as its wings flapped wildly about. I brought my bat down on it without a second thought and was happy to see it break into a mangled twist of clay and a metal skeleton underneath. What didn't make me happy was seeing it fall onto the bound freshman, who had several monsters of his own to contend with.

The bound student was being swarmed by a battalion of pirate skeletons, some of which brandished curved cutlasses. I doubted if they could even do any real damage with those, but the boy was prone and I couldn't just leave the poor bastard there to play pincushion, especially considering he was already bleeding.

"Dammit," I said and jumped back down into the circle. The tiny skeleton pirates shifted their focus from their helpless victim to me. "Back to the boneyard for you, me hearties!" I swung at the closest one and sent it flying off into the darkness where it landed with a shattering sound. "Who's next?"

The answer, apparently, was *all* of them. Before I could pick my next target, the entire group rushed me. The miniature horde was like a track-and-field team as they bolted for me, several of them leaping into the air, climbing up my pant legs. The pokes of tiny swords dug at me along the back of my jacket, but for now they weren't even piercing the fabric.

I grabbed one of the skeletons climbing up my right thigh and tore it off my body. A piece of my jeans went with it, but I didn't care. The little monster writhed in my hand, but I didn't give it time to act. I threw it up into the air like I was coaching little league kids how to play outfield, and then swung at it. The skeleton shattered into tiny pieces, its structure proving to be even more fragile than the Harpies. That gave me hope.

The sensation of the others scrabbling their way up my back started wigging me out. I threw myself backward onto the desk behind me. A mashing *crunch* sounded as my body slammed down onto the desktops. A few of the broken pieces dug into my back, but compared to the thought of their tiny blades poking at me, I was fine with it.

Prone, my legs dangled over the edges of two of the desks and a skeleton head rose up over the crest of my left knee. I kicked my leg straight out as if a doctor had been testing my reflexes, sending the pirate figure up into the air above me. I flashed my bat out at it and it exploded into dust and fragments of wire.

Jumping up to my feet, I was feeling pretty good with the way things were going. I grabbed another one on my leg, swinging it by its head until there was an audible popping sound and its body separated, sailing off with a distant crash.

My moment of triumph was cut short when I looked down at the center of the circle. Two of my pirate attackers had been smart enough to stay clear of me, and had instead taken position by the bound student's head. Their swords were poised over the frantic movement of his widening eyes.

"No!" I shouted, diving for them, but they were already lowering their blades. I wasn't going to make it. I hit the floor hard, skidding into the student with a harsh "oof" as I drove into him.

Connor's feet shot past my head, one landing on the floor next to the student's own head and the other lashing out at the two skeletons. They shattered as his foot connected, their pieces raining down on the student's tightly shut eyes.

"Jesus, Simon," Connor said, "I thought you were trying to save him, not add to his injuries."

I scrambled up to my knees and began untying the poor kid. "What happened to the Harpies?" I asked Connor.

Connor lifted up his hand, displaying a fistful of torn-off Harpy wings.

"Nice," I said. "Remind me never to buy you a bird as a gift."

Connor tossed them to the floor. "As long as it's not an evil bird," he said.

"Where's Darryl?" I asked.

Connor looked away. "He might have escaped."

"*Might* have?"

Connor got testy. "It was a little hard keeping track of everyone, what with the chaos of fighting Harpies and rescuing you."

"You weren't rescuing me," I said.

"On, no?" he said, haughtiness in his voice. "So you could have lived with yourself watching the kid here get his eyes gouged out, then?"

I didn't bother responding and continued untying the student. I undid the final knots, before a thought hit me. "Where's the Inspectre?"

We both looked around but we couldn't see the Inspectre anywhere. "Crap," I said, but Connor held a finger up to silence me.

Off near where we had come in came the sounds of struggle, even though we couldn't see much from where we stood. We hurried our way through the maze of stored stuff while the student finished untangling himself from the coil of ropes encasing him.

Following the sounds, we came across the Inspectre, flat on his back on the floor. He was still clutching his sword cane, but every other inch of him was wrapped up in a writhing sea of movie snakes and sea serpent models, including a mutant octopus-looking thing that had full control of him from the waist down. Muffled cries for help came from behind either a tentacle or snake section that ran across his face. I couldn't tell which.

Without wasting a second, Connor and I made quick work liberating the Inspectre from his monstrous little captors. I pulled the tentacle from around his head, ripping it in two before throwing it off into the surrounding darkness.

"Are you all right, sir?" I asked.

The moment he was free, the Inspectre scrabbled around on the floor until he could get up on his knees.

"What, what?" he said, somewhat flustered. "Yes, yes, of course I'm all right." He found his sword and sheathed it back into the hollow of his cane, and then used it to help himself up. I moved to help him, but he brushed me away.

"It would appear," he continued, "that my fencing skills were a bit lacking, I'm afraid."

"I don't get it," I said, shaking my head. "You routinely clean my clock in the F.O.G. training room."

Connor chimed in, "I'm sure it's not easy trying to fence miniature sea creatures."

"No, I don't suppose it is," the Inspectre said, shaking his head. He stroked his mustache, and then stopped, pulling away with something pinched between his fingers. "There are scales in my mustache."

Something caught Connor's attention back in the center of the room, and he turned.

The student was attempting to lift himself up onto the desks and pull himself along the tops of them while trying to kick his legs free from all the rope. Connor reached the open circle and grabbed one of the dangling ends. "Not so fast," he said. He pulled the student back toward him like he had just roped a steer at a rodeo. "Going somewhere?"

"N-no," the student said, looking a little crazed. "I was just trying to get free of all this."

"Uh-huh," Connor said, not letting go of the rope.

"I *was*," the student said, still sounding uncertain. "What? You think I was trying to escape with the rest of those guys?"

"Trying, yes," Connor said. "Succeeding, no."

The sounds of several Harpy cries came from out in the darkness along with the sounds of a few chairs falling off the tops of desks.

I lifted up my bat and readied it. The Inspectre unsheathed his sword from the cane and looked around.

The student looked at me with recognition. "You again,"

the student said. "The guy from the bar who followed us to our studio the other day."

"That's me," I said, looking around the room for more enemies.

"Relax," the student said. "I don't think you have to worry. Those things won't last long. They lose their juice faster than a laptop battery. That's part of the problem."

"What problem?" I asked.

The student stopped fussing with the ropes and went silent. He must have forgotten who he was talking to and clammed up when he remembered. He shut his mouth and shook his head.

"What problem?" Connor repeated.

"I don't think I should say anything more," he said.

Connor stepped closer to him. "Oh, I think it's in your best interest if you do," he said.

"They were going to kill me," he said, still in shock.

"I might kill you, too," Connor said. "Making me destroy all of this classic memorabilia."

"What?" the student said, snapping out of it. He looked over at the Inspectre. "You look old enough to be in charge here. This one isn't *really* going to kill me, is he?"

"Don't look at me, young man," the Inspectre said. "At least not for sympathy. Your friends were the ones who unleashed those things on us, after all."

"They *aren't* my friends," the student said. "They had me tied up."

The doubtful look on the Inspectre's face got a little doubtier.

"Okay, fine," the student said, looking away. "They *were* my friends, but not after today."

Connor walked back over to him. "You want to tell us what they were about to do with you, then?"

"*Want* to tell you?" he said with a nervous laugh. "No. You've seen what Elyse, Darryl, and Heavy Mike can do. I think I have more to fear in retribution from them than I do from you."

"We still beat them," I said.

"They still got away," the student countered.

I really couldn't argue with that, but I didn't have to. Connor already had him by the front of his bloodied shirt.

"Make no mistake," he said. "Your friends ran like cowards. Trust me when I say you have more to fear from us."

The kid finally looked scared, but he also looked a little pale in general.

"Maybe we should get him to a hospital," I said. "He is bleeding, after all."

Connor looked down at the gash on the boy's side where Elyse had cut him. He reached into his inside coat pocket, pulling out a Departmental favorite when it came to combat in the field, a tiny wound-up piece of cloth that looked like a human digit and bore a sectional crook in two places along it.

"What the hell is that?" the student asked.

"Mummy Fingers," I said.

Connor nodded. He placed it against the student's wound, and at contact, it unfurled itself, running its bandage back and forth over the spot until it staunched the flow of blood. The student squirmed as he watched it wide-eyed, and then looked up once it was fully settled into place.

"Who are you people anyway?" he asked.

I collapsed my bat down and slipped it back into its holster at my hip. "We're the good guys," I said.

"All right," Connor said, grabbing the student by the rope still tangled around him and heading back toward the door we came in. "He'll live, but he's coming with us."

The dazed student stumbled along after Connor, slamming into desks and knocking over chairs as he went. "I'd move faster if I were, you know, untied," he said.

"What's your name again?" Connor said.

"Trent," the student said.

"Okay . . . well, then, Trent," Connor said, "*shut up.*"

Trent turned and looked at me as Connor dragged him off again. "Is he always this way?" he asked, fear in his eyes.

"No," I said, following after them. "Sometimes he's actually mean."

24

By the time we hit the street, we had untied Trent, but Connor and I rode on either side of him once we had hailed a cab, the Inspectre riding up front. When we pulled up outside the Lovecraft Café, Trent looked confused. The Inspectre got out of the front seat of the cab and held the back door open as we pulled the student out.

"You're taking me out for coffee?" he said.

"Inside," Connor said, shoving him toward the coffeehouse doors. Once through the doors, the Inspectre went over to one of the big comfy chairs and collapsed into it.

"Sir?" I asked. "Are you okay? You look a little pale."

"Just winded," he said. "See to our young prisoner, won't you?"

"As long as you're okay . . ."

"Trust me," he said. "Besides, if I expire, at least I'll be doing it in a comfy chair, which is quite preferable to death at the hands of those tiny Harpies and skeletons."

As the Inspectre flagged down a waitress, we left him and escorted Trent back through the movie theater, which was still not operational since Mason Redfield's reincarnation. We kept going and entered the door marked H.P. at the back right corner, but as soon as we entered our secret offices, Trent stopped in his tracks.

"What the hell . . . ?" he said, but words left him as I watched him trying to take in the bustle of activity back here. He looked up and noticed the warding runes carved into the walls of the main bull pen.

"You guys aren't normal police, are you?" he asked.

"No," I said. "The normal police vacillate between laughing at us and fearing us. It's frustrating."

"Come on," Connor said, grabbing him by the shirt. He pulled at Trent and the boy started walking again, still taking in everything around him as we went.

"Are you, like, Men in Black?" he asked, addressing me.

"No," I said. "They're fictional. You know how I know that?"

Trent shook his head.

"Because *they* have a huge budget and unlimited resources."

The three of us continued walking back through the bull pen before passing through the curtain that sectioned off most of Other Division from the main work area. We were approaching our partners desk when Trent started to get back some of his focus.

"I think maybe I should call my dad," he said. "He's a lawyer."

"Sit down and shut up," Connor said, throwing the kid down onto the extra chair at our desks.

"Ow," he said. "I thought you said you were supposed to be the good guys."

"So?" Connor asked, sitting down at his desk. "Doesn't mean were the *gentle* guys, now, does it? So, let's get back to what you were talking about earlier. You mentioned there was a problem with your little operation over at NYU."

Trent shook his head. "Problem?" he asked, trying to feign ignorance. "What problem?"

"Knock it off," I said. "You're not that convincing an actor."

Trent looked hurt. "In all fairness, I *am* only a first-year. They won't even let me pick a specific school of acting until much later on."

Connor leaned down over him. "There's not going to be a later on if you're thrown out of NYU or stuck in jail, is that clear?"

Trent ran his fingers nervously through his hair. "Okay, okay . . ." he said. "You know, come to think of it, I do remember what we were talking about earlier."

"How surprising," Connor said, standing back up.

"So what do you want to know?" Trent asked.

"Why don't you start with what you meant when you said there was a problem with those . . . *things* that came after us?"

Trent settled back into the chair, looking sheepish. "Those creatures that were attacking you," Trent said. "They were a part of an ongoing experiment that the professor had started when he was alive. It was all part of what he called the next level of cinematic achievement—interactive films."

"So you were finding ways to bring things to life using film," I said.

"Yeah," Trent said, "but despite all of the professor's efforts, anything he animated didn't last very long. Whatever he created would disappear back to nothingness after a short time, liquefy. He died before he could find a way to stabilize it."

"Even so, how was he able to do even *that* much?" I asked.

Trent shook his head. "I don't know. The other students didn't really let me in on everything. Said it was because I was new . . ."

"Or maybe they wanted you for something more sinister," I said. "Maybe they needed a little something human to get things stabilized."

"What do you mean?" Trent asked.

"When Elyse cut you, your blood seemed to spark things off," I said.

Trent looked down at his bandage. A little bit of the blood had soaked through to the surface, forming a tiny circle on the top of it. "Don't remind me."

"You said that those manifestations weren't permanent," I continued. "That they'd run out of steam and dissolve away."

Trent nodded. "That seemed to be a very vexing point to Elyse, the professor, and the others," he said.

"You know what I think?" Connor asked, and then pressed on without waiting for an answer from anyone. "I think Mason Redfield found a way to make the manifestations permanent, only he didn't share it with you all. I think he figured out that it would take a full-on blood sacrifice."

"But once he figured it out, he kept quiet and only used it on himself," I said. "Which means that really was him we were fighting the other day."

"Wait," Trent said, leaning forward. "Are you saying the professor's *alive*?"

Connor looked at him, watching his face. "You mean you really don't know?"

The color drained out of Trent's face. "No . . . I mean, we knew he wanted to try and get the whole process to work on humans, but it had never succeeded. When he died, we thought that might be the end of it until Elyse talked us all into continuing on his work. But he's alive?"

"Reborn," I said. "Much younger, too."

"Wow," Trent said, suddenly looking more thrilled than terrified. "Forgive me, but from the practical science aspect of it, it's impressive, isn't it? How did he get it to work?"

Connor gave him a grim smile. "You remember what we said about your blood sparking up those movie creatures earlier?"

"Yeah . . ."

"Have you seen your pal George lately?" Connor asked.

"Oh," Trent said. He sat there in silence as the realization took hold of him.

"So you're saying you didn't know this was Professor Redfield's plan?" I asked.

Trent shook his head. "We were all going to get rich together making films—that's it, as far as I knew. Think about it. If you could take a bank robbing movie and reproduce the contents of a bank vault . . . Well, it wasn't like we were actually hurting anyone, right?"

"I think you're underestimating the power of greed," Connor said. "You know what I think? I think your fellow students had a better idea of what the professor was up to and I think they kept you in the dark. You were getting played, kid."

"But why?" he asked. "Why would they do that?"

"I think the professor taught them something very fundamental about magic," I said.

Trent looked at me, his face searching for understanding in mine. "And what is that?"

"Magic has a price," I said, "and for something like Mason Redfield being reborn, that price is high. You want to achieve the impossible, there's going to be a big price tag on that. This one was written in human blood."

Trent was practically shaking in his seat, his eyes nervous. "I don't want to die," he said.

"We don't want you to die, either," Connor said. "If you help us, we'll do our best to keep that from happening."

Trent nodded, but didn't speak.

"Good," I said. I got up from my desk and stepped out into the aisle outside our work area. "Come with us, then."

Trent stood and followed me, with Connor sticking close behind him. Trent seemed resigned to his fate, but I didn't put it past him to try to make a run for it if we gave him an opportunity to. I headed upstairs, straight for Allorah Daniels's office where Director Wesker was working alongside her. Jane sat exhausted with a ring of empty water glasses in front of her.

"We come bearing gifts," I said. "Yet again."

The three of them turned to look at us, all of them scrutinizing the stranger with us.

"And who is this?" Wesker demanded.

"This," Connor said, slapping the student on the back hard enough to drive him forward, "is Trent. He's our best chance at figuring out what our mad professor was really up to."

"I'm starting to wonder if the water woman killed him so he could be reborn," I said. "He *had* to die to be reborn, right? What kind of deal did Mason Redfield strike with her?"

Trent spotted the coil of film sitting on the laboratory workbench. "May I?" he asked.

Allorah waved him over but gave him a look that was stern warning not to mess with her.

Trent walked over with tentative steps and waited for

her to hand the piece of film over, and then held it up to the light to examine it.

"Recognize it?" I asked.

Trent looked uncertain. "I'm not sure," he said, and then his expression changed. "Wait . . . I *do* know this. I worked on it."

"You did?" I asked.

Trent nodded.

Connor went over to him. "What is it you did for the professor, exactly?"

"I dabble in computers," he said. "Mostly film editing. The professor had asked me to mash up some of these old monster movies with some old footage of him from his early twenties. He said it would help my skills at composite editing once he mastered the magic technique."

"It did more than that," Wesker said. "It helped him come back to life."

Trent handed the film back to Wesker and stepped back. "Sorry," he said. "I didn't know that's what he was planning . . ."

Jane walked over to him and put a hand on his shoulder. Trent flinched.

"What about this?" she asked. She spun around and pulled her hair aside, showing him the tattoo between her shoulder blades in the dip of her tank top. "Can you tell me about this symbol?"

Trent examined it for a moment, but then shook his head. "No," he said. "I'm sorry. I haven't seen that before. What is it?"

"I was hoping you could tell me," Jane said, frowning.

"I think the professor was definitely making a watery new friend outside of those in the film department," Connor suggested.

"We've been poring over the books to try and deal with the professor as much as we have Jane's mark," Allorah said, "but we don't seem to be able to counter the film's magic or destroy it."

"Yet," Wesker added.

"I think I can help you with your film problem," Trent said.

"Let's hope so," Wesker said. "I'd hate to think these Other Division fools spared your life for nothing."

"Way to encourage his cooperation, Director," I said.

Trent ignored us and stepped over to the lab bench. "What do you have in the way of chemicals in your lab?"

Allorah walked him over to a storage cabinet against the wall and threw open the doors. "Help yourself," she said.

Trent scanned the shelves of bottles and powders, and then took one of the bottles. He went back to the bench, grabbed the tub the film was lying in, and filled it with water. He pulled off the top of the bottle, shook it over the whole thing, and then stirred it with a glass rod that was sitting on the workbench. The reaction was instantaneous as the film destabilized and turned to a reddish brown mush in the tub.

"What did you use?" I asked.

Wesker looked a bit angry at the ease with which Trent had dispatched of the film and snatched up the bottle from counter. He spun it around in his hand to read it.

"NaCl," Wesker said, and then threw it down into the sink. "I tried chemicals and acids, not to mention magic, and yet nothing. You just came in here, made salt water, and poof."

"Yep," Trent said, and then shrugged. "I don't know why it works, but it does. We kept trying various experiments with the professor, and when they failed, he had us destroy the footage this way."

"Salt water," Wesker repeated. "So simple."

"Don't beat yourself up too badly, boss," Jane said with encouragement. "Who would have known it would work, right?"

Allorah stood up from her spot at her lab setup. "I should have been able to figure that out," she said. "After all, I have several case samples already that are full of salt water. From Simon's wet coat to the water found in the dead professor's lungs, even."

"And I've certainly been on the receiving end of enough saltwater attacks," I said, "that it's obvious to me that the professor's had a little help in making all his twisted dreams come true."

Jane looked down into the tub, grabbing the sides of it and rocking it. The mush swirled as it broke down even more. "So, what?" she said. "Is that it? Does destroying the film destroy the creations? Is the professor dead?"

She looked to Wesker for an answer, but he waved her off, perturbed. "Don't ask me," he said. "I'm the one who kept failing to destroy the damned thing, remember?"

All eyes turned to Trent. "I'm not sure, either," he said, his voice weak. "The few times we actually succeeded in our test footage, destroying the film took care of whatever we had pulled out of it. But now that he's using blood to sustain it, I don't know. I was never a part of this blood ritual of Professor Redfield's. He kind of raised the bar for crazy on us all, now, didn't he?"

We all stood there in silence for a minute before Jane broke it.

"I could give you some good news if you like," she said.

"We could use some," I said.

"I was able to get a reading off that computer you brought in before it died on me," she said.

"Really?"

"What did it say?" Connor asked.

"It couldn't tell me much," she said, "because it wasn't up and running, but I did get a reading on it as far as the damage it took." She picked up the laptop from the workbench next to her and held it up. "See along here, where it's all crunched in? I could tell at what time the various parts of it stopped working by their last notations before equipment failure. Judging by the size of these marks and what the machine could tell me, I think it was done by something with enormous tentacles. An octopus or something."

"In the East River?" I asked.

"I don't make sense of these things," she said, putting the laptop back down and holding her hands up. "I just report them."

"I'm not attacking you about it," I said. "I'm just surprised. And tired."

"Thing is . . ." she said, "judging by the crush points, I have to say we're looking at a pretty big one at that. Abnormally big."

"I've heard of mutant alligators around New York City," Connor said, "but mutant octopi might be a first."

"Perhaps we will all be better served with a good night's sleep," Allorah said. "I know I've spent too much time on this today with little results. The only plus to it was that now that we're understaffed, I was able to skip out on several Enchancellorship meetings."

"What we need is a way to get ahold of the rest of your fellow students in crime," Connor said to Trent. "We need answers from them."

"I think I know a way to lure them in," Trent said.

"Fine," I said, "but anything we're going to do can wait until morning." I walked over to Jane. She wasn't looking so hot. Whether it was being overworked or the power of the mark draining her, I didn't know, but for once I hoped it was simply the former.

25

The second I got Jane back to my apartment in SoHo, she showered for an eternity, and when she was through she zonked out immediately, but I couldn't sleep. My mind was wrapped up in too many things. Jane's mark was just one in a long list of things bothering me, along with the Inspectre showing signs of his age in the face of dealing with his recently reborn friend. Both those things were out of my control right now, but there was one thing I could help myself with—learning to control my power better. If I was going to absorb downloads of raw emotion from some of my psychometric readings, I needed to learn how to contend with them better.

I went to the built-in bookcase in my living room that took up the greater part of one wall. The backlog of money-making collectibles that I had been nabbing with my powers were starting to take over, not only the shelves but the rest of the room. I *could* work on controlling my powers using them, all the while sorting much of this stuff for return to potential buyers at the same time, but not tonight. I had a feeling that the metal plate I had pulled from the boat-wreck salvage in the lighthouse would be chock-full of all the emotional power I wanted to contend with.

I grabbed a bowlful of Life Savers off one of my end tables and placed it on the floor next to me. I snagged my shoulder bag off the couch, pulled out the piece with *SLO* etched into its rusting form, and pushed my power into it. My one concern was that I might be visited in the vision by Cassie or Mason Redfield as I had back when I started shopping for dressers for Jane, but I had to try. I hoped that slowly coming to terms with hunting down a dresser for Jane, albeit unsuccessfully so far, would help keep it at bay.

The good news was that I didn't feel any panic over the tattooist or Mason Redfield rising up as I entered the psychometric vision. The bad news was that a wave of completely different and instant panic rose over me instead. It was daylight on the river, and whoever's body I occupied was drowning. I felt deep gulps of river water sliding down their throat, filling their lungs. This isn't really me, I thought to myself. I'm not really drowning. Try as I might, the sensations were all too real and I could feel myself giving in to the panic. The person I was flailed their hands and one of them came down on a large piece of floating wood. Their fingers wrapped around it and grabbed on. Using their last bit of strength, they pulled themselves up out of the water onto the sizable piece of wood, coughing up large streams of water and the contents of their stomach.

Now that I had a brief second to catch my breath, I took in what I could. I was male, dressed in clothing styled like those of the turn-of-the-century ghosts out on the Hell Gate Bridge. The board beneath the man bore a full version of the metal plate I held in my hands with the word SLOCUM etched into it. My personal panic started to calm as I slipped into my investigator mind-set, but I could feel that the man was only starting to panic more. I could see why.

Fire and chaos were all around him on this cloudy day. The remains of the *General Slocum* were sinking in large, fiery pieces all around him, the cries of the dying and drowning filling the air. Ships didn't sink this way. I had seen *Titanic* and a few other disaster films. Ships went down as whole objects, maybe even a few pieces. This steamer was *shattered*. Had the woman in green done this? I didn't see her in any of the surrounding chaos, and frankly, I wasn't sure she even had this kind of power over water.

As I sat on the board, holding on for dear life, I got my answer. The surface of the water broke before me and the roll of something gray and slimy passed by until one end of it poked up. A tentacle. It belonged to something *huge*. It rose up out of the water several stories before crashing back down on one of the large pieces of ship that was still floating, tearing it in half.

The man didn't have time to take it all in. Another tentacle rose and wrapped around the floating piece of wood he was on. It tugged it under the surface, dragging him down. This time he was lucky enough to have gotten a deep breath in, but his luck was about to run out. I felt a crushing sensation against his spine from the tightening of the tentacle, and as he went deeper a shape rose up to meet him. Even with daylight up above, it was hard seeing through his eyes in the murk of water, mud, and blood, but one thing stood out as his breath left him and he began to fade. *An enormous yellow eye.*

I never wanted to be stuck in someone's death. I had no idea what effect it might have on my brain or if it would be like needing to wake up while falling in a dream. I pulled myself out of my vision and checked my vitals. My heartbeat was steady, but not thumping in my chest, which was a good sign. The hypoglycemia from using my powers kicked in, but that was to be expected. I still felt a little bit of emotional strain of the victim in my head that I couldn't shake, but I was thankful it didn't belong to any of the other people who had been haunting my visions. When Jane's hand came down on my shoulder out of nowhere, I nearly screamed.

"Got a sec?" she asked. "I couldn't sleep."

I closed my eyes and tried to shake the psychometry-generated emotions off of me, but managed only to make myself dizzy on top of slightly disoriented. "Actually, can it wait?" I asked, trying to control the fear and anxiety in my voice. "I'm kind of in the middle of something here."

"Oh," Jane said. I looked up from the broken piece in my lap. Jane's face was a mix of disappointment and sadness.

I slid the piece of the sign off my lap and got up off the floor. "It can wait," I said, pushing down the remaining raw emotions. I grabbed Jane by the hand and walked with her over to my sofa. "What's wrong?"

"When you started with the Department, did they put you through Undead 103?"

"103," I repeated as I tried to recall it. "Oh yeah. Shamble On?"

Jane nodded. "That's the one," she said. "A lot of zombie-fighting techniques and the philosophical aspects of confronting them. How did it make you feel when you took it?"

"I don't know," I said. "I was so overwhelmed that it kind of blurred into everything else I was learning at the time. Wesker may have just thrown the pamphlet at me and left it at that. Why?"

Jane sighed. "We were going over what to do in the event that one is bitten by the living dead. Wesker suggested that there was only one thing to do in such a case, only one inevitable conclusion. Kill them."

"Leave it to Wesker to take it as dark as he can right out of the gate," I said.

"But he's right, isn't he?"

"I try not to think about it," I said. "I take a more optimistic approach to our jobs than that."

"How so?"

"I do my best not to get bitten in the first place," I said.

"Seems to be working so far," Jane admitted with a small smile. "Still, don't you worry about dying?"

"I didn't *use* to," I said, "but lately? Yeah. Mostly because of the Inspectre. He's looking and acting *old*, more so since Mason Redfield came back all rejuvenated." Jane nodded, but didn't say anything. "Have I been acting more morose than usual because of it? If so, I'm sorry."

"No," she said, quick to correct me. "It's not that."

"What, then?"

She squeezed my hands, meeting my eyes with dead seriousness. "It's just that . . . with this mark on my back, I can feel myself changing. You saw how useless I became on that boat the other night. I can feel it trying to gain control over me. I don't want it to come to that."

I didn't like where this was going. "What are you suggesting?"

"You saw how they protected me," she said. "Those water zombies. They're waiting for me to change. I'm slowly falling under *her* spell."

"So, we'll fight it," I said, and then added, "Together."

"For how long?" Jane asked. Tears began running down her cheeks. "Wesker's not having any luck breaking that woman's hold on me. The magic is too old, too strong. He's been able to slow it with a few counterspells, but we're fighting inevitability here."

"I won't let that happen," I said. "I promise that. We'll find a way."

"Promise me something else," she said. "Please."

"Name it."

"If I become like her . . . or worse, I want you to kill me."

The air went out of my lungs and my heart sped up. "Don't ask me for that," I said. "I can't promise that."

Jane looked angry. "Why not?" she asked. "Don't you love me?"

I wanted to shake her. "That's precisely why you can't ask me to do that to you," I said. "How can you expect me to strike you down?"

"Listen to me," she said, grabbing my face and pressing her forehead against mine. "If it actually comes to that, I won't *be* me anymore. That's the point."

"I'm the glass-half-full kinda guy, Jane. You can't ask me to do that."

"Fine," she said, agitated. She stood up and turned to walk away but I grabbed her arm.

"Jane, don't."

She turned back to me, crying. "What do you want me to do, Simon? Do you want me to end up killing you? Because that's what she'll want me to do. I can already feel it."

"You can?"

"Yes! For days now."

The emotional panic of my vision mixed with my own frustration. "Why are you only telling me now?" I snapped.

Jane softened. "Because I thought if I told you, you'd

want me around here less. I mean, what guy wants a homicidal girlfriend, right?"

"I . . ." I couldn't find the words, which only frustrated me further. "I don't know what you want me to say, Jane. I mean, I've dated girls with far more homicidal tendencies than you."

"Really?" she said, cheering up a little.

"Really," I said, calming down. I could do this. I could separate my emotions from the feedback loop of my psychometry. "You wouldn't be the first. If I had a dime for every time a woman wanted me dead, well . . . I don't think I can count that high, frankly."

She smiled at that. "Just promise me you'll think about the bigger picture if I . . . *change*," she said.

"I will," I said. "I'll think about the bigger picture, but that doesn't necessarily mean I'm going to kill you if it comes to it. It just means I'll come up with something."

"Ever the optimist," she said and hugged me.

She wrapped her arms tight around me, and despite the fact that it felt good, it took all of my nerves right then to fight off the unbidden image rising up of her crushing me until I was lifeless in her arms.

26

I had walked through the theater at the back of the Love-craft Café countless times by this point, but it was rare these days to actually stay in it longer than it took me to get down the aisle and key into the hidden door that led to the Department of Extraordinary Affairs. Several days later, however, I found myself sitting in one of the theater seats, taking in the newly cleaned-up, zombie-free beauty of the place. Gilded fleur-de-lis decorated the walls and an ornate old-world chandelier hung high above. It was really quite beautiful now that I had stopped to take it all in, more so than I had in the past. Jane sat on my left, wrapped up in the ending of *Fright Night*, while Trent looked around nervously sitting on my right.

"So, this was your genius idea?" I asked him. "Hanging out, watching movies? Great master plan, Trent."

"Hey," he said. "At least you're getting paid. I'm not even getting a snack or anything out of this."

"Funny," I said. "I thought payment enough for you would be not sitting in a holding cell."

"I'm the victim here," he said earnestly. "I told you. I had no idea that what they were up to was so sinister."

"We'll see," I said. "Depending on how helpful this is, it may go a long way to getting you back to school instead of prison."

"Shush," Jane said, not looking away from the movie.

I lowered my voice and leaned in toward Trent. "You sure they'll come?"

He nodded. "Oh, they'll come, all right," he said. "Trust me. They won't be able to resist the movie lineup I've put the word out about. A horror film festival? It's going to be impossible for them to pass up."

Connor sat several rows in front of us and turned to look back at me. "How do we know they've even heard about it?"

"We put up ads everywhere," I said. "Online, even on campus. In the old days I would have gotten a Shadower team to do it, but in the spirit of economy the Inspectre hung every flyer up himself. Jane even chipped in, in her own way. She told the computers to help spread the news of the film festival."

"Really?" Connor asked, a fixed look of skepticism on his face.

I shrugged. "Something like that," I said. "I'm out of my element there. You'll have to ask the technomancer."

The credits were rolling now and Jane was finally able to take her attention away from the screen. She nodded. "It was easy peasy," she said. "Even without my power, I could have done it."

"Awesome," Trent said, agitated. "Can I at least get a popcorn or something?" He leaned forward, looking over at Jane. "Is he a cheap date? He is, isn't he?"

"Don't get fresh," I said, pushing him back into his seat. "I'm not going to get you a popcorn. This isn't a date."

Trent looked at me, horrified. "You're so not my type."

"What?" I asked him. "Not evil enough for you?"

"That's not what I meant," he said. "Just the wrong set of chromosomes. Sorry." He turned and looked off into the darkened theater. "What if they notice me?"

"Don't worry," I said. "We've got the situation under control."

"Oh," he said, nodding. "Like when you tried to capture them last time? No offense, Mr. Canderous, but I take very little comfort in that."

"No," I said. "This time we'll get them. Your friends know more about the reborn professor than they let on about, maybe even the water woman. Look at it this way—at least you're not tied up this time. That's an improvement for you already."

Trent looked around the half-full theater. "What about the rest of these people?" he asked.

"We shut down the theater for the day," I said, "and filled it with any available agent we could spare."

"It's far emptier than I'd like it to be right now," Jane said.

"Elyse is so going to catch on to this plan," Trent said. "She's going to sniff them out before they even sit down. She's smart like that."

"Don't worry about your old friends," I said. "Right now, you should be more worried about all of us in here."

"Great," he said, but sounded unconvinced.

"Fine. If you want to worry about something, worry about your pals not showing up. If they don't, there's going to be trouble for you."

"I'm with Simon on this one," Jane said. "I don't think

they're going to show. Why would they come out for this at all when they can just watch them on television?"

"It's not quite the same," Trent said.

"Exactly," Connor said from a few rows ahead of us. "Movies were meant for the big screen . . ."

I shushed him as the coffeehouse curtain opened and Trent's three friends walked in. Jane, Trent, and I sank lower into our seats, doing our best to keep unnoticed, hopefully so we could get the drop on them once they settled in.

The three students were still in the clothes they had escaped in the other day. Elyse wore her hair pulled back in a short ponytail, but Mike and Darryl both looked like they hadn't showered. I could have been wrong, though. Maybe bedhead was all the rage at NYU right now. Mike looked like he was trying to pick the best seat in the house, which made sense considering the fact that he was always carrying a camera on him and probably planned to bootleg the film. He found what he considered to be at least a passable viewing spot, and then started into the row before Elyse and Darryl did. "Hurry," he whispered. "The credits are already rolling."

"So what?" Darryl asked, ducking down as they worked their way across the aisle.

"It's the best part!" Mike said, practically spilling his drink as he tripped over something.

"Shh!" Elyse said, and sat down once Mike stopped.

As they finished settling in, the new film began and the screen filled with a shot of a graveyard. It reminded me of *Good Mourning: How to Tell a Funeral Party from a Zombie Horde*, the short training film I had been shown during my initiation into the Department.

Jane grabbed my arm. I turned to her. She looked worried. "This film is clean, right?" she asked. "I don't want to have a repeat of Mason Redfield's resurrection."

"Looks like we're going to find out, I guess," I said.

Trent leaned forward in his seat, staring ahead at his old friends. "I don't believe it," Trent whispered. "Is Mike . . . *bootlegging* this?"

"Oh," I whispered, "is that where you draw your criminal line now?"

"Stop bickering and get ready," Jane said, standing up. Connor was already up, right behind the group of them, and had his hands on the back of Elyse's seat.

"On behalf of this theater's management," Connor said with some volume behind it, "you're under arrest . . . mostly for being dicks and attacking us the other day."

"Shit," I heard Elyse hiss out. The three students jumped up out of their seats, but Connor grabbed Elyse with both hands. Mike climbed over the seat in front of him. It was like watching a blubbery baby trying to escape its crib and would have been comical if not for the fact that he actually *was* getting away. Darryl turned toward Connor and swung for him, bringing his arm down across both of Connor's. His grip on Elyse broke and the girl pulled away, crouching forward.

Using the agility I had witnessed during her last escape, she pressed herself into a handstand on the seat in front of her, knocking Connor back over the seat behind him as her legs swung up.

"Stay here, Trent," I said. I stood and pulled out my bat, extending it. "Try not to get stabbed this time."

"Yeah, sure," he said. The young student looked stunned by the chaos erupting all around him and stayed in his seat.

I ran down our row after Jane until I hit the aisle, then started down toward the fight in front of me.

Mike had made his way to the front of the theater now, gracelessly but effectively. Elyse continued walking on her hands along the tops of the seats after him. She flipped off the last one when she hit the front row and stuck her landing like a pro before running to join Mike. I ran after her as Darryl ran down his row toward the aisle leading up to the coffeehouse.

"Heavy Mike," Darryl shouted. "Memory card . . . now!"

Several agents were trying to subdue Elyse and Mike, but they were pulling their punches since they were dealing with humans for once. Elyse was a scrapper and gave them as good as she got, her gymnastic flourishes holding them, along with a knife she now held in her hand. Mike was doing his best to push off any of the attackers who got past her, all while holding his camera over his head and out of reach. He popped open a slot on the back of it, pulled the memory card free, and flung it across the theater, aiming high. Darryl, tall as he was, had no trouble plucking it from its trajectory while he reached down with his other hand into his front pocket. He fumbled out his smartphone. The glow of its display along with the film playing gave him enough light to slot the card. He slammed it into his phone and held it straight out in front of him while he backed up the aisle.

Several short movie clips flashed onto the phone's screen—scenes of Central Park and several different shots of subway stations. With each bit of film, the screen gave an audible *pop* and *crackle*, producing a steady stream of creatures into our world. Birds from the park and shots of rats on the subway tracks. The aisle started to fill with them, adding to the chaos all around us.

"That works," Darryl said, examining his work, "but I meant the *other* card."

"I already gave it to you!" Mike shouted.

"Oh, right," Darryl said with an embarrassed shrug. He popped his memory card out of the phone while he fished around in his pocket for the other one. It came out in his hand and he slammed it in the phone. Darryl pressed on the keypad, then, backing away, held the phone out in front of him. I stepped back, waiting for whatever monstrosity they threw at me next.

Nothing happened.

"Crap," Darryl said. He reversed direction, heading back down the aisle and making his way over toward Elyse and Mike at the front of the theater. "Elyse! We're out of juice!"

Elyse looked panicked and her face sank, but only for a moment. She adjusted her grip on the knife in her hand before swinging it around in a wide arc.

It stabbed into the wall of the theater, but not before passing through Heavy Mike's hand, pinning it there. His video camera tumbled to the floor of the theater and shattered to pieces as a howl of pain erupted from Mike. "Elyse!" he shouted in a mix of surprise, shock, and anger.

"Sorry, Mikey," she said. She grabbed Darryl as he pushed his way through the crowd over to where Mike was pinned. Blood was already running thick down the pinned student's arm. Darryl shoved his phone into the stream and a flair of energy sparked from it. A scene flickered on the screen. It was footage of me from the other night when I had come across the students saying their good-byes to the professor at Eccentric Circles. Something looked different about me, but I couldn't put my finger on it. I leaned in closer to the tiny image, avoiding Elyse's kicks with my bat.

"Do I have a *goatee*?" I asked, caught off guard by what I was seeing.

"Computer-enhanced," Elyse said. "Actually, I think it helps hide your weak chin."

Something in my mind snapped and I reared back with my bat. "I do not have a weak chin," I said and swung for her.

A loud crack rang out, accompanied by a blinding flash in front of me, and my bat hit something solid, although it wasn't Elyse. The young actress/gymnast/killer was standing at least five feet away now. My bat had connected with another figure wearing a leather coat identical to mine.

"That wasn't nice," a familiar voice said to me. It was my own. Standing in front of me was another version of me, complete with its phony goatee.

"How 'Mirror, Mirror' of you," I said, looking past him at Elyse. "But I don't get it. How can I be reborn when I'm not dead like the professor was?"

Elyse laughed. "We're pioneers in our industry. He's just a cheap carbon copy. Death isn't a requirement to summon a quick you on the fly to kick your own ass. Just blood."

The other Simon punched me in the arm. "Stop hitting yourself," he said.

"Okay," I said, focusing back on him. "This is . . ."

"Weird," Doppel-Me finished. He pulled out his own bat and extended it. "I know, right?"

"This is going to hurt me more than it's . . . You know what? I think this is going to hurt me just as much as it is you."

"Yeah," he said. "Right."

I swung my bat, going for his knee, but he came around with his bat and blocked it.

"You think you're going to get one over on me?" he asked. "Think again."

"Don't think this is going to be an issue," I said. "I've had years of experience beating myself up."

I swung low, but Doppel-Me jumped high. When I lunged for him, he feinted back perfectly, avoiding the blow or countering it. If I faked left, he faked right, countering my every move.

It was no use. Other than the shoddy goatee, this Simon fought like I fought. I couldn't get an advantage over him no matter how hard I tried.

"Give up," I said.

"*You* give up," Doppel-Me repeated. "I can do this all night."

I shook my head. "No, you can't," I said. "You'll eventually come apart at the seams like all these other playthings."

"Actually, he won't," Darryl shouted out from somewhere behind me. "Like Elyse said, we're pioneers. He's got a better shelf life."

"Well, crap," I said. "Not the answer I wanted to hear. I guess we *both* can do this all night, then."

The other me craned his head and I knew what he was looking for.

"Uh-uh," I said. "There's no way I'm letting you up the aisle and out through those curtains. You'd have to go through me to get out of here and I'm not going to let that happen."

Doppel-Me backed away down the aisle, heading toward the door leading into the offices. Of course! I knew the only other way out was through the creepier parts of the catacombs in the far recesses the Gauntlet, and that meant he probably knew it, too. If he made it down there, I'd never catch up to him in all its twists and turns.

In the hall behind him, something stirred in the darkness.

"I do have something you don't have, you know," I said, pressing toward Doppel-Me.

"Me, too. I've got this stylin' goatee that *you* don't have. What have *you* got?"

The shadow in the hallway moved even closer to my doppelganger.

"Friends," I said, and charged him. With one of my fellow agents behind him, I'd be on the dark version of myself in no time, clashing bat to bat.

Evil Simon spun around to run for the door back to the Department, but stopped in his tracks when he saw his way blocked. Two hands flashed out of the darkness, grabbed the sides of his head, and twisted . . . hard. The audible *pop* of bone and cartilage drove into my ears like daggers. A second later, the other me dropped to the floor, lifeless.

Out of the darkness stepped Thaddeus Wesker. He looked down at the body, and then up at me. He seemed disappointed. "I wouldn't exactly say we were *friends*," he said.

I couldn't stop staring at myself lying there, unmoving. "Holy Hell!" I shouted over the dying sounds of combat all around us. Jane and the Inspectre held Elyse at bay at cane point and Connor had Darryl by the scruff of his hoodie. Most of the birds and rats had been dealt with or were already dissolving on their own. I walked over to Wesker, mindful not to step on prone, dead me. Wesker looked at me with an evil grin.

"That," he said, taking the time to relish each word, "felt good."

"That's disturbing," I said, freaking out at the dead look in my double's eyes. "You did know that was a doppelganger of me, didn't you?"

Wesker shrugged.

"What if that had been the real me?" I asked.

He walked past me. "I guess we'll never know," he said,

heading up the aisle. "I was going to the café to see what they had for fresh pastry. Getting to kill you was just the bonus cherry in my Danish."

Elyse, Darryl, and Heavy Mike—still pinned through his hand to the wall—all started yelling at one another while various members of the Department fought to contain them.

"Everybody, shut *up*!" a voice called out. The room went silent. Trent had come out of hiding from behind his seat. When Elyse saw him, her eyes bugged out.

"Hey, pal," she said, turning on her charm. "How *are* you? Glad to see you made it out of that fracas at the university alive."

Trent came out of his row, walked down the aisle toward Elyse, and shoved her. "No thanks to *you*."

"Hey!" Darryl called out from between the two Shadowers who were holding him. "Keep your hands off her."

"Or what?" Trent exploded. "She'll tie me up again? She'll bleed me out to power your messed-up little project? You might want to listen to these people. They've got some news, and as far as I can tell, it's true. The professor's not dead. He's alive and wandering this city."

Elyse's eyes widened, but there was too long a hesitation before it. "It worked?" Elyse said. "The professor's alive?"

Despite the look on her face, I wasn't buying it. "You're going to need more acting training if you want your surprise to sound more convincing. Knock it off."

"What is that?" Darryl said, puffing up. "A threat?"

"My boy," the Inspectre said, walking up to him. Darryl backed away from him as best he could, but the agents holding him didn't give him much room to move. The Inspectre looked winded from the fight, but there was anger in his voice. "There is a threat, but it is the one that Mason

Redfield himself proposes. His pact for his youth, yes, but I fear it is a debt that will need constant repayment."

Elyse's face finally went serious. "More blood," she said.

"Ours," Trent said.

"Precisely," the Inspectre said. He pulled his sword from its cane once again and started toward her. "I'm sorry, but I believe we are past the point of all civility. Now, why don't you tell me all about this woman in green?"

Elyse stared at him. Her cocky toughness was gone. The girl was scared. Not only was she scared; her eyes were blank.

"What woman?" she asked.

The Inspectre searched her face for a moment before lowering his sword. "Bloody hell," he said. "She doesn't know."

27

Given our need to avoid questions from Thaddeus Wesker, Connor and I dragged our four captives out of the theater on the basis that interrogation always went better when there was less slime to slip around in. Cramped for space and coverage, the two of us were forced to bring the professor's students up to Allorah Daniels's office, with Jane and the Inspectre bringing up the rear, barring any chance of their escaping. When Elyse saw our offices behind the theater, she walked through it all, looking around like a tourist in Times Square.

"What is this place?" she asked. "Are you police?"

I pointed over to a bunch of chairs along one wall. "Consider this your home until we get some answers," I said. "Sit!"

"What are you holding us on?" she said, taking her time sitting down, prim and proper. Darryl sat down next to her, but Heavy Mike sat two chairs away holding his injured hand. Trent remained standing.

"Okay, forget about tonight," I said. "Forget about making me watch one of my least favorite people around here—Director Wesker—take a perverse joy in killing that evil goateed version of me. Let's put that aside for now. Answer me this: Where's your blond friend George?"

The blank look disappeared from Elyse's face. Concern spread across it. "I have no idea," she said. "I think he said he was heading out of town for a few days. I think he said it was his sister's *quinceañera*."

I knelt down in front of her, staring her straight in the face. "You're lying," I said.

"Am I?" she said with a grim smile.

I nodded.

"He used to be a thief," Jane said. "He knows what lying is."

"You're a good actress, Elyse," I said, "but you're not that good."

I walked away from her, went to the workbench, and grabbed George's messenger bag off of it.

"I don't think George is going to turn up anytime soon," I said, walking back over to her. I flipped open the bag's flap and pulled out the crushed remains of his laptop. "See this? See the bend in the middle, the shattered pieces flaking off of it? I have a feeling that your friend's body probably ended up in worse shape than that. And I think you probably knew that George was dead, didn't you?"

Elyse went green at the gills. Darryl did, too, a grayness overtaking his dark skin.

"Yes," she said, letting out a long breath. "And it's my fault." She looked scared for a change, and for once, I was pretty sure she wasn't acting. "I didn't think the professor's plan had worked until a few days ago. When we first took up with him, we knew he had spent years trying to get his magical process to work, but we thought it was only to further his cinematic frustrations with a lack of real fear that he felt was missing from the horror genre. I suspected there might be something more to it, but wasn't sure what. When he 'died' suddenly, I started poring through his notes and at the same time I also discovered instructions he had left me on what he wanted done after his death. I was supposed to go to this lighthouse he mentioned out on Wards Island and play his final film there. He said it was already loaded into the projector and everything, but when I got to the lighthouse, it wasn't there."

"Guess who got there first?" I asked.

"So how does this end up with you trying to kill me?" Trent asked, incredulous. "Why?"

Elyse sighed, dropping her eyes to the floor. "I woke up the other night to discover the professor in my dorm room . . . young again and looking crazed. His notes had hinted at cheating death, but how could he be alive *and* so young? Darryl was with me. He saw the professor, too."

Darryl nodded.

"Did he say what he wanted?" the Inspectre asked.

"The professor confirmed that the magic could work," he said. "He was living proof, but he said that it came with a price none of us had counted on. He came looking for blood."

"Let me guess," I said. "Yours?"

"That's what we thought," she said, "but no. He said I was his favorite. He said he'd spare me."

"*Us,*" Darryl amended. "He said he'd spare us."

"So you offered him someone," I said. "Someone expendable. A freshman."

"George," Trent said, his face turning horrified as he spoke his dead friend's name. "You gave him George."

"I know underclassmen barely earn a blip on your radar," I said, "but this is beyond the beyond."

The shame on Elyse's face was evident. Her brow grew thick with wrinkles as she broke into hysterical sobs. "I'm sorry," she said between gasps of breath. "What do you want from me? He would have killed us instead!"

"I thought you said you were his favorite," Jane reminded her.

"It wouldn't matter," she said. "He was out for blood and if I didn't send unsuspecting George off to him, the professor would have killed us."

I stood there, shaking my head at her. "Don't schools these days offer at least one course on ethics?" I asked.

"I'm afraid an ethical debate would be wasted on this young lady," the Inspectre said, stepping over to the table. Elyse looked up at him. "Why? Why would you do this?"

None of us understood it, but I think it perplexed the Inspectre even more. He sounded as angry as he was confused.

"Have you seen how many of me there are at New York University?" she shouted. "Never mind the cost. All my little Stepford sister actresses are graduated and up to their implants in debt, and the best that any one of them could land was a tampon commercial!"

"So that's how you justify all this?" I asked. "So you could do more than commercial work?"

"Think about what we're talking about here," she said. "Professor Redfield's initial vision was revolutionary! Sure, he was using magic to try and bring it about, but it was only over time that he even hinted that there might be some darker purpose at work. And as far as my career, well . . . to be the first actress ever to appear in this type of film? We were taking reality to a whole new level."

"Congratulations," Connor said. "You've landed yourself on a hit TV show: *America's Most Wanted.*"

"Quiet," the Inspectre said. He leaned over the table. "I couldn't care less for your vanity, young lady. I want to know why Mason Redfield—a man I considered my brother in arms at one time—why would he do all this?"

Elyse fell silent, letting her head drop. After a while, she looked up. "That, I don't know," she said, her voice barely a whisper.

"Me, either," the Inspectre said. He stepped away from the table, disgusted.

Elyse looked up at me. "Sorry we tried to kill you," she said, "with . . . well, you."

"I bet," I said. "I was the last me standing, but don't worry—I'll still have the nightmares for years to come to remember it by."

Darryl had his arm around her. His toughness had left him and he looked to the Inspectre. "So, what happens now?" Darryl asked.

The Inspectre walked over to the couple, staring down at them. "Well, that depends on how cooperative you choose to be."

Elyse started nodding, eagerness in her eyes. "We can be cooperative," she said. "Like I mentioned, there are notes and film footage, computer files . . . You've seen what we can accomplish without a blood sacrifice . . ."

"And *with* a blood sacrifice, too," Trent spat out at them, pointing to the spot on his side where Elyse had cut him and released Professor Redfield's army of tiny office monsters.

"First things first," the Inspectre said, stopping Trent with a reassuring hand on the boy's shoulder. "This process that Mason put himself through . . . can it be reversed?"

Elyse's face sank. "I don't think so," she said. She turned to her partner in crime. "Darryl?"

He shook his head. "No," he said. "We hadn't even got the process working in the first place. There wasn't even a chance to figure out how to, umm, verse it let alone *re*verse it."

"I'm confused," Connor said.

"You're not the only one," I added.

Connor shot me a look that shut me up. "We've seen the professor in his current state. Young, agile, in shape . . . Why would he need you to kill anyone for him? Why not just do it himself? Why kill one of you, his loyal students?"

"I don't know," Elyse said, falling silent as she sat there, dejected.

"I think I do," Trent said. "When you found me tied up on the floor, well . . . it wasn't the first time we had tried to use blood that day."

"Oh, really?" I asked.

"Ask Elyse," Trent said.

I turned back to the young actress. The girl looked guilty. "After we were visited by the professor and . . . sent George off to him, I thought maybe we might be able to use blood for our own gain, too. I thought if we could harness the power of a blood sacrifice somehow, maybe we could use it to our advantage. So I told Trent we wanted a little. He even agreed to it."

I looked over at Trent and he looked down at the floor. "What do I know?" he said with defense in his words. "I'm a freshman. I thought it was a hazing ritual!"

"Problem was, the ritual worked, but just barely," she said. "We could animate certain objects or pieces from tiny bits of film, but they didn't last very long before they quickly ran out of juice."

"So you decided you needed more juice," Jane said. "More blood."

"That still doesn't answer my original question, though," Connor said. "Why use his own people? Why did he use George like that?"

"The professor always talked about the power of betrayal in film class," Elyse said. "To him, it was such a classical theme—betrayal, revenge. I think he saw a real and twisted power in it."

"Betraying his own followers would give their blood more power," the Inspectre said. "Enough, perhaps, to complete his transformation for good."

"Growing his strength, prolonging his stolen life with it," I added. "One of you better be prepared to help us figure this out. It's not just Professor Redfield I want to take down. For instance: you acted like you didn't know about the water woman earlier, the same way you acted like you didn't know the professor was alive. That's my girlfriend who's suffering from that woman's mark. Now, give up some details on her."

"Tell us what you know about that woman," Jane said, her eyes showing her desperation for answers. "Please."

"Like I said before, what woman?" Elyse repeated. "What mark?"

"The green woman," I said. "Stop acting like you don't know."

"I don't," she said, panic on her face.

"Neither of us knows about her," Darryl said.

"Bull," Connor said.

Elyse looked defeated and shrugged. "Fine. Don't believe me."

The thing was, I *did* believe her. I mean, if you were going to cop to almost murdering one friend and handing the other to a recently rejuvenated madman, why lie about not knowing the watery she-bitch?

I stormed away in frustration, heading for the door.

"I think Mason Redfield may have found allies to help him in his rebirth, doing what he and his students couldn't," I said. "We don't know what kind of dark bargain the professor made with that water woman, but I aim to find out."

"Where are you going?" Jane asked.

"To find someone who might actually have some answers for me."

28

I left the rest of the group to deal with locking up the students. I needed a break from the interrogation and I had a few things that still needed checking out with Godfrey Candella, and just as I put my handle on the door leading down to the archives, the man himself sent me a text saying he had some information to share.

Every visit down to the Gauntlet was a new adventure in creepiness, especially when it was dead silent and I found an exhausted Godfrey asleep with his eyes open at his desk, his head propped up on a now-drool-covered stack of books and his cell phone flipped open on the desk. I shook him awake and he sat bolt upright in his chair, startled. When he noticed it was only me, however, he relaxed.

"Wow," Godfrey said. "That was quick."

"I was on my way down, actually," I said.

"Oh," he said. "So, any luck with Director Wesker or Ms. Daniels?"

"Not yet," I said. "We're questioning some of Professor Redfield's students, and even though they were in on his magic, they're maintaining that they know nothing about the woman in green we keep seeing." I paused for a moment, my mind switching gears. "Let me ask you something that's been troubling me the past few days. Do you think you'd be able to take down a loved one if they were transformed into something horrible?"

Godfrey tidied up several of the files and books on his desk as he thought about it. "I don't know," he said. "I suppose I'm grateful that I don't work in the field and will hopefully never have to answer that. On a good day, I only deal in theoretical dilemmas or recording those of other people."

"I'm just asking your opinion."

Godfrey sighed and put down his books. "Fine," he said. "In that case, I'd probably die first. I wouldn't be able to do it. I'd hesitate and that would be my undoing, but don't worry, Simon. That won't happen to you."

"It won't?" I asked. "Why not?"

"Because that's not who you are," he said. "You save people, and that includes yourself as well. It's why you're out there and I'm down here."

Godfrey was probably right. The reason I obsessed over every little thing was my near-constant need these days to be helping others. My issues with Jane, the dresser, and the apartment were only a reflection against that, my last safe haven where I didn't have to defend the world, my Fortress of Solitude. My emotional psychometric outbursts were only an extension of my raw feelings about not wanting to share that, but if I was honest with myself, it wasn't that I didn't want Jane to move in. Hell, she wasn't even asking to. I was simply scared because it would ultimately be the final wall to giving myself over to someone completely. The realization alone was enough to ease some of my tension, and I switched my focus back to the case.

"Have you had any luck tracking down that symbol on Jane's back yet?"

Godfrey nodded. "I came across that marking in some of the older books of New York history. It seems that the older generations of Greek fishermen and sailors carved it into their boats. They believed it would give them good water for safe sailing. It put them under protection from the sea."

"Or something in it," I said. "But what does it symbolize?"

"At first, I thought it might be the symbol for Castalia," he said. "A fairly common figure in Greek mythology, the nymph of poetry."

"What the hell is remotely poetic about this she-bitch who's constantly trying to drown me or turn my girlfriend into something I'll need a fish tank to hold?"

"That's just it," Godfrey said. "Castalia didn't seem like the right fit to me, either. So I kept looking, checking variants of all water-based symbology. It turns out that the mark is used to summon forth a host, a vessel, for the water spirit to inhabit."

"Then that she-bitch *has* been building up her power over Jane," I said, "exerting it to take control of my girlfriend. So, what is it? Who is it a symbol of?"

"Are you familiar with the Police?" Godfrey asked.

"The band?" I asked. "Or the serve-and-protect kind?"

"The band," he said.

"Yes, but do you really think this is the time for a music lesson?"

"In this case, yes," he said. "I don't care much for

modern music personally, but I do try to associate my-self with cultural works that touch on anything mythos-related. When it comes to references, the works of Sting are unparalleled."

"Okay," I said. "So, what song are we talking about here?"

"'Wrapped Around Your Finger,'" he said. "The lyric is, 'You consider me the young apprentice, caught between the Scylla and Charybdis.'"

"Okay, I'll bite," I said. "What the hell are those?"

"I think your woman in green may be Charybdis," God-frey said. "A daughter of Poseidon. A naiad, technically."

"Those are a type of water nymph, right?" I asked.

Godfrey nodded. "Very good," he said.

"Thanks," I said. "Good to see that my time studying *Know Your Unknown* wasn't completely wasted on me. But I thought nymphs were supposed to be sexy. This Charyb-dis is more deadly than sexy."

"I'm sure she started that way," Godfrey said, "but if you—excuse the language—piss off the gods, they tend to exact a punishment."

"Punishment?"

"According to Homer, she stole from Hermes. For her crime, she was turned into a monster of the sea. Another story says she was transformed because she did so much damage on land in the name of her father, Poseidon, that Zeus became irate with her and exacted it as punishment on her. There are several versions of the tale, but any way you look at it, she's marked as a monster of the sea. Part of the description for Charybdis in one of her forms is a giant mouth that takes in vast quantities of water, creating whirlpools."

"Like the ones that have claimed all those boats over the years at Hell Gate," I said.

"Exactly," he said.

"What about the other one you named?" I asked. "What was it called again?"

"Scylla," Godfrey said. "That comes from another tale, but Scylla was also a nymph that the sea god fisherman named Glaucus fell in love with. Apparently, she wouldn't give him the time of day, so he turned to the sorceress Circe, asking her for a love potion. She, however, fell for the fisherman herself, but he spurned her advances, causing her to take vengeance on the object of his desire—Scylla. Using poison, she transformed Scylla into a sea monster that is described differently than Charybdis—twelve legs like tentacles and a ring of snapping dog heads around her waist."

"Tentacles," I said. "That fits what I saw in my vision of when the *General Slocum* went down. That much makes sense, as do the crush marks on one of the student's laptops we found at the bottom of a well leading out to the river."

Godfrey nodded. "Supposedly, these two creatures were the guardians of the Strait of Messina, situated between Sicily and Italy. They still call one of the rocky outcroppings there Scylla. Scholars believe it may well be where the expression 'between a rock and a hard place' comes from."

Despite the hard time my mind was having wrapping around the tale, the last details brought more pressing questions to mind. "Italy? Then what the hell are they doing here in New York?"

"I'm not sure," he said, "but the Greek people are prevalent in America. Why not their gods, too?"

"No offense," I said, "but I'm not sure I buy into this whole pantheistic worldview. I mean, if we're going to go there, let's just call in Thor to take care of it and call it a day, right?"

"He's Norse, not Greek," Godfrey corrected.

"Fine, whatever, but you see where I'm going."

Godfrey sighed. "I hear you," he said. "Look. I don't know if I believe in gods and goddesses the way the Greeks did, either, but I *do* think that much of what they chose to believe in came from things that already existed in the world, something they then interpreted to fit their own worldview. For instance, it's quite likely that supernatural creatures such as sea monsters may well predate the Greeks, but we see them as Greek mythological figures because that's what the Greeks chose to name them. That's what stuck in people's minds."

"Well, we've seen plenty of Charybdis in her female form," I said. "I wonder what's become of Scylla, other than knowing the professor fed it the still-conscious remains of George. Why he's feeding it, I have no idea. Maybe so it grows up big and strong."

Godfrey flipped open one of his books to a page he had marked off with a Post-it. "I think I may have an answer for that," he said. "Remember how I told you that the U.S. Army Corps of Engineers had been blasting away at the strait back in the mid–eighteen hundreds? I think that blasting may have hurt both of the monsters over a century and a half ago, incapacitated them. Charybdis seems to have risen back to some of her power, possibly because she can take aquatic form. I'm not sure. I think Scylla is still mostly dormant. Charybdis is its keeper. Its nurse, in this case."

"Not for much longer, I suspect," I said. "I think Charybdis recovered because Mason Redfield discovered her while investigating the Hell Gate Bridge. In return for his help providing sacrificed students like George to her monstrous companion, she gave him secrets to help him be reborn. I've seen the watery pit where he's been feeding students to something out in the river. A something named Scylla. I imagine that sea monster is probably growing up big and strong."

Godfrey shook his head. "If Scylla is as monstrous as legend and myth has it, it would take more than simply feeding it blood. It's certainly a start, but for something so grand in scale, there would have to be a larger summoning ceremony of sorts. Something to raise it. I think you hit the nail on the head, Simon. The water woman marked Jane so that she herself would have a vessel to inhabit herself once the ceremony is performed to raise Scylla. From what I've read, Scylla, supposedly because she's a daughter of Poseidon, needs a vessel to keep herself material. Something greater than water. Flesh."

"What kind of ceremony are we talking about here, Godfrey?" I asked.

"It would definitely be magical," he said, "but not on the scale we use regularly up in Greater and Lesser Arcana. We'd have to start a whole new division to classify it. Maybe Super Greater Arcana or Godlike Arcana . . ."

"We can name it later," I said. "Focus on the ceremony."

He thought for a moment before answering, but there was uncertainty in his voice. "I would think this type of large-scale ceremonial magic is best performed at liminal times and places, but I'm not sure."

"Liminal?"

"It means being at a crossroads," he said. "On the cusp of great change."

"Like a threshold?" I asked. He nodded. "You said those two monsters guarded the Strait of Messina. That's a threshold of sorts. And isn't a bridge like the Hell Gate another one? I think you may be right about liminality. By their very nature, those two creatures are bound to liminal places."

"You're right," he said, counting off on his fingers. "For instance, the shores of bodies of water . . ."

"We have that," I said. "Check."

"Not just places," Godfrey said. "Time is important, too."

"Like when?"

"There's a whole list," he said. "Solstices, equinoxes, full moons, midnight . . ."

I pulled out my phone to check the time, date, and weather. "We're near the September autumnal point of the equinox." I checked the phase of the moon on my weather app and relaxed when I saw it. "Oh, thank God. We're only at a new moon, not a full one."

Godfrey didn't relax. "I was getting to that on my list," he said.

"I was hoping you wouldn't say that," I said. "Dammit. I think the crossing over of all these various thresholds may be enough."

"Tonight may be the night she attempts the ceremony, then," Godfrey said.

I checked the time on my phone again. "The good news is midnight is almost six hours from now. There's still time, but we have to act now. Any idea how one goes about killing sea monsters, God?"

"Nothing on record that I know of," he said, "but the two of them may be at their most vulnerable right before the ceremony. If that doesn't hold true . . . Well, when in doubt, go for the heart seems to be the advice that works best."

"I'm not all that keen on getting that close," I said. "And as a matter of perspective, I'd need a pretty goddamn big stake to pull something like that off."

"Sorry," he said. "Clearly this is why I don't teach any of the paranormal combat classes."

I nodded and smiled. "Don't worry about it," I said. "I've got to hurry, but thanks for the information, Godfrey. I feel good now."

"You feel good," he repeated with a wary tone. "Why?"

"Because there's a power in knowing what something is," I said. "A power that's going to help me kill it before it gets a chance to rise and take on New York, and most important, a power to save Jane. Do me a favor. Go up to Allorah Daniels's office and let the Inspectre know about this."

I ran off for the stairs.

"Where are you going?" Godfrey called out after me. "What are you going to do?"

I didn't bother to turn back. I was already bounding up the steps, a hint of hope finally in my heart after days of frustration. "Looks like I need to prep the boat with something sea monstery," I said. With all this talk of mythological connections, I only wished I had some Argonauts on my side to go with it.

29

Affixing a pointed ram to the front of the Fraternal Order's boat was a daunting task. It wasn't like there were IKEA instructions on how to mount one, but after a fair amount of Googling, I felt relatively secure with my handiwork when I finished a few hours later. By the time I got back from the docks, I was surprised to see that along with the students, the Inspectre, Connor, and Jane were all still in Allorah's office, each of them off working in separate corners on small piles of files and folders. Allorah Daniels was at her desk and looked up when I walked in.

"Please tell me you are here to take them away," Allorah said.

I nodded. "Not the kids. Just Connor and Inspectre. What's going on? Why are the kids still with you?"

The Inspectre looked up. "Holding is a bit backlogged so we kept everyone here away from Wesker and the like.

In the meantime, I thought we all could get a little work done."

"Way to multitask," I said.

"It is the foreseeable wave of the future," Connor said, standing up and walking over to me. "The cuts and all."

"Did Godfrey come up and tell you about our sea monster problem?" I asked.

The Inspectre nodded.

"Does that mean I get to be a sea monster, too?" Jane asked, looking a bit panicked.

"I don't think so," I said. "I hope not, but I've just spent the past few hours rigging our boat to contend with them, so we need to act fast."

"So what happens to us?" Heavy Mike asked from over in his chair. The hand Elyse had stabbed him through was now bandaged, and he cradled it in his lap.

"That's the good part," Connor said. He walked over and tapped Mike on the forehead. The student flinched back, squinting his eyes shut.

"Ow," he said. "What's that for?"

"Notice how my hand didn't pass through you?" he said.

"Yeah," he said. "So?"

"Well, for one thing, it means you're not a ghost," he said, "which in turn means you're not really one of my cases."

"That's a relief," Mike said.

"Don't be too sure about that," Connor said. "Whether all of you knowingly engaged in dark paranormal activity in the Tri-State area remains to be seen. That will be up to the Enchancellors to decide."

"Dude," Trent said. "I helped you people out."

Connor threw up his hands. "I'm not judge, jury, and executioner," he said, in the worst faux-Stallone accent I had ever heard. "That's for them to figure out."

"We're to be executed?" Elyse said, nervous. She leapt out of her seat and made a break for the door out of Allorah's office before I could grab her. Jane, however, moved with lightning speed and grabbed Elyse by the hair. The actress's body flew out in front of her as her head snapped back and she fell to the floor with Jane still holding on to her. Elyse lay there, writhing around. Jane let go of her hair and gave her a vicious kick to the stomach.

"Jane!" the Inspectre called out, but she wasn't paying attention to him. Her eyes were fixed on Elyse, burning into her.

"It's because of you and that professor of yours that I'm in this mess," Jane said. "People hungry for power, going for the quick fix. When are you going to learn that there are no simple solutions? Power corrupts. Magical powers, doubly so."

I'd never seen Jane like this before—so angry, violent. I went to her and pulled her away from Elyse.

"Easy," I said. "Calm down."

"I'll calm down when I've got this mark off of me," she snapped. "Not a second sooner."

Allorah Daniels looked over at the Inspectre. "Go. I'll try to take them to down to Holding again," she said. "Then I'll gather the Enchancellors to discuss what needs doing about this in the grand scheme of things. I can't not report this threat of sea monsters to the board, but listen, Argyle. I know this thing with Professor Redfield is personal for you. If you want to handle this with any discretion before I drag them all into this, I suggest you and your people leave now."

The Inspectre nodded. Allorah turned from him and headed out the door, leading the four bound students. Once she was gone, the Inspectre turned to me. "Is the boat ready?" he asked.

"I think so," I said. "I've never built a giant spear or ram before, but it's functional. It will hold."

"Good," he said.

Jane looked nervous. "So, now what?" she asked.

"From what Godfrey told me, you think Mason Redfield is in alignment with these creatures," the Inspectre said, "that he traded his help in raising them for the secrets to youth for himself. Saddening, but I am heartened to hear that one of those is still somewhat dormant."

"I hope," I said. "For all I know, Professor Redfield's been providing her with a student a day and George was just one on a long list of monster snack Lunchables. I don't know how regular a feeding schedule Scylla is on, but Godfrey and I think the ceremony could possibly happen as early as tonight."

"We should strike now," Connor said, "before either the creature can rise or the overworked members of the Enchancellors bog this case down in red tape."

The Inspectre checked his watch. "Meet me in half an hour at the docks," he said. "I have a few things I need to take care of first for this. Things of a volatile nature." Without another word, Argyle Quimbley left the room and Connor followed him out.

"Don't worry," I said, turning to Jane. "We'll take care of this tonight."

"Yes," Jane said. "*We* will."

"Wait, what?"

"I'm coming with you," she said.

"Definitely not," I said. "Not in this condition, not the way you were affected last time we were on the water out there."

Jane slugged me in the arm. "Enough of the male macho bullshit," she said. "I'm coming. This is happening to *me*. If there's a chance we can get answers or do something about this thing, I need to be there. End of discussion."

"Fine," I said. "Hell hath no fury greater than a woman marked."

30

Within the hour, the four of us had made our way back to the boat and headed out onto the East River as a heavy rain broke out over the city. All of us crammed into the boat's small wheelhouse as the growing storm raged even heavier on the river, pitching our boat back and forth with the ferocity of an ocean voyage. Jane wanted to stay out in the storm, and even though I had pulled her in, she still stood by the cabin door with her head out in the rain, her hair soaking wet. It calmed her and kept her from freaking out too much, so I let it slide.

"You think the ram's going to stay on?" I asked Connor, who was manning the wheel once again.

"I'm not worried about the ram," he said.

"Oh, no?" I adjusted my Indiana Jones–style satchel out of the way as Jane ducked her head in and moved to stand closer to me.

"No," he said. "I've got bigger things to think about,

like keeping the rest of the boat together right now, at least until we get to the bridge. Then we get to worry about if this summoning ritual is really happening."

Jane squeezed my arm. "I shouldn't have come," she said.

"Seasick?" I asked.

Jane shook her head. "No," she said. "I know what I said in the office, but it was out of frustration. I just wanted this mark off of me so bad, but that was just plain selfish. I'm putting us all at risk again by being here. What if I can't help but get sucked into her ritual?"

"Relax," I said, rubbing her shoulders. "You won't this time. You're stronger than that."

"I won't relax," she said, shrugging me off. "Last time we were out here, I could have killed you and Connor. Now I've got the Inspectre to worry about."

"My dear," the Inspectre added from the other side of the cabin where he held on to one of the interior railings to steady himself, "please don't worry about me. I've dealt with greater horrors than what's happening to you. Fear not. Rest assured we will get that woman in green to release her hold on you."

Jane didn't look too sure about that, but nodded anyway. "I hope so," she said. "For Simon's sake, if not mine."

"It's okay," I said. "Even though I've dated a lot of girls in my time, you'd be my first aqua-woman."

Connor shook his head. "Way to be reassuring, kid."

"So, what's the plan?" Jane asked, impatient. "I take it from the tarp on the front of the boat that we're packing a little extra cargo this time."

"A little insurance," the Inspectre said. "Blasting caps, detonation cords, underwater charges, and a slurry composition of explosives . . ."

"Explosives?" Jane repeated. She turned to Connor at the wheel. "Can you control the roll of the ship a teensy bit more, please? I'd like to get to the bridge in one piece. *Piece*, as in singular."

Connor cranked the wheel of the ship. "Believe me, no one's going to be happier than me if we can keep the boat from capsizing," he said, "but don't worry. Those explosive materials need something a little more powerful than the roll of the ship to set them off."

"Good," Jane said, "but what are they for?"

"My idea," the Inspectre said. "I read the report about unearthing those aqua-zombies. If we encounter any more, we'll be able to take care of them this time."

"Unearth?" Jane asked. "Don't you mean unwater?"

"Whatever," he said. "Either way, we'll be ready for them."

"Brilliant," she said.

"That's not the only reason," Connor added at the wheel.

"No?" Jane asked.

"No," I said. "Connor has a theory."

He steadied the boat before looking over at us. "We blast up some of those sunken ships," he said. "It may just help me in freeing up some of those spirits still lingering on the bridge that died at the hands of both those creatures."

The Hell Gate Bridge came into sight though the pouring rain. The entire expanse was covered with a sea of ghosts, and out on the middle of the bridge was Professor Redfield himself.

"Looks like a double feature so far," I said. "The ghosts of all the shipwrecks and the professor to boot."

"Looks like we have a little company for me," the Inspectre added.

"Crowded tonight," Connor said. "When we get up

there, mind your footing or prepare to be skunked by a ghost."

"That's the least of my worries," Jane said.

"Just get us to the shore safely," the Inspectre said. He clapped Connor on the shoulder and went back to staring out into the storm.

Connor angled toward Wards Island on our left, but he wasn't heading for the docks we had landed at before.

"Where are you going?" I asked.

"Trying not to puncture a hole in your F.O.G.gie boat," he said, wrestling with the wheel. "We're going to need it if we can't stop the ritual up on the bridge. If I go for that broken old dock, we're going to tear apart with the roll of these waves. I've got to go for a deeper part along the shore. I'll need you to jump off and secure us to something more solid." He took one hand off the wheel and pointed off toward another section of Wards Island. "Those trees there, for instance."

I ran out of the wheelhouse. The storm rained down on me and in seconds I was soaked though, but I was still determined. We needed to tie off. I ignored the sting of rain in my eyes and worked my way around the outside of the cabin to the casting line at the front of the boat. Connor brought up the left side of the boat against the shore, and when we were close enough, I leapt for it. I hit the ground and ran for the closest and heaviest tree I could find. I tied the line to it as best I could while Connor killed the engine and the three of them came ashore to the island.

I stared up at the underside of the Hell Gate Bridge and whistled.

"Well?" Jane asked.

"The climb looks treacherous," I said, "especially in this downpour." I looked over at the Inspectre, who was using his sword cane to steady himself as the last one coming off the boat. "You sure you don't want to skip this part, sir?"

He picked up the cane and walked over to me without using it, but I noticed he was a little wobbly despite the brave face he put on. "Nonsense," he said. He tucked the cane through his belt, wearing it like a sheathed sword as though he were a modern-day musketeer. "I'm old, not dead."

"That's the spirit," Jane said.

The Inspectre smiled at her. "However," he said, "why don't the three of you start up first? This may take me a while."

Without another word, I adjusted the strap of my satchel so it lay flat across my back for the climb and the rest of us started up the under skeleton of the bridge. The going was rough but thankfully my gloves kept my hands from slipping as I climbed. I reached the top first and pulled myself up onto the bridge itself. Far out in the center among the swirl of shuffling spirits, Mason Redfield was staring down into the water below, oblivious of our little group's progress. Connor and Jane pulled themselves up next and the three of us waited for the Inspectre together, but he was taking forever. He was still only about halfway up the understructure. At this pace it would be morning before we could pull him up.

Out of the darkness behind him, something blurred into view, grabbing for him. The Inspectre let go of the bridge, but didn't fall. Instead he and the other figure flew up the side of the bridge. They shot up past us, flying into an arc fifty feet over our heads until they both came down onto the bridge right in front of us. The professor landed, stumbling away from the figure carrying him, revealing Connor's brother, Aidan. The vampire's face was drawn and leathery from taking a form that could fly. Aidan almost lost his footing, but caught himself before he fell.

"Aidan?" I asked, running over to him.

The Inspectre turned to him. "Are you all right?"

Aidan nodded, his face returning to its more human state. "Fine," he said. "Just a little too wet out tonight for my liking."

"Thank you," the Inspectre said. "For the ride. It was quite . . . invigorating."

"What are you doing here?" I asked.

Connor walked over to us. "I called him, kid," he said. "Thought the vamps might be helpful in all this."

"Actually," Aidan said, "not so much. We don't really function well around water, remember? It's why I skipped your boat ride and had a little trouble sticking my landing just now. But I'll do what I can. I owe you guys for helping me get rid of that ghost."

"Well, nice Superman entrance anyway," I said. "Let's just hope the water woman doesn't get her green coloring from a Kryptonite infusion."

"Funny," Aidan said. "So glad I came out for this."

"Thank you for joining us," the Inspectre said. "Sincerely."

Aidan smiled, baring his fangs.

"All right," Connor said. "Enough. My brother's going to get an even bigger head on his shoulders."

"Is that possible?" I said.

"Gentlemen, concentrate," the Inspectre snapped. The rest of us fell silent. "Now, then, we have to make sure Mason Redfield doesn't escape. We need to surround him."

Aidan stepped forward. "I'm on it," he said. "I'll block

the other side of the bridge." His features stretched back to his vampiric form once again. "Up, up, and away."

Aidan leapt into the air like he was the Hulk bounding away.

"Let's move in," the Inspectre said.

"And quickly," Connor added, heading out onto the bridge. "There's no telling what my brother may or may not do."

I grabbed Jane's hand and headed after him and the Inspectre, who was already setting a brisk pace.

"Hey, if your brother brings down this woman in green and gets this mark off of Jane, I'll bring him on a Hot Topic shopping spree myself," I said.

"Quiet," the Inspectre said, his mood darkening. Connor and I used foolishness as it had been described in the Departmental pamphlet entitled "Witty Banter to Ease Any Paranormal Situation." I knew that personally it was what kept me from losing my mind and running off screaming on an hourly basis sometimes. Before I could say anything, the Inspectre had picked up his pace and moved ahead, closing in on his old friend. The sea of long-dead spirits parted out of the way as we went, drifting to and fro in their constant wait for a ship that would never come.

Mason Redfield stood at the edge of the bridge, staring down at the chopping waves far below. His hands held him in place as he leaned out over the side, rocking back and forth, totally unaware of our approach. Pushing him off would be so easy if I just took a running start from here. I let go of Jane's hand and reached for my bat in its holster.

I worried that the click of extending it out might draw his attention, but I doubted he would be able to hear it over the whip of the wind and rain out at the center of the bridge. I needn't have worried. Another sound caught his attention instead.

Aidan landed just on the other side of Mason, slamming down into the bridge, cracking a few of the slats. He came down hard, *too* hard, and looked a little stunned by the trouble he was having being exposed to so much water.

Mason spun around, and then noticed the rest of us crowding in on him. Faster than I expected, he reacted, pulling something out of his jacket.

"Crap," I heard Connor say. "Gun!"

Fewer words inspired more panic in the Department than hearing someone was packing heat. Dealing with pedestrian weapons wasn't really our area. Vampires and witches didn't use them, and when I heard the word, I put myself in front of Jane.

Mason looked around him as we spread out to block any escape path he might try to take, all except the one down to the water below. If he wanted to try that hoping to survive the fall, he could be my guest.

"Everyone stop," Mason shouted. "Now!"

Everyone on our side of the bridge stopped, but Aidan continued creeping forward on him, fangs bared.

"I said stop," Mason repeated, and then cocked his head at Aidan as he noticed his teeth. "I've got something to stop you as well." He reached into the collar of his shirt and brought out a wide assortment of chains, all of them with dangling pendants bearing different marks on them. Some of them were definitely religious, some absolutely foreign to me, but they were enough to stop Aidan in his tracks.

"Ever resourceful," the Inspectre called out to him over the wind.

"It pays to be prepared," Mason said. "I'm living proof."

Aidan's face twisted to its monster form. "What do you

want me to do, little brother?" Aidan asked Connor. "I can still probably stop him . . ."

"Don't," I shouted. "I'm not going to risk Jane's life on your 'probably.'"

"Why are you doing this, Mason?" the Inspectre shouted.

"Why?" he asked. "I turned away from the Department years ago because the dark and secret horrors of this life were too much to bear. Only through teaching film did I revisit my love for all things horrifying, only in fictional form. Thanks to it, I learned why people love seeing scary movies. It's a thrill, controlled fear without the actual chaos of it being real. Over time that morphed into something more, a darker fascination . . . I turned to the world of the documentary trying to capture the horrors of real life—in this case, the hundreds of deaths at the Hell Gate Bridge."

"But why?" the Inspectre asked again. "Back in our day, you had everything in control. You were powerful. We were going to fight the good fight side by side."

"You don't understand," Mason said. "Do you even remember the day I told you I was leaving the Department?"

The Inspectre paused in recall, but I stepped forward.

"I do," I said. "That was the day you almost died, yes? There was a fissure in the earth of a graveyard, ghouls pouring out it—"

"Exactly," Mason said, giving me a look of suspicion, "but how do *you* know that?"

I held my hands up and wiggled my fingers. "Psychometrist," I said. "I let my fingers do the walking."

"Fascinating," he said. A spark of interest lit up on his face, the same spark of fascinated curiosity I had seen on it from the vision.

"Look," I said. "I get it. I really do. For the Inspectre

here, that day is but a distant memory, but for me? My powers made it seem like only yesterday. I've even *felt* how you feel. I know the panic you felt that day when you were nearly dragged down into the earth. I understand why you walked away from that life of risk. Hell, I have days in the office where I want to just throw the towel in, too."

Mason was paying attention to me now. He stared at me like I was stupid. "So, why don't you, then?" he asked

I shrugged. I wasn't quite sure of the answer myself

"It's not in his nature," Jane said, speaking up in my defense.

Mason Redfield laughed at that. "Not *yet*, anyway," he said.

"What do you mean by that?" I asked.

"How old are you?" Mason asked. "In your twenties still, yes?"

"What's that got to do with it?" I asked.

"Everything," he said, darkness thick in his voice. "I almost died that day you saw, and every day after that I wondered when the other shoe was going to drop. When was the grim reaper going to show at my door? Over time it built, festered . . . and the years slipped by, age creeping up on me, robbing me of my strength, and I couldn't help but wonder if maybe there was a way to cheat death. There had to be."

The Inspectre shook his head at his old friend. "So you struck a bargain," he said, "with that woman in green. Tell me, Mason, how did you manifest her? You haven't practiced arcana in years."

"Actually," Mason said, "finding her was purely accidental. I unearthed her withered remains while researching the ship graveyard below the Hell Gate Bridge for a perfectly normal documentary I wanted to do about those mundane horrors your friend here suggested. Charybdis was damaged, weakened, and needed my help, which I gladly offered in exchange for some help of my own I wanted."

"This is her weak?" Jane asked. "Geez. I'd hate to see her in tip-top shape."

"No," Mason said. "Once we raise Scylla and Charybdis takes control of her host, she will return to her full power. It took years to return her to her current state. I helped her recover and she promised in return to tell me dark secrets to assist me in pursuit of my rebirth."

"At the expense of others," the Inspectre reminded him.

"No," Mason said. "Not at first, anyway. Originally I only twisted my students to the use of magic trying to make film come alive. Nefarious, but mostly harmless. I kept my grander plan for my youth a secret. When Charybdis was recovered enough to her satisfaction, she finally shared those dark secrets with me. I never knew she would want blood in return."

"Oh, come, now," the Inspectre said. "We both know that's not true. You must surely have suspected. Even with what you had seen in your short time with the Department, you must have known that such a bargain would bear a heavy price."

"Perhaps," he said, admitting it with a slight smile, "but it is a price I've come to live with for the promise of rebirth."

It was the Inspectre's turn to smile, but there was a sadness to it.

"You can't cheat death," the Inspectre said.

"Oh, no?" Mason asked, turning to look at Aidan. "What about him? He seems to be doing quite well at it."

"Make no mistake," the Inspectre said. "Death even

comes to their kind, even if it is staved off by supernatural means. Some give up wanting to live, some are struck down by vampire hunters, but eventually death comes to us *all*."

"Hey!" Aidan said. "Not cool with all this talk about me dying, guys."

Mason Redfield looked around for a way to escape as we argued in the growing fury of the storm, but there was none.

"Come, now, Mason," the Inspectre said, walking after him. "Give yourself up. You can't run anymore. You're surrounded."

Mason spun around, angry. "Are you happy growing old, Argyle? Are you?"

The Inspectre stopped. "Honestly, no," he said, "but it has made me appreciate life all the more for what it is. We get one go-round, Mason. That's all."

"Well, not me," he said, "and once I am finished carrying out Charbydis's wishes, I intend to get right on appreciating my second one."

"How are you helping her with the ritual?" I asked.

Mason fixed me with a sinister stare. "You shall see," he said.

"No, Mason," the Inspectre said, good and pissed. I had never seen him this angry. "This ends . . . now."

As a group, our circle closed in on Mason Redfield. I held the business end of my bat up high, ready to swing. Redfield was close enough that I'd have no trouble dropping him if needed, but a second later that wasn't even an option.

A blast of water shot up through the slats of the bridge itself, shattering some of its structure and flinging shards of it in every direction. The water wrapped itself in a wide circle around Redfield, rising up above him for several feet and staying around him like some bizarre waterfall feature at a mall. One thing was sure: Mason Redfield wasn't responsible for it. Even he looked surprised to see it happening.

Inside the protective circle the water began to solidify until the woman in green stood by his side. Her hair swirled in the chaos of the growing storm.

"Nice Medusa effect," I said.

"Wrong Greek monster, kid," Connor said.

"Sorry." I tested the wall of water with my bat. The rushing water threatened to tug my bat skyward from my hand, but I tightened my grip and pulled it back. Before I could do anything else, the woman's voice boomed out into the night.

"Prokypto," she said, holding her arms out and looking down through the bridge.

"What?" I said.

"It's Greek," Connor said. *"Arise.* She's starting the ritual now!"

I looked down, too. Below, the water churned against the edge of the island like it was boiling. Bits of old, rotted wood rose to the surface, ancient timbers that littered the surface, looking like tiny toothpicks from where we stood.

"I gather those are the remains of the *General Slocum*," Connor said.

"And countless other ships, no doubt," the Inspectre added.

"Aidan," I said, looking over at him on the far side of the water barrier. "Do something!"

He shook his head. "What part of 'not good with water' did you not get, Canderous?"

"Fine," I said. "I'll handle it myself." I rushed the wall

of water protecting the woman and Mason Redfield. The woman was already looking toward me, waiting. She pointed her arms out at me.

No, not at me. *Past* me. Jane screamed, stopping me in my tracks. I spun around. She was doubled over, clutching her arms around her midsection. "Jane!"

"Get her away from here, kid," Connor said. "Now. At least off the bridge, anyway. If the woman can't have Jane, she can't complete her ceremony. Hopefully, anyway."

"Right," I said, grabbing Jane around her shoulders. We ran off as the Inspectre started talking reason with Mason through the wall of water. As we ran farther away from the woman and the professor, a new sound filled the air as we dodged through the swarm of lingering ghosts. A rush of water of tidal-wave proportions filled my ears and I looked down through the bridge. The surface of the river erupted, a greenish gray mass of land rising up, water pouring off it in waterfalls. No, not land, I realized. *Flesh*. Whatever was rising was alive. It rolled as it rose, exposing the familiar yellow eye I had seen in the vision of the *General Slocum* sinking. Scylla was no longer dormant, and even bigger than when I had seen it. A jagged maw of teeth opened to nearly the size of a bus, water running down into its throat. A gurgling roar rose up from it, causing me to grab Jane tighter and run a little faster.

"Who invited the kraken?" Jane asked with weakness in her voice.

"Scylla," I corrected. "Godfrey called it that."

Jane looked good enough to stand again and the two of us stopped where we were to stare at the monstrosity.

"Whatever it's called," I said, "I'm pretty sure my bat alone isn't going to take it down. Good thing I equipped the boat with the ram. I'll see if I can put a nice boat-sized hole in that . . . *thing*. Godfrey told me when all else fails, go for the heart."

"What can I do?" Jane asked. There was concern on her face, but I could see how hard she was still fighting the effect of the green woman's mark on her.

"Stay here," I said, "and don't let her get control of you. Keep fighting her, Jane. I'll be back soon. I promise."

Jane nodded, but the look on her face was pained.

"Listen, Simon," she said. "I'm sorry about the whole drawer thing."

I stared at her, incredulous. "You want to get into this *now*?"

Even in the rain, I noticed tears streaming down her face. "It's just . . . I'm so in love with you and the idea that you didn't want me around all the time, well, it hurt."

I pulled Jane to safety behind of one of the bridge supports. "Jane!" I said. "This is so not the time."

She looked like I had slapped her. "Do you hate me or something?" she asked, hurt. "It's just that I don't know how long I can stop this from overtaking me and I need to get this off my chest."

Given the chaos all around us and the distracting amount of pain she was in, I couldn't believe we were getting into this now. Either way, I had to make this fast or we were sure to die in the middle of it all. I dug into my satchel, pushed past my Ghostbusters lunch box, and pulled out a slip of paper. I handed it to her. "There," I shouted over the noise. "You see, Jane. *This* is how much I hate you."

"What's this?" she asked, looking at it, and then back up at me.

"It's a receipt," I said. "I found a dresser, online. I hate you *so* much that I agonized and searched for days trying to find just the right piece for your stuff in my apartment because I can't stand you." Jane's eyes widened, and I forced myself to stop shouting at her. I hadn't meant to, but the dire situation had me caught up in the moment. I softened my voice. "You know how anal I get about selecting stuff for *my own* needs . . . It took all of my spare time and energy to even come close to finding the exact right one that would be perfect for you. I love you and I realized that's not going to change. What I mean is . . . that dresser is just the beginning. I know you weren't asking me to, but I'm telling you . . . I want you to move in with me. Whatever angry flare-ups or hesitation I had before, that was just me letting the psychometric emotions of another interfere with my own insecurities. I know that now. Like the Inspectre said, we get one go-round. I want mine to be with you."

Jane continued staring at the receipt, a smile slowly building on her face. "Oh, Simon, thank you," she said. "I love *you*."

She wrapped her arms around me and kissed me hard. I melted into it, but after a few moments I felt I had to pull away.

"Not to put a damper on things," I said, "but we kinda need to do something here. Something along the heroic lines."

"Oh," she said. "Okay. Right. Of course."

She handed the slip of paper back to me, hands trembling. When I went to reach for it, it slipped from her hand, the wind catching it and blowing it away. I turned, grabbing for it. It was just a slip of paper, but the weight of everything it stood for was so important that I felt compelled to get it back. It tumbled along the walkway of the bridge and I ran a few steps before catching it, then folding it and stuffing it back into my messenger bag as I turned back to Jane.

She wasn't there. I peered through the dozens of ghosts manifested all along the bridge looking for her. After a moment I caught a hint of movement back where we had all climbed up onto the bridge together earlier. Jane was hurrying to get back to the island below, which meant . . . she had tricked me by pretending to let go of the note too soon. Why? To distract me. To run off before I could stop her.

"The boat," I said, and then started running after her, my heart sinking. "Jane! No!"

I tore along after her, but the small lead she had grew as she monkey-barred her way down the structure of the bridge toward the land below. I climbed down after her as fast as I could, but by the time I had worked my way down, Jane had already reached the boat and was casting off the line, leaving it dangling from the tree we had secured it to.

"Jane!" I screamed above the sounds of the storm. The swells of water coming from the gigantic monster writhing in the river threatened to capsize the boat. Jane raised her hands above her, calling out to the boat, and its systems flew on, it searchlights practically overloading with power as they shone out into the darkness. Her eyes, however, remained on me.

There was no way I could reach the boat now that it was launched. Unless . . .

I looked up at the underside of the bridge. The under support holding up the structure was a web of steel that snaked out over the dangerous waters. If I could get myself out onto it, there was a chance I could jump down onto the boat. I started climbing out onto the steel skeleton until I was back in shouting distance of the boat.

"Jane," I shouted. "Come back! Pull that boat over *now*!"

"I have to do this," she said. "It's too late for me, anyway. I can feel Charybdis pulling at me. She's trying to take possession of me."

"Just get off the boat," I shouted. "We can fight her, together."

Jane turned and pointed up at several of the tentacles crashing down around her, rolling the boat to its near-pitching point. "We have to stop *this* one if you're going to have any chance of defeating her. I can do that."

"Fine," I said, "but do it away from the monster, then."

Jane shook her head, and then slammed her hands down onto the control console of the boat. "Afraid it doesn't work that way, hon. I'm so sorry."

She turned herself away from me and pressed her magic into the boat, the lights on it rising as it gained speed heading for the body of the creature. I gauged my distance to the boat from where I was. There was no chance I'd hit its deck at this angle. I had to get myself back up to the bridge, and started climbing.

When I pulled myself back up onto the Hell Gate Bridge, I immediately looked for Aidan, spotting him off to my right farther along the bridge. I ran over to him, Connor joining me while the Inspectre continued trying to reason with Mason through his protective wall of water.

"Jane's down there," I said. "Go help her. Please."

Aidan shook his head. "I keep telling you," Aidan said. "We're pretty much useless in water. You know, like the way you are when you're breathing."

"So you can't fight that monster?" Connor asked.

Aidan gave a smile. "I didn't say that, now, did I?" he said and sped farther off along the bridge.

Already the enormous creature was making its way up out of the water. I didn't have time to count all of its tentacles, but bunches of them were smashing and crashing against the sides of the bridge already. I steadied myself under its sway as I watched Aidan leap up off the bridge, grabbing one of the tentacles near him. He wrapped it around one of the bridge struts, holding it in place, pinning it.

He looked over at us and smiled. "Happy?" his voice said, unnaturally amplified from where he stood.

"It's a start," I said.

"Well, I think it's safe to say we know for sure what brought the *General Slocum* down," Connor said.

"Crap on toast," I said. "That is one giant octopus thing."

"Steady, kid," Connor said. "Just remember. The bigger they are . . ."

"The more damage they do . . . ?" I finished.

"That's not where I was going with that," he said. "I'll see what I can do with all these spirits up here, see what they can do to help Jane. Let's see if I can get them interested in a little revenge on this monstrosity or the woman."

As the bridge creaked and swayed, I started back to the water woman, Mason Redfield, and the Inspectre out at the center of the bridge. Ghosts were flying across my path and I was having trouble seeing, but when I was about fifteen feet away, I caught sight of the three solid figures. The Inspectre looked like he wasn't having much luck in dealing with either of them.

"Charybdis," Mason shouted, pointing at the Inspectre. "Attack!"

"No!" I called out, racing the last few feet to put myself between them and the Inspectre, who looked resolved to await his fate at their hands. I braced myself for a wave of water coming my way, but when nothing happened a moment later, I opened my eyes.

Mason had turned to the woman within their protective

bubble. "Did you not hear me?" he asked. "I told you to attack."

The woman walked over to him, taking slow, deliberate steps. "I think . . . not," she said. "I serve no man."

"What?" Mason said, fury in his eyes. "What about our arrangement?"

"There is only one arrangement," the woman said. "And that is *mine*."

The woman pulled in her arms, the column of water around her closing in on the two of them. The professor's face filled with horror as water rushed into his mouth and down into his lungs. From the panicked look in his eyes, there was no doubt that he knew his death would not result in his rebirth as it had the last time.

Before any of us could try to reach into the watery barrier, the professor's body imploded from the water pressure, red rushing out of him. It ran into the woman and her body changed, growing in power and strength until the water ran clear and her body turned more solid in the column of water than I had ever seen her.

"Why?" the Inspectre shouted. "Why would you do that to your ally?"

The woman spoke in Greek again, but I didn't bother to wait for the translation from Connor. I thought I knew.

"Betrayal," I said, piecing some of it together from everything I had investigated so far. "It feeds her soul, which is why it took Professor Redfield sacrificing students like George to bring about her rise, but in order to get his help in that, she had to promise him something. His own rebirth. She killed Mason Redfield the first time so he could be reborn first to help her rise and also to awaken Charybdis."

"Taking the professor's life now was all the more cruel and sweet a betrayal," she said, "the power of his blood

growing tenfold from it. In death, his power completes our
ceremonial rebirth."

She dropped what remained of the professor's lifeless
body to the tracks of the bridge and he fell through a shattered section down into the water below. I spied Jane and
the lights from the boat as she headed straight for the sea
monster, aiming for the yellow of its giant eye. I had to act
fast.

I went to charge into the water wall around the woman,
but the Inspectre's hand came down on my shoulder. I
turned toward the far end of the bridge and called out to
Connor's brother.

"Aidan," I shouted. "Do something!"

He looked at me like I was stupid. He let go of the tentacle with one of his hands where he held it in place wrapped
around the bridge support and pointed at it. "I *am*!"

"No," I said. "About Jane!" I pointed down at the boat
below as the spiked ram slammed into the creature. "Down
there. Hurry!"

"I can't let go," he said. "If I do, that thing will destroy
her boat for sure."

Aidan was right. With the creature pinned in place up
here, it couldn't take on Jane or the boat unless he let go of
it. The best I could do was join Connor and the Inspectre
in fighting the green water woman. Maybe the key to stopping the monster lay in beating its keeper, the one helping
it rise to full power.

The three of us turned our attention to the woman
within the circle of water. Connor was busy uncorking
a dozen or so stoppered tubes, rallying a thick swarm of
ghosts all around him. He shouted instructions at them, but
from where I stood I couldn't quite make them out. I hefted
my bat and came in swinging. I landed a solid hit on the

woman through her tower of water, but once she felt it and became aware of my presence, every subsequent swipe of my bat passed through a liquid form of her body.

Another sound rose to meet my ears, one that horrified me. Jane's voice rang out in all its technomantic glory from down below over the fight. With terror filling my heart, I realized it could mean only one thing. Jane wasn't just going to ram the creature. She intended to blow the creature up with the blast materials and depth charges the Inspectre had brought along to dislodge all the sunken ships.

The fight went out of me and I ran to the edge of the bridge. "Jane!" I shouted.

The boat was underneath us and from where I was I could actually see her face. She looked up at me, her face sad but determined. She spoke, but I couldn't hear her over the sound of everything, yet there was no mistaking the words her mouth formed.

I love you.

"Jane, don't," I shouted, but it was too late. She turned her head back to the ship and pressed her power into it. Sparks rose up all over the vessel as she pulled power from the boat itself, sending raw power across the bow like lightning strikes.

All that was enough to set things off, and the ship exploded. The heat of it rose up with concussive force, straight through the bridge. The gas of the boat and blasting caps fed one another, shooting a column of flame up in the air with its fury. Bits of the creature flew through the air, and I tried not to think of the same happening to Jane.

All around me the world slowed. I got back to my feet in time to catch Aidan letting go of the now-severed tentacle, letting it unwind and fall from where it had been wrapped around the bridge. Like a shot, the vampire transformed and shot up into the night sky and then down into the fire-covered river below.

Behind me an inhuman keening arose from the woman as she watched her precious charge dying. The steady stream of water around her faltered and dropped away, yet she herself remained.

"Focus," the Inspectre called out, slicing his cane through her body to no avail, passing right through her. "Don't let up."

His call to arms awoke something dark in the pain of my heart. I charged the woman again. Blow after blow of mine still passed through her as she came at us with a watery fury, unleashing waves of it at each of us. Connor's assembly of spirits swarmed her to the point of distraction that had her firing off her powers in every direction. One of the blasts hit the Inspectre, sending him flying onto his back, his sword cane falling through the slats of the bridge.

"If you got anything better than a bat," Connor said, still orchestrating the spirits in their attack, "now's the time to use it, kid."

The bat was doing nothing more than distracting her for a few seconds at a time. I collapsed it and slid it into its holster. I reached into my satchel to assess my other options. My hand slapped against what I thought was my emergency medical kit, but when I pulled it out I saw it was the Ghostbusters lunch box Jane had given me. Without hesitation, I opened it and shook out the contents. I grabbed it by its handle and lid, thrusting it toward the woman. I had been going about this the wrong way. I thought back to the vision where I had first seen Mason Redfield. He and the Inspectre had tried going for the ghouls' hearts as a first means of stopping them. Even tonight, the Inspectre had tried that tactic, trying to stab her there, but that wasn't the way to go about it. A blade or a bat could pass through water, no problem. What I needed was to take the woman's heart from her in whatever form I could.

I swung the lunch box at her. Her body went liquid and it started passing through her like all my bat attacks had. When the lunch box was fully within the water, I stopped it in the center of her chest, slamming the lunch box shut and pulling it out by its handle . . . full of water. The woman screamed out, her eyes widening and her body stumbling. I stepped back from her, but she kept coming for me, clutching wildly for my lunch box.

I spun around and found Connor off in a crowd of ghosts. "Connor, catch!" I shouted and threw the lunch box over to him, but not before I felt a wave of the water woman wash over me. The fight was going out of her, but not fast enough. I spun back around and all the hate and surprise in her eyes were focused on me. She was going to make it her dying wish to take me with her, and there was nothing I could do to stop it now. With Jane gone, I didn't care.

Falling to my knees on the slats of the bridge, I felt my strength leaving me. I was drowning. My last thought as I drowned was wondering if soon I'd be just another bridge-bound spirit that Connor would be able to talk to in a few minutes.

Then another thought struck me. As my world went dark, I wondered if Jane was already waiting for me on the other side or if Connor would find her standing around on the bridge, too.

31

White light, I thought. That's a good sign, right?

The blur in my eyes roused me and I struggled to awaken the rest of my senses as well. The ringing of an angelic host, complete with accompanying harps, sounded more like the beeps, pings, and whirs of . . .

"Hospital equipment," I croaked out. "I'm not in the afterlife?"

"I don't know, kid," Connor's familiar voice spoke out. "Does your personal vision of blissful eternity include me?"

"Or me?" another voice asked. The Inspectre.

I willed my eyes to fully open, and to my surprise they did, the world coming into focus. I was in a hospital bed, the overhead lights of the room turned off, the white blur that woke me coming from the hallway outside my room.

Connor was already standing at the side of the bed. The Inspectre stood up from a nearby chair, using the empty scabbard of his sword cane to help him up. I tried to turn my head to him but couldn't. I went to speak again but managed only to get out a dry croak before Connor grabbed a Styrofoam cup with a straw sticking out of it from the table next to my bed. I sipped from it, and the hit of refreshing water shot through me like a jolt of energy. Once I was done drinking, I tried speaking again.

My mind stumbled forward slow, the world and everything around me a fog. "Why can't I move?"

"That's probably the pain meds," Connor offered. He put the water back down on the bedside table. "You're probably on enough morphine right now to warrant a rehab program when you leave here."

"What happened?" I asked, feeling like a foreign passenger in my own body. Questions were forming, but slowly, not nearly fast enough, and I was having trouble organizing my thoughts.

The Inspectre stepped closer. "You sustained quite a bit of damage," he said.

"So removing the woman's heart didn't work . . ." I said.

"Quite the contrary," the Inspectre said. "It worked remarkably well."

I forced my head to do my bidding and I felt it shift a fraction to my left.

"Easy," Connor said. "You're in a neck brace. What you did with the lunch box worked, but you still sent that woman into a blind death panic. When she wasn't trying to drown you, she was trying to crush you with all that water. Your body is pretty battered and bruised, but I asked the docs and they say you're going to live."

"What about all those spirits on the bridge?" I asked.

"They moved on," Connor said with a smile. "To wherever spirits go. Once Scylla and Charybdis were dead, their hold over the Hell Gate passage broke."

A new thought slammed into my head, pushing past all of its cloudiness. How had it not been there right away? "Jane," I whispered. "What about Jane?"

Connor's face sobered. "'Fraid not, kid," he said. "I'm sorry."

"She went down fighting," the Inspectre said. "She saved us all."

The meds numbed me. I could barely think, let alone process what had happened to Jane. Fleeting images of her running for the boat and the explosion played themselves over and over in my head, but my mind refused to process the fact that she was gone. I lay there not speaking for a long time. Connor and the Inspectre stood at my side and remained silent themselves as the sounds of life struggled out all around us in the hospital. The figures in the hall passed by until one of them stopped in the doorway. I recognized him, even without his hoodie pulled up.

"Aidan . . . ?"

Aidan Christos stumbled into the room. He was soaked through, his clothes clinging to him, what had survived of them, anyway. Most of what remained of his hoodie was charred or torn. His features, while still human-looking, were drawn and gaunt to the point that he looked like a spectral version of himself. Connor ran over to him and helped him into the room.

"What the hell happened to you?" he asked.

Aidan looked at Connor, but he was so messed up I wasn't sure he could see him in his state. "I told you my kind doesn't take well to water," Aidan said. "Not really our element, and I was in it far too long, I think. I'm having trouble healing."

"At least you can," I mumbled, still in my daze.

Aidan turned and followed the sound of my voice. He

shuffled toward the foot of the bed. When his bony claws of fingers hit the end of it, he grabbed onto it like it was the only thing that could keep him standing. "Simon?" he asked. "How . . . how are you?"

"I'll live," I said. I couldn't hide the darkness in my voice. "What happened to Jane? I saw you let go of the severed tentacle and then dive through the fire into the water."

Aidan tensed. Parts of him were slowly healing, his features turning back to his normal look of a teenager, everything except his clothes. The better his features got, the worse his actual face looked. The young vampire looked pained and worried.

"There was so much going on," he said. "There was the monster. It was dying, but not fast enough. Underwater, I couldn't avoid the tentacles. They were thrashing about everywhere, making it harder to try to find her."

"*Did* you find her?" the Inspectre asked.

Aidan nodded. "Eventually, yeah," he said. "I don't know how long I was under. I don't need to breathe, but still the water was having an effect on me. I felt my body giving in to the river, until I finally struggled to the surface."

I lay there, thankful for whatever painkillers they had given me. My mind filled with sadness, but my body wouldn't react to it in my condition. When I could finally speak, I did. "At least you found her body," I said. "Her family will be able to give her a proper burial."

Aidan looked exhausted, but even through that I could see some hesitation in him. "About that . . ."

"What?" Connor asked.

"Please tell me you found all of her," I said. "Please."

"You have to understand something," Aidan said. "I barely made it to shore. We were both . . . burnt and wet. I could barely pull her after me . . ."

"What the hell did you do?" I asked. "What happened to her body?"

"Tell the boy, for goodness' sake," the Inspectre added.

"I needed to replenish myself," he said. "I . . . I couldn't stop myself."

"You *fed* on her?" I asked, horrified.

"I would have died," he said.

"So you fed on her body," I said, feeling rage rising up in me despite the painkillers coursing through my system.

"Jesus, Aidan . . ." Connor said.

"Wait, wait," Aidan said, holding up his shaking bony hands. "Not exactly."

"Then what exactly?" the Inspectre asked.

"I liked Jane," he said. "A *lot*. She was always nice to me. Whenever Simon or Connor sniped at me, either in jest or whatever, she didn't. She treated me . . . I don't know, normal."

"And that's how you repaid her kindness?" I said, feeling sick to my stomach. "By feeding on her."

"You've got it wrong," he said. "You're not listening. I wasn't trying to feed on her. I was trying to *save* her."

"Save her?" I said. "Bullshit."

"He's not listening to me," Aidan said, turning to Connor.

"I'm not sure I'm listening to you, either," Connor said, getting pissed himself. "Why don't you just say what you're here to say?"

Aidan looked down at the floor, looking unsure of himself. "It just takes humans some time to adjust to it," he said. "To accept it."

Maybe it was the meds clouding my head, but I wasn't getting it. "Time to adjust to what? Accept what?"

Aidan moved to the side of the room, exposing the door

leading out into the hall. A nurse walking by stopped, a startled look on her face as she backed away slowly from something coming down the hall. The wet *squick* of footsteps came slowly toward my hospital room and a moment later the doorway filled with a lone female figure.

Jane stood there, her hair wet and tangled. Her clothes were torn, burnt, and stained with blood. How they even stayed together enough to remain on her was a mystery. They were practically destroyed.

But not Jane herself, though. Everything about her body was perfect. Her skin showed not a scratch of damage, except for a small section of burnt black skin on her cheek, but even that flaked away when she smiled at me. The skin underneath it was just as perfect as the rest of her was.

"The change," Aidan said. "I told you I lost a little blood."

Even in my fragile condition, my heart leapt. Was this really Jane? Was I really seeing her like this, transformed? I could only pray that this wasn't just the pain medication messing with me. "Jane . . . ? We thought you were dead . . ."

"Hey, Simon," Jane said. The pronounced points of her eyeteeth bit into her lower lip as she smiled. "I'm not dead yet. Hopefully your offer to move in still stands . . . ?"

I had spent so much time worrying about the water woman's mark gaining control over her and what I would do if I had had to kill her, but Jane had taken all those choices away from me by running off to take on the sea monster herself. Seeing her alive killed any residual traces of anger, rage, or my own insecurities, all of it replaced with the sudden inescapable fact that my girlfriend was now one of the undead. I wasn't sure how I felt about that, although I was relieved to see her alive, or rather unalive. Still, one thing was for certain.

"I told you I loved you and I told you that wasn't going to change," I said, mustering a weak smile in the hospital bed. "Looks like I'll need to invest in some serious black-out curtains."

ABOUT THE AUTHOR

ANTON STROUT was born in the Berkshire Hills mere miles from writing heavyweights Nathaniel Hawthorne and Herman Melville. He currently lives outside New York City in the haunted corn maze that is New Jersey (where nothing paranormal ever really happens, he assures you).

His writing has appeared in several DAW anthologies—some of which feature Simon Canderous tie-in stories—including: *The Dimension Next Door*, *Spells of the City*, and *Zombie Raccoons & Killer Bunnies*.

In his scant spare time, he is an always writer, sometimes actor, sometimes musician, occasional RPGer, and the world's most casual and controller-smashing video gamer. He now works in the exciting world of publishing, and yes, it is as glamorous as it sounds.

He is currently hard at work on his next book and can be found lurking the darkened hallways of www.antonstrout .com.

Don't miss
ANTON STROUT'S

DEAD MATTER

When the paranormal raises its otherworldly head in
New York City, Department of Extraordinary Affairs
agent Simon Canderous knows he can count on
his mentor, Connor, to help him execute a flawless
smackdown—but Connor's absent, having cashed in
on five years' worth of saved vacation time. Simon
suspects that Connor isn't Club Medding so much
as Club Deading—using his talents as a ghost whisperer to investigate the disappearance of his own
long-lost brother.

M582T1210